The

Kandra

An Immortal MacKinnon Novel

Treasa Klöth

For Information contact:
http:// www.MagickMoonInk.com
Book and Cover design by Magick Moon Publishing
Other art: Victoria L. Kalisiak/Jenn Park
Edited by: Vikki Beck/ Enchanted Editing
ISBN: 978-0-9989563-1-2
First Edition: May 2017
10 9 8 7 6 5 4 3 2 1

Hadin,
I hope you had
a great time today!
Any time you want to be
a Viking come Hang with the
Harrow! Enjoy the Book
&

Always Remember:
Fortune Only Assists the
Daring!
Slàinte!
Theos Kloth

6/2/18
magical Realm
Charlotte, MI

"She Was Fearless.....Until he lay Siege to her Heart...."

"I am used to being out of doors. To be kept in that room is like torture to me." Kandra spoke honestly. She needed fresh air and sunshine like she needed food and water.

"'Tis really so bad for ye?" Lachlan's face softened at the thought.

"Yes, I am not one of your soft Scottish women. I am a warrior." Kandra stood proudly in front of him, raising her chin haughtily. She was proud of who she was, even if there were things she hated about herself.

Being a warrior himself, Lachlan knew her feelings. Perhaps it was the warrior in her that intrigued him. Or was it the woman hidden beneath? "Aye, yer nay like any woman I have ever ken." He closed the distance between them. Lachlan raised his hand brushing his knuckles across her cheek. Though she was a warrior, she had the soft skin of a woman. It was bronzed by the kiss of the sun and gave her an exotic look, "Ye, Kandra of Carlisle, are intriguin'."

"I am not interested in your opinions, laird." Kandra drew away with ice in her eyes. Being close to him muddled her thinking. She would not allow herself to lose control again with this man. "I am only interested in the wellbeing of my men."

"Aye, yer men?" He raised an arrogant brow, "What of 'em?" He eyed her suspiciously. Being so close to her caused a throb within his loins. He tried vainly to ignore it.

"You have no need to hold them." She glared at him. "I am all that you require." Kandra raised a haughty chin.

"Och, lass, ye need to watch what yer sayin' to a man." Lachlan shook his head and laughed at her blush of embarrassment.

Kandra flushed under his words. "That was not what I meant." She tried to push past him, but he caught her to him.

"I will nay give ye up easily lass, I want ye far too much." He raised his hand caressing her cheek as his eyes blazed with passion.

Thank you to all my friends and family, who have supported me through the years.

Thank you to, Tammy, for getting this all started with your faith in me that I could write novels.

Thank you to my mom, my BFF Mindy, my daughters, Alex, and Stephanie for being a part of my editing team and sounding boards.

My Husband, John, for the love through the years!

My Dad, Jim, you are sorely missed and will never be forgotten. I love you and miss you, Dad!

Mom, thank you for all the encouragement you have given me through the years! I love you as well.

Katie, this was originally written for your Sweet 16! I hope you enjoy the story as much today as you did when I originally wrote it.

Alexandra, my beautiful Amazon daughter, who inspired Kandra and her beautiful looks, her fortitude and grit! Thank you for all of your help! I hope your baby girl grows up to be just like her mama.

My daughters Kassie, and Haillie, my son, Jay and my nephews, and niece always follow your dreams and believe in yourself, anything in life is possible.

My Granddaughters, I love all three of you and I hope that you all grow to be successful and have the determination to fulfill your dreams.

Lastly, but surely not least, to my many readers, thank you to everyone who has read and will read this story. I hope you enjoyed it! Without readers, an author is nothing.

Dear Readers,

As a history major myself, I am a fanatic for accuracy in history. However, for this story, I took liberties with people and places. As far as I can find in history, the MacKinnons were never lowlanders, but islanders/highlanders. Being a MacKinnon through bloodlines helped me to research and write about this amazing clan.

The Stafford family of England never appeared to have lived in Cumbria, however, for this story it worked to make Kandra come from this area.

So, please allow me these liberties with history and I hope you enjoy the story, as much as I enjoyed writing it.

For a complete glossary of Gaelic word meanings please visit www.treasakloth.com

Slàinte!

Treasa

Chapter One

*D*o not think to take it easy on me, Jonas." Kandra narrowed her eyes at the younger man facing her with his sword in hand. He was just slightly taller than she was, but Kandra knew he lacked her intense skill with a blade.

"Would the enemy be timid?" She cocked a mocking brow as she taunted him by clanging the end of her sword against his own.

"No," she shook her head as she circled and spoke before he could reply, "They would not be with either of us. If they had half a chance, they would split our gullets!"

"Yes, but Kandra," Jonas shook his head, "If I am not careful I shall hurt you then it will be my head, and well you know it."

"Be passive if you wish, but I warn you. I will show you no mercy," she snarled at him. How could she take him into battle if he'd hesitate to defend himself? She lifted her sword, charging him. He raised his own sword to protect himself. Side stepping, she sliced across his upper arm. Spinning she swept her leg behind his. He fell with a thud onto his back, clutching his arm.

"Kandra!" He looked at her as shock filled him. "You sliced me!" Jonas stared at the blood covering his palm. "You really cut me!" He looked up at her with disbelief.

"I warned you, Jonas, I would show you no mercy." She towered over him with the tip of her sword pressed to his chest. "If I had been meaning to finish you, I would have cut your leg out from under you." She glared down at him with ice in her blue eyes. "Then, I would have run you through before you had a chance to think about it."

"Kandra, I told you to work with him, not maim him!" Raff's gruff voice came from behind her on the other side of the practice field. "Good lord girl, you cannot be cuttin' down our own men."

"I was teaching him a lesson." She shot over her shoulder as Raff approached her. She lifted her sword tip from Jonas's chest. "It is no less than you or father taught me."

"Yes, but that was different." He scolded, his brows furrowed as he watched the boy gain his feet once again.

"Why was it so different," she glared at Raff, "because I am a girl?" Kandra spoke in defense, "Now, this girl can best half, or more, of the men in this castle in a sword fight, and you know as much!" She whirled on him raising her chin haughtily.

"You are hot headed and act without thinking. No knight worth his salt would act thus." Raff countered trying to hold his own temper in check. He'd helped to raise this stubborn young woman. Her father and Raff, himself, had trained her to fight as well as nearly any man he had ever known. He looked levelly into her blue eyes and could read her pride there.

"Then it is lucky I am not allowed into the brotherhood of knights, is it not?" The insult Raff had flung stung, but she wouldn't let it show. She felt just in her actions. If Jonas pulled back in battle, he'd lose his life for certain. The thought of Jonas dying in battle wasn't something she wished to think about.

"You are finished for the day. Return to the keep." Raff waved her off in an angry gesture. "Jonas, head in and have Hannah patch you up."

"Raff…" Kandra frowned at him, feeling her anger beginning to melt away. She hadn't meant to hurt

Jonas seriously. She'd only intended to teach him a lesson.

"Not another word! Go now, before I sorely lose my temper with you, girl." Raff ground out. He watched her flinch at his words. She'd go sulk then apologize to her brother in the end, and God knew why, but Jonas would be her best friend again and dismiss the whole incident. "I do not want to see either of you until the evening meal is served. Do I make myself understood?"

"Yes," Kandra bowed her head turning to leave. Guilt and anger filled her.

"Raff, she didn't mean to hurt me." Jonas frowned at her departing back. He knew her feelings were hurt and it ate at him. Jonas knew he should have practiced harder with her. "I should have been more aggressive."

"That you should have, but she will learn to control her temper, or so help me God, I shall take away her sword!" Raff growled at him. He heard Kandra gasp at his threat, "And I will do it, girl, do not doubt it!"

Kandra straightened her shoulders and held her chin high as she marched back to the keep. Once inside, Kandra made her way quickly to her chambers. Closing her chamber door behind her, she began to pace without even bothering to remove her armor. It was lightweight and almost a second skin to her. She rarely noticed it and often forgot all together that it was still on.

Hurting Jonas had been wrong, she knew that, but she would apologize later for her indiscretion. Raff's wrath was bad enough, but if her father had been home, he'd have been furious with her for injuring one of her own. Luckily, father was in London attending the King and wasn't expected to return home anytime soon.

Sitting upon the edge of the chair nearest the fireplace, she began to remove her armor. A soft knock sounded at the door.

"Enter," she called without bothering to look up.

Mary bustled into the room. "I assume you want to bathe before the evening meal." She moved about the room setting out a bath sheet and soap for her lady. Mary looked closely at her charge for the first time and tisked. "Just look at you! You look like a lady not at all!"

Kandra shrugged a shoulder. "You have known me, the whole of my life, Mary. A little dirt should not be shocking." She continued to remove the rest of her armor.

"A little dirt?" Mary rolled her eyes, "If you bothered to look at yourself once in a while, in your looking glass, you might be a bit surprised." Mary waged a finger at Kandra.

Mary was the closest thing to a mother Kandra had ever known. She was more like family than a servant and she always spoke her mind, be it to Kandra herself, Jonas, or their father. Walking over she bent, placing a kiss upon the older woman's cheek. "Thank you."

"Now, what did you go and do that for?" Mary looked up at her large ward. She loved the girl as if she were her very own child. Though she disliked the idea of her little girl wielding a sword, she'd accepted it long ago because Kandra had always dreamt of being a warrior. Being as tall, if not taller than some men made her perfect for the title of warrior.

"I just wanted you to know how much I love you." Kandra told her with downcast eyes.

"What's wrong?" Mary peered at her through narrowed eyes.

"Nothing," Kandra turned away fingering the silver backed brush and looking glass upon her dresser. They had belonged to her mother once upon a time.

"You are upset about something. What 'tis it?" Mary placed her hands upon her ample hips. "You can either tell me now, or I shall just go pull it out of Jonas later."

"I doubt Jonas wants to even speak of me at this time." Kandra walked over and began picking up her armor then dropped it into the chair, turning to Mary. "I hurt him, Mary. I took a slice out of him. I am so ashamed." Kandra shook her head as tears pooled in her eyes. It was rare for her to cry so Mary knew she was truly upset.

"I am sure he will survive, darling. Your brother loves you, no matter what." Mary came to her, patting her back to console her.

"I let my temper get the best of me." Kandra wiped at the tear that spilled down her cheek. She hated crying, it was an aggravating and useless emotion.

"You always have. 'Tis not the first time and shan't be the last." Mary smiled at her. Kandra had a wicked temper and the entire castle knew it as well. But then, she was her father's daughter after all. "You shall have a bath, dress, then go find Jonas, and apologize to him."

"Do you think he will forgive me?" Kandra appeared so hopeful that it made her look girlish.

"Depends on how big a piece you took out of him and his pride." Mary smiled. "Men do not like to be shown up, especially by women."

"I suppose I will have to grovel, will I not?" Kandra gave a weary sigh.

"That you will, Love," Mary laughed. "Now, we need a bath for you."

Bathed and dressed in a clean pair of breeches and plain blue tunic, Kandra made her way to the great hall. Jonas would be there, as would the rest of her father's men. She'd have to drag Jonas off and speak to him in private.

She entered the great hall and sought out Jonas where he sat with Griffin and Ryan, two soldiers in her father's army. Swallowing her pride, she crossed the hall. Everyone was awaiting her and her brother, to take their seats at the head table so they could begin the evening meal. However, she was determined to deal with what had happened between her and Jonas first.

Striding over to where her brother sat, Kandra frowned down at him. "Jonas, I wish a word with you." Kandra spoke with authority in her voice.

"Yes, my lady?" Jonas gave her a cold hard look. He'd make her grovel for what she had done to him, he thought with a mild satisfaction.

"In private, please." She scanned the table where he sat. She didn't want to make a scene here.

"Oh, I think here would be a fine place to speak, do you not?" He waved a hand around smiling at her brightly.

"No, I do not wish to speak here." She put her temper in check as she bit the inside of her cheek, but it wasn't easy. "It is a private matter." Kandra spoke between her clenched teeth. "Now, Jonas."

"Since it would seem we cannot start the meal before you have had your say, then by all means," Jonas stood, waving her before him.

"Thank you." Kandra led the way into their father's study. She was determined to swallow her pride and apologize to Jonas.

Opening the door, she waved Jonas through it. With an air of arrogance, he sauntered over to one of the high back chairs. Kandra closed the door behind them. With her head held high, she walked over to the desk, leaning on the edge as she faced him.

"This is not an easy thing for me and well you know it, Jonas." She glared at his grinning face. How she would like to swipe that smug look off his face. In a sword fight, she reigned superior, but in a contest of strength, she was slightly inferior and that annoyed her. They had been raised together, played and fought together. Never had a day passed when she and Jonas had been apart. She took in his golden looks that mirrored her own, so much that they could have had the same mother. They each looked at the other with blue eyes, but where Jonas had eyes like the deep blue of water, Kandra's were like the summer skies. If not for the fact that Jonas was younger than her by a little more than two years, she was sure he would wield a sword better than she.

Though Jonas was her father's bastard son, never had Kandra looked at him as less than her brother, or her best friend. Her mother died shortly after she was born and later her father had turned to a village woman for comfort. When Jonas was three, his own mother had become ill and died. Their father had taken Jonas into their home, but by law Jonas could neither inherit their father's title nor lands.

Jonas watched her struggle with her emotions. This was a hard thing for her. Kandra was beautiful with her golden looks, but her size had always bothered her. Being taller than any other woman that she had ever met, as well as being the height of most men, made her uneasy at times. Men who visited the castle often looked at her strangely, for unlike most females, she hadn't a delicate bone in her body. However, she had a kind, soft heart that she guarded well.

He could remember once, when she was eleven and he was eight, the boys from the village had been teasing her about her height, because she stood a full head taller than all of them. They had dubbed her with the title 'Lady Goliath'. Jonas had stood to fight the whole bunch when his sister had punched the ringleader in the nose. When the fight was over, Kandra had cried while he held her and tried to comfort her. He was one of the only people ever to see her tears flow freely. She was determined never to allow anyone to see her weaknesses again.

"I know you did not mean to hurt me." Jonas stood up and began pacing the room.

"No, I did mean to hurt you..." She held up a staying hand as he began to reply. "I meant to hurt you, so that you would never let such a thing happen again. The thought of losing you, Jonas, is something I care to think about not at all." Her voice sounded strangled as tears shimmered in her blue eyes. "I love you Jonas, you are my best friend, and I could not live without you."

Jonas reached her in two steps, pulling her into a tight hug. "Nor could I live without you, dearest sister." He kissed her cheek. "Besides, if I died in battle, who, pray tell, would you argue with?" He touched the tip of her nose with his finger.

"I am sorry." Kandra laid her head on his shoulder, sighing. She took so much comfort in knowing her brother was always there for her. She couldn't imagine life without him.

"I knew that then, just as I know it now. You need not apologize." He squeezed her shoulder once more. "Now what do you say we go eat, as I am starving."

"All you ever think about is food." She rolled her eyes at him as she stepped away.

"And women, do not forget that." He gave her his most charming smile.

"I do not want to think about you and women!" She shook her head in disgust, walking out the door.

Later that evening, the castle was quiet as Kandra and Jonas sat playing a game of chess. Both were intent upon winning.

"Why do we not call this a draw?" Jonas yawned, knowing that neither would win for hours yet.

Kandra's blue eyes twinkled, "Are you conceding to a superior mind, brother?" She knew how to goad him into playing a bit longer.

Before he could answer, the warning bells sounded. Blue gaze met like, both shot to their feet and raced through the castle. Raff met them in the inner bailey.

"The village is under attack, but we have no clue as to how many invaders." Raff jogged alongside the two as they strode for the stables.

"Ready fifty men, send scouts east, north, and west." Kandra ordered, "Catch up to us as soon as you can." She reached her destrier, named Hadwin, and began saddling him.

"Do not be foolish, girl." Raff grabbed her arm, stopping her, "You could be killed if the two of you go alone."

"We could be killed with, or without fifty men," Kandra jerked her arm away from him, "Ready the men and follow behind, but go Raff, before more lives are lost."

Raff muttered under his breath "Foolish damn girl," but he jogged away from them to assemble the men.

Kandra finished saddling her mount at the same time Jonas did. She swung up into her saddle and looked at him. "Ready?"

"Do you not think you should wear your armor," Jonas raised a blond brow. He hated the thought of her going into battle without it.

"Do you not need yours?" She spurred her warhorse out of the stables. She yelled for the gates to open and raced through them toward the village.

The fire loomed in front of them as homes in the village burned. Screams rent the air. Kandra leaned forward and whispered to Hadwin. The horse sped up and left Jonas's mount trailing further and further behind them.

Jonas filled the air with curses as he watched his sister and her damnable horse race through the night, hell bent on reaching the village.

Kandra pulled her sword from its sheath as she reached the edge of the village. On a full out charge, she met one of the Scottish bandits that was raiding their village. With her sword, she made short work of him, lopping off his head as she passed him.

She spied one of the bastards, in the process of trying to rape a village woman that Kandra had known her entire life. Fury erupted. Sliding from Hadwin's back, she thrust out with her sword and impaled the man's back, through the heart, killing him. Ripping the sword from his back, she pushed him off the crying woman.

"It is over, Lindsay." Kandra pulled the woman to her feet. She hugged the woman to her, "Run for the castle. You will be safe there." Kandra pulled a dagger from her boot and pressed the hilt into the woman's hand. "Take this with you. Use it if you must."

"Thank you, m'lady." Lindsay held a tight fist around the tattered ends of her gown's bodice. She gasped as a Scot turned the corner coming around one of the huts.

Kandra turned to face the man, "Run, Lindsay." She flexed her grip on the hilt of her sword.

"I cannot leave you, m'lady." Lindsay shook her head as a second Scot joined his friend.

"Run," Kandra glanced over her shoulder at the woman, "Go now," she commanded. She looked back at the leering Scots. Both men were her height, but held more brawn. "Leave this village, or die, heathens."

The first man threw back his head and laughed, "Yer a bonnie thing, lass." He rubbed a hand over the front of his kilt, "I'll enjoy burying myself betwixt yer thighs."

"You shall be long dead before that can happen," she ground out, "You will die like the dogs you are." She gave them a vicious smile. "And I shall relish cutting you down to size," she let her sneering gaze drop over the front of their kilts.

The second man growled, "I'll show ye how a dog is treated, bitch." He came at her with claymore in hand. The man had no time for a second thought when Kandra took out his leg from under him and slit his throat.

She looked up at the first man, whipping her braid behind her, "Are you ready to join your friend?"

He stared at her in disbelief as the blood dripped from her sword. "Bloody hell!" He roared as he charged her. Quickly, he realized his folly as she ran her blade through his middle and twisted. He died with a beautiful angel of death standing over him.

The bandits had fled the village and Kandra met up with Jonas and Raff. They worked with the villagers, collecting the dead and the wounded. Kandra spent most of her time dealing with stitching wounds of women severely beaten and those that had been raped.

Later after all the fires had been put out and things had settled, Kandra stood in the center of the village with her brother and Raff, "How many dead?"

Raff rubbed the back of his neck, "Twenty-three, as well as four children." His heart constricted at the thought.

Kandra gasped in outrage. The decision was made without another word being said. "We ride out within the hour."

"No, it is too dangerous," Jonas whirled on her with a look of outrage. "You shall not leave the castle."

"Need I remind you that father left the castle and village in my care." She hated to pull rank on him. But she wouldn't be coddled as if she were merely a woman, and not a warrior. No other woman she knew could fight with her skill, for that matter few men could get the best of her. So as long as she had her sword, she'd have the advantage.

"We leave within the hour. Arthur, go with Raff and help him. I want you, Raff, and ten men assembled, and have pack supplies for fourteen ready." She turned on her heels and began striding away. "Leave twenty men to help the villagers. If needs be, house the villagers within the castle walls until we return."

With that, she swung up onto Hadwin's saddle and raced off through the night.

Chapter Two

*H*er brother, Jonas, was furious with her for her decision to lead the group in pursuit of the bandits. After more than eight days of him not speaking to her, except when necessary, it was beginning to irritate Kandra to no end.

Eight days and seven nights of ridding had turned up nothing. If they didn't find the bastards shortly, they'd have to turn back. They had left Cumbria, and entered Northumbria a few days before. Soon they'd be leaving Northumbria and enter the Scottish borderlands, and the Scots didn't take English presence on their lands kindly.

Frustration filled her as they stopped to make camp for the night. Tired and weary, Kandra unsaddled her horse, and began rubbing him down. Once she finished, she walked over to the nearby stream. Kneeling by the water, she began to drink greedily from the icy stream, then splashed it upon her face.

Removing her armor, she dipped a rag into the cold water and began to wash.

The sound of a twig snapping behind her brought Kandra to her feet and her sword ringing from its sheath. Swinging it through the air, her sword clashed against Jonas's. Muttering a curse under her breath, Kandra stared at him. Pulling her sword away, she sheathed it once more, "What do you think you are doing? I could have killed you!"

"Hardly, I was ready for that move. I know you far too well." He smirked at her. It was a typical move he knew she'd make, so he'd countered it easily. "You should not remove your armor while you are alone." He admonished, shaking his head.

"I can protect myself. You need not worry about me." She raised her chin at a haughty angle.

"I must worry about you, for you are my sister, and I care." He reached out tucking a stray lock of golden hair behind her ear. It was an endearing gesture and he watched her swallow hard. "What's wrong?"

"I do not know what to do, Jonas." She admitted. "We have ridden for more than a sennight, we have left Cumbria behind, and will soon be out of Northumbria, and are nearing the border lands of Scotland. If we do not catch up to them soon, then we have ridden all this way for naught." She turned away from him, staring at the stream. "Do we turn back on the morrow or continue on? I am confused as to what I should do?" She pleaded with him for an answer. He was the only one besides Raff, who she was willing to show her uncertainty to. Kandra crossed her arms over her waist, bowing her head in anguish.

"Kandra, do not despair. I say we ride through the morrow and the next, if we do not come across them, we turn back." Jonas stood with his hands upon his hips, scowling across the stream toward the Scottish border. "Those Scottish bastards need to die for their crimes."

Kandra glanced over her shoulder at him. The taut set of his body told her of the fury that he held just beneath the surface. "Then we ride through the marrow and the next if needs be, and I am sure we shall find them." She nodded her head and began to turn away, but stopped next to him. "I am sorry, Jonas. I should have listened to you."

Jonas laid a hand upon her shoulder, "You were right to pull rank, and you know you could never have stayed behind." He flashed her a knowing smile.

Kandra smiled back with mischief dancing in her eyes. "You are right. I would have followed behind you anyhow."

They broke camp before dawn then continued their journey. Kandra's confidence kept them going through the day and into the next morning, she was sure they couldn't be far behind the bloody bastards.

The riders didn't stop once they broke camp that morning. Kandra and her men rode until late afternoon before they stopped to rest their horses. Frustrated, Kandra watered her warhorse then sat on a log to eat some of the salted meats they'd brought with them.

'*It is hopeless! We are never going to catch those bloody Scots!*' She thought in frustration as she kicked at the dirt with her toe.

"Do not be so hard on yourself. We will catch them." Raff came to sit down beside her.

"It is of no use, Raff, we might as well turn back." Her shoulders slumped in dismay.

"If that is your wish, then why not turn back now?" Raff looked up at the sky as he asked the question.

"Because, I cannot seem to get the sight of those villagers out of my head, I want justice for them. I cannot go home empty handed!" Kandra's determination spilled forth. She wanted those bandits with a vengeance.

"Then what do you suggest, my lady?" Raff smiled at her.

"Catch those bloody bastards!" She gave him a cold hard look as fury burned in her bright blue eyes. "Mount up!" She bellowed. Kandra swung up on her horse, looking around at her men, "We cannot be far behind them. We shall catch them!" She placed her helmet back on her head, wheeled her horse around, and set off at a neck-breaking pace.

A roar of enthusiasm and vengeance filled the air from the group of fourteen at her words. Mounting their horses, they charged off after the thieves.

They rode hard and fast for two more hours. However, there was no sign of the bandits. Kandra was about ready to give up. The day was waning and the men were weary. Slowing at the top of the next rise, she was going to turn back when she saw them in the valley below.

Nineteen Scots, mounted, and wearing vibrant colored plaids of red were just below them. The leader rode a pitch colored destrier that looked as if it where at least twenty hands high. The man seated upon the beast, looked powerful and angry. Without a second thought, Kandra drew her sword, charging down the hill toward the leader.

Jonas kicked his horse into motion and tried to follow her. Raff and the rest of the men took up arms and followed.

Kandra watched as the leader spurred his horse into motion. His long, raven black hair flowed behind him as he charged to meet her in battle. She determined to bring justice to these heathen, Scottish bastards.

The lad had to be insane, Lachlan MacKinnon thought as he spurred his mount into motion. He didn't want to kill the boy, but the lad had charged upon him. Lachlan quickly took in the lad's silver and gold armor, along with the boy's matching helmet. Lachlan sized the boy up as the son of a nobleman. He was an Englishman and Lachlan hated the English, the thought of teaching this whelp a well-deserved lesson pleased him greatly.

Kandra braced herself for the impact of their swords crossing, but she was not prepared for the total force behind their meeting. As his sword struck hers, the clang of metal against metal was thunderous. The Scotsman thrust out his elbow and unseated her in one quick motion. The world spun as she tumbled from her mount. The earth rushed up at her. With a bone-jarring thud, she hit the ground and rolled to her back as the wind was knocked from her body. Gasping she looked up at the blue sky above her.

In her head, she could hear her father's voice telling her to get to her feet. '*Do not just lay there on your back girl, get up and defend yourself!*' Her father bellowed loudly in her head. She sighed inwardly, but lying there seemed, oh so much better. Then an image of Jonas came into her thoughts. With great effort, she rolled over, grunting as she gained her feet.

Lachlan shook his head as he watched the boy stagger to his feet. He had to give the boy credit. He was certainly persistent. Dismounting quickly, Lachlan strode toward the lad as the boy still staggered to his feet. He couldn't wait to teach the lad some manners. It wasn't right for him to charge upon them without cause. The lad didn't know whom he was dealing with. Lachlan shook his dark head at the thought. No one within his right mind would take on Lachlan MacKinnon, War Chieftain of the Clan MacKinnon, especially on his own lands.

Kandra watched the leader of the thieves, stride toward her. She quickly cleared her head and evened her breathing, but she continued to stagger a bit. As he came to stand over her bent body, she smiled beneath the mask of her helmet. He thought her injured and unable to fight. She'd show him that he had met his match this day.

With claymore in hand, he stopped, looking down at the lad, bent at the waist. "Do ye yield, lad?" Lachlan smiled down at the staggering boy. When the boy didn't answer, or look up he placed his hand on the boy's shoulder and peered at him. In the next instant, Lachlan found himself hitting the ground and saw the boy swinging his sword. In one fluid motion, Lachlan swept the boy off his feet and jumped to his own, trying to gain the advantage. This boy was tricky. Lachlan smiled and relished the fight ahead.

Kandra took the force against her shoulder as she hit the ground once again. Gritting her teeth, she rolled away from the thief, and gained her feet with sword in hand, as the heat of battle fired her blood. Standing at her full height of six feet, she realized that this man was over a full head taller than she. He must be six and a half feet tall, and nearly twice as wide as she with his muscular frame!

Lachlan watched the lad with narrowed eyes and swung his claymore. As steel clashed against steel, Lachlan knew he could out power the boy and that was his advantage. As the boy whirled away from Lachlan's powerful blade with swift agility, he soon realized that the boy may be weaker, but he was much quicker. That could be a huge disadvantage.

Over and over, their blades clashed, as time and again Kandra pared with him and whirled away from him. She could neither out power him or out maneuver him, but she would not surrender. Win or lose, she was in this battle until the end. And damn her, if a Scot would claim victory over her! From the corner of her eye, she saw Jonas making his way toward her.

Lachlan saw the moment of distraction and his opening as the boy looked away. He struck out swiping the boy's arm. Victory would be his, of that he was sure. The lad was good, no doubt, but he was no match for a Scotsman's skill.

Kandra hissed in pain as the blade sliced her left arm just under her shoulder plate. She tried to focus her attention back on the fight at hand. This giant was cocky and over sure of his skill. In a quick movement, Kandra gave as well as she got, when she ran her blade along his thigh as she spun around him. Then to add insult to injury she kicked him in the butt.

He bellowed in an angry roar. The lad was good, but it was time to end this battle. Lachlan swung strongly in several powerful blows, driving the boy to his knees. Swinging his claymore high, he brought it down intending to knock the sword from the boy's hands.

Kandra knew how to counter this move just as Raff and her father had taught her. She rolled between his spread legs in a move that surprised him completely. Regaining her feet, she turned to face her opponent and Jonas caught her eye again. As he was heading her way to help her, a Scot came from out of nowhere and sliced her brother from the side across his stomach. Jonas never saw it coming. Kandra's throat locked as a scream choked her, only a small whimper sounded.

From the corner of her eye, she saw the leader of the thieves swing his claymore toward her. Spinning away, but not quiet out of reach, he sliced along her right side. A searing pain gripped her as she stumbled. The giant swept her feet out from under her and rolled her over placing the blade of his claymore at her throat as her sword met his belly.

"Surrender or die!" His deep rich voice thundered stopping the fighting around them.

Kandra glanced around her at her men who looked on. They would fight to the death if needs be, then her gaze slid to Jonas's crumpled form. She closed her eyes then roared as she threw her sword. Kandra had no choice but to surrender, and now she had sealed their fate.

Lachlan removed the tip of his claymore from the lad's throat, and stepped back, picking up the boy's smaller broadsword, "On yer feet, lad."

Kandra struggled to her feet and felt the pull at her side. She wouldn't let them see her pain. Turning, she looked to where her brother lay on the ground. A whimper escaped her. Without a word to the giant she raced to her brother's side kneeling. "Jonas," she whispered as she removed her helmet.

As the long golden braid tumbled out of the helmet Lachlan gasped, as did his men, "She's a lass? She's a lass!" Horror filled his face as his heart seized in his chest. Swearing under his breath Lachlan kicked a rock in anger.

"Oh Jonas," she cradled her brother's head in her lap and with a shaky hand, she swept his hair off his brow. He couldn't be dead, he just couldn't, her mind screamed over and over as fear seized her. She couldn't lose him, she thought as tears shimmered in her eyes.

"Do not dare cry in front of these bastards," Jonas cracked his eyes open as he smiled weakly up at her.

Tears pooled in her eyes, "You are not dead?"

"No, if I died then who, pray tell, would you have to argue with?" He reached up, wiping away a stray tear. "Show no fear, do not let them have that."

"I will not show a thing. I shall make you proud." Her chin jutted up as she laid his head back down. "Griffin, see to our wounded."

"Yes, m'lady," Griffin walked quickly to Jonas first and began to tend him.

Kandra turned back toward the leader of the thieves. Her head was high and her back ramrod straight as she walked. The wounds on her side and arm, along with her bruised shoulder, were on fire, but she wouldn't show weakness, not to these bastards.

"What are we to do with 'em, laird?" A tall redheaded man spoke to the giant.

"I have nay decided as of yet, Gavin." Lachlan watched the lass walking back toward him. Anger filled him, what man in his right mind would allow a woman, nay, a mere lass, to ride with them? Was her father or husband a mad man? Watching her, he realized he could have killed her. The thought of killing a woman, armed or not, staggered him.

"I am Lady Kandra, my father is Lord Stafford from Carlisle in Cumbria." She announced herself with pride and dignity as if she were holding court. For the first time, she really looked at her nemesis. He was tall and his golden, sun-kissed body was laden with rippling muscles. His midnight, silky, black hair was longer than she had ever seen a man wear it. His hair hung well past his shoulders and down his back, with two long war braids down the sides of his face, and other braids scattered throughout his glorious hair, all ending with silver beads. He looked wild and heathen. His magnetic green eyes were breathtaking, as they looked her over from head to toe and back. He was the most beautiful man she had ever seen in her life.

"I am Lachlan MacKinnon, War Chieftain to the clan MacKinnon, and laird of the clan MacKinnon of the low lands. And yer on my lands, lass." He stared down at her through narrowed eyes. "Why in the… name of saints did ye attack us?" His voice was a deep and demanding rumble with a brogue that made her heart beat a bit faster.

Kandra realized her mistake right away. This man was a Scottish lord, not some common thief. "I mistook you for the Scottish bandits that plundered our village over a sennight ago." She gave him a haughty look. "We have been in pursuit of them since."

Lachlan looked this girl over. She was as tall as most men, some may call her unnatural, but as he studied her, he realized he would call her more woman than girl. Her hair was the color of spun gold and if the armor she wore told true, she was well formed. Her eyes were summer sky blue and hard, but of her features, it was her mouth that drew him. It was full, with a slightly pouting bottom lip. The word plunder brought the image of his mouth on hers to mind. Pulling his gaze from her mouth, he narrowed his eyes again.

"And this gives ye the right to attack us, *Sasunnach*?" His voice bellowed with rage. Most cringed when he was angered, but not this young warrior woman, she didn't so much as bat an eyelash.

"I believe I explained that it was a mistake." Kandra rolled her eyes at him. He was certainly the densest creature she had ever had the misfortune of meeting, but then what did one expect for a Scottish heathen, even one as gloriously beautiful as him?

"Well *Sasunnach*, ye seem to have found yerself in more trouble than ye ken what to do with." Lachlan peered down at her with hard eyes that made her want to shiver. He had no clue as to what he would do with her and her men, but he was certainly not going to shrug his shoulders and walk away.

"I am sure we can come to a reasonable accord, can we not?" Kandra looked impatiently up at him. She studied his masculine beauty as she awaited his response. It was rare for her to have to look up at anyone. This man made her feel small in comparison. Good lord, but any normal women must feel completely dwarfed, she thought with an inward sigh.

As if the Gods were blessing him, Lachlan found an answer to his lack of money problems, and here she stood before him. With the weather destroying their crops in the last few years and the feuding between the clans, it had depleted most of Lachlan's coffers, or left them completely empty. So, there was no money for much needed seeds to replant and homes to repair. If he ransomed the lass to her noble Da, he would gain the coins he needed to refill his coffers.

"Aye, and here it be," Lachlan sneered down at her, "Yer to be my guests until yer noble Da arranges a reward for finding yer sorry hide."

Kandra narrowed her eyes at him, "You are making an enormous mistake. I would release us if I were you."

"Well yer nay me, lass. Ye'll return with me to my home by yer own power, or by pure force." He growled down at her. He would enjoy another tussle with this feisty woman if for no other reason than to see if she was as well formed as her armor suggested.

Kandra had no choice but to concede to this barbaric man's demands. She would find a way out of this for her men and for herself. "Fine, but let it be said that you shall regret this, my lord."

With that she turned, striding to her horse. In one graceful movement, she swung up onto the saddle. "Pray, lead the way, my lord."

Chapter Three

Well past midnight, the group rode through the gates and into the inner bailey of the MacKinnon castle. Lachlan dismounted, shouting orders in Gaelic for Kandra's men to be placed in the dungeon. As Kandra began to follow them, Lachlan grabbed her arm, pulling her to him.

"Yer nay goin' with 'em, *Sasunnach*," he looked down at her surprised face. He could not justify to his own conscience the idea of putting a woman in the dungeon. Besides, his mother would surely be fit to be tied if she were to find out.

"Those are my men and I am going with them. Now, release me." She raised a haughty brow as she gave the command.

"I am laird here. Yer aught, to my people. Ye dinna give commands around here, ye ken?" He pressed his fingers slightly tighter and she hissed in pain. Looking at the cut in her shirt his brows furrowed and he shook his head. "Yer hurt, we need to have yer wounds tended to."

"I need nothing from you." Kandra jerked her arm away from him. "If you would but show me to my chambers." She was issuing commands once again as she threw her haughty chin in the air.

"This way, yer highness," Lachlan gave a mocking bow as he waved her up the stairs leading to the solar.

"At least you recognize nobility when you see it, but you may address me as my lady, or your ladyship, either shall do nicely." She threw over her shoulder in an icy tone that matched the icy glare she sent him.

Lachlan threw back his head roaring with laughter. She was as amusing as she was beautiful, he thought, following behind her as she climbed the stairs.

Once shown into the room that would be her prison, the door was locked. Kandra moved to the window. Looking out, she knew she was too high up to attempt escape this way. A key scraping in the lock brought her attention around. Facing the door as it opened, Kandra was confronted with a small young woman with ebony hair. A tall broad Scotsman with flaming red hair flanked the young woman. He was one of the men from their earlier battle.

In a stance prepared for battle Kandra scowled at them. "Get out!"

"Yer wounded, m'lady." The woman hesitated. "The laird sent for me to tend yer wounds."

"Get out, or I shall throw you both out!" Kandra raged at them. "You will not touch me."

The Scot gave Kandra a cross look, but stood his ground. A pottery pitcher was near at hand. Kandra hefted it and began swinging it toward the man. The little women yelped and fled the room. Kandra threw the pitcher at the man as he left the room. It shattered in the hall just before the door slammed shut and relocked. Kandra smiled in satisfaction.

She felt the warm sticky ooze of blood running down her side from her wound. Taking the sheet from the bed, she tore it into strips making a pad and wrap. Removing her armor, she lifted her jerkin and shirt to examine the wound and winced. It was deep and in need of stitching, but she would have to make do. She placed the pad over the wound then wrapped the strips as tight as possible around her midsection and tied them off. Pulling her shirt and leather jerkin back in place, she refastened her armor. It would have to do for now, she thought with a sigh. She had lost a great deal of blood. She was tired and badly in need of some rest.

Crawling upon the bed, she sat with her back against the wall. Laying her head upon her updrawn knees, Kandra tried to relax. Rest would help her regain her strength and perhaps on the morrow she would figure out how to get her and her men out of this.

She fell into a fitful dream filled with her brother and the giant Scotsman.

The sound of a key scrapping in the lock brought her awake with a jerk. Blinking, she realized it was morning. She hissed in pain as the movement pulled at the wound on her side. Rolling off the bed, she was on to her feet as the door swung open.

"Food to break yer fast, m'lady," an older lady with midnight hair, streaked liberally with silver, was carrying a tray laden with food.

"Allow me." Kandra put out her hands. The woman let Kandra take the tray. She looked down at the delicious food and smiled haughtily. "Tell your laird I am not hungry." Kandra pitched the tray into the hall, laughing wickedly as it hit the opposite wall.

The older woman shook her head, tisking, and walked from the room. Kandra smiled after her, this older woman didn't scare easily, but Kandra had made her point.

Lachlan returned to the castle as food was being served for the evening meal. He sought out his mother, Ferran MacKinnon. She was in the kitchen helping to prepare the evening meal. Lachlan embraced the small woman in a hug that lifted her clear off the ground. "Mam, how is the most beautiful MacKinnon woman this fine day?"

"Busy Lachlan," she sighed, "And the extra mouths ye've brought me is nay helpin', especially that She-Devil!" Ferran rolled her eyes, shaking her head.

"She can nay be so bad, she is but one wee, *Sasunnach*." Lachlan shook his head grinning down at his small mother.

"Ha! Then ye take her, her tray and we'll see what ye have to say!" Ferran shoved her son the tray before he could say a word in protest. "And while yer at it, see if ye can get her to let someone tend to her wounds. Lord knows we can nay get near her."

Kandra came off the bed and held onto one of the bedposts to steady herself as the key rattled in the lock of the door. As the door started to open, she rammed it shut with her uninjured shoulder. Pain assailed her side from the force of hitting the door. She forced herself to stand with her weight placed against the door, as her knees began to buckle.

As the food and ale ran down the front of Lachlan, shock was replaced by the anger that consumed him. With a roar of rage, he shoved the door open to find an empty room. He looked this way and that, turning around just in time to duck as a candleholder barely missed his head, "Yer insane woman!"

"Then let me and my men go and I shall no longer be your problem!" She raged at him and threw another candleholder at his head as she made her way to the side of the room where the washstand stood.

He ducked as the other wooden holder whizzed past his head. Through his anger, he took in her pale complexion and glassy eyes. She was injured worse than she was letting on. He'd have to coax her out of her armor if he were to help her. She was like a cornered, injured animal and he had been the one to injure her, he felt guilt weigh upon him.

"Remove yer armor, lass, and I'll look at yer wounds." He took a step toward her and she grabbed the water basin to use as a weapon. "I am nay gonna hurt ye."

"Stay away from me or I shall hurt you!" She threatened him. The weight of the basin made her tired arms ache and she wished he'd just leave so that she could sleep. Then the throbbing in her head, shoulder, arm, and side would lessen a bit.

"What will it take to get ye out of that armor?" He looked her up and down as if searching for a hint.

"Where are my men? What have you done with Jo... with them?" She tried to keep the tremor out of her voice as she thought of Jonas' wound.

"Ah, yer men, would ye like to see to their welfare?" He walked toward the window looking out.

"I shall strike a bargain with ye," he glanced over his shoulder at her as she lowered the basin. "Ye remove yer armor and let me look at yer wounds and I shall let ye see yer men." It was the injured man that concerned her and now Lachlan knew he had his bargaining tool.

"No, I do not make deals with barbarians." She shook her head then swayed. Kandra placed a hand upon the washstand to steady herself as the room reeled for a moment.

"Nay even to see yer man and check on his wounds?" He had found her weakness and was using it against her to gain what he wanted.

"Have any of them died?" Her face paled even more. Please don't let Jonas be dead, she prayed silently as her eyes pled with her captor.

"Remove yer armor and ye shall see for yerself, yer highness." He turned to look at her fully as he raised a brow. He watched the thoughts and weight of indecision play over her face. Her glassy blue eyes pled with him when she asked the question, but he could not give into her until he was able to treat her wounds. He watched her gnaw at her lower lip, making it redder and plumper as she thought.

She thought about it for several moments before she spoke, "Agreed, but I shall only remove my armor."

"Agreed, but once yer armor is removed ye can nay put it back on." He added, eyeing her, and decided he would settle for what he could get. The rest would come soon enough.

"Agreed," she was desperate to check on Jonas. He just had to be alive. She couldn't wait to see him and to know how he faired.

"Well?" Lachlan prompted. "Do ye need a hand?" The idea of touching her in such intimate ways made his loins tighten. Not that he was interested in this woman. It had just been a long time since he had, had a woman to ease himself with. Though, he had to admit at least to himself, that this woman thoroughly intrigued him with her skills with a sword and her unique beauty.

"No, I can do it myself." Kandra shot him a menacing look. Carefully, she unfastened her breastplate, but as she raised her arms to remove it over her head, the pain shot through her side as her wound opened wider. Her breath hitched in a ragged gasp.

Lachlan was at her side in two large steps. He removed the platting from her, as worry creased his brow. Dropping the breastplate, he closed his eyes and sighed at the sight of blood soaking her shirt and jerkin. The whole side of her breeches was stained with blood and Lachlan felt a wave of sickness at the pain he had caused her. He began to pull at her shirt and she smacked his hands away. "Let me look at yer wound, lass."

"No, we agreed to armor only. Are you going back on your word?" She tried to reach for the armor on the floor.

"Nay," he pushed at her shoulder to stop her from retrieving it. "But if 'tis nay taken care of soon, ye'll bleed to death or die of septicemia."

"It is not your problem, but if you are that concerned, allow me and my men to leave, then I shall have it cared for by my people." She glared up at him. Looking up at anyone was an unfamiliar sensation and made her dizzy and light headed. This laird made her nervous, and it caused her to be on the defensive.

Without another word, Lachlan helped her remove the rest of her armor. He'd find a way to convince her to have her wounds tended to. If he tried forcing her, she would likely cause herself more harm than good. She was a stubborn wench for sure.

With the armor removed, she could move and breathe a little easier, but her body was still achy and sore. The wound on her side throbbed as it continued to bleed. Three times since the previous night, she had changed the bandage, but still she couldn't staunch the blood flow completely. "I wish to go to my men, now."

"As ye wish, *Sasunnach*," he shot her a worried glance as she walked ahead of him, a bit wobbly, clutching her side. Quickly, he took hold of her arm to give support.

"I am in no need of your assistance to walk." She tried to pull away, but his grip held firm.

"I would nay want ye to run away on me now, lass." He smiled challengingly down at her and she felt her knees grow weaker. She wasn't sure if it was from her loss of blood, or from his smile.

"I would not leave without my men. You need not worry." Sarcasm dripped from her words. She had never met a more annoying man before in her life. As they reached the base of the stairs, Kandra stopped worrying her lower lip.

"Is there aught amiss?" He raised his brows as he stared into her frowning blue gaze.

"Yes, I am in need of a cloak." She knew that if the men saw blood on her, they would worry and get themselves killed if they thought her in peril.

"'Tis nay a problem," he waved a man over, speaking in Gaelic to him, the man scurried off, only to return in moments with a hug dark cloak. "'Tis a bit large for ye *Sasunnach*, but I think 'twill do." He draped the cloth across her shoulders then turned her slightly so that he could fasten it. Standing this close to her, he could see that her eyes were the color of bright blue, summer skies, with flecks of gold through them. Her mouth was deep pink and looked as luscious as sweet ripe fruit. It made him think of nibbling and suckling them.

As he wrapped the cloak about her, she felt a thrill course through her as the scent of him wrapped around her. It was earthy, male and absolutely provocative. She wanted to lean in and fill herself with his scent. Kandra looked up into his rugged dark features and felt her knees wobble.

"Steady, lass." He reached out touching her arm to steady her. She winced from the pain as he touched her wound, but said not a word. His heart clenched at the thought of hurting her. Lightly, he brushed his fingers across her cheek. His breath caught at the contact and his blood stirred as she closed her eyes for a moment.

The feel of his fingers against her skin brought a fluttery sensation to her stomach as warmth spread through her. Closing her eyes at the unexpected comfort his touch invoked, she reveled in the sensation for a moment. No man had ever touched her in such a way. With that thought, she opened her eyes and pulled away from him, looking away.

Lachlan furrowed his brow as she moved away from him. She was his prisoner, so why did he have the urge to touch her, to taste her, to have her? He asked himself. '*Because ye've been without a woman for far too long, ye daft bastard!*', he thought silently.

"Are ye ready?" He spoke to her more harshly than he had intended.

"Yes," she looked straight ahead with a concerned look upon her face. The thought of Jonas being injured made her worry her lower lip. He just had to be all right. The thought of him dying was too much to stand.

As Lachlan walked beside her, he could see her tiring. Each step was an effort, he was sure. Under her eyes were darkened circles and her skin was pale. Her wounds and the lack of food were already taking a toll on her. Though she was not a fragile woman he was sure, she was still human. As she stumbled, he reached out and steadied her. "Easy lass, perhaps ye'd like to sit a spell and rest."

Her head was high as she shot him an indignant look. "I am quite all right. I am not feeble, nor am I weak."

"Aye, but yer human, lass."

In silence, they reached the dungeon. It was damp, dark, musty, and gave her the shivers. Sadness filled her at the thought of her men locked within this awful place. It broke her heart. If it wasn't for her and her impulsiveness, they wouldn't be here, imprisoned by a heathen, Scottish lord. It was up to her to find a way to gain their freedom.

Lachlan glanced over at her as she peered around the dark dungeon. Sadness filled her features, but pride kept her moving. He watched determination take over as she walked toward the cells, her back was ramrod straight and her chin raised a notch higher.

"In which cell is the severely wounded man?" She turned a cold set of eyes upon him. She was desperate to see Jonas, but wouldn't allow the laird to see her eagerness.

"I dinna ken, lass." Lachlan shook his head then grabbed a set of keys from a high hook upon the wall. Walking to the first cell, he unlocked it while two guards flanked the sides of the open door. Kandra inclined her head then ducked into the cell. She scanned the darkened room, furrowing her brows when she didn't see Jonas.

Griffin stood upon her entrance. The other five men in the cell came to their feet as well, all hurrying to encircle her and ensure themselves of her wellbeing.

"Griffin!" Kandra stepped to him and the rest of the men in the cell.

"M'lady, how fares thee?" Griffin searched her over with his eyes. "Has the barbarian touched you?" He was seething.

"No, I am well." She waved his concerns away. "Tell me how all of you fare? Are you being taken care of?"

"Yes, m'lady," Griffin paused then furrowed his brows, "How fares Lord Jonas?"

"I do not know, I am visiting his cell next, but I fear for him." Kandra bowed her head, trying to hide her concern for her brother's life.

"He is strong m'lady, he will survive." Griffin took her hand in his and squeezed it lightly. "We stand behind you, Lady Kandra, do not fear."

"Thank you, Griffin." Kandra squeezed his hand in return. "I shall return as soon as I can."

She left the cell, focusing her attention on finding her brother. "Where are the rest of my men?" She demanded, upon emerging from the dank cell with fire burning in her eyes.

"This way, lass," Lachlan escorted her to a room farther down the row. He stopped in front of a large door, unlocking it, swinging it wide. "In here."

Kandra entered the second cell containing her men. Her gaze darted from face to face. Raff stepped forward. "Where is he?" Her voice was horse and sounded slightly strangled, but she didn't care that her desperation showed through. She had to see Jonas.

"Here," Raff waved her over to a dark corner.

"Is he...all right?" Tears pooled in her eyes as she hurried to where her brother lay on a pile of straw.

"For now, but he is not well and being in here is not going to help him." Raff spoke from behind her as she knelt beside her brother. "He needs a healer."

"Jonas?" She spoke in a desperate plea. Kandra brushed the hair from his forehead. It was hot and feverish. "I will not let you die! Do you hear me, Jonas?" She leaned forward brushing a kiss upon his forehead as she grasped his limp hand in hers. "Hold on, I shall find a way to save you. I swear it to you. I love you."

Lachlan stood in the doorway and watched her whisper with the older man. His brow furrowed as the older man motioned to the corner and she hurried over to it. He watched her kneel over the injured young man. Sadness filled her voice, but he couldn't make out her words. He watched her place a soft loving kiss upon the man's forehead. The gentleness and her concern for him showed her love for the young man. He must be her betrothed, or perhaps he was her lover, Lachlan surmised as he watched her with the young man.

Kandra wiped away her tears angrily as she stood, turning to Raff. "How fare, you and the rest of the men in here, Raff?" She spoke in a calm voice that belied how she truly felt.

"We are fine, Kandra. My concern is for you and Jonas." He eyed her carefully and took in her tired features and pale complexion. "How are you faring?"

"I am well Raff, have no concern for me." Kandra stood tall and proud, looking him squarely in the eyes. "I am sorry for this and I shall find a way to set things right again."

"Have you any injuries from the battle with the heathen?" Raff scanned her and took in the cloak that covered her from sight. She didn't own this garment and it wasn't so cold in the dungeon that she'd need to wear such a thing. She was hiding something from him.

"No, I am uninjured." She shook her head and tried to smile at him. "You know me, Raff." She tried to reassure him.

"Yes, that's what worries me so. I do know you and I know you are hiding something from me. What?" he looked at her through narrowed eyes.

"Trust me, Raff, I will find a way too free us, stand ready." Kandra leaned forward brushing a kiss upon his leathery old cheek. Raff pulled her into a tight hug and it took every ounce of her self-control not to yelp from the pain.

Chapter Four

K andra removed the barrowed cloak, folding it carefully, then she lay it over the foot of the bed. The laird had returned her to her room without a word, locking the door once again. She had to think of something to get herself and her men away from this place, she thought wearily. But oh, she was so tired. She wanted a moment to rest, she thought as she crawled upon the bed.

Her body ached from the beating it had taken during the battle, and her wounds were paining her something awful. Resting her back against the wall behind her, she sat back upon the bed. With her knees drawn up, she folded her arms, resting her head upon them.

With her head pounding, and her body screaming, Kandra allowed herself to fall into a light sleep. If she rests for a few minutes, she was sure she would think with a clearer head.

Lachlan returned to the great hall as the meal was ending. A squeal from the far end of the room caught his attention. A blur of arms, legs, and pitch colored hair launched itself at Lachlan. "Da!"

"Bry!" Lachlan tossed her into the air. "Where in the name of Saints have ye been, lass?"

"I was at the MacGregor's with Aunt Blair. Visitin' the old laird and his daughter," Bryanna was grinning from ear to ear. "Guess what I got, Da?"

"A goat?"

"Nay," The little girl giggled as she shook her dark head. Lachlan loved the bright sparkle he saw within his daughter's eyes. She was his whole world now, and he would do anything within his power to protect her.

"A sheep?"

"Da!"

"All right, all right, tell me 'afore I can stand it nay, more." Lachlan told her dramatically, then tickled her mercilessly. Bryanna's enthusiasm made her beam and Lachlan loved the sound of her laughter more than anything in the world. She was all that was left of the dream he had, had for a family of his own. When his Kerra and their son had died, that dream had vanished along with her spirit.

"I got a new doll from Kerry, the old laird's daughter. She made it just for me! Do ye wanta see her?" Bryanna squirmed in his arms to be set down.

"Aye, aught would please me more, dumplin'." Lachlan set her on her feet and she scrambled out of the hall. He watched her set out after her newest treasure and smiled.

"She has been missin' ye sorely." Ferran walked up beside her son, wrapping an arm around his waist as she leaned into his bulk.

"Aye, and I've been missin' her as well." He placed a large arm over his mother's shoulders.

"So how did ye fare with yer She-Devil?" Ferran gave him a knowing look. "Did ye get her to agree to eat, or have her wounds tended?"

"Nay, she's a stubborn wench." He flashed Ferran a wicked grin, "Though I did manage to get her out of her armor at least."

"If we dinna attend to her wounds, she could die from septicemia." Ferran tisked, "I dinna believe ye'd be getting' a reward for a dead woman. More than aught ye'd be gettin' a war over her."

"Aye, I ken Mam, but she's the devil's own." Lachlan rubbed his chin. "If I were to try and force her then she would probably only harm herself worse." He looked thoughtful for a moment. "Nay, I need to find a way around her prickly pride."

"How did ye get her to remove her armor?" She looked at him with curiosity. Her Lachlan was a cunning one just as his father had been and with those devilishly handsome looks, he was dangerous to any woman's heart.

"I bargained with her. I allowed her to visit her men..." He trailed off as a twinkle lit his green gaze. "Aye, that would be it. I think I ken how to bend her to my will." He turned to his mother grinning devilishly.

Kandra stood at the sound of the key scrapping in the lock. Pain gripped her side as she sucked in a harsh breath. Her head spun and it took all of her strength and resolution to remain on her feet and not give into the pain.

Lachlan stepped into the room with another tray of food along with a jug of ale and a skin of wine.

"Are you asking to wear it again?" She snarled at him.

"Nay, I wish to strike another accord with ye, lass." He told her flatly, as he sat the tray upon the table.

"An accord? What type of accord?" She sent him a suspicious look. Her brain was still far too fuzzy for her to think clearly.

"Well that would depend on ye." He looked her over, wincing at her bloody clothing. "If ye die from nay eatin' then I'll have a war on me hands, so what besides yer freedom could get ye to eat?"

She didn't even have to think twice before she spoke, "I want Jonas moved out of the dungeon." She stated quickly, then worried her lower lip. Kandra knew she shouldn't give into this heathen, but she was worried over her brother. If he died, a part of her would die also.

"He 'tis the wounded one, aye?" Lachlan knew which one he was, but wanted her to confirm it, "Why him? Why do ye nay seek freedom for some of yer men?"

"Would you release all of my men and allow them to take him home?" Her face held a hopeful look.

He couldn't allow them all to leave for they may try to rescue their lady and he wouldn't let her go at any cost. Because his people needed the coin this woman would bring him, not because he wanted her, he reassured himself.

"Nay, I will nay allow it." He shook his dark head. "I do believe yer man would die 'afore they reached yer home."

"Then I want Jonas removed from the dungeon and taken care of by a physician or a healer, someone to help him. I shall eat once I know he is safe." She raised her chin haughtily.

"Nay, I'll move him to a room, then ye eat. Then ye'll swear to me that ye'll nay starve yerself again while yer in my home." Anger edged his voice. "After that we'll see about yer healer."

Kandra thought about it. All it would take is for her to eat a little food then Jonas would be in a warm dry place and get some help. She could save Jonas for now. What good was she to him if she let herself die? She asked herself.

"All right, once he is moved and is seen to, we have an accord." She nodded her head in a curt gesture, "But only if you promise to have him seen to as well."

"Durell," Lachlan bellowed over his shoulder. A man smaller and much older than the laird appeared behind him. "Durell, I want the wounded prisoner moved into one of the unoccupied chambers and seen to, tell my Mam, to do whatever 'tis necessary to tend him."

"Aye, laird," Durell hurried off without another word.

"Does that meet yer approval, *Sasunnach*?" Lachlan raised an arrogant black brow as his green gaze pierced her blue one.

"Yes, but I wish to see him with my own eyes." She gave him a sharp look.

"My people shall take care of yer man." He retorted. "Now ye must honor yer part of the agreement."

"He is not moved as of yet." She raised a haughty challenging brow. "When he is, I shall eat."

Lachlan reached her in three strides. "Stubborn wench, ye may as well eat 'afore it grows cold." Standing toe to toe with her, he glared down at her as his patients stretched to its limits.

"We made an accord," she replied tersely, not weakening under his furious gaze.

"Yer infuriatin'," he began to throw Gaelic curses at her.

"If you are going to curse my name, at least do so in a manner I can understand, instead of yer heathen tongue," Kandra became furious with him. Did he really expect her to easily capitulate? Prisoner or not, she'd never surrender to him.

Lachlan glowered at her, then ran a hand through his long hair. She was stubborn to say the least. But looking down at her, he had the strongest urge to pull her into him, and crush his mouth over hers until she surrendered to him.

She couldn't help but to notice his missing braids. The longing to reach out and touch the black, silken strands that hung over his shoulders engulfed her. When he spoke, her eyes snapped back to his.

"I'm havin' him moved, can ye at least start to, eatin'? When all is well, I shall take ye to see yer man." He sneered the last part of his promise.

"Agreed, but I expect you to hold to your word." Kandra curled her lip at him in a matching sneer.

"This way with ye, lass," he waved her over to the table, which held the tray laden with food.

She turned with a grimace of pain, but made her way to the table. Settling herself in the seat by the food, she lifted the cover off the first bowl. Thick venison stew filled the dish, a large slice of bread slathered in butter and honey sat to the side. It looked delicious and smelled like heaven to her empty stomach.

Kandra looked up as Lachlan settled himself on the other side of the table from her. She shot him an icy glare, "I neither need, nor want your company to eat, heathen."

"I dinna care what ye be wantin'." He shrugged. "I want to make certain ye eat every bite." Lachlan looked at her with a devilishly wicked smile that made her stomach flip flop.

"Suit yourself," Kandra shrugged, picking up the spoon next to the bowl. The stew tasted just as heavenly as it smelled. "This is delicious." She could barely talk around her mouth full of food.

"Would ye care for some wine, or ale?" He leaned forward to pour her whichever one she chose.

"Wine," she stopped eating long enough to speak. She bit into the bread and raved, "Mmmm, your cooks should be praised for their abilities." Then she licked the sticky honey from her lips.

Lachlan watched as her small pink tongue glided over her lips in a seductive move that made his body clench with need. His blood heated as his loins tightened. He wanted to taste the honey on her lips, and explore the sweetness in her mouth. One type of pillaging and plundering surged through his mind. With an effort of control, he focused his attention on pouring her wine. "I'll tell my Mam and the other MacKinnon women yer well pleased."

"Thank you," she reached out, taking the mug of wine he offered. "Are you not going to eat, or drink anything?"

"Nay," he shook his head, "I've just finished my meal below stairs, in the great hall." Truthfully, he hadn't eaten a bite since morning. At that moment, he didn't think he could sit here and eat with her, without chocking on the food. She was by far too distracting.

He watched her as she continued eating. When she took a deep drink of wine that finished off more than half the mug, then licked her lips again, he thought he would lose his mind. His loins tightened to an excruciating point.

Silence spun out around them as he watched her eat in the candlelight. Her golden hair shimmered in the halo of light. Those blue eyes of hers were the shade of a clear, Scottish summer sky, he thought as he watched her. They were rich and vibrant, yet soft, and made a man lose himself in their depths. Her soft skin was sun kissed from hours spent outside and the wine that passed over her delicious lips as she drank, deepening her luscious, sweet, pink lips. He was sure if he were to taste them at that moment they would be honey sweet and graced by a nip of wine on them. If he were to take even a sip of those lips, he would be sure to lose himself in her.

Her body was muscular and well honed, yet he was sure it was soft in all the right places. She would be a powerful lover. They would fight for control if he were to take her. She would be a remarkable lover he was sure, and a pleasure to look at as well.

"Yer beautiful," he spoke in the silence that had settled between them, before he could stop himself.

Kandra blinked, then just stared at him as if he had sprouted a third eye. "Ye look surprised. Does nay one tell ye such things often?" Lachlan searched her eyes.

She shook her head as a slight blush crept up her cheeks. "No, never men," she looked back down at her food, studying it intently as she scooped up another spoon full of stew.

"Does yer lover nay tell ye such things?" Lachlan raised a questioning brow, as unwarranted anger surged through him at the thought. How could the man neglect to tell her such things? He must be an arrogant *arse*, Lachlan thought, furrowing his brows.

Kandra choked on her food at his words and was forced to gulp down more of the wine in her mug to help her. "What did you say?"

"Does he nay say such things to ye?" He shook his head at the thought of her surprise. How could the man ignore such a beautiful woman? Why would he nay tell her such things?

"I do not wish to discuss such things with my captor!" She was mortified by his words, yet she was thrilled at the thought that this man found her beautiful. He was a confusing man and his words made her head spin.

To distract herself from him, she stood up from the table and the room swayed. Kandra grabbed the table to steady herself as the world spun around her, licking her suddenly dry lips. Dizziness assailed her. She looked at Lachlan as he sat watching her. She watched his image go in and out of focus as he stood.

"Stay away from me!" She pushed back from the table. "What did you do to me?"

"Calm yerself, *Sasunnach*, 'tis all right." He moved around the table toward her. The drug was working just as he had planned.

Realization dawned. She gave him an accusing look that held an underlying hurt in it. "You... You drugged me?" She watched him go in and out of focus again as she blinked her eyes. Kandra shook her head trying to clear it, but only stumbled.

"Aye lass, I'm afraid 'tis true, but I did it for yer own good." Lachlan moved forward as she crumpled. Catching her, he swept her into his arms and took her to the bed, where he laid her down gently. Sitting on the edge of the mattress, he stroked her cheek and smoothed her hair from her face. "I truly am sorry, lass."

Slowly, carefully, Lachlan unfastened her jerkin and pulled her shirt free of her breeches. He winced as the dried blood stuck to her skin. The wound was wrapped and padded with pieces of sheet that were soaked through with blood. Gently, he removed the pad and surveyed the damage. Guilt filled him as he looked at the deep slice in her side. Stitching would be required and she would bare a scar there for the rest of her life. A scar he had given her.

He'd have his mother check her from head to toe, then tend to her wounds. They'd need to keep her drugged and quiet for the next few days if she was to heal.

Chapter Five

*K*andra felt weighed down as she swam through the darkness. She wanted to find the surface, too reach the light, but no matter how hard she tried, it seemed just out of her grasp. Worry over Jonas, was her guiding light, as his image floated through her mind. He was hurt and she needed to be with him.

The light of day hurt her eyes and her vision was blurry as she forced her eyes to blink open. Her mouth was dry and her throat was raw. The room spun as she fought the drug that had kept her silent for God knew how long. No more of their evil drinks, Kandra told herself as she slipped back into the darkness again.

"Lachlan," Ferran walked into his study without knocking. She glared at him openly, as only his mother would dare. "Yer She-Devil 'tis beginnin' to awaken."

"Give her more of the sleepin' draught," he shrugged his shoulders in dismissal to an easily solved problem. In the past few days, he had had blessed peace and didn't want it disturbed.

"We can nay, she'll nay drink any more of it." Ferran shook her head, frowning at her son. With this woman, Lachlan was in over his head.

"Let me try," Lachlan rose with a look of annoyance upon his face. This English woman was proving to be a trial on his patience.

Kandra's body felt heavy and weighted, but she shook it off. The key jangled in the lock at her door and a woman entered the room. "Who are you?" She crooked from her dry throat as her head reeled.

"Aleina, I see yer awake now, m'lady. 'Tis time to check yer wounds m'lady." She came near the bed.

"Do not touch me!" Kandra rasped, and began to get up only to realize she was completely naked beneath the blanket. "Where is my clothing?"

"Please m'lady, I must see to yer wounds." The young woman pleaded.

"If you come near me, I shall kill you!" Kandra threatened, menace lacing her roughened voice.

"'Tis nay verra ladylike, to be sayin' such things, ye ken, *Sasunnach*?" Lachlan spoke from the doorway where he stood leaning against the door jamb.

"You, heathen bastard! You drugged me!" Kandra came out of the bed, groping for the blanket. She swayed on her feet, stumbling as the world tilted around her.

Lachlan reached her in three long strides, scooping her up in his arms. Quickly, he laid her upon the bed, "Yer nay ready to be up yet, lass."

"Let me go." Her voice was weaker then she meant it to sound as she struggled in his hold.

"Nay lass, ye need to stay abed," he kept a firm hand upon her to keep her lying down.

"I need nothing from you! Let me go!" She began to sit up when he raised his hand and he pushed her back down on the bed. Kandra swung out with a fist connecting with his jaw.

"Leave us!" He bellowed at the young woman who stood watching them intently. As the door closed behind her, Lachlan turned his attention to the woman he held down on the bed. "I give ye a choice, ye may stay abed willingly, or I shall tie ye to it."

"Let me go, you, heathen bastard! You have no right to do this." She began to fight him with all the strength she could muster. Kandra hated to be told what to do, and she was not about to bow down to this man, he would not win.

Lachlan grasped her wrists in one of his larger hands and pinned them over her head as he covered her body with his own. "Cease this, wench." He growled at her.

"Get off me!" As she struggled with him, she felt a searing pain, as the stitches in her side wound ripped open. The pain froze her as she gasped for air.

As her struggles ceased, he looked down into her face as she panted. "Are ye all right?" His breaths also came in heaves from fighting Kandra, she was no weak woman. She was a wild minx. He looked at her with concern as he read the pain in her gaze.

Tears shimmered in her eyes and she looked away from him. "I am fine, just leave me be."

"Nay, I'm afraid I can nay do that, *Sasunnach*. If ye'll stop strugglin', I shall release yer hands." Lachlan turned her face to his, he looked down into her pain-filled gaze. A tear escaped, slipping from the corner of her eye and he wiped it away with the pad of his thumb. Guilt filled him, but he pushed it aside.

"Let me go." She rubbed her cheek where the tear had been, against her shoulder to dry it. Crying showed weakness and the last thing she wanted to let this heathen see was any sign of weakness in her.

"Will ye behave yerself?" Lachlan looked down into her beautiful face and noticed the softness of her lips once again. He was sure they would feel like the finest of silks beneath his and taste of the sweetest fruits. The feel of her body under his was threatening to undo his well-honed control. He could feel the soft supple curves of her body. Gazing down at her, he could see the high swells of her breasts just under the blanket. If said blanket slipped just slightly her breasts, in all their splendid glory, would be bared to him. The thought appealed to him greatly.

The weight of Lachlan's body pressing hers into the mattress made her pulse race and a tightness form in her stomach. The feel of his fingers wrapped around her wrists branded her skin. As his gaze lingered on the tops of her breasts, she felt her nipples pebble while her breasts felt heavier and fuller. Her breath came in short labored pants. No man had ever looked at her with hunger in his eyes before.

She noticed how very green his eyes were and how delicious his mouth looked. Outside of her father and her brother, Jonas, or perhaps Raff who would give her a quick peck on the cheek, no man had ever even chastely kissed her at all. She wondered what it would be like to have a man, such as this heathen laird, kiss her and touch her.

By the Saints, Kandra thought furiously, she had to get him away from her, to stop the contact and feelings he was stirring up inside of her. These desires were like nothing she had ever felt before. No man had ever made her yearn for their touch, or their kisses. And to have that with her captor was not a very sane idea. "Fine, I shall stay in bed," she spat out with a glare.

He searched her face for a moment. "I'll let ye go, but I'm goin' to have a look at yer wound. I promise to be gentle. Ye ken?" Lachlan loosened the pressure upon her wrists.

She would do anything to get him away from her. "Yes, fine, just get it over with." The wound on her side was burning in a fiery pain.

Slowly, and with great regret, Lachlan removed himself from covering her. The feel of her under him had been provocative and completely arousing. She was nearly as tall as he was and well formed, her body was hardened with muscle, but soft in all the right places, it was an intoxicating and heady mix.

Once he was off her, he sat upon the edge of the bed looking down at her bare shoulders and the creamy swells of her breasts, with her golden locks spread around her. She didn't even bother to pull the blanket up to cover her exposed cleavage. It was as if she weren't aware of the sensuousness of her own body. Had no man ever paid homage to her body? Did her lover nay worship her? Did the blackguard just rut her like an English dog?

"Do not look at me thus." She glared at him through narrowed eyes. He had no right to look at her as if he wanted nothing more than to...to... She wasn't sure, what was the right word for the way he was looking at her, but she knew it was wrong.

"And just how would I be lookin' at ye, *Sasunnach*?" He gave her a broad devastating smile that sent her pulse skittering.

"Like that!" She glared at him accusingly. The way he looked at her unnerved her. It was as if he found her a very tasty morsel he would very much like to sample.

"Like what?" He was striving for innocence even though he looked like the very devil himself.

But oh, what a gorgeous devil he was, she thought, then pushed it aside. This man was a heathen who had taken her and her men prisoner. She couldn't let herself get confused by his looks. This man wanted money from her father in exchange for her, pure and simple. He was her captor and was not interested in her as anything more.

"Never mind," she shook her head looking away from him. No man would, or could look at her with wanting in their eyes. She had imagined the look he gave her.

"I need to be lookin' at yer wound. Turn on yer side." He urged her gently.

Slowly, Kandra turned on her side, careful not to expose anything of her person to this man. She may be a warrior, but she was still modest.

With great care, Lachlan uncovered Kandra's side to look at her wound. Slowly, he removed the bandage. Two of the stitches had indeed been pulled free during their struggle. Using the edge of the blanket to dab the blood from the wound, he examined it carefully. He could see the soft curve of her hip and felt himself growing hard at the thought of her being naked under the blanket. Gently, he swirled his fingertips over the silken skin around the wound. The skin was ivory colored, warm, and soft as silk. He was sure her skin would taste sweet and savory if he pressed his lips against it, then swirled his tongue over it for a sample.

The feel of his fingers tracing a pattern upon her bare flesh made her breath catch in her chest. His fingers were hard and callused. He had the hands of a warrior. The image of those hands touching the rest of her body made her shiver. Kandra tried to push those wicked thoughts from her mind. She failed.

He felt her shiver and grinned. The urge to press his mouth to her side and taste her was far too great. "We need to get ye a bath and repair the stitches in yer side. Ye've pulled two of 'em free." He rolled her onto her back looking down at her blushing face. It pleased him that he had such an effect upon her.

"A warm bath would be heavenly." She surveyed him from under her lowered lashes unaware of how sultry she looked. Her embarrassment caused her to bite her lower lip.

Lachlan groaned inwardly from the look she sent him. Lying back against the white bedding, with her golden locks spread around her, she watched him from under her lashes like a siren. The thought of her naked, with warm water caressing her ivory skin, made him ache for her. This was insane! She was his prisoner! He couldn't allow himself to want her. "I'll give instructions for ye to have yer bath," he snapped.

His voice was gruff and angry. What could she have done now to anger him, she wondered with a frown. "Thank you." Her words were curt as she looked away from him.

He rose from the side of her bed, heading for the door. "May I have my clothing back?" She called before he could leave the room.

Lachlan turned and looked at her as she leaned on her elbow, watching him. Her hair cascaded down around her shoulders and over her luscious breasts. The Gods were testing him, he thought sorely. "Aye, I'll have somethin' sent to ye. Perhaps one of my kin's women would be havin' somethin' to spare." Slowly he turned back to the door.

"I will not fit your women's garb." Her voice was small, with embarrassment coloring it. Kandra hated to point out her oddity, but she had no choice, for no woman she had seen here had clothing that would fit her. Not for the first time in her life, did she wish to be dainty and small. The type of woman men looked at and wanted, instead of a giant to be gawked at, or for men to be repulsed by.

Though her father had always told her proudly that she favored her Viking ancestors, it did nothing to take the sting out of the comments men made about her size, or the looks they cast upon her. Why was it that the thought of this man seeing her in the same light as other men tore at her?

"Dinna fash yerself, *Sasunnach*, I'll take care of ye." He promised her, with a glance over his shoulder to where she lay upon the bed looking angelic and too beautiful for words. Even though she wasn't looking at him, he could read the pain in her expression. Without another word, he left her room and sought out his mother.

The bath was refreshing and the pain of repairing the stitches in her wound brought her world back into focus. She was insane to let herself worry over what any man thought about her, let alone the man who was her captor. With her side stitched and wrapped once more, she was ready to dress. "Your laird promised me clothing." Kandra looked down at the smaller older woman who had stitched her side.

"Aye, he did. Lachlan has sent ye somethin' he hoped would make ye more comfortable." She looked Kandra over then shook her head. "If ye wish it, I could make ye a gown instead of yer men's garb. Do ye never wear dresses, lass?" Ferran eyed her then smiled, "Blue and gold would do wonders for yer skin and yer eyes."

"I have had dresses before. Father had hopes that I would wear them when other lords visited." Kandra told the woman with a shrug as she sat taking in the older woman's black hair that was liberally streaked with silver. "Though I rarely did wear them, dresses are cumbersome."

"Trust me lass, ye'd look a vision in blue trimmed with gold to match yer eyes and hair." Ferran smiled at her.

Kandra shook her head, "I could never be a vision as you say. I am neither frail, nor small enough to be such. Beauty is not something I have been blessed with." Kandra looked sad for a moment. Then hard determination filled her face. "But I am good with a sword and bow, and that makes up for it."

"Aye, that 'tis a handy thing, but do ye nay wish to attract men?" Ferran looked at her with watchful considering eyes. "Do ye nay want a husband and wee bairns of yer own, lass?"

Her stomach clenched and pain filled her as this woman asked about her most private fantasy. Kandra pushed her feelings aside. "It matters not. I care not how men see me."

"Aye, I see. Ken this, Kandra of Stafford, yer a beautiful young woman and any man 'tis a fool if he thinks otherwise. My Lachlan 'tis nay a fool." Ferran grabbed a white shirt from beside her and held it out to Kandra. "He sent ye one of his own shirts."

Slowly, Kandra reached out and took the linen shirt. Ferran stood smiling down at her. "Put it on while I'll see to yer noon meal and have it sent up to ye. My name's Ferran MacKinnon, and if ye be needin' anythin', send for me."

Kandra watched Lachlan's mother turn to leave the room. "Lady MacKinnon?"

Ferran stopped turning back to look at her, "Call me Ferran." She smiled softly at the younger woman.

Kandra inclined her head, "All right, Ferran, it is."

"What can I do for ye, lass?" Ferran raised an aristocratic brow.

"Can you tell me how Jonas fares?" Kandra furrowed her brows in concern. Jonas was her biggest concern right now. She had to get to him and soon.

"Yer man? He's recoverin' quiet well." Ferran looked away then turned back. "Are ye wishin' to see him?"

"Yes, very much," Kandra's face held a sad, but anguished expression.

"I shall speak with Lachlan, but I can make, nay promises to ye." She shook her head then turned and left the room, closing the door softly behind her, but not locking it.

Kandra rose from the bed and begun to don the shirt the laird had sent her. As she draped it over her head, she could smell the soap used to wash it and another scent. A smell that was strictly male, it was earthy, yet airy. She pressed her face into the fabric of the shirt and breathed in his scent. It smelled like the laird himself. The muscles in her stomach clenched as she remembered the feel of his fingers on her side and his body covering hers.

With a sigh, she finished dressing. Amazed, she looked down at herself draped in the laird's shirt. For the first time in her adult life, she felt dainty. The shirt hung almost to her knees and the sleeves dwarfed her arms, hanging well past her hands. She laughed at the feeling of being too small for it.

This was how Lachlan found her as he entered the room, standing by the bed laughing as she examined the shirt. Her hair hung damply down her back. She was beautiful as her face lit up with laughter. "Ye practically swim in it, lass. I can find ye somethin' smaller if ye like."

Heat rose in Kandra's face as she turned to stare at him. "No, thank you, but I was hoping for some breeches to go with this shirt."

"I fear my breeches will nay fit ye, lass, the shirt 'tis big enough, aye? It looks good on ye though, *Sasunnach*." He told her as he closed the distance between them. Lachlan stopped in front of her. He let his gaze slide over her.

She could feel the heat of his gaze like a warm caress. Kandra tipped her chin up to look into his dark handsome face. Her lips felt dry, she slowly swiped her tongue over them then parted her moist lips in unconscious anticipation. "Why do you call me that? What does it mean?"

"*Sasunnach*?" Lachlan asked while he watched her soft pink tongue dart out of her mouth. The slight part of her lips was inviting. "It means Englishman or outlander," he told her softly. Lachlan placed a finger under her chin to tip her face farther up, bending his head, softly touching his lips to hers. She was just as soft and sweet as he had known she would be. Slipping an arm about her waist, he pulled her closer, pressing her into him, with a hand at her back. Lachlan deepened the kiss letting his tongue trace the line of her lips. His body thrummed with need and desire, he was holding onto his control by sheer threads.

Kandra wasn't sure if the moan she heard was his, or hers, as the sound of her heartbeat roared in her ears. As he pulled her into him, fitting her body to his, she placed her hands upon the hard planes of his chest. Instinct demanded that she open to his probing tongue. She let herself sway into him farther, pressing her body to his.

Lachlan breathed in her scent, moaning deep in his throat. She smelled of the wild heather that grew over his lands and under that sweet scent was simply her, the vibrant yet sultriness, of Kandra. He crushed her to him feeling her pebbled nipples pressing against his chest through the thin material of their shirts.

This had to stop, Kandra thought with her head spinning. Her heart was racing and she couldn't seem to catch her breath. She pulled away from him, leaning back to look up at him. Panting as her breath came in heaves, she searched his eyes a moment then jerked out of his hold. "Why did you do that?" Her voice was accusing, but shaky.

He read the anger and puzzlement in her eyes. He gave her the truth. "Because yer beautiful."

"Do not say that!" She stepped back from him.

"Has, nay one ever told ye thus, lass?" He frowned at her. Was she playing coy with him?

"You lie! You are trying to deceive me and to confuse me." Kandra took another step back from him. "Men do not find me beautiful!" She wrapped her arms around her waist as she took deep calming breaths and turned away from him.

"What of yer man? Does he nay tell you such things?" He stared at her back and read her tension.

"Jonas?" She turned looking at him in bewilderment.

"Aye, is he nay yer lover?" He accused.

Kandra started to deny it, but stopped herself, perhaps if she didn't correct his mistake then he would leave her be. Lifting her chin to a haughty angle, she spoke. "I wish to see him."

It was not a question, but a command and it angered Lachlan. Even after the kiss they had shared, she thought of her pale little English dog of a lover. "Nay!" He roared as jealousy surged through him.

"Why?"

"Did yer English father never teach ye to do what yer told?" Lachlan glared at her, anger burning in him. He knew it was selfish, but he didn't want her to see her lover.

"My father taught me to fight for what I want! My father is a great man, who is also a great warrior. You will be lucky if you do not get a war, rather than a ransom from him." Kandra raged at him. How could this man be so mean as to deny her to see her brother when he might be dying? "If either myself or Jonas dies, you shall have a war on your hands, make no mistake about it."

"Yer precious Jonas, 'tis nay goin' to die," Lachlan growled. "I sent word to yer father four days ago, but have heard, aught, as of yet. Perhaps, he is nary as concerned about yer welfare as ye think, *Sasunnach*."

"No, you, oaf! You have not heard from him because my father is in London attending the King. It will take nearly a sennight to reach the castle then another fortnight, or more, to reach London. Once he receives the missive then he will have to wait for the King to dismiss him, after which he will take another fortnight or more, to reach the Carlisle castle." She shot him a smug look. "So, it will take much time for you to receive your ransom."

"Then we're to be stuck with each other for a while 'twould appear, *Sasunnach*." Lachlan looked her over with anger in his gaze. Though he wanted to throttle her, he still wanted to have her, take her in every way a man possesses a woman.

Kandra turned away from him angrily, crossing her arms over her chest as she walked to the window. How could she let herself be pulled into this man again and again? How could this man make her heart race and her pulse pound? She was disgusted with herself for the way he made her feel. "I want to see Jonas. I wish to be assured of his wellbeing."

Lachlan watched her walk away, but when she stopped near the window lifting her arms to cross them under her ample bosom, pushing her breasts higher, his heart skipped a beat. The back of her shirt pulled upward revealing more of her strong warrior's legs. His loins tightened as he cocked his head and traced the length of her legs with his eyes. They would fit nicely wrapped around him. Damn, but he needed a woman! He had to stop thinking of this English woman in this manner. "All right, ye may see yer man."

Chin held high, she inclined her head regally, her back still toward him as she looked out the window. "Thank you. I wish to see him as soon as possible."

"I dinna say what I want in return." He eyed her quickly, then smiled.

"I have nothing to give you." She snapped as she rounded on him.

"Aye, but ye do, *Sasunnach*." He gave her a look that warmed her skin making her pulse skitter. "I want yer word that ye'll behave civilly and curb yer miserable tongue while yer in my home. Nay more threatenin' my people when they're but trying to help ye."

"Are you included in that?" She raised an arrogant brow. A part of her felt relief at his request, but another part of her felt a twinge of disappointment that he hadn't asked for something more personal.

"Nay lass, ye can threaten me all ye wish. I'm nay a'scared of ye." He gave her a crooked smile, as he looked her up and down. "Besides, yer nay so big I can nay handle ye, if needs be."

"Are you calling me little?" She stared at him in disbelief. No one had called her little in ages, not since she had been but a child. At six foot, she was as tall if not taller than most men. Kandra narrowed her eyes at him. "Or are you thinking I am weak, because I am a woman? If that be the case, we can rematch our skills with swords anytime you wish, my lord."

"Nay lass." He shook his head. "I'll nay fight ye. I dinna fight women, nor do I hurt 'em, ever."

"Things would have turned out differently had I not been distracted." She gave him a challenging look. This man was by far too arrogant and she couldn't abide men who were too full of themselves.

"Aye, I could have killed ye." His voice held a note of warning in it, "Yer lucky to be alive, lass."

She scoffed at this ridicules notion. "I fear laird, that you are quite mistaken. I can best any man I have ever met." She sighed as if weary of his absurdities, "If you wish to try your luck once more, I shall be more than happy to cross blades with you again."

Her tone and manner enraged him. "We will nay fight! Yer a woman, 'tis a shame yer father never taught ye to act like one!" Without another word, he turned, striding from the room and snapping the door shut behind him.

Angry and hurt, Kandra grabbed a wooden candleholder from the table and threw it at the door with a scream of rage. She didn't know why his words hurt her so much. Any other man who had referred to her as an oddity couldn't put a dent in the armor she had built around her feelings. Tears glistened in her eyes, but she blinked them away, she was addlebrained to let this man get to her and hurt her.

Chapter Six

As the early morning light spilled through the window, Kandra knelt by the bed where Jonas lay sleeping. With a teary smile, she reached out, brushing a lock of golden hair from his forehead. Slowly, his eyes opened. A weak smile brightened his pale features.

"You are a sight for sore eyes." Jonas reached out, stroking her cheek. Since he had awakened two days before, he had been asking after his sister as he drifted in and out of sleep.

"As are you," a tear trickled down her cheek as she pressed her face into his open palm. His living brought such joy to her heart. She had feared his death more than she let herself believe.

"Are you all right?" Jonas felt concerned by her show of tears. "That heathen bastard has not harmed you has he?" He began trying to sit up. A frown creased his brow. "I swear if he has, I shall kill him!"

"No Jonas, calm yourself, the laird has not harmed me." She dipped her eyes from him and frowned. It was true the laird hadn't harmed her, but what was it he did do to her? Confuse her? Anger her? He caused her many odd feelings, but she couldn't say he had truly hurt her.

"What? What has he done to bring tears to your eyes?" Jonas placed a finger under her chin to make her look at him as he searched her face.

"Oh Jonas, 'tis not him that makes my tears, 'tis joy that you are alive and sorrow that I am the cause of your pain." Kandra worried her lower lip in guilt.

"Listen to me," he grasped her shoulder, giving her a soft shake. "None of this is your fault, you must not blame yourself."

"But I am to blame and I shall find a way to free you from this place." She grabbed his hand in both of hers and brought it to her cheek. "I swear it to you, Jonas."

Jonas was healing well, Ferran assured Kandra as she walked her back to her room. Perhaps by the week's end he could be made ready to travel, Kandra thought. He needed to be home, not in the clutches of a Scottish laird. At home the servants would do everything possible to see to his wounds. Not that she thought Ferran wasn't.

As she lay in bed later in the day thinking of a way to convince the laird to release her brother, the door to her room slowly opened. Kandra sat up and turned to the doorway to see a beautiful raven-haired girl staring at her. By her height Kandra guessed she could be no more than nine or ten, but something in the girl's eyes told her the child was younger than her height led Kandra to believe.

"Hello," Kandra spoke softly from where she sat up upon the bed studying the child.

"Who are ye?" The little girl cocked her head, then spoke again before Kandra could reply. "Are ye my Da's she-devil?"

Kandra couldn't help but to laugh, "I suppose that depends on who your father is."

"The laird, 'tis my Da." she spoke with pride filling her little face as she made her way into the room fearlessly. *'For a devil, she was verra pretty',* Bryanna MacKinnon thought.

"Then I suppose I must be." Kandra grinned at the title she had been dubbed with. "Is that what your father calls me?" She couldn't stop her curiosity from peeking through.

"He calls ye many things when he speaks to my Gram." She looked ashamed for a moment. "I listen to 'em sometimes when they dinna ken I'm there. Ye will nay tell 'em, will ye?" The girl's large green eyes were identical to her father's, and were currently rounded with worry.

"I will not betray your secret. Even in torture I will not tell them." Kandra looked at her seriously. "Would you like me to swear an oath to you on it?"

"Nay," Bry shook her head, "My Da, does nay torture people."

"Ah, well that is certainly good to know." Kandra took the girl in from head to toe then patted the bed next to her. "Would you care to sit and visit awhile?"

"Aye," Bry beamed with happiness. She had very few friends in the castle, and was not old enough to go to the village and play. "What's yer name?" She quickly settled herself upon the bed.

"I am the Lady Stafford of Carlisle, but as the rest of my friends do, you may call me, Kandra." Kandra could read the girls loneliness. A kindred spirit she thought.

"My name 'tis Bryanna, but my friends call me, Bry." She smiled brightly up at Kandra as she tried to mimic her.

"How old are you, Bry?"

"Seven winters," Bry informed her proudly then sighed and shook her head. "Though, I wish I were older."

"Being older is not always so great." Kandra shook her head as she spoke to the girl solemnly. "When I was seven, I began shooting my first bow." Kandra remembered her father spending hours with her to teach her how to be a warrior.

"Ye shoot a bow?" Bry looked at her with amazement clearly on her face.

"Yes, I shoot a long bow. I am also an excellent swordsman or woman. However, you wish to phrase it." Kandra informed her, waving the terminology away as if it were no major thing.

Bry's eyes were wide with awe and wonder, "Yer Da lets ye use a sword, a real sword?"

"My father taught me, along with Raff, he is my father's head guard." Kandra looked down at the child and saw wonder in her eyes.

"My Da, would never allow me to use a sword." Bry shook her head sadly.

"I was two years older than you when I began my training. I have all the skills of an English knight." She could remember all the hours she had spent with her father and Raff, to be better than any of the others training.

"I wish I could learn to be a lady knight." Bry was silent a moment then turned excited eyes upon Kandra. "Could ye teach me to shoot a bow?"

"I am afraid I cannot leave this room." Kandra shook her head slowly.

"But the door 'tis nay locked. We could go into the yard and you can teach me." Bry spoke brightly.

"Oh Bry, I am sorry I cannot. You see," Kandra paused at a sound in the doorway. Looking up she saw Lachlan standing in the doorway scowling. She looked back at Bry. "I am wounded and your father has been good enough to help me and my men who were wounded in battle." She couldn't bring herself to hurt this little girl's image of her father.

"Bry, lass, what are ye doin' in here?" Lachlan stepped into the room.

"Da! Kandra 'tis my new friend, she's gonna teach me to be like her!" Bryanna bounced up and down on the bed excitedly.

Lachlan walked in, scooping Bry up in his arms. "Is she now? And just what is she gonna teach ye, lass?"

"To be a she-devil just like her," Bry laughed wildly.

Lachlan blanched at the phrase. He glanced at Kandra and she gave him a droll stare, as she cocked and eye brow. Before he could respond, Bry gave him a sad look. "When she gets better, Da, can she come out to play with me in the gardens?"

He looked down into his daughter's hopeful little face. "Of course, dumplin', but it may well be awhile 'afore she's better." He set her upon her feet and swatted her bottom, "For now 'tis time ye were runnin' along to help yer Gram."

"Aye," Bryanna smiled over at Kandra, "I'll come back to see ye verra soon."

"I would like that," Kandra smiled, waving after the little girl.

Lachlan was silent for a long moment as he looked at the woman before him, dressed in men's clothing. She was like no other woman he had ever met before. She had the skills of a warrior, but something told him she had a soft heart beneath that tough exterior. "Why did ye nay tell her the truth, lass?"

Kandra stood then walked over to the window. She stood looking out into the sun-filled day. "What's between us is not for a child to know of."

Lachlan stood there, watching her as she twisted a piece of her long golden hair around her finger. Her thick tresses fell, down her back nearly reaching her bottom. He had the urge to walk over and comb his fingers through her hair.

"A father is very special to his little girl," Kandra glanced over her shoulder at him. "I can see that she adores you, much as I do my own father, and I could not break her heart like that."

"I thank ye for that," Lachlan inclined his head.

"If you really wished to thank me, you could let me and my men go." She raised a haughty brow at him.

Giving her a flat look, "I dinna think so, lass." he turned to leave the room.

"You have chosen a battle you cannot hope to possibly win." She spoke sharply from behind him.

Lachlan turned back to her with an arrogant smile, "Trust me lass, I never lose in battle." With that he left the room and her fuming behind him.

Kandra paced the room restlessly. She threw glances at the door. Though the door was unlocked, two guards were placed outside it in the hallway. As the day wore on, she became more and more restless. Never had she spent so much time indoors. She yearned to stretch her legs and feel her sword in her hand. She clenched her sword hand and stared down at its emptiness.

Her mind turned from her captivity to Jonas and her men. She had to find a way to get them out of here. Her father was too far away to offer her any hope of immediate aid. They had not nearly enough troops at the castle to mount an attack, even if she could get word back home. If only she had left Jonas or Raff behind, they would've been able to assist her someway, somehow.

When the door opened and a young girl entered bringing a tray of food with her, Kandra sighed. The young girl gave her a weary look. "Please, just set it upon the table."

Giving Kandra a wide birth, the girl scurried over to the table, quickly placed the tray upon it, and left. Not interested in the food, Kandra ignored it and continued her pacing.

She wanted to see Jonas and hold council with him. But she knew the laird would never allow her that much freedom. Pacing, she grumbled as she thought of and discarded plan after plan. Stopping, she stared at the late sunlight shining through the open window. It was far too high for her to try to escape through it.

Walking to the window, she leaned on the sill and looked out over as much of the castle and the land as she could see. Perhaps, if she could get a lay of the land and the castle, she could come up with a plan to escape.

When the girl came back for the tray of food a short time later, Kandra paid her no mind. She was far too involved in forming an escape plan. It would be a couple of days before she could attempt it, but it was worth a try.

Lachlan opened the door of the room to find his guest hanging half way out the window. Though it was an intriguing view of her derriere, he was afraid if he spoke he would startle her and she'd fall. On silent feet, he walked up behind her. Quickly, he grasped her around the waist pulling her inside.

Kandra didn't let it faze her when her head hit the top of the window case. Acting on instinct she turned, swinging on her attacker. Before she even saw who held onto her, she landed a fist to his jaw. Her hand stung from the impact, but she was out to defend herself.

Lachlan wasn't prepared for the blow she delivered and stumbled back with his hands still around her waist. The motion caused both to crash to the floor with Kandra sprawled atop him. For a quick moment, she knocked the wind out of him.

When she reared up to deliver more blows, Lachlan used his weight and strength to his advantage, to quickly roll her under him. Capturing her hands in his, he pinned them on either side of her head, glaring down at her.

"Enough, lass," Lachlan growled down at her.

"You!" She accused, glaring back at him. "Get off me."

"I think nay, ye nearly knocked my head off with that punch, och." He shook his head. "I'll nay be lettin' ye swing at me again."

"I would not have hit you if you had not snuck up on me," she narrowed her eyes. "You deserve much worse. If I had, had my sword you would have been run through."

Lachlan shook his head as he looked down into her beautiful angry face. The fire in her blue eyes lit them and made them mesmerizing. Her face held a slight flush and she was panting under him, making her breasts clearly defined under her shirt rising and falling. The neck of the shirt was twisted enough to show the upper most swell of her left breast. He stared at it for a long moment then his gaze slid back to her face. Her eyes were wide and she was biting her lower lip. When she released her lip, it was slightly swollen and red, begging to be kissed.

"Do not look at me like thus!" She tried to sound firm, but for some reason her voice came out sounding thick and slightly husky.

Lachlan couldn't take his eyes from her lips as he growled, "Like what?"

"Like..." Her words were cut off when his mouth captured and plundered hers in ravenous hunger. It was a punishing kiss that made her shiver under him. The taste of him excited her and the feel of his body pressing against hers made her breasts swell and her stomach jittery. She wanted to push him away and pull him closer at the same time.

She gasped for breath and he plunged his tongue into her mouth, ravaging her senses. A heavy fog veiled her thoughts, and she could think of only his mouth on hers and the heat he was making her feel inside. It coiled in her belly, pooled between her legs, and in her neither regions. Confusion reigned in her brain.

Lachlan wanted to devour her. Releasing her hands, he cupped her cheek and slid his hand down her throat feeling her pulse pounding under his fingers. Her skin was soft as silk and she smelled of wild heather. Letting his fingers explore her farther he cupped her breast. Her soft breast, fit his large hand perfectly, he thought with satisfaction. He wanted to bed this woman. He wanted to feel himself sheathed inside her. He wanted to possess her.

At the feel of his hand on her breast, Kandra's mind cleared and came back to reality. In a quick movement that took nearly every ounce of her strength, she flipped him over so that she ended up straddling him.

Surprise was Lachlan's first reaction. However, as he looked up into her beautiful face looming over him, while her silken hair surrounded him like a golden veil, he felt the need to have her pull at him even stronger. He would have this woman until he purged himself of this obsession with her. He would have her until he could sleep a night without thinking, or dreaming, of her.

When she pulled away from him, jumping to her feet, Lachlan watched her. She glowered down at him with temper bright in her eyes.

"How dare you touch me," Kandra looked down at him with murderous eyes. If she had, had her sword, she would run the knave through twice.

"Ye dinna seem to mind to much at first, lass." He grinned arrogantly at her as he watched her standing there with a rosy flush to her skin, and her breasts heaving. His loins ached painfully at the sight.

"You are a blackguard." She spat at him as she swiped her hand over her mouth as if to wipe away the taste of him.

Lachlan gained his feet, watching the emotions pass over her face. True fear and disbelief filled her eyes. "So ye fear me, lass?"

Kandra's chin rose in defiance as her heart thundered in her chest. "I have no fear of you."

Lachlan advanced on her and was amused when she didn't so much as flinch let alone back away. She was a brave lass at heart, he would give her that. "Then perhaps ye should."

"You do not frighten me, laird." Kandra glared up at him with challenge in her narrowed blue eyes. "I have faced down much more powerful men then you, and not yet has one bested me."

"Then perhaps 'tis time ye've met yer better." He growled down at her.

"When he comes along be sure to introduce him to me." Kandra shot back at him as she crossed her arms over her chest cockily. She would not let this man daunt her.

Lachlan couldn't hold in the mirth that bubbled up in him. He threw back his head letting out a roar of laughter. "Yer a cocky one lass, I'll give ye that."

"I would prefer it if you gave me my freedom instead." Kandra flashed him a sarcastic smile as her temper held firm.

"Ye ken, I can nay do that." He shook his head at her. "I need what ye can bring to me."

"Then free me, or Jonas, and we can get you the reward you requested much faster." She gave him a hard stare. If she could just get one of them out of there then they would have a chance to get home before her father could be notified. There was still time.

"Nay lass, we'll wait for yer father to send for ye." He shook his dark head. Even if he believed her, Lachlan knew he couldn't let her go. Not yet, not until he had, had her, for she was fast becoming an obsession for him.

Kandra huffed out a breath, "Then if you will not listen to reason, go away and leave me be." She waved him off turning her back to him in dismissal.

Lachlan felt first shock at her dismissal, then anger.

He was laird here, not this woman. No one dismissed him. "Well, yer highness, I'm here to remind ye, we struck an accord."

"What bargain would that be?" She sighed as she looked over her shoulder at him, with boredom clear in her eyes.

"Ye swore ye would nay starve yerself while ye were here so long as yer man was being cared for." Lachlan frowned at her. "An ye dinna eat yer evenin' meal."

Kandra felt a spot of hope as she frowned, shaking her head. "I was not hungry."

"Ye gave yer word, lass."

Raising her arms, she turned in a slow circle, "Do I look as if I am starving, my lord?"

Swallowing hard he took in every curve, every inch of her as she turned for him. He wanted to reach out and touch her, stroke her, so instead he curled his hands into fist. "Nay, lass ye dinna look it."

"I apologize that I did not eat." She turned away from him again, frowning. "I will force myself to take at least a bit of something from each tray, so as not to insult your cooks, but I cannot predict rather I will get my appetite back or not." She gave a dramatic weary sigh, "If only I were not…" She cut herself off with a shake of her head.

Lachlan couldn't help but to let his curiosity slip out. If there was something wrong he would fix it, he was not a man who could stand to see a woman suffer. "What bothers ye, lass?"

Kandra shook her head as she waited on baited breath. She saw the waiver in him and knew she could and would play upon his weakness. For some unbeknownst reason, this laird saw her as a woman, not a warrior.

She ignored the flutter in her stomach and the way this knowledge set her heart to tripping. So, what if he was the first man to see her as a woman, the first man to want her, desire her, touch her. She gave a mental shrug, telling herself it meant nothing to her. She would use his weakness against him. He was a softhearted fool when it came to women.

Lachlan stepped forward, furrowing a brow, he reached out touching her shoulder. "Tell me, lass."

After a healthy pause, she frowned up at him, "How can you expect me to eat when I am trapped inside this room night and day?" She shook her head as she charged on. "Tell me, do I look as if I am used to inactivity?" She held out her arms, doing another slow turn for his inspection.

Lachlan felt as if his tongue had swollen in his mouth, which had gone as dry as dust. His green gaze was riveted to every curve and sleek muscle he could see. With his loins burning for this woman, he let his gaze travel the length of her, from head to toe. Groaning inwardly, he knew that it would be another sleepless night.

"Well?" She demanded, when he just stood there looking at her as if he were the village idiot.

"Nay," he croaked, then cleared his throat, pulling his gaze from her breasts back to her face. "Ye look as if yer used to riding and such."

"And such," she spoke mockingly. Kandra rolled her eyes. "Whether you believe it or not, laird, I am as much a warrior as you are."

"Yer a woman," Lachlan shook his head as fire lit in his eyes.

"At home I am not seen as a woman," She spoke softly, meeting his gaze boldly.

He shook his head, "Is every man ye ken dense or blind?"

"Neither," she walked back to the window to look out, "I have proven myself their equal. I can do everything a man can do and some things even better."

Lachlan snorted, "Then they are weak men. No woman can best one of my men."

Kandra looked back at him with a glint of challenge in her blue eyes. "I can."

"Nay, lass..."

"I would have beaten you, my lord, if I had not been distracted." She turned to him, raising a brow. "If you are afraid to face me yourself allow me to face one of your men and I will prove myself to you."

"Nay..." His voice growled now with temper.

"If you give me no chance to prove myself, then how can you dispute my claim?" She knew she could give this man a challenge, if not beat him in a sword fight. Even if she didn't win she would gain his respect for her fighting ability.

Silently, he contemplated her words. After a heavy silence, he nodded. "Fine, ye can prove yerself, but ye'll nay face me, for I'd harm ye." He stepped up to her, looking down into her brilliant blue eyes, "On the morrow, I'll give ye yer chance to show me yer skills with a blade, but ken 'tis for practice alone and nay for death. I'll allow nay, harm to befall ye, lass." He reached up, stroking a finger down her cheek, causing a shiver to race through her.

She couldn't ignore that fluttering in her stomach this time. Her lashes drifted down to rest on her cheeks for a moment, but snapped back open when she felt his thumb on her lower lip. Her blue gaze locked with his bright green one and she felt lost.

"I want ye, lass." He murmured as he leaned down to replace his thump with his lips. The kiss was light and feathery, belying the need clawing inside him.

Kandra allowed her eyes to drift shut at the feel of his warm lips upon hers. Heat coiled inside her. Laying her hands upon his chest, she had to fight from bunching her fingers in the material of his shirt and yanking him closer. Her common sense took over as she pushed him away from her.

"Do not do that!" She hated that her voice sounded weak and shaky to her own ears.

Lachlan looked into her eyes once more, "Do ye claim nay to like my attentions?"

She shook her head in denial as her heart screamed to pull him closer and hold on to him. *'He is the first man to ever see you as a woman, a woman who is desirable*!' "No!" She denied heartily, "I do not want you to touch me."

Lachlan released her, stepping back with fury and desire blazing in his eyes, "Make nay mistake about this, lass, I will have ye and ye'll give yerself to me willingly enough."

Kandra narrowed her eyes. "That will never happen, my lord."

Chapter Seven

S he slept fitfully, as her dreams were filled with images of a giant, dark, devil of a man. Lachlan had come to her, atop his midnight black beast of a horse. His hair hung thick and loose down over his massive shoulders except for the braids throughout his silky black strands, all of them ended with tiny silver beads, that clacked and shimmered in the light as he moved. He was bare from the waist up with only the sheen of sweat covering his muscular arms and chest. Two silver bands encircled his arms. Each band held strange writings and symbols on them. During her dream, the bands glowed eerily.

In her dream, she stood in an open field, dressed in a thin white night rail, her hair blew loose around her shoulders. She felt wanton and desirable, for she knew he was there to claim her as his, and she wanted to give herself up to him with a need she had never known before.

She watched him rein in the destrier then dismount in one fluid motion. He towered over her, looking down into her blue eyes. His green eyes seemed to glow as they held a mystic power over her, making her body hum with need for him. She wanted him to touch her in all the ways he already had and more. When his arm snaked around her waist, pulling her hard up against his body, she let out a gasp. His mouth captured hers in a searing kiss, as her hands splayed over his bare muscular chest.

Kandra could feel the warmth of his slick skin under her fingers. She traced his rippling muscles as she met him with absolute desire filling their kiss. Her heart pounded and her breath heaved. Her nipples harden as they brushed against the hard plains of his chest through her thin gown. Liquid heat pooled in the base of her stomach as the dull aching need pulsed at the junction of her thighs.

Lachlan's hand fisted in her golden tresses, pulling her head back roughly, so that he could look down at her with the fires of desire burning in his eyes. "I told ye I would have ye, lass."

Kandra woke with a start as the gray light of dawn filled the world around her. Her bare skin was slick with sweat, her heart raced and her breasts felt heavy, hot and full. She ached in her womanly places as she had never ached before. Sitting up and pulling her knees up, she rested her chin upon them. This laird was having wicked effects upon her.

She was no stranger to men. Kandra knew in general what they did with women, but never had she had such wanting to experience those things, with any man before this laird. Perhaps she should give into the laird, give into the sensations he stirred within her. He was the only man within all of her score of years to have noticed her in such a way, she thought with a frown.

Closing her eyes, she sighed, "No, I would be a fool to even think such a thing."

Pushing the blanket from her body, she climbed from her bed. Walking over to pour the cool fresh water from the urn into the basin to bathe, she sighed. With the sweat of her dream washed from her body, she dressed in her own shirt and breeches that Ferran herself had kindly mended.

Moving about the room, Kandra stretched her sore and achy muscles. Being cooped up for more than a sennight was making her stiff and she longed to work the kinks out.

She stood in the early morning light, clenching her fist, anticipating the feel of her sword in her hand once more. The thrill of the combat to come made her smile. It would feel good to work out her aggressions on her opponent.

A rap at her door had her turning around. Ferran, along with the timid serving girl, entered the room with a tray of food and Kandra's armor.

Kandra couldn't suppress her smile, "Ah, a sight for sore eyes." She walked toward them, taking the armor from Ferran's arms, hugging it to her chest. "I have sorely missed this."

Ferran rolled her eyes, "I had hoped the tray of food was what ye were happy to see."

"I will not eat all of that anyhow." Kandra shook her head as she scanned the tray laden with food. "It would slow me down."

"Ye must to eat somethin', lass" Ferran walked over, cupping Kandra's cheek, "'Tis nay good, for a warrior to go off to battle with nothin' in her belly."

Kandra looked down on the smaller woman and smiled softly. "Thank you, Ferran."

"Poosh, dinna thank me yet," Ferran waved her gratitude away, "I'll tell ye when ye can thank me."

"For now, put somethin' in yer belly," Ferran pulled the armor out of Kandra's hands and pushed her toward the tray of food. "Even if 'tis but a few bites of food. Make this old woman happy."

Kandra pulled out a chair then waved Ferran to another. "Please, join me."

Ferran inclined her head and waved off Margaret, the young serving girl. Silence stretched out around them. Kandra nibbled on this and that, but nothing seemed to hold her interest. Ferran could see that something was weighing on the younger woman's mind. She watched Kandra pick up a slice of fresh bread and pull it apart. "Are ye nervous?"

Kandra shook her head, frowning at the bread she was ripping to shreds instead of eating. "No, combat has never made me nervous."

Thoughts of her dream from the previous night were creeping in on her. Her brows furrowed. Why couldn't she shake the images that had plagued her in the night?

Ferran reached out, covering the younger woman's hand before she could finish mutilating the piece of innocent bread. "Tell me what weighs so heavy upon yer mind, lass."

Kandra started to shake her head then looked into Ferran's kind green eyes. "I am not like most women." She pushed away from the table and prowled the room restlessly.

"Ye can be anythin' ye wish to be," Ferran sat back in her chair smiling.

"Men do not find me…" She waved her hand around as she searched for a word. Lachlan's term popped into mind, "*Beautiful.*" Kandra said sarcastically then flopped on the edge of the bed to frown. "I am not beautiful, I am not desirable, but I am a warrior and an equal to men."

Ferran got up from the chair she had been sitting in. Slowly, she crossed the room to sit next to Kandra on the bed. Reaching up, she took Kandra's face in her hands, "Yer a warrior, aye, but yer still a woman, and yer verra beautiful. A man would have to be blind or addled in the head, nay to see ye as all three." She smoothed a stray lock of hair back into Kandra's braid, "I think yer already seen as a woman, but today ye must prove yer a warrior. Mayhaps, in time he'll see all sides of ye together."

Kandra looked into her kind face, "No man can see me and accept me for all that I am." Determination set in her. "But by God he will see me as a warrior and as an equal."

Ferran stood up, pulling Kandra into a quick embrace. "Yer a fighter, and 'tis just what we need around here." She stood, cupping Kandra's cheek once more. "I pray the Gods keep ye safe and give ye what ye deserve, lass."

With that, Ferran walked out of the room. Kandra sat for a long while, thinking about what the older woman had said. She could never make a man see her from all sides. If he saw her as a warrior, he couldn't accept her for a woman then he couldn't see her as an equal. Time and time again, men had proven this to be true. Once she proved herself a warrior in this laird's eyes today, he would no longer acknowledge her as a woman. However, he would have to give her the respect she was due.

Resolution settled over her. She had always been and would always be a warrior first. She did not need, nor wanted, a man in her life. She would prove herself once more today and to hell with Lachlan MacKinnon.

Kandra made quick work of putting her armor in place.

Lachlan slept poorly as dreams and images of his captive plagued and tortured him through the night. As the gray light of morning crept through his window, he pulled himself from bed and bathed. He could swear the English woman was a witch with the way she haunted his dreams, and occupied his every thought. He was becoming obsessed with the damned woman.

Dressed for the day, he headed off to find Rogan. As was usual, he found his friend in the outer bailey already practicing with his sword.

"How fairs the day, laird," Rogan called out to Lachlan as he approached.

"'Tis well enough," Lachlan walked over to straddle a large log as he watched his oldest childhood friend practice. "I have somethin' I wish ye to do for me this fine day."

"Aye, and what would that be," Rogan stopped his practice to give Lachlan his full attention.

Lachlan looked around, not meeting his friend's eyes. "I want ye to pick a couple of yer younger men to match skills with my guest."

"Surely ye mean one of the Englishmen in the dungeon."

"Nay, the English lass." Lachlan shook his head and grinned.

"Have ye gone daft man?" Rogan gapped at him. "She could get hurt."

"I dinna want them to hurt her, just to show her that a woman is nay match for a man." Lachlan shook his head.

Rogan rubbed a hand on the back of his neck, "I'm nay sure I can find men who will face a woman, in sword play at least." He narrowed his eyes at Lachlan, "Why, are ye nay facin' her yerself?"

"I can nay risk hurtin' her again," Lachlan shook his head. "I marked her pretty well the first time around."

"Then why are ye lettin' her have another go at it with different men?" Rogan frowned.

Lachlan stared at him long and hard for a moment, "She insists she can take any man. And she's well trained, I grant ye that, but underneath she's still a woman and she needs to learn so."

"I think I ken what yer sayin'" Rogan nodded. "I'll pick a couple men myself."

"Be sure they ken their nay to injure her severely. Bruises at the worst." Lachlan nodded his approval, leaving Rogan to do his job.

Making his way down to the dungeon he went to the cell holding the older knight who had ridden with Kandra.

"Ye come with me." Lachlan gestured to the knight.

Once outside the cell, Lachlan stopped, crossing his arms over his chest as he glared down at the man. "Yer woman, yer lady, ye serve her, aye?"

"Yes, my lord," Raff frowned at the large man. "What has she done now?"

"She is to fight one or two of my men this morn'.." Lachlan smiled as anger bloomed in the older knight's face.

"Damned fool girl, she's so hot tempered, she's bound to get herself killed." Raff ranted and raged reverently.

Lachlan held up a hand to silence him. "I thought perhaps she would feel more at ease to have one of her own with her, then to face my men alone."

Raff sighed, "She's a proud one. Perhaps if she gets her ass kicked by one of your men, my lord, she'll learn to control her tongue and her temper." Raff toed the dirt as he frowned then looked up at the laird, "Your man, he is not to hurt her, is he?"

"Aye, I've left word he's nay to injure her, beyond perhaps a couple of bruises." Lachlan assured him.

Raff snorted, "Too bad you cannot get her to abide by the same. She tends to cut her own men down." Raff held out his hand, "Raff."

"Lachlan," the laird grasped his hand. "Ye speak with pride about her."

"That's because I helped to train her." Raff grinned with beaming pride. "She is one of my best knights."

"If a woman is one of yer best knights, it makes me wonder what a sorry lot ye are." Lachlan clapped the older man on the shoulder.

"You fought with her once, but she was distracted. Today, she won't be." Raff smiled. "I hope your men can handle defeat well."

The door to her room swung open with a crash. Kandra jumped at the sound. Her mouth hung open at the sight of the man standing in the doorway.

"What the bloody hell have you gotten yourself into now, girl?" Raff bellowed at her.

"Raff?" Disbelief colored her voice.

He stormed into the room, slamming the door behind him. "What got into that thick head of yours to challenge these men?"

"Raff?" Tears swam in her eyes. Though he raged and bellowed at her, she ignored it. Dropping her helmet, she raced across the room to Raff, throwing her arms around him.

Raff's stiff stance dissolved under her fierce hug. Shaking his head, he wrapped his arms around her, hugging her to him as he rocked her back and forth. "What am I to do with you, girl?" He stroked a hand down her braid giving it a light tug. She was more like a daughter than a soldier to him. He loved this thickheaded little fool.

"Oh Raff, I have missed you." She leaned back, placing a kiss upon his weathered cheek. "Everything is so confusing. Jonas is doing better. I am trying to find a way out of here." She prattled on until Raff set her away from him.

"Enough. Let's sit and talk for a few moments." He led her over to the bed. They sat facing each other. She filled him in on nearly everything that had happened so far.

Once she was done, Raff stood up and swore. "And just how did you think this would help us?"

"I...I do not know." She shook her head. "I just had to prove to him..."

"Prove what?"

"That I am not a woman, I am a warrior." Her chin rose in defiance.

"Kandra, sweetest, you are a woman." Raff took her hands in his as he sat on the bed again. "A beautiful young woman."

She shook her head adamantly. "No, I am a warrior, just like you and father trained me to be."

"Being a woman is not a bad thing," Raff reassured her. But he could see by the stubborn look in her eyes that she wouldn't believe it. He switched tactics. "All right, for this morn, you will need to be a warrior. Christ, you're going to have your work cut out for you."

"Now that you are here, I am not worried." Kandra gave him a level look.

"I wish I could say the same." Raff muttered, frowning.

The morning air was cool and refreshing. Kandra held her sword in her hand swinging it in combat movements, reacquainting herself with the weight and feel of it. Her sole focus was on her opponent who stood across the field sneering at her and strutting around in his cockiness.

"Are ye ready, lass?" Lachlan walked across the field.

"Yes," she inclined her head, but didn't look at him as she watched her opponent strut across the field. His movements were jerks and his steps plodding. He would use strength instead of speed. His swordplay would be powerful blows instead of agile, graceful ones.

"Care to make a wager, before ye start." Lachlan moved closer to her to give them a bit of privacy.

Kandra turned to him raising a brow. "What type of wager, my lord?"

"Would ye care to wager, yerself?" He spoke low so only she could hear him.

"And if I win would you free me and my men?" Kandra gave him a level look. She would not let his bold wager shake her confidence.

Lachlan frowned shaking his head, "Nay lass, nay even a woman like ye is worth what I'd lose for freein' ye."

Kandra thought for a moment, perhaps she could work this to her advantage in the long run, "All right, how about just moving my men out of the dungeon. Is that worthy, my lord?"

Lachlan studied her for a moment, "If ye lose ye must give yerself to me freely, but if ye win, I move yer men out of the dungeon?" He mulled this over for a moment then nodded, "Aye 'tis agreed." He held out his hand.

Kandra placed her hand in his expecting him to shake hands. She gasped when he lifted her hand and brushed a kiss over her knuckles.

"I can nay wait for ye to lose, lass." Lachlan smiled devilishly.

Kandra brought her chin up in defiance, "You shall have a long wait, laird." She jerked her hand free of his, turning away from him.

As she walked across the field to meet her opponent, she mentally shook off the feelings Lachlan had stirred inside of her. She couldn't let him distract her from her goal.

Kandra met her opponent face to face, he was a large man who stood nearly half a head taller than she did, but that did nothing to deter her.

"I am Kandra, daughter of Lord Stafford." She inclined her head.

"I'm Kraig," her opponent flashed a ferocious look.

Kandra raised her sword to the man, "I wish you luck."

"'Tis ye lass, who will be needin' luck, for I'll have ye whimperin' under my blade in no time." He shot her a cocky smile, "Perhaps, if yer lucky, I'll show ye some mercy if ye beg real pretty like."

"Perhaps, I shall show you the same courtesy if you beg prettily." She flashed him a quick confident grin. With that she clashed her sword against his to start the battle.

As she suspected, Kraig came at her, time and time again with powerful thrusts and blows. She pared and blocked easily. She was quicker and by far more agile then this man. It took little effort to stay out of the way of his sword, he lacked her skills with a blade.

Within minutes she had him heaving and snarling at her. He had expected to win by now. As he thrust out at her, she deflected and spun away.

"She is good is she not?" Raff grinned at the laird from the sidelines. "Like grace in motion, huh?"

"Aye," Lachlan grunted. He could see she out skilled this man easily. His hopes for having her this night were flittering away with each meeting of their swords.

"You do realize, she is but playing with him, do you not?" Raff smiled then shook his head.

"How 'bout we see how good she really is?" Lachlan challenged getting his back up.

"What do you propose, my lord?" Raff smiled at the laird. These Scots weren't as well trained as his own men it would seem. Pride filled him.

"Let her match as many of my men as she can, one at a time." Lachlan smiled, "If she holds her own with ten men, then ye feast tonight in new accommodations, her along with ye."

Raff thought about it for a long while then spoke, "Agreed."

"Kraig, enough!" Lachlan called their battle to an end. "Shamus, you have a go at her." He ordered.

Kandra turned to Raff, raising a brow. When he simply smiled, and nodded, she turned back to the man coming at her. With a shrug, she met him blow for blow and out skilled him within minutes.

By the time, she had matched ten men she was becoming annoyed. When they sent in the eleventh, she was seeing red. Her arms where getting tired and she had been at this for more than an hour, steady. With a snarl, she out maneuvered her newest opponent, spun around him, sweeping his legs out from under him. Once he hit the ground, the tip of her blade met his throat enough to hold him in place.

"Enough!" She cried. "Yield, or die!"

Her gaze shot to Lachlan's as she called to him, "I have won your contest, have I not laird?" She raised a brow, "Or do you wish me to defeat your men, one by one until I reach you?" She was heartily tired of his games and wished only to face him as her temper grew by leaps and bounds. Now he would call this game to a halt or she would goad him into a fight.

Lachlan pushed away from the log he had been sitting upon next to Raff. Walking across the grass, he came toward her.

She watched his every step. "Are you going stop this foolishness then laird, and fight me yourself?"

Lachlan smiled shaking his head, "Nay lass. I've come to beg my man's life from beneath yer blade." As he stopped in front of her, he could see the weariness in her eyes. She was exhausted.

"Do you concede then, my lord?" She glared at him.

"I do lass, yer a fine warrior, for a woman." He laughed at her snarl. "I mean ye nay disrespect, *Sasunnach*."

"Then our bargain is met?" she raised a brow.

"Aye," he inclined his head, "Ye and yer men shall dine well tonight."

"Very well," she removed her blade from her opponent's throat, turning away from him. "I hope the food is plentiful. I am sure my men are ravenous."

"Do ye think I nay feed my prisoners?" Lachlan frowned at her as he turned to walk with her.

Before she could answer she caught a movement out the corner of her eye. Her last opponent had decided that their match wasn't over yet. She raised her sword to defend herself, but her opponent's blow was blocked before it ever reached her sword.

Lachlan stood with his claymore locked against her attacker's own claymore. Anger glowed on his face. With a primal growl, he shoved his man's sword back. Angry words spoken in Gaelic shot between the two men as they faced off.

As the man motioned toward Kandra, Lachlan stepped in front of her. More words were shouted, then Lachlan pointed his sword to the man's chest. His opponent spat what sounded vaguely like a curse then stormed away.

When Lachlan turned back to her, sheathing his sword a scowl to match her own etched his face.

"I do not need you to defend me!" Kandra spat at him.

"He would have killed ye," he growled, even as the thought made fear clench in his gut.

"I can take care of myself." She shoved at him causing him to step back a step. "I do not need any man to defend me!"

"Dinna push me, lass." Lachlan gritted his teeth as rage filled him.

"Or what? You shall strike me down?" She shoved at him again, this time having no effect.

"That's it! I can take nay, more!" He grabbed hold of her, tossing her over his shoulder. She dropped her sword as her world turned upside down. He turned, marching for the castle.

"Put me down, you blackguard!" She cried in outrage.

"Nay," Lachlan smacked her hard on the bottom when she pulled at his hair. "A warrior ye might be lass, but yer still a woman. And sometimes a woman needs to learn her place."

"You are a heathen bastard!" She struggled to get out of his hold, kicking and hitting him.

Raff watched the two head for the castle and laughed. "'Twould appear she's met her match." Rogan stood beside Raff.

"And about damned time, too," Raff shook his head. He was coming to like the laird of this castle.

Chapter
Eight

L achlan carried her through the castle still dressed in full armor, screaming like a banshee at him. Not once did he glance right or left, nor did he see the smile upon his mother's face. Ferran shook her head, smiling as she watched him climb the stairs to the solar with Kandra slung over his shoulder.

If ever there were two people alike it was these two, Ferran thought happily. She was sure the English woman could make her Lachlan happy once more. She prayed to the Gods that all would work out between the two.

Reaching Kandra's room, he threw open the door, marching through, he kicked it shut behind him. Striding to her bed, he dumped her upon it unceremoniously. "If ye even dare to get up from there..."

Before the words were completely out of his mouth, she was on her feet, lunging at him. Fists flying, she hit him in the jaw and would have connected with his eye as well, if he hadn't been faster. Grasping her wrists, he wrestled her to the bed.

"You, heathen bastard!" Kandra struggled wildly as she fought to break his hold, "How, dare you manhandle me like that!"

Lachlan swore in Gaelic as he tried to pin her to the mattress. She was madder than a raging bull, but he was none too thrilled himself. If she'd been a man, he'd have hit her back. He probably should have knocked her *arse* over tin cups, but warrior or not, he couldn't hit a woman without guilt cutting his knees out from under him.

"If you are going to curse at me at least do it in a civil tongue!" She got one hand free only to have it captured again. Her strength was waning, but she would fight until there was nothing left.

"Christ, woman, I spend more time wrestlin' with ye than anythin' else." He finally managed to pin her arms beside her head and her body under his. "There are more pleasurable ways in which to wrestle, if yer willin' to give it a go."

"Beast!"

"Nay lass, I'm just a man." Lachlan smiled down at her as the last of his temper began to fade away. He enjoyed watching her eyes as they fired with anger. Though she was sweaty and had dirt smudged on her cheek, there was something primal and alluring about it. Lachlan dipped his head, capturing her mouth in a kiss that silenced her when she would have cursed his head.

He swiped his tongue over the seam of her lips, begging entrance. Surprise rocked him as she opened for him, not in surrender, but in wanting. Eagerly, she met and matched his tongue stroke for stroke, thrust for thrust.

Slowly, his grasp on her wrists loosened, until he was no longer confining her. Releasing her wrists altogether, his hand cupped her cheek then speared his fingers into her hair as he deepened the kiss. Passion flared between them and heated until neither could get enough of the taste of each other. Lachlan tore his lips from hers as he nipped at her jaw and throat. She tasted both salty and sensuous at the same time, and he wanted more.

His hand slid down, finding the fastenings for her breastplate. Quickly, he released the plate. Capturing her mouth once more in a deep heated kiss, he pulled her to a sitting position. Breaking their kiss again, he removed her plate of armor. Before she could utter a sound, he had her lying back upon the bed, with his mouth tasting and teasing hers once more.

Kandra hands fisted in his hair as she feed upon his mouth with a fevered frenzy. The anger she had felt toward him melted into an over whelming need for him. The primal need in her to meet him and match him, even on this level, was overwhelming. She wanted to feel his hands on her as well as feeling him under her hands.

Her eagerness was a siren's call to him. His hands stroked and caressed until she was gasping. When his hand cupped her full heavy breast, she cried out. Capturing her mouth with his once more, he swallowed her soft gasps and moans as he rolled her nipple between his thumb and forefinger.

She wanted, no needed, to touch him, to feel his bare skin under her hands. Yanking his shirt from his kilt, her hands touched his heated skin as she shoved them under the fabric. Kandra fingers traced the rippling muscles of his back, the ridged pack of muscles across his stomach. Her nails raked his sides as he teased and tortured her aching breasts.

Her touch seemed unskilled, but aggressive. It burned him as it branded him. His hand left her breast to push her shirt up exposing both of her breasts to him. Tearing his mouth from hers, he kissed, licked and laved a trail over her exposed nipples.

His wet hot mouth closed over her nipple and she arched wildly under him. Heat flared through her as desire filled her. Need blinded her and drowned out what her head was telling her, until his hand slipped

inside her breeches. She hadn't even realized he h[...]
unlaced them.

Reality of what they were doing hit her like c[...]
water. She could not allow this, could not allow [...]
to take her. Pushing at his shoulders, she strug[...]
beneath him.

"No!" she shoved at him, "Stop this." Panic seize[...]
her, and for the first time in her life, she felt real fear.
This man was so much larger than her and she
couldn't match his strength. If he wished to finish
what the two of them had started, he could do so and
she would be no match for him. Shoving harder, she
managed to push him away farther.

Her cries and pleas finally broke through the haze
of passion that wrapped around him. Lachlan looked
up into her frightened eyes and pale face. Reining in
his lust, he pulled away from her. Looking down into
her face, he could see the caution in her eyes. Never
had a woman looked at him thus, and never had he
frightened one with his need for her. Closing his
eyes, he sighed.

"I cannot do this," Kandra spoke in a voice that was
barely above a whisper. "I cannot. It is wrong." She
bit her lower lip.

"But ye want to, lass." Lachlan met her gaze when
she started to shake her head. His harsh words
stopped her. "Dinna lie to me lass, I felt yer passion
and wantin'."

She looked at him long and hard, "I cannot."

With a growl, Lachlan rose from the bed, looking down at her as she straightened her clothing. "I want ye lass, as well ye ken it. Make nay mistake, I will have ye."

Kandra watched him leave the room, closing the door behind him. The lock clanged loudly in place as she lay frowning at the door. Curling onto her side, she gave into the tears of confusion that pricked at the back of her eyes.

A bath and clean clothing was brought to her. Kandra languished in the hot water that was scented with the sweet-smelling heather. No matter how hard she tried to push thoughts of Lachlan MacKinnon from her mind, he crept back into her thoughts, torturing her heart.

Sitting down on her bed after her bath, she began combing her fingers through her wet hair to help it dry faster. When the lock in the door turned, she dropped her hands, prepared to face the laird once more. To her great surprise, a small dark head popped around the door to peer in.

"I was just hoping you would drop by for a visit." Kandra smiled brightly at Bryanna. She waved the girl in, "Come in."

Bry walked into the room, looking at Kandra with awe. "Ye truly are a warrior." She spoke reverently.

"Yes, I am." Kandra patted the bed next to her. "Come sit and we shall have a nice chat."

Bryanna scrambled onto the bed and settled herself cross-legged, facing Kandra. "I watched ye fight this morn, ye were so verra brave."

"No," Kandra shook her head, "Bravery had nothing to do with it. It was skills I have learned and honed for years."

"I want to learn to fight just like ye." Bry smiled brightly. "Then Robby will nay be so mean to me anymore." Her little face screwed up in disgust at the boy's name.

Kandra frowned at the little girl, "Is Robby bigger then you?" Concern filled her, for she knew how boys and men could be.

"Aye, he has ten summers on him." Bry's shoulders sagged in dismay. "I'm nearly his size, but he's stronger."

"Strength means nothing, if you have skill and speed." Kandra shook her head. "What does he do that is so mean? Maybe we can find a way for you to thwart him and teach him a lesson."

Bry smiled brightly, "Do ye really think we can?"

"We are women, are we not?" Kandra flashed a wicked grin. This little girl reminded Kandra of herself when she was a child. The idea of helping little Bryanna fight her bullies and possibly win was too tempting to pass up.

The two females put their heads together, forming a battle plan against Robby MacKinnon. Kandra taught Bry a few simple fighting moves and wished her luck against her nemesis. Bry promised to return the next day to tell Kandra what had happened.

With a smile, Kandra watched the little girl walk out of her room. A strange longing and pride filled her.

Sharing the evening meal with her men boosted her spirits, but they were not left alone enough to talk of escape plans.

"How is Jonas fairing?" Raff swirled his ale in his mug as he surveyed her.

"He grows stronger by the day." Kandra nibbled on a bit of meat. Her brows furrowed, "I just wish I could free him of this place. I would feel much better if he was at home healing."

"Yes, but there is naught you can do that will accomplish that." Raff reassured her. "We'll have to wait until your father arrives."

Kandra groaned at the thought and dropped the piece of meat she had been nibbling on. "Must you remind me?"

"What, afraid to face your father girl?" Raff laughed at her.

"You know he will have my hide for this," Kandra glared at the older man, "And you just love the thought of it."

"I figure his wrath will be well spent." His grin faded, "But it is not only you who will feel his wrath."

"That is not my concern." Anger filled her, "This laird gets what he deserves."

"You are a hard girl," Raff shook his graying head, "And you still have much to learn about life."

As Kandra lay in her bed later, she recalled their conversation. She couldn't help but to wonder what Raff had meant by it. What had she left to learn? She was a skilled warrior, and she didn't think there was anything left for her to learn about fighting. She could handle herself in nearly any situation. Confidently, Kandra drifted off to sleep.

Bryanna came back the next day with a bruise on her cheek, but a smile filling her face. "Ye should have seen him, Kandra." Bouncing upon the bed, Bry recounted the action for her friend. "He took Arlene, my kitten, from me and held her over my head. He was so surprised when I hit him in the stomach that his eyes nearly popped outta his head."

"Did you grab Arlene and run like I told you?" Kandra gave the bruise on her cheek a serious look.

"Nay," Bry shook her dark little head. "I pushed him then I stood there glarin' down at him as you would have."

"And just how pray tell did you end up with the bruise upon your check?" Kandra raised a haughty brow, as she took the girl's chin in her hand turning her face back and forth, surveying the bruise in all of its glory.

"Robby got back up and hit me really hard." Bry lifted her chin with pride, "But I dinna cry."

Kandra felt anger course through her. "That boy should be whipped for hitting you like that."

"Ye sound like my Da, when he found out." Bry laughed. "Shamus broke up our fight and cuffed Robby a good one. He hauled me off to my Da." Bryanna frowned. "I've never seen Da so angry 'afore. Not even when ye fight with him, does he get so angry."

"Well, I hope he beat that boy for what he did." Kandra frowned. She knew if she could get her hands, on Robby MacKinnon, she would give him the scare of his life. Looking back at Bry, she reached out and cupped her cheek. "Being a warrior gets you many more bruises then this and some hurts are much worse. It's not an easy life to live."

"I'm goin' to be a warrior just like ye." Bry smiled brightly with pride and determination shinning in her beautiful green eyes.

"If you are determined enough then nothing can stop you." Kandra spoke earnestly. She herself was determined to escape her prison and free her brother, no matter what it took to achieve it. She pulled Bry into a hug for a long moment, then released her.

The sound of the door opening had both woman and child turning. One smiled brightly as the other frowned. Lachlan MacKinnon stood in the doorway with his raven black hair tied back and a scowl upon his face.

"What are ye doin' in here, Bryanna MacKinnon?" Lachlan growled at his daughter as he stood with his hands on his hips looking at the two.

"Visitin'," the girl stood up placing her hands upon her hips, mirroring her father's stance. She raised a brow, tilting her head just as he would do.

Lachlan's anger melted just looking at her arrogant stance. "You're a retched child, dumplin'" Lachlan held out his arms to her.

"And yer a beast of a Da," Bry ran to him, allowing him to swing her up into his arms. She placed a smacking kiss upon his cheek then hugged him to her.

Lachlan ran a loving hand over his daughter's dark head then nuzzled her playfully. When he pulled back to look at her, he frowned at her bruised cheek. Gently, he ran a large finger over it. "I should have whipped Robby within an inch of his life."

"It hurts nay, more, Da." Bry assured him then smiled brightly, "'Sides I gave him a beatin' he'll nay likely forget soon."

Lachlan threw back his head laughing. Kandra watched the interaction between father and daughter and her heart ached at the sight as a soft smile lifted her lips. Looking away from the two, she continued to run her fingers through her partially dried hair.

"If she has been botherin' ye, lass, I apologize." Lachlan spoke to Kandra for the first time. He watched her continue to comb her fingers through her golden tresses. His own hands itched to bury his fingers in her silken strands.

"No, she does not bother me." Kandra turned to the pair, smiling brightly at Bry, "I enjoy visiting with her."

"Da, can I take Kandra out to play with me?" Bryanna begged her father, cupping his cheeks in her hands she turned his face to hers, "Please Da?"

"She's nay a pet for ye to play with." Lachlan frowned at his daughter.

"But she's my friend." Bry smiled over at Kandra, "A'sides she is goin' to teach me to be a warrior just like her."

"Really?" Lachlan shot Kandra a skeptical look. "It would depend upon how she's feelin', Bry. She might nay be up to goin' out of doors with ye."

"Actually, I am feeling rather well. Perhaps Bry would like to take me for a walk around the keep?" Kandra smiled at the little girl. She knew it was not right to use her, but after all, Lachlan did refer to her as a she-devil, didn't he?

"Aye, but I think I shall accompany the two of ye." Lachlan shot her a narrow-eyed look. He was nay about to chance her escaping or using his daughter to escape.

"Can my Da come with us, so that yer friends as well?" Bry gave Kandra such a hopeful look, that she couldn't help but to give in.

"Yes, he may." She inclined her head, but kept a solemn look upon her face as her eyes met Lachlan's. "I'd like that, very much."

"Well, thank ye, m'lady." Lachlan set his daughter down and bowed regally, "Yer far to kind to a retch like me."

The trio turned to the door making their way out of the castle. Both adults allowed Bryanna to lead them on their way.

In the garden, excitedly Bryanna raced off, leaving them alone so that she could fetch her pony to show Kandra. The adults strolled through the gardens leisurely in the wake of the little girl.

"If yer thinkin' of usin' my daughter to escape, ye can forget it." Lachlan spoke from behind her as soon as his daughter was out of earshot.

"I do not plan to use your daughter for escape. I could never leave my men to your heathen mercy." Kandra rounded on him with eyes blazing.

"Then why did ye want her to take ye for a walk?" He growled at her as they stood facing each other on a flowered path in the gardens.

"I am used to being out of doors. To be kept in that room is like torture to me." Kandra spoke honestly. She needed fresh air and sunshine like she needed food and water.

"'Tis really so bad for ye?" Lachlan's face softened at the thought.

"Yes, I am not one of your soft Scottish women. I am a warrior." Kandra stood proudly in front of him, raising her chin haughtily. She was proud of who she was, even if there were things she hated about herself.

Being a warrior himself, Lachlan knew her feelings. Perhaps it was the warrior in her that intrigued him. Or was it the woman hidden beneath. "Aye, yer nay like any woman I have ever ken." He closed the distance between them. Lachlan raised his hand brushing his knuckles across her cheek. Though she was a warrior, she had the soft skin of a woman. It was bronzed by the kiss of the sun and gave her an exotic look, "Ye, Kandra of Carlisle, are intriguin'."

"I am not interested in your opinions, laird." Kandra drew away with ice in her eyes. Being close to him muddled her thinking. She would not allow herself to lose control again with this man. "I am only interested in the wellbeing of my men."

"Aye, yer men?" He raised an arrogant brow, "What of 'em?" He eyed her suspiciously. Being so close to her caused a throb within his loins. He tried vainly to ignore it.

"You have no need to hold them." She glared at him. "I am all that you require." Kandra raised a haughty chin.

"Och, lass, ye need to watch what yer sayin' to a man." Lachlan shook his head and laughed at her blush of embarrassment.

Kandra flushed under his words. "That was not what I meant." She tried to push past him, but he caught her to him.

"I will nay give ye up easily lass, I want ye far too much." He raised his hand caressing her cheek as his eyes blazed with passion.

The sound of Bry's voice had him releasing her and stepping away. Both turned to smile at the child, rushing toward them clutching the reins of a dapple pony.

Chapter
Nine

*K*andra smiled up at the sunlight streaming down upon her face, as she sat in the garden watching Bry play with her little gray kitten. She was so happy, she felt as if she were near to bursting. She had found the way out.

The laird had given her more freedom by allowing her to go adventuring within the castle walls with Bryanna, so long as she was accompanied by her two guards. Usually Colin and Rory would stay some ways back, or lounge by a wall while she and Bry played in the garden or walked.

It was because of Bry's adventures and her wish to show Kandra everything, in and outside of the castle, that she had found the way she and her men would get out of the castle. They had been on their way to visit Bry's dappled pony in the stables when Kandra had spied a young woman coming through a gate near the kitchen entrance.

"Where does that gate lead to, Bry?" Kandra spoke quietly to the little girl. She glanced over her shoulder to make sure that Rory and Colin were well behind them, and hadn't overheard them.

"Do ye mean the one Aileen came through?" Bry smiled up at her.

"Yes, that one," Kandra bit her lip, praying they were talking of the same gate.

"Nay where special," Bry shook her head. "It leads to a path behind the castle that goes into the woods. Aileen goes there to pick berries for pastries and such. I've helped her a few times." Looking up at Kandra hopefully, "Would ye, like to go pick berries?"

Sadness filled her at having to refuse this little girl. "I don't think your father would allow that."

"Why?"

"Why do we not go see your pony, and perhaps I can watch you ride," Kandra changed the subject holding out her hand. A feeling of longing washed over her, as Bry slipped her smaller hand within hers.

She had steered them past the gate several times over the last four days. She was sure it was left unlocked. Now, she had but to lay her plans for freeing her men. She would get them out of this Scottish laird's hands and back home where they belonged soon enough.

Leaning back on her elbows, she sat upon the green grass with the sun warming her. Her eyes closed as she thought of her impending escape, Kandra frowned at the thought of leaving Bryanna behind. She hated not being able to say goodbye or explain why she had to leave, she only hoped the little girl would not be hurt too badly when Bry discovered she had left.

Lachlan stood across the sun-drenched garden watching his daughter playing with her kitten while his captive lay back in the grass upon her elbows. Her golden hair was in its usual braid, her body was stretched out, long and lithe, with her ankles crossed. Her face was tipped up to the sun and her eyes were closed, as she smiled up at the sun's warmth.

Pushing away from the archway in which he had been leaning, he crossed the gardens. As he reached the spot where Kandra lay in the grass, she frowned up at where the sun had just been. Standing over her, he took in her sculpted features. Her cheekbones were high and defined. Her nose was thin and slightly upturned at the end. Brows that were now furrowed were usually arched aristocratically. However, it was her sensuous mouth that drew him. Her lips were made to be kissed and savored.

His gaze trailed from her face down over her high, full breasts. He knew them to be firm and large enough to fill even his extra, large hands. Her flesh was silky and tasted sweet. His loins tightened at the thought of touching her, tasting her.

"Do ye find displeasure in the sun, yer highness," Lachlan smiled wolfishly down at her. He wanted nothing more than to smooth the frown from her brows.

Squinting up at him, Kandra sneered at his greeting, "No, I find displeasure in barbaric company."

Unable to resist the temptation she laid before him, he sat upon the grass next to her. Stretching out his longer frame, he looked over at her.

"I'm afraid you are mistaken. That was not an invitation for you to join me." Kandra looked over to where Bry was running after the kitten. She had to look at something else, so as she wouldn't be caught by his captivating green eyes. Or stare at his handsome face. Never had she seen anyone with such black hair. She had to bite her lip to fight back the urge to reach over and run her fingers through it, making it shift in the sun, washing blue highlights through it.

"'Tis my castle, I need nay invites, yer highness." Lachlan also looked over at his daughter and smiled as she chased the kitten under a bush.

Kandra turned to look at him and watched the slow, love filled smile slid over his face. Her heart tripped at the sight. His powerful features softened as love for his daughter warmed them. For a brief second, she wanted this man to look at her with that same soft look.

Panic seized her at the thought. No, she didn't want this man to look at her at all, her mind screamed. She had no use for men or for love. She had use, least of all, for this heathen man who had taken her captive. He was an ill-tempered and ill-mannered barbarian, but oh, he was so handsome.

"I care not what you do, laird." Kandra growled as she looked back up at the sky.

"Is that so, lass?" Lachlan gave her a leering look as he raked his gaze over her luscious body. "And what would ye like me to do?"

She gasped at his suggestion as her eyes whipped over to look at him. Grasping a rein on her shock at his words, she arched a brow and spoke sweetly, "For you to go to hell."

Kandra got to her feet nimbly and began brushing herself off. She kept her back to him, giving him a pleasant view of her derrière. In long strides, she reached Bryanna, where she was still trying to coax the kitten from under the rose bush.

Looking up with her father's green eyes, Bry frowned at Kandra. "I think she's stuck."

"Perhaps I can reach her." Kandra knelt down, looking under the bush at the feline huddled in the middle of the roses. "Come here, you scoundrel."

Reaching into the bush, she couldn't quite get a hold on the kitten, lying flat, Kandra crawled partway under the bush. Grasping the kitten around the middle, she began working the kitten through the tangle of thorns. Scooting out from under the bush with kitten in hand, she smiled up at Bry as she handed the furry creature over to her. "There you are, safe and sound."

Bryanna cuddle the kitten as she scolded it for going under the bush. Looking up at Kandra as she gained her feet, Bry frowned. "Look Da, she's hurt."

"Aye, that she is," Lachlan stepped closer to Kandra, taking her hand in his. He raised it to examine it closer. He frowned then lift her hand to his lips. Brushing a soft kiss over the scrap as his eyes met her brilliant blue gaze and he could see the spark of passion in them. "I think she shall live, Bry."

Kandra's breath caught as his lips brushed softly over her skin. The gesture was sweet and endearing, but also provocative and sensual at the same time. Her heart raced at the look in his intense green gaze. The hunger in them took her breath away.

Pulling her hand from his, she stepped back. She was too close to be able to think. She needed space between them to stop the dizziness he caused her and to be able to breathe freely.

"I shall ... I shall be fine, 'tis nothing," she glanced down at her hand, "It is but a scratch. I have had worse."

"'Cause yer a warrior," Bryanna beamed proudly as she held tight to the kitten. She turned her bright eyes upon her father once more. "I wanna be a warrior just like her, Da."

"Do ye now," Lachlan scooped his daughter up in his arms, "But yer nay more than a mite of a thing."

Bry raised her chin in challenge, "I'm the same years that Kandra was when she learned to shoot a bow." She turned to Kandra for confirmation.

When Lachlan raised a brow in question, Kandra inclined her head, "Yes, I was taught by my father how to hit a target at twenty paces. Now I can manage much more than that."

"I'll just bet ye can, lass," Lachlan shook his head. "I fear yer too little to handle a bow, Bry."

"I'm plenty big enough, please, Da," she pleaded with her father then turned hopeful eyes upon Kandra for support.

"She is by far large enough to handle a small bow." Kandra confirmed as she saw the longing and the cry for help in Bryanna's eyes. "I think she could manage it."

"I dinna ask for yer opinion, yer highness." Lachlan growled at her.

Kandra narrowed her eyes at him, "Well, if you were not so narrow minded, you would see it for yourself and I would not have to point it out."

With that, Kandra turned on her heel, marching away from him. Rory and Colin fell in behind her as she stormed toward her chambers.

Bryanna tisked as she shook her dark head, "Ye should nay make her mad, Da."

Lachlan looked back at his daughter's solemn face, "And why nay?"

"'Cause she likes ye and if ye keep on a makin' her mad, she'll be yer friend nay, more." Bry spoke sagely as she looked at her father in dismay.

"Ye think?" Lachlan raised a brow.

"Aye," she spoke solemnly, "Gram says we have to be nice to Kandra, if'n we want to keep her."

"Does she, now?" Lachlan narrowed his eyes. His mother was up to mischief again and he would be having words with her, soon.

Throughout the evening, Lachlan heard not a word of the conversation around him. His mind was on the woman above stairs, just as it had been for the rest of the day. His mind kept drifting back to her laid out upon the grass, the sun turning her hair into light shiny gold, and making her sun kissed skin look radiant. Her eyes when she looked at him held glints of gold and brightened with the sunlight. Those eyes set in that tanned face made them, bewitching, and he was under her spell.

Every moment of his day had been spent thinking about her. No matter how hard he had tried to rid his mind of the blasted woman she always crept back in. He was beginning to truly wonder if she were indeed a witch, and she had cast a spell over him.

"Ye seem to be elsewhere, laird." Rogan, who sat next to him grinned, "Would it be with a beautiful *Sasunnach*, above stairs?"

Lachlan began to shake his head, but thought better of it. This was one of his best friends after all. If he could tell anyone what plagued his soul, it was Rogan. "Aye, I have begun to fear she is a witch." He shook his head. "I can nay seem to get her out of my head."

"Obsessed are ye?" Rogan laughed lightly. "Perhaps ye need to ease yerself with another woman."

Lachlan snorted in return. "I dinna seem to want anyone else." He glowered at his food. "Every other woman seems to have somethin' nay quiet right."

"Ye mean they are nay like yer, *Sasunnach*?" Rogan smiled knowingly.

Before Lachlan could respond, a sounder from the castle walls blew. Scowling, Lachlan rose from the table. Accompanied by Rogan, he met a young lad sent with a message.

"Laird, Angus MacNair is outside our gates, biddin' entrance." The lad announced.

Lachlan looked at Rogan, "Ye think he's heard about our guests?"

"Aye," Rogan frowned. "I smell trouble a brewin'."

"Let's take a look for ourselves, shall we?" Lachlan spoke grimly.

"After ye, my laird," Rogan motioned him on.

Reaching the wall, they looked down upon the party of thirty MacNair's, all mounted. They looked harmless enough, but Lachlan knew looks could be deceiving.

In the courtyard as the MacNair's entered, Lachlan waited for Angus to dismount. Walking to the younger man, Lachlan held out a hand. "Welcome, MacNair."

"I brin' greetin's from my father and brothers." Angus took Lachlan's hand, shaking it hardily.

"And what brin's ye here this day?" Lachlan released the man's hand, stepping back. He hoped Angus would come to the point, but he was to be disappointed.

"We're passin' through, headin' home." Angus shook his head. "We hoped to find hospitality with the MacKinnon's for a day or two, 'afore we finish our journey."

"Yer welcome here," Lachlan inclined his head. "Come join us." He waved them toward the hall, where the evening meal was still being served.

Angus sat to Lachlan's left and Rogan to the right. Lachlan was not interested in his meal as he surveyed his guest. He had no doubt the man was on a mission, but as to what, he was sure he would find out soon enough.

"Yer meal, does nay hold yer interest, MacKinnon?" Angus raised a brow as he took a large swill of ale. He couldn't help but to wonder if it was the English woman he had heard tale of MacKinnon holding that was disrupting this laird's appetite.

Lachlan shook his head. "I was near through when yer presence was announced." He shot the other man an inquiring look, "Have ye and yer men traveled far?"

"Aye, we have come from visitin' the MacDonalds, who are kin by marriage to me sister, Bonnie, last fall." MacNair hoped by mentioning the MacDonalds it would show MacKinnon that the MacNair family was in the rank of his own family.

"And how did ye find the laird and his wife?" Lachlan disappointed Angus by not batting an eyelash at the man's name-dropping.

"They have a healthy son." Angus boasted, then swirled the ale in his cup, "But talk around their keep is that the MacKinnon's are holdin' a *Sasunnach* woman."

Lachlan raised a brow. Word certainly did travel fast. "And where did ye hear such a rumor?"

"I can nay say for sure, passin' gossip mayhaps." Angus met Lachlan's bright green gaze with his own darker one. "Is it true, MacKinnon?"

Lachlan knew that if Angus and his men were here for more than one night, they would learn the truth. Better it come from his mouth. "Aye, 'tis true."

MacNair leaned back in his chair, "And how did ye come across such a treasure."

"'Tis a long story as well as a rather painful one." Lachlan thought of the gash Kandra had made in his leg during their first encounter. "She's nay yer usual *Sasunnach* woman."

When Angus raised a brow in question, Lachlan laughed and shook his head. "Be on the practice field in the morn' ye'll see for yerself."

The sun was barely up when Lachlan burst into Kandra's chambers carrying her armor, her shield, and helmet. She was already seated near the window watching the gray day take shape outside her prison.

"I've come bearin' gifts, yer highness." Lachlan set the items upon the bed.

"If it is not to release me and my men, then leave." She scowled at him. Her mood matched the gray, misty day outside her window. She had slept fitfully through the night. Dreams of a tall, handsome, Scotsman had plagued her.

"Ye ken I can nay do that, lass," Lachlan frowned at her back. She sat in the wooden chair with her arms wrapped around her updrawn knees. "I thought perhaps ye would want to feel the weight of yer sword in yer hands this morn'."

"Go away and leave me be." She waved him away. Laying her chin upon her knees, she sighed.

Now, Lachlan began to feel real fear churning in his belly. Where was the woman who would spare with him at the drop of a hat? Perhaps she was ill? Striding across the room, he knelt beside her chair. "Are ye ill, lass?"

When she merely turned her head from him, his frown deepened. "Tell me what bothers ye, lass." He reached out, touching her golden hair.

Her blue eyes met his with anger in them, "You, you bother me. Go away and leave me be." She pushed out of the chair. Kandra began to pace the room, looking to release some of the tension this man caused inside of her.

Lachlan breathed a sigh of relief to see the fire back in her eyes instead of the despair he saw in them moments, ago. "And who are ye, to be commandin' me, yer highness?"

"If I am to stay in this God forsaken place, at least you can give me is some privacy." She raged at him.

Lachlan strode to where she stood shouting out her demand. "'Tis my castle and I'll go anywhere I bloody well please." It felt good to spar with her again.

"You are an arrogant ass," she fumed, "A heathen who has no decency."

"Well, yer a woman who has nay, idea of her mind." Lachlan bellowed at her. "I came in here to offer you some sword time, but perhaps yer beginnin' to realize lassies can nay be warriors."

"I have already shown you differently." She glared at him. "I can best any man in this castle." She stood on her tiptoes to be face to face with him as she poked him in the chest, "Even you, Lachlan MacKinnon."

It was the first time she had spoken his name, though she said it in anger, he liked the sound of his name rolling off her tongue in that sweet clipped English accent of hers. He wanted to pull her to him and crush his mouth over hers, but restrained himself.

"Ye can nay best me, lass," Lachlan shook his head as he looked down at her. "But if ye can defeat every man I put ye against today, I'll make ye a bargin."

Kandra narrowed her eyes at him, "What?"

"If ye best every man I put ye against this morn'" Lachlan grinned, "I'll give Bry her bow, and allow ye to teach her to shoot it."

She gasped at the thought. She had not meant to teach the child to shoot a bow. Sure, she wanted Bry to have one and be allowed to learn the skills, but she wouldn't be here long enough to teach her.

"No, I shall best any man, including you, laird, but you must promise to teach Bry to shoot the bow, no matter the outcome between us." Kandra stepped back, eyeing him carefully, "Your word laird."

"Ye've my word, as a MacKinnon, I'll teach her." Lachlan held out his hand to her.

Hesitantly, Kandra placed her hand in his. He grasped her hand, but she wasn't prepared for him to tug her forward, slamming her against his chest. She gasped, but before she could get a word out in protest, she was wrapped within his embrace and being thoroughly kissed.

When he released her, she wasn't quiet steady on her feet. "Easy lass," he steadied her. Smiling, he let her go.

"I'll see ye on the field shortly." Before he left he smiled at her, "Wear yer helmet, or nay bargin."

Chapter Ten

*K*andra paced the field waiting for her next opponent. She knew the reason for the laird wanting her to wear her helmet. The giant redhaired man standing next to the laird was a new face. She had no idea who he was, but for some reason Lachlan didn't want this man to know she was a woman.

He was showing off her skills, and that sparked an emotion she had yet to identify. She brushed the feeling aside as she focused on the man coming across the field to challenge her.

When the redhaired giant drew his sword, Lachlan shook his head. Kandra could feel the strength just beginning to wan in her arms. She had faced more than a dozen men. Now, the giant wanted to fight her, but Lachlan wouldn't allow it.

"The lad's good, but cocky, MacKinnon." Angus argued. "Someone needs to show him his better."

"In that, I agree with ye, MacNair, but it'll nay be this day." Lachlan gave a sharp whistle waving Kandra over to him.

When she reached him, she was furious. She had wanted to fight the redhead without the advantage of him knowing she was a woman. Though she was tired, she was sure she could take the man.

"Angus MacNair, meet Kandra, or should I say, the Lady Stafford." Lachlan introduced them as Kandra removed her helmet, "My *Sasunnach* woman."

"I am not your anything, laird." Kandra glared at him.

At first, the sight of her long golden braid swinging free from under her helmet shocked Angus, but it was her piercing blue eyes that left him truly speechless.

"Yer… Yer… a lass for cryin' out loud!" Angus found his tongue at last. His eyes swept over her. In her armor, he could tell she must be well formed. He couldn't wait to see her out of it.

"No, I am a warrior." Her eyes were cold and hard as she looked Angus over. "My being a '*lass*', makes no difference. I can best any man I have met." She shot a deliberate look at Lachlan.

Lachlan couldn't help but to laugh. Turning to Angus, he smiled broadly, "Would ye care to have a go at her, MacNair?"

"Nay, I can nay fight a woman." Angus looked aghast at Lachlan. "I would surely hurt her."

Kandra snorted in return, "I highly doubt that, my lord." She looked the redheaded man over. Though he was nearly the same height as the laird and nearly as thick, he was not honed, he was soft, running to fat. He would be slow and cumbersome on the battlefield.

"Yer good lass, I'll give ye that, but I will nay fight a woman." Angus shook his head. He didn't want to harm this *Sasunnach* woman, for she could prove to be far too valuable to him and his father.

Kandra turned to Lachlan, "And what of you, laird? Do you intend to cross blades with me this day?" She shot him a challenging look.

Lachlan narrowed his eyes at her, "Ye ken I'll nay risk hurtin' ye again, lass."

Kandra looked him over with contempt and arrogance in her eyes, "Just because you got lucky once does not mean it will happen again." With that she turned on her heels, heading back for the castle.

"Remember our bargain, MacKinnon." She threw over her shoulder at him, in her most haughty commanding voice.

"She's an arrogant, prideful woman." Lachlan shook his head. "She's infuriatin'."

"Aye, she appears to be a handful at the least." Angus grinned as he watched her strut away. "Perhaps we should talk."

Kandra wondered through the gardens by herself, Bryanna had yet to make an appearance. She was probably off somewhere playing with friends. Thoughts plagued her, thoughts of her men and escape, thoughts of the laird and his daughter. She wanted to go home, she wanted to leave this place, yet Kandra knew she would wonder about these people when she was gone.

"M'lady," Angus MacNair stepped out from behind a tree.

"My lord," Kandra stopped where she was, inclining her head. She didn't like this man. Though he had done nothing to truly offend her, she disliked him.

"Where are ye headed?" Angus matched his pace to hers as she continued, on her way.

"Nowhere, I am just wondering." She didn't bother to look at him. "I am used to being much more active then I have been here."

"I'm surprised MacKinnon allows ye such freedoms as to roam about his castle." Angus eyed her speculatively. Now that she was out of her armor, he looked her over. She was striking with her golden features and her other female attributes. If he were to breed with a woman such as her, he would be guaranteed strong sons to honor him.

"The laird does not take my skills serious. He does not see me as a threat." She looked back over her shoulder to where Colin was following her today. "But he takes no chances."

"Yer his prisoner," Angus shook his head. "He's a fool." He smiled wolfishly at her. "I have made him an offer to turn ye over to me. I'd nay keep ye as my prisoner if he agrees."

Kandra stopped, raising her chin as she looked at the other man, "And just what would I be?"

"My wife," Angus spoke firmly, "Ye could give me fine sons, as well as English ties."

"What I would give you is a sword through your gullet." Kandra growled through clenched teeth. When she found Lachlan MacKinnon she was going to kill him for offering her to this heathen as if she were a brood mare. "I would never give myself to the likes of you."

Before he could reply, she turned on her heels, striding away from him. She was in search of a bigger oaf then she had just left behind. When she caught up with the laird, she would give him a lesson he would never forget. Women were more than bargaining tools.

Storming through the castle, Kandra found no trace of Lachlan. When she was on her way out to the practice field, she came across a young boy arguing with Bryanna. Already annoyed by MacKinnon men, Kandra strode over to the pair, just as blows were being exchanged.

Snatching the boy by his collar, Kandra hoisted him off his feet. "Robby MacKinnon, I presume." Kandra looked at Bry who had tears shinning in her eyes from the confirmation.

"Let me go, ye wench," Robby struggled as his feet peddled air.

"He... he..." Bryanna sniffled, "He threw rocks at my kitten. Now she's runaway." Tears began streaming down her face.

"You should be ashamed of yourself, Robby." Kandra spoke harshly giving him a slight shake. "What you deserve is a good thrashing."

"Hey now, what are ye doin' with me boy there, wench?" A burly man dressed as a blacksmith came hurrying toward the trio shouting.

"He is your son?" Kandra spoke haughtily as she looked down her nose at the man.

"Aye, he is." The man growled, snatching his son away from her. His face was filled with anger.

"You should thrash that boy and teach him some manners." Kandra informed Robby's father. "He is a terrible child who torments animals and hits little girls."

"Who are ye to be tellin' me anythin' about me boy." Robby's father's bellowed, "Yer an unnatural woman, who does nay ken her place." He sneered at Kandra, "I have seen ye on the field." He spat.

Kandra felt the words slap her. She turned the hurt to anger quickly, "At least I am skilled with a sword, unlike you who has no skill at being a father." She spat venomously. She stepped up to look him in the eye. She would not back down from any man. "Your son is a bully, and has no respect for women. But perhaps, he gets his ill-mannered behavior from his equally ill-mannered father."

The burly man went red faced as he bellowed in rage. Kandra prepared for the blow she knew he would attempt to deliver. Her eyes narrowed to slits as she prepared for battle with this man.

Robby's father swung at her, she dodged his ham-sized fist and landed a blow to his nose. Though this man was stronger than she, Kandra knew she could move quicker.

She heard the roar as the man swung again. Before the blow could strike her, she was shoved out of the way landing on her bottom in the dirt. Lachlan had Robby's father by the throat shoving him back against a nearby wall. She watched in amazement as Lachlan lifted the huge man clear off his feet.

Rage contorted Lachlan's face as the other man struggled for his life. Bryanna was now sobbing wildly, as was Robby. Kandra jumped to her feet, running over to Lachlan.

"Let him go." She tugged at his powerful arm, but it wouldn't budge. She hit at his arms several times. His muscles were bulging rock and she knew she couldn't break his hold.

She prayed reasoning with him would work, "Lachlan, let him go," she begged, "For God sakes, do you want Bry to see you like this?"

Lachlan turned to look at her, murder was clear in his eyes and for the first time, she shivered at the rage and something else she saw in their green depths. "Please, do not do this. Please Lachlan, not in front of Bry, I *beg* you."

Lachlan let go of the man, letting him fall to the ground, gasping for breath. He turned his rage filled eyes upon Robby, "Dinna ever let me catch ye strikin' a female again, lad. Do I make myself clear?"

Robby nodded fearfully then ran to his father's side.

Kandra raced over to where Bryanna stood with tears streaming down her face. Scooping the girl in her arms, Kandra cradled her and marched away from the whole scene.

When at last she reached the peaceful setting of the garden, Kandra sat upon a bench and rocked the little girl. "Hush, Bry. You are fine, sweetie." She stroked the little dark head. "Let me look at you." Kandra set the girl back from her. She had an angry red mark upon her cheek from Robby smacking her, but otherwise she was unharmed.

"Are you hurt anywhere else," Kandra spoke as she gently ran her fingers over Bryanna's face. In that moment Bry looked less than her seven years and Kandra's heart went out to her.

"I thought Robby's Da, was goin' to hurt ye," Bry's eyes refilled with tears. "I'm sorry he said such awful things to ye, Kandra. Please dinna be mad and go away." She sobbed, throwing her arms around Kandra's neck.

"Oh Bry," Kandra rocked her. "I am all right. Robby's father would not have hurt me." She set the little girl away from her once more. "When I go away it will not be because of you, or anything you have done."

"Please dinna go away, promise me." Bryanna begged as tears streamed from her green eyes.

Kandra felt her heart lurch and twist. She closed her eyes sighing. "I cannot make promises I cannot keep."

Lachlan chose that moment to make his presence known. Striding over to the bench, he sat next to Kandra. His brows were furrowed and his face was etched with concern as he looked at his daughter.

"Are ye all right, Bry?" Lachlan held out his hands to her. She lunged for him and he embraced her tightly. He stroked and kissed her dark little head. "I dinna mean to scare ye, dumplin'."

Kandra looked away as the sight of father and daughter, caused a lump to grow in her throat. Without a word, she stood from the bench and quickly made her way to her room. She didn't want to see her captor as a person, or a loving father. She didn't want to become attached to this little raven-haired child, but in her heart, she knew it was already too late.

Lachlan soothed Bryanna then went after Kandra. He found her in her chamber, pacing restlessly. Standing in the doorway he wasn't sure if she noticed him.

"How dare you?" she rounded on Lachlan with fire in her eyes.

"Come to see if yer all right, lass?" he gave her a puzzled look.

"How dare you speak to MacNair about selling me off." She raged as he shut the door. Walking up to him, she thumped him on the chest, "You, arrogant pigheaded man! I will not leave my men behind!"

Lachlan caught her wrist as she made to hit him again, "I told him nay."

She tugged at her wrist and hit him with the other hand, "If you dared to sell me off to him, I would come back here and run you through, so help me God."

Lachlan grunted then caught that hand. He turned them, backing her against the door, "Will ye listen to me..."

"And if I died before I could, I would haunt you..." She cut him off only to have him cut her off in return.

"Bloody hell will ye listen to me..."

"Do not..."

He could think of only one way to shut her up, so he kissed her long and hard until she was breathless. When, at last, he pulled back too look at her, he smiled at the soft look upon her face. "I told the bloody bastard, I would nay sell ye and he was nay happy."

Kandra's blue eyes fluttered open, "Oh I thought..."

"Ye thought wrong, lass." Lachlan caught both of her wrists in one of his large hands and traced a finger over her cheek, "Now, are ye all right?"

She gave him a puzzled look when all she could think was that he was asking her if she was all right from their kiss. "I...Um..."

Lachlan laughed that soft deeply sexy laugh he had, "Did Robby's Da hurt ye?" He let his finger trace her lips then her jaw and down her throat to the opening of her shirt.

"Um…" She couldn't think with him touching her, "No, I am fine." She stammered as her pulse raced and her blood roared in her ears.

"Aye, ye are." With that, Lachlan pulled back and sighed. He moved her from the door and opened it. Looking down at her, he grinned with mischief in his eyes, "Will ye try to stay out of trouble, Kandra lass?"

He walked through the door, closing it behind him quickly. Then laughed as he heard her curse and throw something at the closed door behind him.

That evening, Kandra paced her chamber with restless anxiety. She barely touched her food tray. With the walls of her room closing in on her, Kandra stuck her head out her door to look at Gavin, who was standing guard for the night.

"Gavin, could we go for a walk?" Kandra pleaded with him. "I cannot stand being cooped up in here a moment longer."

"Aye, if ye wish, m'lady." Gavin inclined his head. He waved Kandra before him. He liked Kandra greatly, she was nice and she gave him no trouble.

Kandra paced the east wall of the castle. From here, the village spread out before her. The moon and stars shone brightly, making the nearby loch and the moot below her shimmer. Walking to the edge of the wall, she took in the moonlit land laid out before her. She missed her home and her father.

She heard the approach of footsteps but didn't turn. She knew if she were to look over her shoulder the laird would be there, watching her with his intent green gaze. She could feel his eyes surveying her. Heat spread through her.

Lachlan took in her unbound hair hanging down her back in golden waves. The wind lifted stray strands, making it look like a golden cape. She stood rigid, with her ramrod straight back and her feet braced apart as if she were ready to battle.

"What do you want?" Kandra snapped, though he had done nothing to cause her anger, yet she could feel it bubbling inside of her.

"I've come to thank ye, lass." He watched her shake her head and her golden hair sway with the movement. His fingers itched to plunge into that silken mass.

"You have nothing to thank me for." She didn't want his thanks. Kandra didn't want this man here. She wanted to be left alone.

"Ye defended my daughter when ye could have walked away." He pushed away from the wall where he had been leaning. He came to a stop not a foot from her.

Kandra whirled around to face him. Fire lit her eyes. Her anger surged through her. "No, I could not walk away. I could not let that bully hurt her." She railed at him as she struck him with her fists on his chest, "And I did not need you to defend me. I can take care of myself! I do not need you! I do not want you!"

Lachlan caught her wrists before she could hit him again. He took in the fire sparking in her eyes, her rigid stance, and her golden hair blowing loosely in the wind. Her features washed in moonlight made her ethereal.

"Yer bloody beautiful, lass," his voice was husky as he pulled her to him. His lips hovered over hers, less than a breath away.

Kandra closed her eyes as the words washed over her. "Do not say that..." She trailed off as she stretched up to meet his lips. Kandra didn't want this man to have the power to make her feel, but he held it. He could make her feel, want and need. He could make her feel desirable. This man could almost make her believe she was beautiful.

The smell of the wild heather on her skin and in her hair, along with her own womanly scent, was a heady mix. Lachlan traced the seam of her lips with the tip of his tongue. When she moaned into his mouth, opening for him, he pulled her closer as he plundered her mouth.

Kandra reveled in the feel of his arms wrapped around her. Her senses spun out of control at the feel of his body pressed tight against hers. The heat he caused in her was addictive and she craved more.

The feel of his manhood pressed against her abdomen had desire coiling tight within her. Twining her arms around his neck, she feasted hungrily on his mouth, letting the essence of him seep into her, filling her.

Plunging his fingers into her golden locks, he cradled the back of her head as his other hand cupped her bottom, lifting and pressing her into him. He wanted to mark this woman, brand her to him and claim her for his own. Pulling his mouth from hers, he rained kisses upon her jaw as he whispered soft Gaelic words to her.

Kandra felt the heated brand of his lips all the way to her toes. She wanted to stay in this man's arms forever. The sound of his foreign words propelled her heart. Though she knew not one syllable that passed his lips, her heart raced with promises of the feelings he could create in her.

Lachlan pulled back from her looking down into her blue eyes. "Let me love ye, lass."

Kandra looked into his green gaze, and though her heart screamed for her to give herself to him, she knew they were thinking about two very different things. She would give anything to have this man love her, but she knew love was not a part of her destiny.

Closing her eyes against the tears that stung at the backs of her eyes suddenly, she shook her head that was cupped in his large wide palm. "No," she spoke weakly as she opened her eyes to look into his once more.

"Dinna deny what we feel, lass." Lachlan pressed her more firmly against his erection and nearly groaned. "I want ye like nay, other man ever has."

Closing her eyes once again, Kandra leaned her forehead against his chest. Never could he have spoken truer words to her. No man had ever wanted her. '*This man wants you!*' Screamed her racing heart.

When she looked back at him, her eyes were filled with the desire she felt. "What I feel means nothing."

"What of what ye want?" Lachlan frowned down at her. He was so close to having her, but he felt the wall slide in place between them.

"What I want, you are unable to give me." She shook her head. "And I cannot give you what it is you seek."

"Damn ye, *Sasunnach*, I could take what I want." Lachlan tightened his hold on her. He saw the tinge of fear creep into her eyes and guilt filled him.

Raising her chin arrogantly, Kandra met his eyes. "You would not do such a thing."

Lachlan met her eyes, "How can ye be sure?"

Kandra searched his eyes and spoke from her heart. "You are far too honorable."

"That does nay change the fact that I want ye, lass." He raised a hand, cupping her cheek as he traced her lower lip with his thumb. Her tongue darted out to follow the path of his thumb.

"Then I am afraid, laird, we are at an impasse." She pulled out of his arms.

Kandra stepped around him to leave, but paused when she stood beside him. She looked over at his hardened expression. "For that impasse, I am truly sorry." She bit her lower lip. Reaching up, she cupped his cheek, feeling the rough texture and the warmth of it in her palm. Lowering her hand, she walked away.

Chapter
Eleven

K andra spent a restless night, full of shadowy dreams, filled by a dark Scottish warrior with mesmerizing green eyes. Before the sun had even broken the horizon, she threw off her covers and dressed for the day. Restless energy filled her and pacing didn't seem to help. Her chamber was far too small for the amount of room she needed to release the tension her dreams had coiled tight within her.

Poking her head out the door, she smiled at Gavin dozing next to it. On silent feet, she slipped out of her room and down the hall past him.

Making her way through the stables, she stroked the head of her own destrier, Hadwin. He was well cared for and exercised regularly. She whispered to him as he nuzzled her hand. Kandra wished she had apple slices to feed him.

Oren, the stable master, greeted her with a bright smile upon his entrance.

"Morn' lass, have ye come to ride yer beast?" Oren raised a brow, looking around her for her escort.

"I left Gavin sleeping by the door this morn'. Please, do not tell Lachlan, Oren. I just needed to move around a bit this morn'." Kandra smiled softly at the older man.

"Yer secret's safe with me, lass, but 'tis the laird ye best be worryin' about." Oren shook his head as he continued to feed the horses. Kandra picked up a pail and gave a helping hand. It was a menial task, but she enjoyed the company.

When they were finished, she bid Oren good day. Turning toward the gardens, she ambled through them, picking a flower from a bush aimlessly as she strolled. Plucking the petals as she wondered through the garden paths, her thoughts wound around the night before.

The laird was having too great an effect upon her. She wasn't sure how much longer she could keep herself from acting upon the want he could make her feel. When he was near, she couldn't seem to keep her mind on anything but him. Even her dreams were now haunted by his image nightly.

She needed to get herself and her men far from this place as soon as possible. If she didn't, she feared what would come to pass.

With a sigh, she watched a bird wheeling through the early morning sky. She couldn't wait to feel such freedom once again.

Noticing the height of the sun, she turned back toward the main house. She didn't want Gavin to suffer because she had snuck out. Walking into a dark corridor, her eyes looked into blackness for a moment, as she waited for them to adjust.

When a hand slipped over her mouth and she was propelled back into the wall with a jarring thud, she was momentarily dazed. Kandra looked up into Angus MacNair's face, next to him stood two of his men, smiling villainously. Kandra began to struggle in a vain attempt too free herself, she lashed out, kicking, hitting, and punching. Her hands were captured and tied, but still she struggled. She would not make this easy for them.

Angus raised a gleaming silver dagger to her throat. Kandra froze as the cold steel pressed against her skin. She felt its point dig slightly into her flesh. She looked belligerently up at him, "You will not make it out of here with me, and even if you do, you will die."

"Think again, lass." Angus laughed quietly, the sound sent shivers down Kandra's spine. "I get what I want, and from the moment I looked at ye, I thought of ye as mine."

A gag was quickly placed in her mouth before she could reply. She knew she had to get away from these men, or she would be in serious trouble. She could only hope that someone saw them taking her, and sent word to Lachlan, but then she couldn't be sure he would even care enough to come after her.

"Take her out the back gate. We'll meet in the forest beyond." Angus instructed his men. Throwing a cloak over her shoulders and covering her head with the hood, he grabbed her chin forcing, her to look at him. "Do as he tells ye, lass, and ye'll be fine, but if ye get any wayward notions he'll stick ye." He waved the blade in front of her face.

Kandra merely raised an arrogant brow, pulling her chin out of his grasp. When Angus's man propelled her forward, she walked with him. With her hands tied and weaponless, it would prove harder to get out of this situation. However, it wasn't impossible. Walking toward the kitchens, Kandra spied the gate up ahead. Looking over at her captor, she saw him darting glances back and forth, not paying her any mind and not seeing her as a threat.

Kandra pretended to trip, stumbling forward. When he grabbed for her, she turned and struck him with both of her hands fisted together. Pain shot through her hands, but she ignored it. Throwing off the hood of the cloak, she prepared to fight. Out of nowhere flew Lachlan, diving at the man. Both men fell to the ground, knocking Kandra off her feet. Struggling, she regained her footing just in time to see Lachlan rolling over and over with Angus's man. When the man took, the top and struggled to plunge the knife in Lachlan's chest, Kandra felt the icy fingers of fear race over her. Without any thought except saving Lachlan, she kicked the man with all of her strength.

Her assailant rolled off Lachlan taking him over with him. Kandra watched as Lachlan came away with blood on his hands. The dagger had impaled the other man when they had rolled.

Lachlan wiped his hands on his breeches as he walked over to her. His eyes glared with anger. She reached up to pull out her gage, but his quick hands grasped hers. "Leave it!" Before she could do more than blink an eye, she found her world tipped upside down, as Lachlan swept her off her feet, tossing her over his shoulder.

Being thrown over his shoulder, not once, but twice was not only humiliating, it was infuriating. As she struggled against his hold, she swore he would pay for this trespass against her person, and pay dearly he would.

Lachlan marched through the castle, anger lengthening his stride. Anyone within his path took one look at his face and scurried out of his way.

Taking the stairs at a jarring pace, he paid no heed to his cargo's discomfort.

Kandra was bounced and jarred by his carelessness. Angrily, she clenched her fists and struck his back. She gasped when he merely grunted then shifted her position and struck her bottom firmly. The sting from his hand enraged her more, kicking her legs she tried in vain to free herself.

Lachlan marched through her door, kicking it shut behind him. He walked to the bed, dropping her upon it. Kandra lay sprawled upon the blanket glaring up at him.

"I should have let them take ye," Lachlan spoke with rage glinting in his eyes, "The Gods ken yer more trouble than yer worth, *Sasunnach*."

Kandra drew back her leg to kick him. Lachlan grabbed her ankle holding it firmly.

"If ye dare to kick me, *Sasunnach*, I swear I'll beat ye," Lachlan growled down at her. The fire in her big blue eyes matched his own anger. His anger wasn't so much built upon the early morning stroll she had taken, as it was the fear that had raced through him when he had seen MacNair hold the dagger to her throat. Fear and anger had raced through him, knowing that he could do nothing to help her in that moment. Then waiting for a chance to rescue her had eaten at him.

Looking down at her on the bed, his gaze focused on the scratch upon her neck the dagger had left. The sight of blood there nearly brought him to his knees. He had failed to protect what was his to protect.

Dropping her ankle, he spun away, walking to the window. Rage roared through him. He would kill MacNair when he got his hands upon him. Lachlan heard her sitting up on the bed, but he didn't turn to look at her. If he didn't get his anger under control first, he knew he would act foolishly.

Kandra sat up on the bed. Reaching the back of her head, she struggled to untie the gag knotted there. When it slipped free, she pulled the cloth from her mouth and worked her jaw. Glaring at the laird's back, she looked around the room for something near at hand to throw at him, or use for a weapon. There was nothing handy.

"If I am so much trouble, you should have let them take me." Kandra spat. "I would have killed the bastard."

"He would nay have given ye the chance." Lachlan felt his rage boiling. "He would have forced himself upon ye."

"I would have stopped him." Kandra stood up, striding over to him. "I can take care of myself."

Lachlan's rage came unleashed. Whirling on her, he grasped her throat backing her to the wall. His fingers pressed against her throat, but just enough to show her he had the upper hand. He wanted to punish her, to teach her, to make her surrender. "If a man wants a woman enough, there is aught that will stop him."

Before she could reply, his mouth crushed over hers as his kiss plundered and punished. Her hands shoved at his chest, but he used his superior strength and size to trap her against the wall. His free hand cupped her breast through her shirt and kneaded.

Kandra's fear spiked as she fought him. Getting a handle on her fear, she began to feel desire at his touch and taste. Another type of fear raced through her. She didn't fear his touch, but feared her own need, her own desire, her own longing. She feared she would bow to this man, and he would rule her.

Lachlan felt her struggles cease, felt her turn submissive. The fire in him turned to hunger. He went from punishing to savoring. His kisses turned softer, but still possessive. He wanted this woman, wanted her withering under him. Never, had wanting a woman wrapped him in such a tight choking obsession.

Kandra knew she had to get away from him, before she surrendered to his will. Letting herself feel for this man was dangerous, not only to her heart, but to her fate. When his kiss turned tender and his hands began to trace the line of her, she shivered. Tracing her hands down his chest, she reached his waist and heard him growl deep within his throat. The sound made the heat inside her flare. She felt her own womanly power over him.

Lachlan slid his hand under her shirt, cradling her bare breast in his palm. Rubbing his thumb over her hardened nipple, he felt her knees tremble and breathed in her sigh of pleasure.

He was taken by surprise when he felt the cold steel against his own throat.

Kandra pulled from their kiss as she pressed his eating knife to his throat. "I can take care of myself, MacKinnon."

Never had he expected her to use his own weapon against him. Lachlan looked into her eyes, searching, "Aye, lass, yer good at getting yerself into trouble, but I've yet to see ye truly get out of it."

"I do not need you to get me out of anything." She hissed as he smiled down at her.

"Ye'll nay use that on me."

"I will."

In a movement, so fast, Kandra barely saw it. Lachlan had her bound wrists and the knife over her head. "Ye won't."

Using his body to hold her still, he used his free hand to take the knife from her. Never taking his eyes from her face, he cut the rope from her wrists. Sheathing the dagger once again, he caught her freed wrists.

Kandra frowned at him. He raised her hands, studying the bruises already forming on her knuckles, from the blows she delivered to her captor and to him as well. Raising her hands, he brushed soft kisses across them.

His green gaze held hers captive once more. "I want ye, lass."

She shook her head. "You cannot have me."

"Give yerself to me." Lachlan pressed forward, brushing a kiss over her lips, then nibbled. "I'll pleasure ye, worship ye and cherish ye."

A thrill of longing raced through her at his words. "You cannot have me, MacKinnon." She breathed against his lips.

"I will have ye, *Sasunnach*." Lachlan pulled away.

"Only if you force yourself upon me," She shook her head defiantly. "I shall never surrender to you."

Lachlan stepped away from her, but his eyes never left hers. "I will have ye lass, make nay mistake 'bout it."

With that, he left the room without looking back. The anger and fear he had felt still rolled through him. Making his way to the practice field, Lachlan took out his emotions on his men. When his arms ached and he was winded, he finally called a halt.

Rogan walked over to lean against the log next to his laird. "Feelin' better?"

"Nay," Lachlan shook his head in disgust. "'Twould feel better if I could wring her beautiful neck."

Rogan raised a brow. "I dinna think wringin' it is yer first choice." He let out a laugh at Lachlan's scowl.

"Ye ken aught of how I feel." Lachlan frowned at his friend.

"I've ken ye long enough to see what the English woman is doin' to ye," Rogan shook his head. "Ye want her, any fool can see that. But she will nay have ye. Perhaps, ye would be better off to let her go."

"I can nay do it." Lachlan growled. "I need her."

"Ye want her, but ye nay need her." Rogan countered. "If ye keep her, it will make it impossible to let her go later."

"Nay," Lachlan lied to them both. "When her English father shows, I'll readily give her troublesome hide up."

Lachlan turned, walking back to the keep. He would give her up when the time came, but he would have her long before that time arrived.

Rogan watched his laird walk away. Shaking his head, Rogan turned back to training his men. He had seen the obsessed look upon Lachlan's face, and the golden haired, warrior goddess had surely bewitched the poor man.

Chapter Twelve

K andra knew she had to leave this place and leave it soon. She could wait no longer. Kandra had to get away from this man. Pacing her chamber, panic closed in on her. She had been so close to giving herself to him. How she had wanted to let him do all of those wondrously wicked things to her. To make her feel the pleasure he offered. To make her feel cherished and to know his touch intimately.

These feelings were dangerous not only to her body, but to her heart. If she found all of the things he promised, within his arms, could she ever leave this place when the time came? Could she go back to her life?

No, she wouldn't be able to go back to the same warrior she had been. A piece of her would remain here in this place, with this man, with these people. If she were not whole, she wouldn't be able to stand her life of loneliness. She would fall apart when other men snubbed her and looked at her with contempt and disgust.

Jonas was doing better each day when she visited him. She could risk moving him. Tonight, she would make their escape. Kandra needed to get Jonas home where he belonged. If she focused upon that, she wouldn't feel the sorrow of leaving her one chance at knowing what it was like to be wanted as a woman, instead of a warrior.

The moon was a waning sliver. With the candle extinguished, leaving the room drenched in darkness, Kandra lifted the water urn in her hands. It had good weight, she thought with a smile. With one good whack, it should knock the guard out and not kill him. She prayed it would knock him out long enough for her to reach Jonas and to get her men freed.

Once she had them out, they would need to move swiftly. She could only pray that they did nothing to alert the other sentries. If they could reach the garden gate, they could make good on their escape.

Taking a deep breath, she walked to her door, lifting the latch, letting it swing open on its own. The slow creak of the iron door hinges made her bite her lip. She said a silent apology to Rory, the sentry on duty.

The sound of the door hinges creaking had Rory look toward the lady's doorway. He waited a moment to see if she would stick her head out to speak with him as she did often. The room appeared darkened. Curiosity got the better of him as he pushed away from the wall, walking to the doorway.

"M'lady?" he called, as he pushed the door wider to peer inside. "Lady Kandra?"

Squinting into the darkness, Rory gnawed at his lower lip. Should he risk going in to check on her, or should he leave her be. He knew that if anything happened to her the laird would have his head on a pike. With a sigh, he crept into the room. Standing half way inside, he peered at the bed. "M'lady," he whispered toward the bed.

On silent feet, Kandra crept forward with the urn in hand. 'Forgive me Rory,' she pleaded silently as she raised the urn and brought it down on his head. Biting her lip, she looked down at his body lying upon the floor. Kneeling, she checked to make sure he was still breathing. "You will live Rory, but you shall hate me later for the knot upon your head." She whispered to him.

Taking his sword from its sheath, she left her room, locking the door behind her, and making her way to Jonas's chamber. Slipping through the door quietly, she made her way to his bed. Kneeling by it, she shook him gently. "Jonas, you must awaken."

"Kandra?" He blinked in the darkness then narrowed his eyes, trying to see her better. "What are you doing here?"

"I have come to get us out of here." Kandra pulled back his covers. "We need to get you up. Can you walk?"

"A little, though I am not yet very steady on my feet." He sat up with her help. Through duel effort, they managed to dress him and get him to his feet.

"I know this will be painful, but we must hurry before our escape is detected." Kandra shouldered as much of his weight as she could take.

As silently as possible, they made their way through the castle and out into the dark night. Racing from shadow to shadow, Kandra with Jonas in tow, made her way toward the building holding her other men.

Stumbling, both she and Jonas fell. "Just leave me behind." He gasped, clutching his injured middle, as he lay sprawled in the dirt.

"No," Kandra gained her feet. "I would rather give up my soul than leave you behind." She pulled him to his feet. "We can do this. I know we can."

From high upon the wall Lachlan looked out over his land, sighing. The sight of the village and rolling hills, in dark or light, had once brought him contentment, but no longer. A golden, haired hoyden had brought him unrest with her fiery eyes and lithe body.

Pacing upon the wall, he thought over his problem regarding his captive. He was having a hell of a time keeping his hands to himself where she was concerned. She was disrupting his entire life. He hadn't slept a decent night through since she'd arrived.

His every thought seemed to be wrapped around her. How many days in the last week had he been caught in a lurid fantasy about her, when someone had nudged him out of it? Too many by far, Lachlan shook his head frowning. He wanted her and she wasn't as averse to his touch as she claimed. Besides, the Englishman obviously wasn't treating her as she deserved. So why shouldn't he press her?

Because she wasn't his to have, and he was afraid that once he had a mere taste of her, it wouldn't be enough to satisfy him. He wanted this woman, but he needed the gold she would bring his people more.

A movement from the courtyard caught his attention. Turning his gaze upon the darkened area, he watched as two figures hurried from shadow to shadow. When the pair fell together and struggled to get up, Lachlan cursed under his breath.

'*The woman was insane*!' He thought as he marched off the wall to find Rogan and recapture his guests.

Desperate to keep Jonas moving, Kandra carried most of his weight. Praying they had not been discovered yet. She stopped them at the end of the storehouse in which her men were being held.

Panting, she whispered to Jonas. "Stay here, I will get Raff and the others out then I shall come back for you."

Jonas caught her hand in his as she started away, "Be careful."

"As always," she flashed him a cocky smile. Pulling her hand from his, she turned the corner of the storehouse, hugging the shadows as she made her way the length of the building.

The sentry was leaning back against the wall next to the door. Kandra looked around and found a small log, about the size of her lower arm. She could use it as a weapon and she picked up a fairly good size rock for a distraction. Standing, she hugged the side of the building once more.

Inching closer on silent feet, she could see the sentry dozing where he stood. She threw the rock past him on the other side of the door. The clatter had his head snapping up and him turning.

On a silent apology, Kandra moved in, striking him over the head. She watched him crumple. Leaning down, she made sure he was no more than unconscious then took his sword.

Swiftly, she unbarred the door. Slipping into the storeroom, she smiled when her men came to their feet.

"Girl, what are you doing here?" Raff rushed to her, followed closely by the others.

"Rescuing you, but we must hurry. We have not much time." She hugged Raff tightly. "We have to get Jonas, I left him..."

"I am here." Jonas spoke from the door where he leaned, holding his stomach.

"Bloody hell, Jonas, why did you not stay where I left you?" She frowned at him. "You never listen."

Raff intervened before they could start bickering. "Enough the both of you," Raff glared at them. "How do we get out of here, girl?"

"I have found a garden gate, but getting there will be tricky." Kandra frowned, "We will have to move quickly and silently. If we can make it out of the castle walls they will have a devil of a time finding us in the forest beyond." She looked from man to man. "The only weapons we have are this sword and the one I took from the sentry outside."

"Then I suggest we move out." Raff motioned to the door.

Kandra walked through the door only to draw up short and gasp. The laird stood in front of her with his claymore in hand. His pitch colored hair blew loose in the night breeze. His eyes held a murderous glint as he stared her down.

Raising her sword, Kandra meet his gaze evenly. She tightened her grip upon her weapon and prepared her body to fight.

"Dinna be a fool, lass." Lachlan rasped as she took a fighting stance. Rage pulsed through him.

"Put it down, girl." Raff growled, stepping in front of her. "You will not fight him this night."

Kandra raised her chin indignantly, "I can take him. He is just one man."

"No, he is not a foolish man, Kandra." Raff thrust his chin toward the shadows. Twenty Scots came out to surround them, each was armed and Kandra knew it was hopeless.

"Drop the sword, *Sasunnach*." Lachlan growled menacingly as he tightened his grip on his own sword. Anger surged through him. The woman had used his kindness and betrayed him.

Reluctantly, she threw the sword at his feet then spit on it. "Take it, but know that I will never give up."

Lachlan narrowed his eyes dangerously at her, as his temper flared at her words, "Choose a man to pay for yer stupidity, lass."

Kandra pushed her way past Raff as Jonas came up beside her. She met Lachlan's gaze evenly. "Me."

"Nay," Lachlan bit out. Though he was angry, he would not harm a woman in any way. It was beyond him to do so. "Pick a man, lass."

"You will take me if you are in need of punishing someone." Kandra lifted her chin stubbornly. "I will not allow one of my men to pay for my doings."

Anger billowed through him. This woman was trying him to the end of his patience. "Then I will pick one."

When his eyes darted to Jonas beside her, she stepped in front of her brother. "It is me or no one," she spat at Lachlan.

He took a menacing step toward her, "Fine, if ye wish to take the place of a man, then ye'll suffer a man's punishment!"

"No!" Jonas and Raff spoke at the same time, stepping in front of her to shield her.

"Show her mercy, my lord." Jonas spoke to Lachlan, furrowing his brow as he stood in front of her.

Lachlan felt his anger surge at this boy, jealousy had him wanting to run this boy through and take the woman behind him.

"Will ye take yer woman's place?" Lachlan sneered at the young English knight.

"I will..."

"He won't!" Kandra pushed between the two men. "Take me or take no one, MacKinnon."

As Jonas and Raff began to protest once more, Kandra silenced them with a steely look. "None of you will dictate this. I led each of you in this." She turned back to the laird, looking down her nose at him. "And it is I, who will take whatever punishment this heathen shall inflict upon me."

Lachlan had heard enough. "Take her," he growled to his men. "If the lass, wishes to learn what it is to be a man, then I shall teach her." He knew his anger was getting the best of him, but she infuriated him.

Kandra didn't so much as flinch as the Scotsmen seized hold of her. Turning cold eyes upon the laird, her voice held ice in it. "I have no fear of you, MacKinnon."

"Then yer a fool, lass," Lachlan growled as he stepped up to her. "When I'm done with ye. Ye'll ken yer place as a woman."

"I will never surrender to you." She snarled, glaring into his hard, green eyes. Her bravado was running high.

Lachlan conveyed orders in Gaelic to his men, never taking his eyes from hers. This woman held far too much pride for her own good, and he would remove some of it for her.

His men jerked her away from where she stood. She didn't struggle, but only raised her chin regally and walked with pride. She would not let them see her falter.

"If you hurt her, I swear I will kill you." Jonas glared at the MacKinnon laird as he watched them take his sister away. Letting loose of his aching stomach, he stood to his full height.

"Dinna threaten me, lad." Lachlan growled, turning on him. He hated this boy, he wanted what this boy had, and perhaps if he killed the

English dog here and now, he could take what he wanted.

"It is not a threat. It is a promise. I assure you, MacKinnon." Jonas narrowed his eyes. He didn't flinch when Lachlan stepped forward pressing the tip of his sword to Jonas's throat.

"Dinna make promises ye can nay keep, English." Lachlan removed his sword, turning away. He threw a command over his shoulder in Gaelic that had his men jumping into action.

Kandra kept her head high as the Scots led her through the castle to the damp, dirty, dungeon. The smell of mold, mildew and stagnation assailed her nose. She wanted to gag at the stench, but fought it.

Setting out at a jog, Lachlan caught up with his men and Kandra as they entered the dungeon. Speaking in Gaelic to his men, he led them past the cells where her men had been kept when they had arrived. She couldn't help but to notice Lachlan's men's weary looks as he spoke. The shocked expression upon Durrell's face made her feel the first tickles of fright.

Fear churned in her stomach, but she kept her chin up and her expression indifferent. She refused to let this heathen laird see her fears.

With his temper hot, Lachlan led the group into the bowels of the dungeon. The stench became thick in the air, the floors became damp and slippery. A fine coat of slime shined in the torchlight one of the men carried.

He hated the idea of placing a woman in this hellhole, even a stubborn woman such as this, but his temper wouldn't allow him to back down from the path she had chosen. Though he had to give the woman credit where credit was due, she was keeping a brave face. He sincerely hoped the sight of what lay before her would have her begging mercy. Then he would perhaps show some lenience.

Her stomach heaved at the stench that filled the air, but she swallowed her sickness down. Her feet slipped on the slime covered floor. She couldn't help but to wonder what type of hell was awaiting her. Whatever it was she would face it bravely, she promised herself.

Stopping before a large, solid wooden door with a heavy iron bar, Lachlan lifted the bar, swinging the door open on creaking hinges. Walking into the room, he took the torch from his man, placing it into a holder on the wall. Turning, he faced her with a grim look.

Kandra walked into the cell and wanted to shudder as she surveyed the room around her. The floor and walls where coated with a film of slime. She wanted to cringe as a large rat scurried across the far side of the room. Her gaze finally came to rest upon the manacles hanging in the middle of the room from a rusty chain.

Turning to face her, Lachlan raised a brow, "Have ye come to yer senses yet, lass?"

When she met his gaze unwaveringly and remained mute, but lifted her chin defiantly, he growled as his anger exploded. "Yer a bloody fool, *Sasunnach*, if ye think ye can take this."

The same remote haughty expression stayed on her face as she kept her cold hard gaze fixed upon him. She knew that if she spoke, she wouldn't be able to keep her voice steady and it would belie her bravado, and the laird would see her fear.

Kandra squelched the shudders that wanted to claim her. She fought to keep her breathing steady and even. She held herself stiffly so as not to give these Scots the pleasure of seeing her fears.

Lachlan frowned at her, "Yer a stubborn wench." He inclined his head to one of his men as he issued commands in Gaelic. Walking over, he grasped the chain and manacles in his hand.

One of his men prodded her toward the laird. Her feet didn't want to move, but she forced them. Fear crawled through her. Walking to him, she didn't let her blue gaze slip from his green one.

"Hold out yer wrists, *Sasunnach*." For a moment, Lachlan was sure he saw true fear in her eyes, but just as quickly it was gone.

Holding out her hands, Kandra wanted to cringe as the cold heavy metal was clamped tightly around her wrists. She could not stop the shiver that escaped. Closing her eyes for a moment, she remained silent until she found her calm. Opening her eyes, she refocused upon the laird.

Lachlan spoke over his shoulder, stepping back, as he watched her hands stretched above her head until she was standing with the toes of her boots barely touching the ground. Her hair lay loose, hanging down her back like a golden cloak. He watched her muscles strain and bunch at the weight of her body against her arms. Furrowing his brows, he turned, leaving the room.

When the torch was taken from its holder and the door was slammed shut, Kandra nearly cried out. The room was plunged into absolute darkness. Panic gripped her as she was left hanging there in the dark alone. Fear made the breath back up in her lungs and she could not breathe.

Lachlan paused outside the door for a full minute. He fully expected her to cry out, but when only silence met him, he shook his head. Prideful English woman, she would be much more, tame when she came out of there.

Kandra's shoulders and arms were on fire, the dampness was beginning to soak into her clothing. She wanted to scream every time something scurried by her feet. No matter how she tried, she couldn't seem to remove her mind from where she was. She didn't know how long she had been hanging there. It could be minutes, hours, or days, for all she knew.

She would kill him, or at least she would die trying. She thought grimly, as she let her head rest upon her aching arms. Her thoughts turned to her brother then to her father. At last, she drifted off for a few minutes as exhaustion claimed her.

Chapter
Thirteen

L achlan growled and snarled at everyone he encountered. When morning came after a sleepless night, he headed for the practice field to get some exercise. One by one, he took out his aggressions upon his men. When Rogan faced him, he was sweat soaked and shirtless.

"Yer in a fine mood," Rogan pared with him.

When Lachlan merely growled, Rogan laughed and shook his head. "If yer so bothered over the lass hangin' in the dungeon, why do ye nay let her down?"

"I'm nay out here to have speech with ye, Rogan." Lachlan growled as he took aggressive action with his sword. The two pared and thrusted, evaded as they circled.

"Then what are ye here for?" Rogan avoided him easily and nearly knocked Lachlan's sword from his hand. Lachlan's anger was making him careless. His mind was clouded with thoughts of his *Sasunnach* woman, and Rogan knew it.

"To practice with my sword." Lachlan snapped

"To assuage yer guilt," Rogan laughed. "Ye never were one to mistreat a woman."

"She asked for this. Ye were there." Lachlan frowned at his friend as he clashed swords once more with Rogan.

"Aye, I 'twas there." Rogan nodded. "But ye ken, nay matter what she claims to be, she is still verra, verra much a lass."

Lachlan lowered his sword, "Are ye sayin' I was wrong?"

"I'm sayin' perhaps ye should ease yer own conscious by checkin' on her." Rogan lowered his own sword. "If she has begged for mercy, then grant it."

"I'd be weak if I did." Lachlan frowned.

"Ye'd be a fool if ye didn't." Rogan shook his head.

Kandra's arms and hands were numb, but the pain in her legs and back made tears course silently down her cheeks. As another rat scurried across her feet, she bit her lip to keep from crying out. The sound of water dripping endlessly from some unforeseen place in the cell made her want to scream.

Dampness pervaded her clothing, her skin, and into her bones. She couldn't help but to shiver as the cold sank into the morrow of her being. Surely, she would die in this dark hell.

She wanted to cry out to anyone who might be on the other side of the door, but her pride kept her from doing so. She wouldn't give Lachlan MacKinnon the pleasure of knowing she was suffering. She would be damned if she would give him that satisfaction.

Lachlan sat at his desk, trying to focus upon the sheaves of parchment in front of him, but his mind kept wondering down to the dank, dark cell where Kandra was hanging. Was she ready to concede to him? Would she beg his mercy? After two days, most men were calling out to be released, begging in fact, but the guards had reported no sounds coming from within.

Had something happened to her in there? Fear at the thought clutched in his stomach. Lachlan sat up in his chair ready to bolt from the room. Then his pride kicked in, he would look weak if he ran down there releasing her. No, he couldn't show weakness in this.

Lachlan had no sooner turned back to his sheaves of papers, when his door burst open. Ferran MacKinnon bore down on him with fire in her eyes.

"Ye!" she pointed her finger accusingly. "Ye will get yer stubborn *arse* down to that dungeon and release that pur girl, or so help me I'll march down there myself."

"I will nay release her yet." Lachlan narrowed his eyes at his mother.

"Ye will release her now, or so help me, I will turn every MacKinnon woman against ye and every one of yer kinsmen to boot." Ferran threatened. "There will be nay food, nay nothin'"

"Ye can nay threaten, yer laird!" Lachlan bristled. "I'm nay threatenin' my laird. I'm promisin' my son he will pay for this injustice." Ferran glared at her oldest son. "I dinna raise my sons to abuse women."

Lachlan blanched at the statement. "She asked for it, Mam," Lachlan looked away from his mother, feeling like a guilty five-year-old.

"'Tis nay an excuse, Lachlan," Ferran frowned at him. "Release her, now." She spoke sternly.

"Aye Mam," Lachlan rose from his chair on a sigh. As he walked by Ferran she thumped him on the back with a solid whack. "Och."

"Dinna every let yer stubbornness let ye do something so foolish again. If yer Da was still alive, he would have yer hide." Ferran scolded as she marched behind Lachlan to the door. She shook her head as she sighed, "Leavin' that pur lass hangin' there for two days, let alone puttin' her in the dungeon. Shame on ye, Lachlan MacKinnon!"

Lachlan muttered under his breath, but felt relief that his mother had intervened. Marching to the dungeon, Lachlan ordered the door to Kandra's cell opened.

Kandra squinted at the light coming through the door, as a torch was brought in and settled into the wall scone. She glared at Lachlan as he entered the cell. If she had the strength she would kick at him, but her arms were numb and her legs were on fire.

Lachlan nearly gasped when he walked into the room and saw her damp clothing sticking to her. Her skin was pale, and she was shivering from the cold dampness of the room. Her blonde hair was wet from the moisture and hung heavily down her back. He could see the trails down her cheeks from her tears and his heart twisted. What had he done to her?

Lachlan spoke in Gaelic as he walked over to the wheel holding the chain. Two of his men held her as he lowered her. Walking over he took the manacles off her wrist and winced at the red welts and cuts the metal had left.

"Let go of me!" She rasped, in a dry voice from lack of water. "Let go of me!" Kandra pulled from their hold, falling to the floor. Pain flooded her entire body.

The two men reached down for her, to help her back to her feet.

"Do not touch me!" She gave a snarled croak as she tried to ignore the pain. With enormous effort, she pushed to her feet. Though she was not steady, she looked Lachlan in his eyes. "You will never break me." She vowed before darkness claimed her as she spiraled forward into Lachlan's arms.

Lachlan caught her as she passed out. Scooping her into his arms, he held her close. What had he done to her? He hadn't meant to truly harm the lass. He prayed she would be all right.

Marching to her chambers, Lachlan laid her upon her bed. Ferran came bustling in with salves and linens. Closing the door behind her, she frowned down at Kandra.

Lachlan backed away to let his mother work, but Ferran motioned him forward.

"Ye'll have to help me undress her. She is far too large for me to manage on my own." Ferran touched her icy skin. "She's freezin', Lachlan. We have to warm her, and quickly."

"I can nay undress her, Mam," Lachlan shook his head.

"Ye have seen plenty of women's bodies, Lachlan. She is nay different," Ferran frowned as she soaked a rag in warm water. "Remove her clothin' so that I may cleanse her."

Reluctantly, Lachlan began removing Kandra's shirt and breeches. He tried to keep from noticing her slender, well-honed form and her generous breasts, but it was impossible. Her skin, though cold from the dungeon, was pale and silky smooth where the clothing covered her.

Ferran washed Kandra and wrapped the cuts on her wrists from the manacles. Looking at Kandra, she clucked her tongue, "The lass, is far too cold. If we dinna get her warm soon she will likely take sick."

Lachlan lifted Kandra's hand and began rubbing it vigorously between his own. He hadn't realized she would get so very cold being locked down there.

"That will nay work," Ferran shook her head, "We must get her under the covers and ye'll have to lay with her, to warm her."

Lachlan nearly groaned at the thought. "I can nay do that!"

"Then I shall have one of yer kinsmen do it instead." Ferran threatened. She knew her son would never stand for that.

He gave a resounding sigh, "All right, but ken I dinna like the idea." Lachlan lifted Kandra while Ferran pulled the covers of the bed back. He placed her on the bed and brought the blankets to her chin. With a sigh, he removed his boots, but left his kilt and shirt on.

As he began to climb in the bed, Ferran shook her head, "Remove yer shirt, 'twill help warm her faster."

"Ye push me, Mam." Lachlan growled at his mother.

"'Tis yer own fault, Lachlan," Ferran placed her hands upon her hips, glaring at him. "Yer the one who did this to her."

Lachlan felt the barb of guilt she threw at him, "Aye, and this is my penance for it."

Ferran shook her head, "Yer penance has barely begun. Yer gonna take care of the lass, until she's over this ordeal."

With a long, suffering sigh, Lachlan stripped his shirt off. Wincing, he crawled under the covers and pulled Kandra to him. Her body was icy cold. Lachlan cradled her to him as he ran his hands up and down her back.

"When she awakens, send Rory after me. She'll be needin' somethin' for the pain and a hot bath." Ferran turned to leave the room. Smiling, Ferran left her son to his punishment. She knew he wanted this girl, but was reluctant about taking her. Lachlan needed the lass if he were to live again. She also knew that the lass needed her Lachlan just as much. Perhaps this would help to push them together.

Kandra felt the warmth surrounding her and wanted to snuggle deeper into it, but the pain that began wracking her body pulled her from the glorious nothingness of sleep. A cry torn from her lips as the pain surged through her. She was sure death would soon follow this agony.

"Hush lass, 'twill be all right." Lachlan cradled her closer as he stroked her back. "I've already summoned my Mam, she'll give ye somethin' for the pain."

Kandra came fully awake to find herself wrapped in Lachlan Mackinnon's arms. Feebly she struggled against his hold. "Let go of me, do not touch me."

Lachlan reached up stroking her hair. "I'm sorry lass, but I have to keep ye warm."

For the first time, Kandra realized that Lachlan's chest was bare and she was not wearing any clothing. "Get away from me." She attempted to turn away from him and pain ripped through her. Every muscle in her body was on fire, causing her to cry out. Tears sprang to her eyes.

Lachlan's gut twisted at the sound of her quiet sobbing. '*Such a strong woman should nay be brought to tears,*' his conscience screamed at him. Her head was cradled against his chest and her wet hot tears fell upon him, branding him. Carefully, Lachlan laid her back upon the pillows. He rose above her looking down into her golden face.

Kandra couldn't stop her tears from falling as pain racked her body. When the laird looked down at her, she tried to look away. She hated this weakness and hated him seeing it.

Lachlan caught her chin forcing her to look at him. Gently, he reached up, he caught a single tear. Rubbing it between his thumb and forefinger, he studied it for a long moment.

Looking into her tear filled blue eyes, he frowned. Seeing her in pain brought a tight feeling in his chest. Knowing that he was the cause of her pain made him ache. He wanted to take away her agony. Bending down, he let his lips brush hers softly.

He pulled back, looking down at her once more. "I am sorry, lass, for yer pain." Lachlan looked as if he wanted to say more, but the chamber door burst open, admitting Ferran.

Lachlan surged from the bed, donning his shirt once more. His brows furrowed as he turned to his mother. "She is in terrible pain, can ye help her?"

"Aye, ye must have her drink this, while I get somethin' soothin' for her bath water." Ferran thrust a tiny bottle in his large hands then turned and strode from the room.

Kandra didn't listen to a word spoken between them. When Lachlan surged from the bed, she rolled onto her side as pain ripped through her. Clenching her teeth, she curled herself into a ball. Her breath hitched as she waited for the pain to abate or for death to claim her.

Lachlan walked back to the bed, looking down at her curled into herself protectively. Setting on the edge of the bed, he leaned over her. "Drink this lass, 'twill help with the pain."

Kandra shook her head as she spoke through gritted teeth, "Leave me alone. Go away!"

Lachlan reached out, stroking her golden locks soothingly. "Trust me, lass, 'twill take the pain away."

When she remained stubbornly silent, he shook his head, frowning, "Dinna make me force it down ye, Kandra."

Reaching out, he rolled her over onto her back. She hadn't the strength to fight him as the pain slashed through her, making her cry out once more. Lachlan held her, cradling her to him. Her body shook as she sobbed. Her hot tears bathed his chest. Brushing her hair back from her face, he pressed light kisses to her temple as he spoke soft Gaelic words to her. Taking the stopper from the bottle, he held it to her lips.

"Let me ease yer pain, lass." He whispered softly.

Kandra drank the foul, tasting potion, praying for a miracle to take away the agony she was in.

As Ferran bustled back into the room, servants carrying buckets filled with hot and cool water for the bath followed her. A large tub was set in the middle of the room and was filled quickly. When the tub was to Ferran's satisfaction, she shooed the servants away. She turned to Lachlan, setting upon the bed holding Kandra to him. A smile brushed her lips. Whether her son wanted to believe it or nay, he had a soft spot for this bonnie lass.

"Ye must put her into the tub to help ease her sufferin'." Ferran waved toward the tub. She walked over, sprinkling herbs into the hot water. "It will help to ease the pain in her muscles."

Lachlan's eyes snapped to his mothers. "Ye can nay be serious."

"I am." Ferran narrowed her eyes at him. "Ye will heed me on this, boy, or so help me..." She left that statement hanging, letting him make what he wanted of it. With that, she turned on her heel, marching to the door. "I'll check on her later. If ye need somethin' 'afore then send Rory to me."

Lachlan watched her walk out of the room, closing the door resoundingly behind her. With a sigh, he looked down at the woman in his arms. "I have to get ye into that tub, *Sasunnach*."

He started to lift her, but she pushed him away weakly. "No, you cannot do this."

With a sigh, Lachlan pulled back the covers and ignored her feeble protests as he picked her up in his arms. He tried to ignore her woman's body in his arms as he cradled her to him. Carrying her to the tub, he gently set her into the bath, gritting his teeth as she cried out in anguish. "Relax lass, this will help ye."

Even through the haze of pain, Kandra felt modest. With the last of her strength, she raised her knees, wrapping her arms around them. As misery washed over her, she laid her head upon her knees, letting her tears have free rein. The laird couldn't see her face and it helped hide her shame.

Kneeling by the tub, Lachlan picked up a cloth. Dipping it into the warm water, he soaked it then brought it over her bare back and arms, letting the water wash over her. Kandra stiffened at his touch. "Have ease, lass, I'll nay hurt ye."

Kandra had no choice, but to let him continue. She was too exhausted and weak to fight him. She couldn't even stand if she tried, let alone wash herself. As the soothing water and the potion Lachlan had given her began to work their magic, Kandra felt her pain easing and herself relaxing.

Her mind drifted and grew light. As the pain was numbed, she sighed when Lachlan ran the cloth over her arms. Slowly, she turned her head to look at him. He was a powerful man, yet gentle, she thought with a frown. He was defiantly the most beautiful man she had ever seen.

Lachlan looked into her frowning face. Gently, he reached his fingers out, brushing a strand of golden hair from her cheek. "Dinna frown, lass."

"You are so very beautiful. Do you know thus?" She looked into his green eyes and sighed, "Beautiful is not right, for a man..."

Lachlan laughed, placing a finger over her lips. "I'll take beautiful and thank ye, lass, for the compliment."

Her eyes were still sunken and shadowed. Gently, he rubbed a thumb over her cheek. "I need to wash yer hair. Will ye let me?"

"Yes," Kandra sighed again as he wiped the cloth over her shoulder.

Lachlan grabbed a bucket of tempered water and gently poured it over her hair, wetting it. Diligently he rubbed heather scented soap into it, removing the smell of the dungeon from her tresses. He rinsed her hair then sighed. "I have to wash the rest of ye."

She shook her head, "That would not be right."

"I need to get the smell of the dungeon off ye." Lachlan gently pushed her back. At the sight of her lithe body he nearly groaned. Instantly, he was hard under his kilt. Gritting his teeth, he soaped the cloth and began rubbing it over her in soft, gentle strokes.

"This is not right," she repeated softly, sighing as his hand slid over her breast.

"Right or nay, it must be done." He spoke in a husky voice as he fought his desire. He forced himself to quickly finish the task. "Can ye stand, lass?"

The potion he'd given her for the pain made her light headed. Closing her eyes, she tried to make it stop. "I do not know, but I can try." As she began to struggle to her feet, she gasped as Lachlan grasped her under the arms raising her to her feet. The room spun and tilted around her.

Keeping one hand on her, Lachlan grabbed the bath sheet left for drying her. Quickly, he wrapped it around her. Knowing she wouldn't be able to walk to the bed, he scooped her up in his arms. Gently, he laid her upon the bed, leaning over her.

Her heavy lidded blue eyes searched his green gaze. Reaching up, she placed a hand upon his cheek. "Are you going to kiss me?"

Lachlan searched her gaze and knew the potion was affecting her, but shrugged it away. "Do ye want me to kiss ye, *Sasunnach*?"

"Yes, I like your kisses very much." Kandra spoke honestly in her drugged state of mind.

Slowly, he leaned down, brushing soft kisses over her lips. Lowering himself to the bed he took her into his arms, brushing butterfly kisses over her delicate mouth.

Pulling back, Kandra sighed as sleepiness plagued her. She laid her head upon his shoulder, reveling in his warmth. Drug induced sleep washed over her. Sighing, she slipped into contented slumber.

Chapter
Fourteen

L achlan stayed with her the night through. From time to time, he gave Kandra medicine to take away her pain. He held her and stroked her body to soothe the aching muscles until she was fast asleep once more. For hours, he lay next to her, watching her sleep as moonlight washed over her golden features.

By the time morning's first light began to creep through the windows, Lachlan knew he'd give anything to have this woman. Her beautiful features were etched in his memory for eternity. Her soft feminine scent was wrapped around him, imprinted upon his mind. Never again would he be able to look upon the heather filled hills of his home, without seeing Kandra's sweet beautiful face.

Easing himself from the bed, careful not to wake her, he walked to the window looking at the land beyond it. What would it cost him to have her, even for a little while? Never had he wanted a woman as much as he wanted this troublesome *Sasunnach*.

Slowly, he turned back to the woman sleeping upon the bed. She lay on her side with her hands tucked under her cheek. Her long blonde lashes made soft half-moons upon her cheeks, while her lower lip stuck out in a tiny pout. She was no longer the warrior she tried to prove herself to be. At this moment, she was a soft beautiful woman, whom Lachlan found desirable. A shudder slid through him. This woman had the power to bring him to his knees, and she must never learn that she held such powers, least she wield them against him.

He watched as her lashes fluttered and she sighed. Slowly, Kandra stirred to wakefulness. Her vibrant blue eyes met his green gaze. She looked soft and warm, and absolutely gorgeous in her sleepy state. He felt his loins stirring.

Kandra felt his warm gaze upon her as she lay sleeping. Her dreams through the night had been wrapped around this man and his gentleness. Now that she saw him standing here in her room, washed in the early morning light, she wasn't so sure all of it had been just dreams. Had he bathed her? Had he kissed her? Had he stroked his hands over her body? Had he slept with her?

He watched her brows furrow in thought, "Why do ye frown, *Sasunnach*?"

"How long have you been in my room?" Her throat hurt slightly as she spoke, making her voice sound slightly rusty.

He walked over, pouring a drink of watered wine into a mug. Taking it to her, he settled on the side of the bed. He looked her in the eyes and smiled, "All night lass, do ye remember, aught?"

Kandra started to sit up only to realize she was naked under the blanket covering her. Her face paled, her voice shook as she spoke, "Where are my clothes?"

"Being laundered, but I've somethin' for ye to dress in until they're returned." Lachlan reached out, helping her sit up. She cringed away from him. "What's wrong, lass?"

"You have been here all night, and I have been unclothed this whole time?" She frowned up at him as images whirled through her mind. Had she dreamt he bathed her, his kissing her, and touching her?

"Nay lass, ye've the wrong of it, we stripped ye out of those damp clothes too warm ye," he smiled at her. He could read her unease, but wasn't about to set her mind to rest.

Kandra tried to sit up on the bed and groaned at the aches throughout her body. She started to protest and Lachlan set the mug upon the floor, and reached out helping her. She scrambled for the blanket to cover herself from his sharp gaze.

"I did not need your help." She glared at him. "I can take care of myself."

He handed her the mug of watered wine, grinning. "I see ye have nay lost yer fire, *Sasunnach*."

"I told you, you could not break me." She took the wine, drinking greedily.

"Easy lass," Lachlan pulled the cup away from her lips. "If ye dinna slow down, ye'll make yerself sick."

"I do not need you to take care of me." Kandra raised her chin defiantly. "Go away, you have done enough to me."

He was quiet for a long moment as he considered her, "Yer right, I should nay have put you in that place. I should have picked one of yer men to stand in yer stead." He gave her a sincere look, "For that I am truly sorry, lass."

Before their conversation could go any further, Ferran bustled into the room. "Good morrow! How are ye feelin' this morn?"

Kandra merely looked at her for a long moment. Then looked away as a blush crept into her cheeks at the thought of being caught sitting there all but naked with Ferran's son. "I am well enough."

"Yer lookin' a might peaked." Ferran shook her head. "Lachlan, would ye go fetch her food to break her fast?"

"Aye Mam," he looked back at Kandra, "I'll return shortly."

"Please do not hurry on my account." Kandra glared at him as sarcasm dripped from her voice.

Lachlan shook his head, smiling as he left. Her little stay in the dungeon had done nothing to tame her fierce spirit. Of that, he had to admit he was glad.

Ferran watched him leave then began bustling around the room. "How's yer aches and pains this morn'?"

Kandra looked at the older woman and sighed. "I am sore, but nothing a little moving around will not fix."

"Good," Ferran placed her hands upon her hips, smiling, "Then we'll get ye up and dressed, for a little lass has missed ye sorely."

Kandra paled at the thought of Bryanna, "Does she know where I was?"

Ferran raised a brow. "Would it matter if she did?"

"Yes, she has no idea I am her father's prisoner." Kandra frowned. "She thinks so highly of him. It would hurt her to know otherwise."

Smiling, Ferran walked over to the bed, settling upon the edge. She took Kandra's hands in her own, "Ye care about my granddaughter a great deal, aye?"

"Yes," Kandra smiled softly, "We have become fast friends. She reminds me of when I was young. I lost my mother when I was born, but I never really noticed. I had the love of my father."

"Bry certainly loves her father," Ferran shook her head. "And my son loves his daughter greatly. To him the sun rises and sets upon her head."

Kandra couldn't curb her curiosity, "Why has he never remarried?"

"Ye'll have to ask him that question." Ferran frowned, shaking her head. She patted Kandra's hand, "For now let's get ye up and dressed, before Bry finds out ye can have visitors."

Once admitted into Kandra's room, Bryanna rambled on and on for nearly an hour.

"And Robby apologized to me." Bry clapped her hands as she bounced upon Kandra's bed. "He even climbed a tree to get my kitten down when she got stuck up there."

Kandra nodded and smiled. "I think perhaps Robby and his father learned a lesson after all."

Bry flopped on her belly, plucking at the string hanging from the blanket. "Are ye goin' to leave us?"

Kandra was caught off guard by her question. Furrowing her brow, she considered how to answer. "Why do you ask?"

"'Cause Robby says yer gonna leave as soon as yer Da pays money to my Da." Bry frowned up at her then looked down at the blanket once more. "But I was thinkin' that ye could tell yer Da ye wanna stay with us and ye could marry my Da."

Kandra could only stare at the child open mouthed. Oh, good lord, she thought silently. How was she to answer this? Carefully she cleared her throat, "Bry, I... I..."

Thankfully she was saved from answering as Lachlan himself came into the room. Standing over the bed, hands on his hips, he was an impressive site to see. "What are ye doin' in here, now?"

Bry gave him an angelic look, "Nothin' Da, we were just havin' us some woman talk 'tis all."

Lachlan cracked a smile then threw his head back in a roaring laugh, "Yer but a mite of a thin' dumplin'. Ye hardly count as a woman."

"I am so a woman, 'tis that nay so, Kandra?" Bry sat up on the bed defensively and looked to Kandra for backing.

Kandra reached over, pulling Bry to her in a hug, "Aye, a beautiful young woman, but I am afraid your father will see you as a little girl the whole of your life."

"Well," Lachlan bent, scooping Bry into his arms, "'Tis time for this young woman to go help her Gram." He held her up over his head then brought her back down to him, nuzzling her cheek with his whiskered face.

The sound of little girl laughter filled the room. Lachlan set her on her feet. He patted her rear as he shooed her toward the door, "Off with ye now."

"I'll see ye again verra soon." Bry called over her shoulder to Kandra as she left the room, waving cheerfully.

"I cannot wait." Kandra smiled at her.

The silence in the room after Bryanna's departure was heavy. Kandra looked down at the blanket spread across her lap, plucking nervously at the thread Bry had abandoned. She didn't want to look at this man, she didn't want to be alone with him, but stuck here she was. Bry's words kept playing through her mind in an endless circle.

"How are ye feelin', lass?" Lachlan watched her absently pluck at the little string.

"I am well, but I am tired of being in bed." She threw off the covers. Swinging her long legs over the side of the bed, she began to stand, only to stop when Lachlan grasped her arm. "I do not need your help, MacKinnon."

"Sorry yer highness, but I would nay want ye to fall on yer *arse*." He growled at her. His eyes were locked on her bare legs and body, clad in one of his own shirts.

"I would not be in this state if it were not for you." She shot back with a glare as she rose from the bed.

"I would nay have had to place ye there had ye nay tried to escape." He shot back angrily.

"I would not have tried to escape if you would just be reasonable and release us." She stood toe to toe with him.

"If ye'd been reasonable and ye had nay charged upon me and my men then ye would nay be here." Lachlan grasped her arms, lifting her slightly as he walked her back toward the wall behind her.

"Well... Well..." She stammered as she tried to think of a response.

"Aye, *Sasunnach*?" Lachlan raised a brow as he trapped her between his body and the wall.

She couldn't think with him this close. His hands trapped her where she stood. Her head was tipped up to look him in the eyes and she was lost in his incredible green gaze. Her mind drew a blank as she looked from his eyes to his lips. She knew just how wonderful those lips could taste and feel.

"I... Um..." She trailed off as his head bent forward, catching her lips with his. Heat raced through her, scorching her. Her hands were on his tight, bunched biceps.

Lachlan released his hold on her arms. Sliding his arms around her waist, pulling her into him. His hands ran up and down her back. He wrapped her golden braid around his hand until he reached the base of her neck then cupped her head in his large palm.

Kandra's hands slid up his arms and wide shoulders until they wound around his neck. Her fingers slid into his loose, silky, black hair. Though she knew she should be pushing him away, she couldn't help but to pull him closer. When his tongue swept across the seam of her mouth she opened eagerly to him.

His hand traced her back, down over the globe of her bottom, pulling her into him, pressing her against his erection. The moan that slipped from him was tortured. He wanted to lose himself in her. His fingers slid under the shirt as he cupped her bare bottom in his hand, kneading her silken flesh.

She was drowning in his taste, in his body pressed against hers. His calloused warrior hands heated her bare skin with just a single touch. The earthy smell of him, as well as the scent that was uniquely male, wrapped around her.

His fingers slid across the damp folds of her sex, causing him to pull his mouth from hers as he nipped and kissed her jaw and neck. She shuddered in his arms and her own small moan pushed him on. Parting her silken folds, he found her pearl of desire. Slowly, he stroked it, pushing her desire higher and higher. Her head fell back, giving him free access to her throat and swells of her breasts.

She knew she should push him away, she should fight him, but she wanted him. Wanted him to touch her, stroke her, more than she had ever wanted anything in her life, she wanted to feel what other women felt.

When he touched her intimately, as he was doing now, she felt herself melting in his arms. He was making the need inside her coil tighter and tighter. She couldn't stop the little whimpers that escaped her. Her fingers dug into his shoulders as she tried to urge him to release this tightening inside her.

Lachlan wanted her naked and withering under him. He wanted to watch her come to completion, watch her slip over the edge into ecstasy. Reaching between them, he released the laces on the shirt, allowing him better access to her breasts. Fondling one breast, he pressed his mouth to it, paying homage to the perfection of her breasts.

He held her in his arms as she shattered. The taste of her skin and the scent of her arousal overwhelmed him. Removing his hand from her, he swept her into his arms. Marching to the bed, he laid her upon it then stretched out along side of her.

Kandra felt herself coming back down to earth as Lachlan laid her upon the bed. When he joined her on the mattress, reality came back with a jolt. His artful mouth and skilled hands had already begun assaulting her senses once more.

"No," her voice was husky, as she pushed at him.

"Dinna deny us this," he raised up to look down at her. "'Tis what we both wish for."

"Yes, but we are enemies." She shook her golden head as she tried to pull away from him, but she couldn't break his hold. "I cannot betray my men in this way."

"But ye want this as much as I, admit it, *Sasunnach*." When she remained stubbornly mute, he crushed her mouth under his in a searing kiss. "Tell me ye want me, lass."

"Yes, but what I want, and what I can have are two entirely different things." Kandra strained to resist the temptation he laid in front of her. "You hold my men and I prisoner, and I am not about to give in to what I feel."

Lachlan considered her for a long moment then shook his head. "What will it take for ye to give yerself to me?"

"Free my men." Kandra knew it was irrational to barter herself for the freedom of her men, but it was a small token to pay for their release. "Free them and I'll be yours as long as you want."

"I can nay do it, what yer men and ye will bring to me is worth a great deal." He pushed up from the bed to pace the room. He had to have her, but he couldn't sacrifice his people for his wanting. An idea formed and he smiled wickedly. "Yer man, would ye trade yerself for yer man's return home?"

"Jonas?" She sat up on the bed clutching her shirt together as she stared at him.

He nearly groaned as the shirt slipped off her shoulders, showing her silky skin beneath. "Aye, yer precious Jonas," he sneered. "Would ye trade yerself for his freedom?"

"Yes, him and five of my men," Kandra came off the bed to stand before him.

"Just him."

"Four."

"One and yer man, 'tis my final offer, lass." Lachlan growled at her.

"Three, Raff, Griffin, and Ryan, as well as Jonas," She dropped the sides of the shirt she had been holding closed so that they fluttered open revealing her long, lithe, naked body. She stepped closer as he gave a low throaty growl while his eyes scanned her bare skin. She slid her hands up his chest, wrapping them around his neck pulling him closer.

"The last two and yer Jonas, but nay, more." He growled against her mouth.

"And you cannot have me until they are safe within my father's castle walls." She breathed against his lips.

"Ye drive a hard bargain and dinna play fair, *Sasunnach*." He spoke against her lips, barely tasting her.

"Take it or leave it, MacKinnon." Kandra smiled, because she knew she had won a small battle, but the war was hardly over.

"We've an accord," he growled against her lips then took them in a crushing fury. At any price, he wanted her. Giving up two of her men plus her man was a small price to pay for the feel of her in his arms.

Chapter Fifteen

J onas frowned harshly at her as he stood next to his mount. "What have you promised the bastard, in order to free us?"

"I only convinced him, that you would be able to hasten the funds to secure our freedom." Kandra lied to him, not meeting his eyes. She hated lying to him, but she felt giving herself to the laird was a trifle token to secure the release of her brother. It was not as if she was placing herself in danger. She had nothing she could lose in this bargain.

"You are lying to me," he shook his head as he cupped her cheek. "Why will you not tell me?"

"Because, you would worry," she placed her hand over his. "Please, just go before I give in to the tears I am trying so hard to hold onto. You know how I hate them." She gave him a weak smile.

"I shall hurry home and send back the funds to free you." Jonas promised with a worried frown. He pulled her into his arms, hugging her hard as he brushed a kiss over her golden hair.

"That is why I have to do this." She brushed a soft kiss upon his cheek then released him. "Ride fast. Be safe."

Jonas laid his forehead against hers as he cupped her face in his large hands, "Take care, do nothing foolish. I shall have you home soon."

She smiled softly, "I never do anything foolish."

"That is what worries me." Jonas planted a kiss upon her forehead then released her. Quickly, he mounted his destrier.

As he wheeled his horse away to head for the portcullis, Kandra wiped a stray tear from her cheek. Never had they been separated, but she knew she would survive it, as she counted the days to her freedom.

Lachlan walked up behind her, grasping her shoulder, he turned her. Jealousy raged within him at the affectionate parting between the two. She was his now, the English dog had abandoned her.

"Swear to me, ye'll nay try to escape, until yer release is secured." He growled down at her.

Raising her chin, she met his cold green gaze evenly. "I have no reason to escape now."

"Aye," he spoke roughly as he reached out, pulling her to him as he entwined his fingers into her long golden hair, his mouth crashing over hers.

Kandra struggled against his hold until he pulled back. "You swore not to touch me."

"I swore I would nay take ye, but I said aught about touchin' ye, *Sasunnach*." He brushed his fingers across her cheek, "Yer my leman now, and I will enjoy ye."

Kandra jerked back as if he had struck her. Anger surged through her. "I am no whore." And never would she be one.

"Nay, but ye are my woman now." Lachlan released her, stepping back. "And it pleases me to touch ye."

"You will not touch me unless I give you leave to do so." She scowled at him.

"I'll touch ye and often, until I can have ye, and ye will enjoy it, lass." With that Lachlan walked away, leaving her sputtering at his back.

Four days had passed since Jonas' departure, and Lachlan had kept his word. She was now expected to sit next to him at the high table in the great hall during meals. He touched her, and often. Sometimes it was a quick stolen kiss, others it was his hand, stroking her leg under the table during meals.

Kandra sat in her room, looking out the window at the gloomy gray skies, and frowned. The laird was driving her crazy with his touches. He was entrenched in her dreams at night and plagued her thoughts during the day. At times when she was in his presence, she found herself hoping he would touch her in some small way at least.

This was not how things were meant to work. He was not supposed to touch her before Jonas sent the gold back to free her, with Lachlan's men who had escorted him. Then she would be free and not have to honor their bargain. If the laird kept up the way he was going, long before the funds arrived she would be begging him to break their bargain.

Lachlan was in his study when Rory burst in, beaming, "We've company, laird."

"Aye?" Lachlan glared up at the younger man, irritated at being disturbed.

Lachlan had gotten little to no work done in the last two hours, as his mind was dull from lack of sleep. To surmount his already existing problem, his constant interactions with Kandra were affecting him nearly as badly as they were her. He couldn't keep thoughts of her from creeping into his mind every few moments, causing him to get absolutely nothing accomplished.

"Aye laird. The MacKinnon, as well as Duncan and yer brother Aidan have come to visit." Rory grinned brightly as he imparted his news.

A smile lit Lachlan's face. His cousins and his younger brother would be a welcomed distraction and a joy to see. Lachlan rose from his desk and strode out into the bailey.

Three brawny Scots atop pitch-black, powerful destriers rode forth through the portcullis, reigning in at the stairs to the keep. Dressed in the MacKinnon tartans, the three men swung down from their mounts to approach Lachlan.

"What in the name of all hell are ye three doin' here?" Lachlan embraced his cousin Ian, slapping him on the back.

"We've come to visit and find out if yer truly keeping a *Sasunnach* woman prisoner?" Ian slapped him on the back in return. "'Tis all over *Alba* that ye are."

"Are ye so fool hearty brother, that ye would tempt the English to storm yer doors?" Aidan MacKinnon embraced his brother firmly.

"I dinna wish to discuss this out in the rain," Lachlan embraced Aidan firmly. "What say ye, we have us some fine Scottish whiskey and discuss it by a warm fire?"

"I think ye have the right of it, cousin." Duncan nodded his agreement.

A commotion in the outer bailey caught Kandra's attention. More than thirty men on horseback came through the gate. All of them dressed in tartans that matched Lachlan's. They didn't look to be his men, because the three leading the group sat upon giant destriers as black as night, much like Lachlan's.

She watched Lachlan come from inside the keep greeting the new arrivals. Enthusiastically, he embraced each man in a backslapping hug. Arms slung around each other, the men entered the keep together, leaving Kandra's view. She worried her lower lip as she wondered who these men were. Had these other Scots come to offer money for her?

Pushing back from the window, Kandra began pacing her chambers, wondering about these new visitors. She was worried about what Lachlan had planned for her. She only prayed that Jonas hasten Lachlan's men in returning with the gold to free her.

The four men ducked indoors to find a quiet place by a warm fire to discuss Lachlan's prisoner.

Ferran MacKinnon came bustling from the kitchens, beaming at the four men. She held out her arms to Aidan. "Aidan, my boy, how I've missed ye!"

Aidan took her hands and engulfed her in a fierce hug, twirling her around. "I've missed ye sorely, Mam." He pressed a kiss to the top of her head as he tucked her under his chin in a loving embrace. "Yer just as beautiful as ye were when last I was here." He looked her over.

"Yer a shameless flatterer, Aidan," Ferran swatted at him playfully. "Ye've a bit of yer father in ye, that's for certain."

"Aye, I love beautiful women." Aidan smiled rakishly.

Duncan snorted, "He loves all women, dinna matter their age, or even if they're married."

"Aidan MacKinnon! Ye'd best nay be chasin' after married women." Ferran scolded firmly as she frowned up at him.

"Duncan exaggerates, Mam." Aidan tried too placid her as he sent Duncan a scathing glare.

Ferran gave him a knowing look, "We'll discuss this later, for now I've to go make our guest aware of yer arrival, so she may make herself ready for the evening meal."

"Yer guest? I thought she was a prisoner?" Ian spoke to his aunt then raised a questioning brow at Lachlan.

"All of ye will clean up before yer presented to her ladyship." Ferran gave them each a meaningful look.

"Aye," all three men spoke in unison. It was easier to agree then to face Ferran MacKinnon's wrath.

Ferran turned on her heels, heading for Kandra's room. She had plans brewing now that Aidan, Ian and Duncan had arrived. With a light step and a smile on her face, she went to visit the younger woman.

Kandra sat upon her bed, brooding over the events of the last few weeks. She had made serious mistakes since the day she attacked the MacKinnon War

Chieftain and his men. And, it seemed, her recent decision to exchange her virtue for her brother's freedom had been as foolhardy an endeavor as the attack that had landed her where she was at the moment.

Now MacKinnon assumed he could make her his strumpet. She could only pray that Jonas sent Griffin, Ryan, and the MacKinnon men back with the money to free her and the rest of her men. If they didn't return soon she would be forced to honor the ill thought agreement she and Lachlan MacKinnon had struck.

Lachlan believed she and Jonas were lovers, she cringed at the thought. Would he know she was still a virgin? Should she tell him the truth? She sighed in frustration, perhaps he wouldn't care, or wouldn't notice that her maidenhead was still intact, if he took her.

Kandra looked up as Ferran came bustling into the room, a cloth wrapped bundle in her hands. A smile nearly split the older woman's face.

"Up with ye, lass." Ferran beckoned her from the bed. "We've nay time to waste."

"For what?" Kandra rose from the bed as she was bid.

"To dress for the evening meal, of course." Ferran thrust the wrapped package at her. "I made this for ye and ye'll wear it tonight."

Kandra raised a brow at the smaller woman's commanding tone. Laying the bundle upon the bed, she carefully opened it. She smiled when she saw the soft light blue material. Slowly, she lifted the gown from the bundle. Tears prickled at the backs of her eyes for the thoughtfulness Ferran had shown.

She hugged the dress to her chest as she turned to Ferran, "It is beautiful."

"Well let's try it on ye." Ferran waved impatiently.

Smiling, Kandra laid the dress upon the bed and began removing her knee-high boots and stripping out of her shirt and breeches. She quickly donned the dress, running her hands over the soft blue material to smooth any wrinkles out of it.

Ferran quickly fastened the laces then surveyed her work. With a few quickly made alterations it would be perfect. "Ye look like a Fae princess. Yer a vision and will certainly turn a few heads in the great hall this eve." Ferran hoped she would turn at least four male heads.

"It is beautiful, Ferran!" Kandra hugged the smaller woman. "Thank you."

"Yer more than welcome, lass." Ferran hugged her back then stepped away. "We need to make a few adjustments then 'twill be perfect."

Seated within Lachlan's study, the four MacKinnon men raised tankards of Scottish whiskey in a toast to long lives and good health.

Ian sat back, stretching his long form out in the chair. Crossing his booted ankles, he watched his cousin pour more whiskey for each of them. "So, are ye goin' to tell us about yer *Sasunnach*, or keep us in suspense, cousin?"

Lachlan snorted, "She's nay like any lady ye have ever ken before, I'll guarantee ye, that."

"Is she ugly?" Duncan leaned forward.

"Nay, she's down right bonnie, ye'll see that for yerselves, at the evenin' meal. She sits at the high table with me." Lachlan smiled proudly.

"If she is nay ugly, brother, then what's wrong with her?" Aidan couldn't help but anticipate meeting a beautiful woman. He loved all women, young and old, tall and small, thick and thin.

"She's a wicked wench, stubborn as a mule," Lachlan's smile widened and his eyes gleamed. "And she could damn near best any of us with a sword."

"What?"

"Nay!"

"Impossible!"

All three men sat forward, shaking their heads disbelievingly at Lachlan.

"I swear it to ye, let me tell ye how I came to acquire the bonnie Lady Stafford." Lachlan sat back and began weaving his tale, starting with the lad that so boldly attacked him and his men.

When his story was finished, Ian shook his head, "She sounds fascinatin', I can nay wait to meet her."

"Aye, I would nay mind seein' if she can fight as well as ye claim she can." Duncan grinned broadly.

"I myself, can nay wait to see if she is as lovely as ye claim," Aidan sat back with a wolfish grin.

"Dinna, think ye can have her, little brother, she is my prisoner. Ye will nay touch her." Lachlan growled.

"Ah, I see." Aidan smirked. "I dinna ken the way of it."

Before the two could go at each other's throats, Ian interrupted. "I think we should be gettin' ready for the evenin' meal, 'afore Aunt Ferran comes lookin' for us."

Nods circled the room. The four men went off to ready themselves for the meal.

Kandra was nervous as she entered the great hall. She was late and she was feeling self-conscious for wearing a dress. Long ago she had stopped wearing gowns and dressing up for meals. It had become a nuisance.

Nervously, she clasped and unclasped her hands. Her gaze met Lachlan's as she entered the great hall. She couldn't discern what his gaze meant, but she didn't think it was pleasure at seeing her in a gown. Before she could turn and flee, Ferran was shoving her into the room.

"Go on with ye, lass." Ferran shooed her.

Lachlan watched Kandra enter the room. She was absolutely stunning in the pale blue gown, her hair seemed more golden, and her skin held a sun kissed glow. Even her blue eyes appeared deeper and more enticing.

"Is that yer English, lass?" Ian spoke roughly then cleared his throat. "I want to meet her."

Lachlan shot him a fiery glare then turned to greet Kandra as she walked up to him.

"MacKinnon," she spoke softly, but couldn't stop the tremble in her voice. She bit her lower lip nervously.

"*Sasunnach*," Lachlan reached out, taking her hand in his, he brought it to his mouth and gently brushed his lips across her knuckles as he tugged her closer to him. "Ye look beautiful, lass."

She could feel the blush that crept into her cheeks as she replied, "Thank you, MacKinnon."

"I'd like for ye to greet my kinsmen. My cousin Ian, here, is the MacKinnon, Chieftain of our clan as well as laird of our clan on the Isle of Sky in the highlands." Lachlan presented Kandra to him. "This, cousin, is the Lady Stafford."

"My lady," Ian bowed artfully. "Allow me to say how divine ye look."

"Thank you, my lord," Kandra inclined her head regally. This man was every bit as tall and dominating as Lachlan. Their looks were similar with the same pitch black hair that fell past their shoulders, but where Lachlan's flowed just past his shoulders, Ian's hung down to the middle of his back, but also held braids with tiny gold beads at their ends. Ian also wore the armbands identical to Lachlan's except his were gold and Lachlan's were silver. Their features held their family resemblance, but their eyes were what set them apart. Where Lachlan had mystical green eyes, Ian's were dark, deep, pools of blue. She could read kindness in his eyes and smiled back.

Lachlan drew her to the next man awaiting introductions, "This ox, is Ian's younger brother, Duncan."

"A pleasure, my lord," Kandra inclined her head once more as Lachlan held a firm grip upon her hand. This man was a warrior through and through. She could see his battle edge in his sharp, deep blue gaze. That gaze took in everything at once, not missing a thing, of that she was sure. Though he looked much like his older brother, Duncan was slightly fairer in coloring. Instead of the pitch colored hair, his was a deep, deep mahogany, and hung nearly to the middle of his back. Long braids graced his hair and had small golden beads at the ends of them. He too wore golden Celtic armbands around his powerful biceps. The man was impressive to say the least.

"My lady, yer even more bonnie than we were led to believe," Duncan bowed quickly over her hand. She was nothing like he had imagined, with her long, lithe body and angelic face. She was certainly more beautiful than he had assumed. He could see why Lachlan was enamored with her.

"And this rogue 'tis my younger brother, Aidan." Lachlan didn't let her move over in front of Aidan, instead he slipped a possessive arm around her waist to keep her anchored at his side.

Inclining her head regally, Kandra smiled brightly at Aidan as she extended her hand. "I am pleased to make your acquaintance, my lord. I was unaware the laird had a brother." She was knocked nearly breathless by the sight of Aidan MacKinnon. The man was surely forged in the image of an ancient Celtic God. His shiny, pitch black hair hung down past his waist, silver beads held the ends of braids that were scattered throughout his hair. His face was strong, but absolutely gorgeous, like a dark angel, with silver eyes. His golden body rippled with muscles and like all of the MacKinnon men, he wore armbands with ancient Celtic symbols and words carved in them. The silver bands that matched his brother Lachlan's were wrapped around his powerful biceps.

Aidan stepped forward, taking her hand in his. He could see why his brother was so protective of this fair lady. Though she was well over a head shorter than he, she was taller than any woman he had ever met. Her body was lithe and athletic, perfectly sized with luscious breasts. Her golden hair and sky blue eyes drew a man's attention, as well as the warmth she radiated.

Brushing a lingering kiss over her knuckles, Aidan decided to goad his brother. "'Tis my absolute pleasure to make yer acquaintance, m'lady." He gave her a flirtatious grin. "I hope to get to ken ye better while I am here, lass."

Lachlan gave his brother a narrowed eyed glare. He'd have to keep a closer eye on his brother while Aidan was in residence. He hadn't told them of the arrangement between himself and Kandra. They had no knowledge that she was to become his leman, he wondered briefly if he should tell them.

Lachlan seated her to his left at the head table, with Ian and Duncan next to Kandra. Aidan and Rogan were seated to Lachlan's right as well as his mother. He wanted to keep Aidan as far away from Kandra as he could.

Ian and Duncan dominated Kandra's attention throughout the meal. They talked about battle strategy, weapons and horses. Both men were suitably impressed with her knowledge and couldn't wait to meet her on the practice field.

Kandra had not enjoyed a meal more thoroughly, she thought as she bit into a piece of sweetmeats that was served with their meal. She watched the camaraderie between Lachlan, his brother, and his two cousins and laughed at their antics. She could tell they were close, even though Ian and Duncan lived so far way.

Her mind turned to Jonas and she wondered if he had made it home yet, or if they were still traveling in this rain and cold. She worried her lower lip, worrying that Jonas would catch sick in this cold, damp weather.

"What's amiss, lass?" Lachlan asked quietly. He had noticed she had grown solemn and had watched her as she bit her lower lip.

She shook her head, "Nothing."

Lachlan reached out and brushed his knuckles down her cheek, "If aught 'tis amiss, then why do ye frown?"

She sighed, "I was thinking about my men and wondering if they were riding through this horrendous weather."

His eyes flared with quick anger, "Ye mean 'twas yer precious Jonas ye were thinking of, aye?" He raised an angry brow.

"Perhaps it was," Kandra gave him a hard glare.

Chapter Sixteen

*A*s the last of the meal was finished, Ferran called for the tables to be cleared and moved out of the center of the room. Instruments were brought out and the music began.

Dancers filled the floor, laughing and singing. Kandra stood next to Lachlan, clapping in time with the music. She loved the sound of the music and the swirl of the dancers.

Lachlan glanced over at her and her beauty hit him once again. The fitted blue gown showed off her generous breasts, her slender waist, as well as her luscious body. Her golden hair was pulled back in two braids that encircled her head like a golden circlet. While the rest of her honey colored hair hung loose, spilling down her back and shoulders, falling to her waist. The waves and slight curls in her thick golden tresses made him think of golden waterfalls.

His hands itched to touch her silken strands, running them through his fingers like water.

Her face was animated with joy while her brilliant blue eyes sparkled with amusement as she tracked the dancers spinning around the floor. Her jubilant smile warmed his heart.

Before he could ask her to dance, Ian was bowing before her. Lachlan ground his teeth as possessiveness roared through him.

"Would ye honor me with a dance, my lady?" Ian held out his hand to her as he smiled brightly.

A blush crept over her face, "I fear, my lord, that I will have to decline," she looked down at her clasped hands, "I am afraid I cannot dance."

Ian raised a brow, "Can nay or will nay?"

"I am afraid I have never danced before and would not know how to dance to this." She nibbled her lower lip as apprehension filled her eyes. For years, she had watched the dances at her father's castle, but never had a man asked her to join him for a dance, not even her brother or father.

"Then my lady, 'tis time that ye learned," Ian reached out, snagging her hand pulling her behind him to the dance floor.

"No...I..." Her protests died as he pulled her onto the dance floor, twirling her into his arms.

Ian placed one hand at her waist, the other grasped her hand. He took in her stricken expression. "Dinna fear me, lass, I'll nay bite ye."

"I am not afraid of you biting me, my lord..."

"Ian."

"Ian, I am afraid I may embarrass us both, quiet thoroughly." Kandra frowned up at him. Her heart was racing and she felt wooden as she stood there looking up into his fathomless blue eyes.

"Nay lass, ye just need to relax and follow my lead." With that, Ian began moving them to the rhythm of the music. Within minutes he had her relaxing and moving easily to the musical beat.

"See lass, yer a natural. Ye were born to dance." Ian smiled broadly down at her as the song ended.

Kandra was smiling with pure delight, "I never knew dancing could be so much fun. You are such a wonderful teacher, thank you, Ian. I'm sorry I stepped upon your feet so many times."

"Yer welcome," he bowed slightly. "Tell me lass, does yer family nay hold dancin' for entertainin' their guests?" He frowned down at her.

"Yes, but I have never been asked to dance before." Kandra shook her head at his appalled look, "In my home men tend to find my height odd and intimidating."

"Then they're fools, the lot of them, for yer a verra unique and bonnie woman, Kandra of Carlisle." Ian squeezed her hand lightly.

As the next song began, Duncan came to take Ian's place. Lifting her hand, he brushed a kiss across her knuckles. "Now, I shall show ye how a real man dances, my lady."

Kandra looked around at the people dancing with complicated steps and shook her head, laughing, "I am afraid I do not know how to do this, my lord."

"Duncan," he grinned, "And it's easier than it looks, my lady."

"If I am to call you, Duncan, then you must call me, Kandra." She smiled brightly up at him. She liked these MacKinnon men she'd met tonight. They made her smile, laugh, and feel as if she were a desirable woman. Never had she had a better time than with these men.

By the time, Aidan took his turn to dance with her, her sides ached from laughing and her face was flushed from excitement. Her eyes sparkled with merriment as she took his hand.

Lachlan leaned back against the wall, scowling as his eyes tracked her movements. Anger surged through him as Aidan leaned down to whisper in her ear and she smiled brightly up at him then laughed joyously.

Ian leaned against the wall next to his cousin, watching the interaction between Kandra and his younger cousin. "*Tha I glè àlainn*, but she does nay see it."

"Aye, she is verra, verra beautiful." Lachlan's scowl deepened when Aidan toyed with her hair. He would beat his brother bloody if he continued touching her in such a manner. Kandra was his and no other man beside him had the right to touch her.

"Why did ye nay tell us ye were so taken with her?" Ian smiled brightly, meeting his cousin's furious gaze. "I can nay say I blame ye. If ye were nay interested in her, I would take her to wife myself."

"I am nay taken with her, but she is to be my leman." Lachlan growled. "She is nay free."

Ian held up a staying hand, "Ye can deny it all ye wish, but I see different. Yer taken with her." Then he frowned at his cousin. "To treat her as yer 'hore is nay right. She is a lady of breeding, and nay a common strumpet."

"What she is, is aught of yer business." Lachlan growled, pushing from the wall to claim her from his lecherous brother's hands.

Duncan took Lachlan's place, frowning after his cousin, "He's mad for her."

"Aye, but he needs his *arse* kicked for the way he's treating her." Ian growled as his narrowed eyed gaze watched his cousin.

The dance had come to an end, Kandra was laughing happily as she looked into Aidan's beautiful face. "Thank you, Aidan, that was most enjoyable."

He lifted her hand, pressing a kiss into her palm, "'Twas all my pleasure, Kandra."

With a low growl, she was pulled from Aidan's grasp. Lachlan spun her toward him as he grasped her arm painfully. His angry eyes glowered down at her accusingly. "'Tis time ye retired, yer highness."

Kandra winced at his bruising grip. She raised her chin as her eyes turned hard and cold, "Perhaps, MacKinnon, but I am not currently tired."

"I dinna care, *Sasunnach*." He raised her up as he leaned down to whisper near her ear. "Ye can either walk out of here on yer own feet, or I can carry ye o'er my shoulder once again."

She was furious at his indignant treatment. "As you wish, MacKinnon," she inclined her head, started to turn away, but his grip on her arm kept her where she was. "I can see myself to my bed."

"I'll make sure ye get tucked in properly." Lachlan turned, propelling her along with him. He didn't release his grip on her arm as he guided her through the castle.

Aidan took several steps after his brother as anger ripped through him. He had no clue what was wrong with Lachlan, but Aidan wasn't about to let his brother treat a sweet lady in such a manner. Ferran blocked his path with hands on her hips. "Where do ye think yer goin'?"

"After my daft brother," Aidan scowled in the direction the two had gone. "Someone needs to beat him for treating the lass in such a manner."

"Ye'll stay right here and let them work it out for themselves." Ferran crossed her arms over her chest as she glared up at her younger son.

"He can nay treat a lady in such a way, Mam." Aidan protested as he turned his scowl on his mother.

"Trust me, she can handle yer brother. She does nay need yer help." Ferran shook her head. To pacify Aidan's sense of protectiveness, she sighed as she spoke, "If he truly harms the lass, then ye've my blessing to rally yer two cousins and beat him senseless."

"Believe me, I shall." Aidan growled then turned from his mother to find himself a deep cup of ale.

When they should have turned toward her chamber, Lachlan guided them in the opposite direction. With her chin in the air, she shot him a quelling look. "I believe you are lost. My chambers are in the opposite direction, MacKinnon."

"We're nay goin' to yer chambers." Lachlan ground out as he stopped in front of a large wooden door. He pushed it open, propelled her through, closing it behind them and latching it.

Kandra drew up short, when she saw the massive four-poster bed. She whirled on him, mustering all of her indignation and burying her fear. "What is the meaning of this?"

"I want ye lass, and I plan to have ye tonight." He pushed away from the door advancing upon her. His green gaze was dark and hungry and she shivered under its intensity.

Kandra retreated, walking backward through the room. She glanced at the bed and moved as far away from it as possible. Holding her hands out to ward him off, she swallowed hard, "You swore, you would not touch me until Jonas was home safely."

"And I'm sure he is, but never did I say I would wait for a message back." Lachlan walked her back to the wall behind her. When her back came up against the solid stonewall he caged his arms on either side of her.

"You cannot do this." She whispered as she looked up into his brilliant green eyes and she felt her own desire heating. Slowly, she licked her suddenly dry lips.

Lachlan watched her tongue dart out, tracing her luscious lips. "I can and shall." He leaned forward and breathed against her lips as he lowered his mouth, claiming hers in a punishing kiss.

His hand slid into her loose hair as his other slid behind her bottom, pressing her into his erection. His tongue traced the seam of her lips and she opened for him. His hand at her bottom traced over her hip, up her side until he cupped her breast. He toyed with her nipple through the material of her dress, making it go taut and hard.

Kandra opened to him, arching her back, pressing her breast into his palm. Heat scorched through her as fire burned at the junction of her thighs. He pressed her into the hard, cold stone behind her, but she ignored it biting into her back.

His mouth left hers to trace kisses along the line of her jaw, down the column of her neck. Her breasts felt heavy and full. Her heart raced as his hands fumbled with the laces of her gown. Sliding her arms across the wide berth of his shoulders and down his chest, she yanked his shirt up out of his kilt to feel Lachlan's bare skin beneath her hands. She traced the line of crisp hair that lead down to the waist of his kilt.

He heard her gasp when he ripped her dress trying to undo her laces. Quickly, Lachlan bared her breasts. He bent his head, taking one taut pink nipple into his mouth as his other hand kneaded the creamy flesh of her other breast. Suckling, licking and laving, his skilled mouth tortured her, making her whimper, and he loved the sound.

His hand crept down over her flat stomach to cup her through the material of her gown. She cried out and he smiled. He would have her this night and nothing would stop him. Her protests would fall on deaf ears, for she was his and he would claim her.

His hand slid under the skirt of her gown, up her thigh, rubbing in sensuous circles. Her skin was soft and silky. He cupped her bottom, kneading and gently squeezing.

Kandra tried to stop the little cries of delight and the soft moans of desire from escaping her. The thought that she should stop him floated in and out of her mind as she licked her lips and spoke in a husky voice, "We cannot do this..."

Lachlan ignored her words as his hand lifted her leg, wrapping it around his hip. He pulled his mouth from her breast and recaptured her lips to silence her. His tongue thrust into her mouth as his fingers parted the soft petals of her sex. She was wet and silken, he groaned his pleasure.

She whimpered into his mouth, matching his kiss frantically as his fingers stroked her. Her hands slid into his hair, pulling him closer as she feasted upon his mouth hungrily. Her hips arched against his fingers as they moved of their own accord.

His deft fingers stroked and teased her into a wild frenzy. Sliding his fingers down, he circled her entrance. She withered against him as she clawed his shoulders pulling him closer. He slipped one long finger into her, reveling at her tightness.

He groaned into her mouth as he slipped a second finger within her, stretching her for him. She pulled her mouth from his and cried out. He pressed his mouth to her neck, suckling and nibbling. His thumb found her tiny bud of desire and stroked it until she came apart in his hands.

Cupping her bottom in his large hands, he whispered in her ear. "Wrap yer legs 'bout me, lass." He lifted her and smiled as she obeyed his command, wrapping those long legs around his hips.

Her face was pressed into his shoulder as she kissed and nibbled. The taste of him was driving her insane. His touch was making her melt. She could no longer deny her longing for this man. She could only pray he wouldn't discover her virginal state, for then he would know she had misled him.

Lachlan braced her against the wall as he moved his kilt and her gown out of the way. His long, hardened length pressed against her and she stiffened.

"Lachlan..." He cut off her words with a quick kiss.

"Say it again." He growled against her lips.

"What?" she asked softly.

"My name, say it again." He liked the sound of it on her lips in that husky clipped English accented voice.

"Lachlan," she smiled at him and his heart melted.

"Tell me ye want this, ye want me." He laid his forehead against hers.

"Yes, I want this very much." She looked into his green gaze then lowered her mouth to breathe her next words against his lips. "I want you, Lachlan, very much as well."

With that Lachlan thrust up into her. She pulled her mouth away from his and cried out as he breeched her maidenhead. She had no idea this would be so painful.

Lachlan froze then laid his forehead against hers as he held utterly still to ease her discomfort all he could. "Kandra lass, why did ye nay tell me ye were a virgin?"

Her voice trembled, "I did not think you would be able to tell the difference." She looked at him with watery eyes and his heart melted. A single tear escaped and he pressed his lips to it, tasting its saltiness.

"If ye'd told me ye'd never been with a man 'afore, I would have been more careful with ye." He shook his head. "Tell me when it hurts nay, more."

"I think I am okay," she sighed then wiggled a bit. She smiled at him, "Yes, I am well now."

"Wrap yer legs tight around me and I'll carry ye to the bed." He kissed her lips gently as she obeyed.

Carrying her carefully to the bed, he silently cursed himself seven ways from Sunday for not realizing she was an innocent. Climbing upon the bed with her, he gently laid her down with them still connected intimately.

Kandra nearly sighed at the feel of the feather mattress pressing into her back as he laid her upon the bed and knelt over her. This certainly beat the hard cold stonewall. She reached up to toy with a strand of his black hair that fell over his broad shoulder.

Raised up on his hands, he looked down into her face that was illuminated by the golden candlelight. He smoothed her hair back from her face as he took in her glowing beauty. Her blue eyes held his gaze as he began to gently move inside of her. His other hand slid down the column of her neck until it caressed her breast. His fingers rolled and gently tugged at her pebbled nipple.

She felt the heat rising in her once more, as he gently slid in and out of her, never quite leaving her all the way. She reveled in the pleasure of him filling her completely. Picking up the rhythm he set, she began matching him as he taught her a dance as old as time itself.

The desire coiled in her once more. Winding tighter and tighter, until she became frantic with need, but need of what she had no clue. She whimpered and dug her nails into his shoulders and back. "Please Lachlan..." She begged in a desperate whisper.

He pressed a kiss to her neck then whispered in her ear, "'Tis all right lass. Let go, and I swear 'twill be worth it." As if she needed more encouragement he assured her, "I'll catch ye when ye fall."

With that, Kandra gave herself up to the sensations he was creating within her. She trusted him and she was right to, for when she finally reached out to touch a piece of heaven he was there to catch her when she fell.

Lachlan watched her find euphoria as her muscles clenched around him. Then, finding his own release, he threw back his head, roaring as he emptied his warm seed inside of her.

Chapter Seventeen

London, England

L ord Stafford had just settled down with a tankard of wine, in his chambers within the King's castle, when a knock sounded at the door. Sighing in frustration, he bid the intruder to enter.

"M'lord," the page bowed as he entered. "Forgive this disturbance, but a messenger has arrived with urgent word from your home."

Lord Stafford sat up quickly, "Where is he?"

"In the hall, I shall send him in." The page walked back to the door and bid the man entrance.

Stafford watched as Hugh, one of his most trusted knights, strode into the room.

"My lord," Huge bowed before his lord and master. "I bring news from Castle Carlisle."

"Hugh," Stafford waved him into the room, "Tell me, are my children well?"

Hugh looked at the floor and drew upon his courage. Bravely, he met his lordships eyes, "I regret to report, my lord that they are not."

Stafford closed his eyes briefly to control himself then looked back at the younger man, "Tell me everything you can."

"Yes, my lord," Hugh began his tale, "Lord Jonas and Lady Kandra are being held prisoner by a Scottish border lord." He held the parchment that the Scottish laird had sent to the castle, demanding a reward.

Lord Stafford quickly perused the letter. Sighing, he set it aside. This Scottish laird was a smart one, but if he harmed one hair upon his children's heads, the Scottish bastard would pay with his miserable life.

"Sit, Hugh, for I tire of looking up at you," Stafford waved him to the chair across from him. "Tell me how this came to pass."

Hugh took the chair with a grateful sigh. He had ridden hard to reach the kings castle and Lord Stafford as quickly as possible. With a saddened look, Hugh began to weave the tale of the misadventure that led his lordships children to the peril they now faced. "When I left, my lord, there had been no further word from the border lord."

Lord Stafford was quiet for a long moment, "I will inform the king of our dire situation. We shall be prepared to depart at first light on the morrow, if I am given the king's blessing."

"Yes, my lord," Hugh inclined his head.

"Seek your own bed Hugh, for you will need the rest." He frowned. He had planned to return home in a few weeks, but had not planned to make it a hurried journey. Now there was no avoiding it.

Hugh quit the chambers and Lord Stafford sat silent for a long moment. A hand upon his shoulder had him looking up, "I did not mean to wake you, my love, but it is best you hear this tonight."

"I heard Sir Hugh's tale from our bedchamber." Rowena of Wales pressed a kiss to her husband's golden head. "I will be ready to leave first thing on the morrow."

Lord Edward of Stafford gapped at his wife, "You will not go with us. I will not have my wife pushed at such a brutal pace, especially in your condition."

Rowena stood back with her hands on her hips, glaring at him, "You will not leave me behind, my lord husband. Though I'm a woman, I can ride just as well and as hard as you." She raised her chin, "Besides, our children are in trouble."

Edward smiled at her as he pulled her onto his lap. Though she was little more than ten years older than his beloved daughter, Kandra, she would be a fine mother. He only hoped Kandra and Jonas saw it that way. "You are a remarkable woman, Lady Rowena."

"I love you, Edward." She bent her red head to brush a soft kiss across his mouth.

"And I love you, my darling." Edward's hand cupped the nape of her neck as he deepened the kiss. He had fallen hard for this beautiful, high-spirited woman. She was completely opposite of the other two women he had loved. They had each given him a child that he held precious and now this wonderful woman was not only letting him feel love again, but was giving him another child to cherish. He laid a hand upon her slightly rounded belly. Pulling back from the kiss, he rested his forehead against hers. "I do not wish to endanger either of you on this journey."

She placed her hand over his, "We will fair fine. Besides I have no wish to stay in this castle without my husband by my side."

Edward felt himself cave in. "As you wish my lady wife, but I will extract a promise from you."

"Name it, my lord husband." She smiled as she brushed a kiss over his lips.

"You will tell me if you experience any discomforts during our journey." He gave her a stern look. "I will not risk you or our child."

Rowena narrowed her eyes at him, "Think you I would do anything to harm our child?"

"Nay, my love, but I would not have it on my heart to lose one child trying to reach the other two."

Edward cupped her cheek. "Those two tend to get into all types of mischief, but they take care of each other and can take care of themselves. This one has only us to protect it for now."

"And we shall. He will be healthy and well when he arrives." She smiled, stroking her husband's stubble covered cheek. "I swear I shall tell you if there are any issues."

"Thank you, my love." Edward nipped at her neck then set her away from him. "Now, I must go disturb the king and inform him of our plight."

"I'll await you in our bed, Edward." Rowena gave him a sultry smile.

"I will return as soon as I am able." He captured her hand in his, brushing his lips over it. "Get what rest you can, my love, for we will be on a long journey with little rest."

"Aye, my lord." Rowena smiled as she walked him to the door of their chamber. "Hurry back, my husband."

"Rest Rowena, I will not be any longer than I must."

Edward returned from his visit to the king two hours later. The king had granted him leave, for that Edward was thankful, the king could have delayed his leaving for as long as he wished, but had granted him kindness.

Removing his tunic as he strode into his bedchamber, Edward smiled in the candlelight at his wife's sleeping form. Her luscious red hair was spread across the pillow and her ivory skin glowed softly in the candle's flickering light. Her dark lashes formed half-moons upon her cheeks as she sighed softly in her sleep. She shined with her pregnancy, she was a rare beauty and Edward loved her whole heartedly.

Removing his clothing and blowing out the candle, he slipped into bed next to her. Gently, he pulled her into his arms. When she sighed his name, he smiled, "Shh love, go back to sleep and let me hold you."

"All right," She sighed, "I love your body." She cuddled into him, "So warm." She sighed as she slipped back into slumber.

He laughed softly as he stroked her hair and slipped into his own slumber.

Border Lands Scotland

Kandra reveled at the feel of Lachlan's body pressing against hers. She stroked her hands up and down his shirt clad back. She wanted to strip his clothing from him and feel his heated skin under her hands.

Lachlan lay collapsed on top of her, breathing in her scent. Never could he remember feeling quite so content. Though she was a novice at this, she had matched him thrust for thrust and passion for passion. Sighing, he rolled off her, pulling her with him until she lay sprawled on top of him. Lachlan looked at her as he toyed with her hair. Her face held a soft satisfied smile.

Propping herself up she looked into his dark, handsome face. "Is it always like this?"

Lachlan frowned, "Like what, lass?"

"The pain then the pleasure," she sighed, furrowing her brows in thought, "I can handle the pain if I am expecting it and if I know there will be pleasure to compensate."

Lachlan laughed in a deep rumbling sound that she enjoyed hearing, "Nay lass, 'twill nay hurt the next time. It will be only pleasure."

Kandra smiled wickedly, "Then can we do it again now?"

"Are ye out to kill me, *Sasunnach*?" Lachlan shook his head as he chuckled, "Perhaps, if ye give me a minute or two, and yer nay too sore."

"I am not sore in the least." She assured him then scowled, "Have you forgotten, I am not like your soft Scottish women?"

"Nay, I have nay forgot that," he caught her hair and gave it a tug until she leaned forward to kiss him. "I'm verra, verra glad for it as well."

She pressed her lips to his for a kiss then decided to deepen it by thrusting her tongue into his mouth. She wanted to tempt him into giving her more pleasure. The thought of feeling his skin under her hands had her trembling.

Lachlan growled deep in his throat then set her away from him. "Ye have to slow down a bit, lass." He shifted her back to the bed. "We need to do this slowly this time."

He knelt on the bed beside her and carefully removed her gown. Lachlan frowned down at the rips, "I dinna mean to be so rough with ye."

"You did not hurt me," she looked up at him and smiled, her light blue gaze laughing at him.

His gaze went to the bruise that was forming on her arm from where he had dragged her from the hall. He reached out, tracing the marks his fingers left. "I did, and I'm verra sorry for it."

She looked at the light bruising on her arm and shrugged her shoulder, "It is nothing, I have had worse." Kandra flashed him a cheeky smile. "But if it will make you feel better I could hit you."

"I'll consider it." He shook his head as he grinned at her. Sliding from the bed, he walked across the room, where he removed his own clothing.

Kandra watched him with avid fascination. When he pulled his shirt over his head and stood with his bare back facing her, she chewed her lower lip.

Muscles rippled across his back as he moved. As he quickly unwrapped his plaid, letting it fall to the floor, she nearly groaned. The laird was a fine man indeed. Her gaze roved over him as she studied every aspect of him. His powerful legs were spread wide in a warrior's stance. His hips were narrow and from this angle she could see there wasn't an ounce of him that had run to fat.

When he turned toward her, she didn't avert her gaze. She took in his broad shoulders, the dark crisp hair that was on his washboard stomach, and the trail of hair that eventually led to the curly thatch of dark hair. From that mass of hair sprang his manhood. She nearly gasped at its size. There was no way that had been inside her, it could not possibly fit, she thought as she studied it.

Lachlan allowed her to study him, when she frowned at his manhood, he looked down to see if something was amiss. Looking back at her, he frowned, "What's amiss?"

"It is huge!" She exclaimed, giving him a wide-eyed look.

"Aye, it is." He spoke proudly, then laughed, "Yer a bold one, Kandra."

She gave him a soft smile, "Say it again."

"Say what, lass?"

"My name, I like the sound of it when you say it." She grinned at him.

"Kandra," he stalked toward her with the water basin in his hand. "Let me love ye, Kandra lass."

"I think I would like that." She smirked.

Lachlan sat the washbasin on the floor next to the bed and knelt. Grasping her ankle, he pulled her to him. She gasped and smiled. "Trust me." He winked at her.

She swallowed hard then nodded. "I do." She bit her lip as she watched him wring out a cloth from the basin. When he gently pressed it to her womanhood she jerked away and tried to close her legs.

"Nay lass, let me wash the virgin blood from ye and I promise ye much greater pleasure when I've finished." Lachlan stilled his hand, looking up at her. He could read her indecision and embarrassment, but when she let her thighs fall apart once more he smiled at her.

Gently, he continued to wash away the blood that stained her creamy white thighs and the soft flesh of her womanhood. As his hand moved over her, he felt himself growing hard with wanting her, but he made himself take great care in touching her.

Kandra felt the heat fill her face at his touch, but as his fingers, covered by the cloth, continued to probe and caress, she felt herself heat. Her womanhood began to throb as her breasts began feeling hot and heavy once more. When he removed the damp cloth, she wanted to cry out and beg him not to stop. But when his mouth replaced the cloth, kissing her intimately she cried out, "Lachlan, you cannot do this."

"Aye, I can." He grinned up at her then buried his head between her legs once more, making her moan with the delight of his wicked touch.

She grasped the bedclothes as she pressed herself against his skilled mouth and rode the waves of pleasure he gave her. Higher and higher she rode until she was sure she was going to shatter. As his finger slid inside her, she fell over the edge of ecstasy and into the bliss he created for her.

As her world began to refocus around her, she felt his weight dropping onto the bed next to her. She looked over at him with a sated smile, "Surely that was a sin. For nothing that wonderful could be otherwise."

Lachlan raised her hand to his lips pressing a kiss to her palm. "I'm glad ye enjoyed it, but I'm nay through with ye yet."

"Surely there cannot be more." She sighed as she rolled toward him, snuggling into his warmth. She felt sleepy and content.

"Ah but there is," Lachlan rolled her onto her stomach and began pressing soft kisses and light caresses to her back.

She shivered with pleasure and sighed, "I like this very much."

He laughed lightly as he continued. Sliding his hand between her thighs, he began to play and pleasure her, drawing her desire to a tight coil within her.

Rolling her over, he suckled her breasts, rolling the taut nipples around his tongue. He pressed kisses over her stomach and side. When he reached the scar, he had given her with his own sword, he traced it with his finger then pressed soft kisses across it. He would regret marking her in such a way for the rest of his life. He had marred her creamy skin with this angry red line. He had given her a flaw, an imperfection, when she had so perfect a body. Her muscles were battled honed, but yet she was soft where a woman should be. She was an interesting woman, an interesting warrior, and she was turning out to be an interesting lover.

When at last he had finished paying homage to her body and could take no more, he rose up over her, spreading her thighs wide as he slid into her, filling her completely. She arched against him and rode the waves of passion with him, meeting him stroke for stroke.

As she reached for heaven, she cried his name, clinging to him as she clutched him with her inner muscles, causing him to find his own release.

Chapter
Eighteen

K andra woke feeling warm and content. She couldn't remember ever sleeping better. As she began to stretch, she felt the heavy arm draped around her, cupping her breast. She couldn't help the grin that slid easily into place. For the first time in her life, she truly felt like a woman.

This was what women whispered and giggled about. She was sure her own face held a sappy smile of contentment.

She tried not to move as she savored this moment and the feel of this man wrapped around her. For a long moment, she lay with her eyes closed thinking of what it would be like to wake up in this man's arms every morning for the rest of her life, to bare his children, to share his life, to be his wife.

Reality crashed around her, she was to be his whore and when the money to free her arrived, she would be nothing to him. She would return home and to the life she had known before. This man would be nothing but a memory for her, a memory she would cherish in her lonely world.

His arm tightened around her as he whispered in her ear, "What are ye thinkin', lass? I can nearly hear yer thought's they're so strong."

Kandra tried to pull away, but he didn't release his hold upon her. She sighed then spoke, "Nothing of importance."

"Then I'll give ye better thoughts." He nuzzled her neck, sending shivers of pleasure down her spine. Rolling her under him, he covered her body with his own. Looking down at her, he smiled roguishly.

Kandra smiled softly up at him. Even though it was wrong for her to give her body to this man, she enjoyed this thoroughly. "I do not think we have time for this, I should be getting back to my chambers before it gets any later."

"Ye can bathe here. I'll have yer things moved in here this afternoon." Lachlan assured her as he brushed a hand over her collarbone and shoulder.

She scowled up at him, "I am not moving in here with you, in your private chambers."

"Of course, ye are, lass." Lachlan glanced up, taking in her expression, he sighed.

She shook her head, "It is improper." She huffed in indignation.

"Yer my leman, does nay matter what 'tis proper." He assured her as he leaned down to press a kiss to her neck.

Anger surged through her. With strength drawn from that anger, Kandra shoved him off her. "You need not remind me that I am your whore."

She rolled to her knees, glaring down at him. "But I will not suffer the indignity you suggest. I will not have people talking behind their hands about us."

Lachlan came to his knees as well, staring at her, "'Twould make more sense for ye to stay here with me, I would nay have to be sneakin' across the castle to be with ye."

"I am not your wife, and only a man's wife should share his chamber." She frowned at him. "People would talk and what of Bryanna? What would she think?"

"I will explain things to her." He shrugged his broad massive shoulders.

Kandra's eyes blazed with anger, "Damn you!" She screeched in frustration as she leapt off the bed. Snagging Lachlan's shirt from the floor, she threw it over her head then turned to glare at him. "What are you going to explain to her, that I am your whore, how are you going to get her to understand that?"

When Lachlan frowned at her, she shook her head and continued. "Will you tell her that as your whore I am to allow you into my bed at any time you deem it, and that I shall spread my thighs for your pleasure when you bid it so? Do you honestly want your daughter to see how women are degraded in this manner? Well I do not! You, stupid oaf!"

With that said, she slammed out of the room, storming through the halls toward her own chamber. Anger blazed in her eyes when she threw open her chamber door.

Pacing the room, she frowned in frustration. Anger surged through her. He was a buffoon if he thought she would share his bed every night.

On a sigh, she turned as the chamber door opened. Ferran came bustling in, smiling brightly. "How are ye this morn?"

"Frustrated, angry and...and...I do not know, confused, perhaps." She frowned at the older woman. Walking over, she flopped on the edge of the bed and buried her face in her hands. "He makes me so very angry. We just cannot quit fighting. We never see eye to eye on anything."

"Well ye surely won a battle with him this mornin', for he asked for a bath to be sent up here for ye." She shook her head, tutting happily. "But ye must nay give into him, make him fight for ye, and he will fall for ye, as sure as I'm standin' here. He's just afraid to let anyone into his heart once again."

Kandra stared at the older woman for a long moment, disbelief colored her voice. "Are you trying to say I should get him to marry me?"

"Of course, nay! He should fall in love with ye first. Ye can nay have marriage without love, now can ye?" She shook her head as if Kandra was a silly young girl.

Kandra nearly choked at her words. Fall in love? She shook her head and gave an unladylike snort. "I am afraid men do not fall in love with me."

"The heart 'tis a tricky thing, lass." Ferran studied her intently. "Why do ye believe men can nay fall in love with ye?"

Kandra was quiet for a long moment then looked the older woman in the eyes. "Look at me." She held her arms out wide as she stood to turn in a circle. "What do you see?"

"I see a beautiful young woman, with a gentle and lovin' heart, that any man would be a fool to nay love her." Ferran smiled gently.

"Then you see wrong." Kandra dropped her arms, "I am a warrior, a woman who should have been a man. I am an oddity. And I am cold hearted and have feelings for no one."

Once again Ferran tutted, walking over to Kandra, shaking her head, she reached up, cupping the young woman's face. "Ye have but to open yer eyes and see what others see of ye. When ye do, ye'll realize that aught is wrong with ye, lass. And that any man worth his salt would treasure a woman such as ye."

Before Kandra could respond, a knock sounded at the door. Ferran hurried away from her, opening the door for two men carrying a large wooden tub. Following those men were several young men carrying buckets of hot and cold water.

When at last Kandra was finally alone, she sank into the steamy water and acknowledged the tiny aches throughout her body that the previous night had caused. The heat of the bath helped to sooth most of them away and whatever remained she would work off on the practice field later in the morning.

Dressed in her usual breeches and shirt, hair braided, Kandra strode down to the great hall to break her fast. Few remained in the hall. She looked for the laird and was relieved not to see him. Walking to an empty table, she seated herself.

Quickly, a plate of food and a mug of ale were set in front of her. She picked up a piece of bread and began tearing it apart as she frowned down at her plate.

"Is the food nay to yer likin'?" Aidan MacKinnon slipped onto the bench next to her. His gaze surveyed her and when he saw she was no worse for the wear, he smiled at her.

Kandra gave him a soft smile, "I am not very hungry this morn'."

Aidan shook his dark head sadly. "He's done somethin' to offend ye already has he?"

"The laird?" Kandra raised a brow.

"Aye, my mule of a brother," Aidan grabbed her mug of ale and took a deep drink from it. "He has nay, idea what women want."

"And you do?" Kandra shot him a disbelieving look.

"I ken women, even a woman like ye." Aidan smiled broadly. "If ye were my woman, ye would nay be frowning into yer eggs."

"So, what is it I want?" Kandra smiled at him as curiosity guided her.

"Ye want to be treated with respect, with tenderness but nay entirely as if ye were delicate. Ye want a man to make love to ye like yer fragile and precious, but sturdy enough to grasp onto." Aidan flashed her a knowing smile. "Ye want to be a man's wife, ye want to be his equal, and be looked at as thus."

Kandra was silent for a long moment then looked away. "You are wrong, what I want is to go home and never see your brother again."

"Yer a woman who needs to be romanced and taught about her own beauty," Aidan reached out, caressing her cheek. Before he could say more the squeal that came from the far side of the great hall had them both turning to look in the direction of the dark haired little girl racing through the room toward them.

"Uncle Aidan! Kandra!" Bryanna shouted in her charge toward them. When Aidan stood, she threw herself at him. He caught her in a crushing hug, whirled her around, laughing.

"Ye've grown into a beautiful young lass, yer Da must be beatin' the lads off with a stick." Aidan smiled at the young girl in his arms.

"He is nay doin' such a thing," Bry giggled as her uncle tickled her tummy. "Did Gram havta beat the lasses with a stick to keep 'em away from ye when ye were young, Uncle Aidan?"

"Aye, by the droves," Aidan spoke seriously, causing the girl's eyes to widen.

"If they bother ye now, ye havta tell me, or Kandra, cause we're warriors and we'll defend ye." She took his face in her small hands, looking at him seriously as she whispered, "Cause ye can nay be hittin' lasses, but we can cause we're lasses."

"Are ye now?" Aidan sat on the bench with Bry in his lap.

"We are, right Kandra?" Bry turned to her for confirmation. "She even got Da to teach me to shoot a bow. She's gonna stay with us and marry him, so I can have a Mam." Bry preened proudly as she looked at her uncle, "Then she can teach me to be a she-devil like her."

Kandra's mouth opened and closed then opened once more, but no sound came forth. She was flabbergasted at the idea this tiny girl had put together.

"I have to go!" Kandra shot off the bench, striding from the hall as quickly as possible.

Aidan threw back his head and roared with laughter. His adorable little niece had just scared the daylights out of the fierce warrior. He would have to have a talk with his brother later about Bry's notions.

Kandra strode out to the practice field where men were training. Even in the early morning, some were stripped bare to the waist as they clashed swords, trying to disarm their opponent.

Spying Rogan, she strode over to him, "I wish to have my sword and practice."

"I have nay heard permission from the laird." Rogan growled down at her then shouted in Gaelic at two young men training.

With hands on her hips, she scowled up at him. "I do not care what he has or has not said. I want my sword, or so help me I shall march out on that field and take one of theirs." She frowned over her shoulder at the two young men, "They're not very good anyway."

"Yer in great spirits this morn', lass," Duncan walked over to where she stood. He was sure by the look on Rogan's face that he was seriously considering throttling her soon.

"I want my sword and this big oaf will not give it to me." Kandra growled through bared teeth. "I am considering running him through with his own sword."

Now Rogan growled down at her, "What ye need is to be turned over the laird's knee and beat."

"As fun as that sounds, I shall have to decline," she glared at him, "I am in the mood for a good sword fight instead."

Before they went to blows, Duncan decided to interject. "Rogan, get her sword for her. She can take her anger out on me instead of takin' a piece of yer hide."

Rogan muttered under his breath as he walked away, but returned from the armory with her sword in hand. Tossing it at her feet, he strode away to work with his men.

Kandra snatched up her sword and started after Rogan's retreating form.

Duncan grasped her arm, spinning her around to face him. "Dinna try him, lass. He'll only make ye sorry ye did."

"I am not afraid of any man." She informed Duncan haughtily. "I can best any man I go against."

"Then it'll be my pleasure to knock that chip from yer shoulder, lass." Duncan grinned as he touched his sword to hers.

"And I will apologize in advance for making you look the fool in front of your men." Kandra grinned impishly at him as she assumed a fighting stance.

They circled each other, learning the others body language. Duncan clanged his blade against hers, trying to rattle her but it failed. "Ye have fine form, lass, but ye lack courage to jump into a fight."

Kandra raised an arrogant brow, "Really, I was trying to take it easy on you, so that you would not get hurt."

Duncan threw his head back and laughed. She was a spirited lass and he was enjoying her thoroughly. Shaking his head, he stepped into the fight beginning it and determined to end it.

Kandra knew he out powered her, but she was slightly quicker, because of her size, she could brazen moves most men wouldn't dare. Twice she knocked the legs out from under Duncan, and twice he retaliated in kind. She didn't stay down for long though.

She was bolstered by the sound of the clanging metal as sword struck sword. The concentration of footwork and gauging her opponent helped her to focus on something other than Lachlan and Bryanna. In the area of swordplay, she was on solid ground, but when it came to the laird and his daughter, she was sinking in quagmire.

Nearly an hour after they had started, they were both panting and feeling battle weary.

"I'll give you a chance to surrender," she smiled at him with her light blue eyes alight with mischief.

"Nay a chance, my lady," he grinned at her as he raised his sword, coming at her.

She ducked under and around him, tripping him in the process. As she turned to hold her sword to his throat for surrender, he caught her leg, sending her to land on her bottom. Sword pointed at each other's throats, they panted and grinned.

"Draw," they spoke at once and flopped back on the dirty field.

"I admire yer skill with a blade, lass." Duncan grinned over at her.

"And I admire yours, Duncan MacKinnon." She grinned at him. "I would fight at your side any time."

"And I would welcome ye," Duncan spoke earnestly.

Kandra turned her face back up toward the sky. Closing her eyes for a moment, she let the heat of the sun wash over her. When a shadow fell across her, she squinted up.

"What do ye think yer doin', *Sasunnach*?" Lachlan glared down at her, with his legs set wide and his hands upon his hips.

"Resting," she informed him, closing her eyes once more dismissing him.

Anger raged through him. Reaching down, he grasped her arm, yanking her to her feet.

Kandra raised her sword, pressing it to his throat. "Release me if you do not wish me to spill your blood, laird."

"Do ye think yer brave enough, *Sasunnach*?" Lachlan growled down at her, not releasing her. "I would hate to have to embarrass yer in front of everyone out here."

Before she could figure out his meaning, he had his hand over her wrist of the hand that held the sword. She cried out as he gave it a quick twist, causing the tip of the sword to scratch him.

In another quick motion, he had her hauled over his shoulder once more.

Duncan watched the altercation between them and grinned. They were quite a sight, the pair of them. Never had he seen two people who challenged each other more. They would rub along well together, Duncan surmised.

Kandra raged as she beat on Lachlan's back. Not again, she wouldn't allow him to embarrass her in this undignified manner again. She should have killed him. She berated herself for her hesitation.

When he set her down again there would be hell to pay and she intended to wallop him a good one. He would be lucky if she didn't beat him bloody.

Lachlan turned angry eyes upon his cousin. "We'll speak of this later." With that said, he strode for the keep once more with Kandra struggling in his arms. As she viciously yanked his hair, he slapped her bottom hard enough to bring tears to her eyes.

Reaching his chambers, he flung the door wide, kicking it shut behind him. Striding to the bed, he upended her upon it.

Kandra hit the mattress of the bed, and would have come up swinging, but his body trapped hers on the bed and her wrists were pinned on either side of her head.

Lachlan knew that if she got up there would be hell to pay. Though he was twice her size, she would attempt to pommel him. Once he had his say, he would deal with her anger.

"Let me up, you great buffoon." Kandra spat at him.

"What were ye thinkin' goin' out there like that?" He jerked his hand and her wrist away as she made to bite him.

"I was practicing. What did it look like, you bloody ass?" She snarled at him. "You are going to pay for this as soon as I get free."

"I'm sure I shall, yer highness." He glared down at her. "But for now, I want to ken why ye were out there practicin' without your armor?"

"Without my armor?" She stopped struggling against his hold to look up at him in bewilderment.

"Aye, without yer armor?" He growled, "Ye could have been hurt, Duncan could have killed ye."

Kandra looked at him for a long silent moment, "Were you worried, laird?"

"Aye *Sasunnach*, ye could have gotten hurt." He glared down at her. As an afterthought, he added. "Then where would I be?"

She felt a small thrill surge through her. This man was concerned for her. He was worried about her! Never had a man besides her father, Raff, or Jonas, showed concern for her.

"I am fine, Lachlan." She spoke softly as she looked into his green gaze. "I can handle myself on the battle field."

"Ye could die." He spoke quietly. Just the thought made his gut clench with fear for her. Lachlan couldn't imagine life without her already.

When she tugged her arm, he released her. She reached up, cupping his cheek, "And so could you. I am a warrior, Lachlan, the same as you. I have to practice, to keep my skills up."

He turned his head as the anger died in him, leaving only the cold fear inside of him. He pressed a kiss into her palm. "Then swear to me, ye'll wear yer armor from now on."

"I don't need..."

"Swear it to me, or I shall destroy yer sword myself, I swear it to the Gods." Lachlan threatened. "I want nothin' to happen to ye."

"All right, I swear it." She looked up at him, smiling softly.

Lachlan sighed in relief, leaning down he brushed a soft kiss over her lips. He grunted as he felt himself pushed off her and over the side of the bed. With a thud, he hit the floor.

"That is for carrying me over your shoulder, and bruising my bottom." She smiled serenely down at him from the side of the bed to where he lay on the stone floor.

Lachlan lay where he was and laughed, "Yer a wicked wench, *Sasunnach*."

Chapter Nineteen

*K*andra walked into the great hall for the evening meal, dressed in an elegant gown of red, trimmed in gold. Her gold hair was plaited around her head, forming a golden crown. She stopped in the doorway as her gaze sought out Lachlan's.

Lachlan watched her as she stood in the doorway. He surveyed her attire and his mouth nearly watered. His loins tightened with wanting. He would have to thank his mother for making Kandra the gowns. Lachlan watched her standing there across the room, fidgeting, her hands knotting together then releasing to smooth imaginary wrinkles from the skirt of her gown. She was nervous, he realized with a slight smile.

His green gaze was fastened upon her. She wanted to shiver under the intensity of it. Kandra could feel his eyes taking in everything about her, from her plaited hair to her leather boots. She hoped he liked what he saw.

Straightening her spine, she strode across the room. Walking to the high table, she inclined her head to Lachlan, greeting him formally. "Laird," she smiled brightly.

Lachlan took her hand, lifting it to his lips. "Ye look stunning, lass."

Kandra blushed at his words. "You exaggerate, laird."

"I would nay lie to a beautiful woman," Lachlan smiled as he led her to the high table and the chair he now thought of as hers.

Once they were seated, Lachlan signaled for the meal to begin. Kandra was ravenous. Everything Lachlan lay upon her trencher, she ate heartily. She had fled in the middle of the morning meal then missed the noon meal, as she was occupied by Lachlan in his chambers.

"I should nay have kept you from the noon meal. Yer half starved." Lachlan leaned over, whispering in her ear.

A blush crept into her cheeks as she remembered her wanton ways and the feelings she felt with his hands upon her. The sensation of his warm breath tickled her ear, sending shivers down her back as thoughts of his clever mouth made her blood sing.

Lachlan noticed her blush and brushed a hand over her thigh, lightly, teasingly. When he felt her tense, he nearly laughed. She was an intriguing lover. Never had he met a woman who matched and yet challenged him in so many areas.

"Your behavior is very inappropriate, Lachlan." She admonished in hushed tones as she tried to concentrate upon her meal.

"Ye dinna mind my behavior earlier." Lachlan chuckled as he toyed with her hip, running lazy circles over it with his fingertips. His thoughts turned to new ways he could worship her body when he had her naked upon his bed later.

Trying to ignore him, she turned her attention to Ian sitting beside her. This only proved to further Lachlan's amusement as his deft fingers found other ways to torment her.

She was surprised when Lachlan himself called for the tables to be cleared and for dancing to take place in the great hall once again. Delighted, she listened as the musicians began to play a lively tune.

Lachlan watched her smiling and clapping along with the music. Walking over he claimed her hand. "Would ye dance with me, lass?"

Smiling softly, Kandra looked up into his luminous green eyes. "I would be honored Lachlan, but I fear I do not dance very well. You could certainly find a better partner."

Lachlan gazed down at her, "I dinna think I could." He took her hand, leading her to the dance floor. Lifting her hand to his lips, he pressed a kiss into her palm then smiled down at her. "I dinna get a chance to dance with ye last eve, and I wish to change that now."

"And lucky you are that you did not dance with me." Kandra laughed, "I fear poor Ian, Aidan, and Duncan's feet sadly shall never be the same."

"I'm a fairly brawn lad, I think I can handle it." He laughed as he took her into his arms. She felt good there, he had to admit silently to himself.

The couple laughed and twirled on the dance floor. Kandra had never felt so treasured in all her life. This man held her as though she were spun glass and barely winced when she stepped on his foot for the fifth time. As the dance came to an end, breathlessly, she slipped easily into his arms when he pulled her closer.

He would have kissed her there in front of the whole castle had Bryanna not appeared at his side frowning.

"Da," Bry tugged at the edge of his kilt to gain his attention.

Looking down at her, Lachlan released Kandra, "Aye, dumplin'?"

"Will ye nay dance with me?" Bry smiled at him.

"I would be honored, Lady Bryanna." Lachlan bowed deeply then swept her up in his arms as she squealed with delight. He looked at Kandra, "Do ye mind, lass?"

"Not at all," Kandra smiled back at him. Turning, she started to walk away, but Bry's words drew her up short.

"Nay Da, I wanna dance with ye both." Bry smiled at him.

The little girl's words from earlier rang in Kandra's mind. Was this part of her idea that Kandra was to become her new mother? She didn't want to encourage Bry with this idea of hers, in fact she needed to speak to Lachlan about it and have him set Bry straight.

Kandra turned back to the pair. Looking at Lachlan, she shook her head, "I would not want to intrude, the two of you should dance."

"But Bry wants ye too." Lachlan held out a hand to her. When she hesitated, he wiggled his fingers at her then smiled.

Kandra shook her head, "Really Lachlan, I..."

"Please Kandra, please dance with us." Bry begged with pleading little green eyes that matched her father's.

Kandra felt herself giving in. How could she deny that little face? With a sigh, she took Lachlan's out stretched hand. "All right, but it is your feet at risk." She warned Lachlan.

He smiled down at her, "I'll risk it, lass, if it makes ye both happy."

As the music started once more in a lively jig, Kandra stepped to the music, and upon Lachlan's feet from time to time. By the end of the song, all three were laughing and smiling.

"'Tis time for ye to seek yer bed, dumplin'." Lachlan swung Bryanna around, making her giggle.

"Will ye tell me a story, Da?" Bry pleaded with him.

Looking down upon the sweet face of his daughter, he could refuse her nothing. "Aye, I'll see ye to yer bed, but only a short story this night." He turned to Kandra, "Do ye mind, lass?"

Kandra looked from father to daughter and back, she smiled softly at Lachlan. "Not at all, take your time."

Lachlan reached up and brushed the backs of his finger over her cheek. "I'll nay be long, I'll have Ian keep ye company, until I return."

"There is no need, I shall be fine on my own." Kandra smiled as he tugged her hand to make her walk in the direction where Ian was standing by the far wall.

Left standing next to Ian, Kandra watched Lachlan carry his daughter from the room. The laird was a man who was a contradiction in terms. On one hand, he was a hardened warrior, a leader, a tyrant at times, but with his little girl's eyes upon him he became a softhearted, cuddly bear. Kandra couldn't help but to smile at the thought.

"A coin for yer thoughts, lass." Ian grinned at her. "Ye can nay be thinkin' about my cousin and smile in such a way." He teased gently.

"He is an unusual man, your cousin." Kandra sighed softly. All these MacKinnon men were unusual, but great men in their own rights. She was glad to have met them all.

"I see ye care for him a great deal, as well as lil' Bry." Ian laughed at her shocked look. "Yer good for them, lass."

"Lachlan is a wonderful father," Kandra skirted the subject of her feelings. She wasn't at all sure of how she felt about Lachlan and his daughter, and until she did she planned to keep her feelings in check, at least until she had time to examine them further.

"Aye, he 'tis at that, he loves that girl more than life itself. They're good together. I have nay seen Lachlan and Bry so happy in a long time," Ian agreed with her, then sighed, "But they are both missin' somethin' that neither can give the other."

Kandra gave him a long look, "I think I shall take a walk."

Ian laughed as she turned away, "I never took ye for a coward, lass."

Kandra looked over her shoulder and stuck out her tongue. She heard Ian roar with laughter as she made her way from the great hall.

The summer air was warm and refreshing. The night sky was clear and bright overhead. Kandra made her way up to the battlements. Walking along the wall, she looked out over the darkened village and countryside. How she missed her home, but yet she wouldn't give up what she had found in this place one second sooner than she had too. Lachlan made her feel things that she had never felt before. He made her feel beautiful, cherished and...and? Loved?

Her thoughts turned to Lachlan and all they had shared so far. Was Ian, right? Did she have deeper feelings for Lachlan then a woman and her captor, more than lovers? Could she be in love with him? Never had she felt this way about a man. Of course, she loved her father and Jonas, but it was different with them. How did it feel to love a man?

How she wished she had a mother she could turn to at a time like this. Giving a resounding sigh, Kandra looked up at the waxing moon and the twinkling stars laid out on a blanket of midnight blue velvet.

"Yer stunnin' in the moonlight," Lachlan leaned against the wall watching her.

Kandra looked over at him. A smile lit his face as his eyes danced in the light of the moon. He was so utterly handsome that she felt her breath quicken at the sight of him. He was her captor, her enemy, her lover, and her heart burst at the thought of him. This man could make her touch the stars in the heavens above, and burn with the fires of desire until she thought she would burst into flames. Raising a brow, she smiled seductively, "You should not let the wine go to your head so."

"'Tis nay the wine that has gone to my head, lass, 'tis yer beauty." He watched her look back at the stars above.

"I do believe you are either drunk or blind, my lord." She turned to look at him fully, and what she saw made her desire flare to life. She wanted to touch this man, to explore him and make love to him. "Perhaps you forget, men do not find me beautiful."

Never could he remember a woman who could take his breath away with a single look. As Kandra stood, bathed in moonlight, his heart fluttered. She could be the Goddess Danu herself, with her golden hair washed in moonlight, making it glow and shimmer. Her usually sun kissed skin was washed pale and translucent, giving her an ethereal look. But it was her eyes that stole his breath, the look of longing and desire within them that made his heart pound and his loins stir.

"I am nay drunk, but I am completely blinded by yer beauty, lass," he crossed his arms over his chest as he watched her, "And by my desire for ye."

Slowly, she walked toward him. Standing toe to toe, she smiled up at him placing her hands upon his chest as he dropped his arms to his sides. "I want to touch you, I want to taste you, I want to make love to you." She stood on tiptoes and brushed a soft kiss across his lips. "Will you show me how?"

"Ye've a good start," he met her mouth for a searing kiss that set the flames of desire licking higher in each of them. Taking her hand in his he led her through the castle to his chambers.

With the door closed and secured, Lachlan leaned back against it. He watched her walk gracefully into the room before him. Her golden plaited hair shimmered in the candlelight, her red gown showing every enticing curve as it swished around her legs.

Lachlan was hungry for her, but he held tight the reins of his lust, and would allow her the freedom she asked for. He would let this woman love him this night, perhaps it was a folly to allow her so much power over him, but he couldn't deny her her wish, no more than he could deny a request from his daughter. Gods save him if this woman ever found out that she could bring him to his knees with little more than a look.

He spread his arms wide as he looked at her, "I am at yer mercy, m'lady. Do with me as ye will. I am yer's to command."

Kandra stood across the room staring at him. She thought of all the delectable things he had done to her. Was it possible to do some of the same to him? Raising a brow, she crooked her finger at him. "I want you here, standing before me."

With his eyes fastened on hers, he walked over to stand in front of her. Slowly, Kandra drew her gaze over him from head to toe. "What am I to do with you?" She mused aloud as she walked around him, taking in his marvelous warrior's body.

Again, this night, he was dressed in a kilt and shirt. It left his powerful legs bare to the eye. What Kandra saw, was pleasing indeed. Gently, she let her fingers trail lightly over his broad chest and shoulders. Tracing a path down over his stomach, she reached the waist of his kilt. Slowly, she grasped his shirt, pulling it free.

Kandra slipped her hands under the material as she sought his bare skin. Her hands splayed over his heated chest, pushing his shirt up. Tugging at the hem, she smiled up at him, "I am afraid I am not tall enough to remove your shirt without some assistance."

A grin lifted a corner of his mouth. "Are ye askn' me to strip for ye?"

She shot him a sultry look from under her lashes, "Just the shirt, for the moment."

Quickly, he removed the shirt and stood before her, looking down at her with his hungry green gaze. He wanted to reach out and take her into his arms. He wanted to strip her and worship every valley, curve, and plain of her body. He wanted to show her more of the sensuous lovemaking he had begun to tutor her in.

Kandra stared at his broad chest. As she reached out to trace the lines of his chest, she rejoiced in the quiver of muscles under her fingertips. Though she had seen countless men shirtless, she had never had the chance, or the desire, to touch one of them, nor explore the mountains and plains of their bodies. She was fascinated with the strength in this man's body and wondered at the way he could be so gentle. Leaning forward, she pressed a soft kiss to his broad chest. The light, crisp, springy hair on his chest tickled her face. She rubbed her cheek against his chest. When she felt his deep in draw of breath, she glanced up at him.

The hunger in his eyes had grown. She could see him fight for restraint, to keep from grabbing her and having his way with her. Gently, she trailed her fingers over his chest once more then traced the line of his shoulder. Walking behind him, she traced the muscles of his back. Smiling softly, she pressed open mouth kisses across his back and shoulders. As his muscles quivered and bunched, she traced them with the tip of her tongue. His breath became more labored and Kandra felt her power grow.

"Kiss me," she whispered against his skin.

Lachlan turned and snagged her around the waist. Leaning her back, he captured her mouth in a searing kiss, and caught her sigh in his mouth. His hands cupped her bottom, lifting her, he pressed her against his hardened length. He throbbed for her. He needed the relief only she could give him.

Sliding her hand between them, she pulled from the kiss. "I am not through with you yet, my lord."

He watched her as she dropped to her knees in front of him and begun unlacing his boots. He shook his head, "Nay lass, I shall do that."

Kandra shook her head, "No, I want to do this."

Helping him from his boots, she sat back on her haunches and studied his kilt. She commanded him to unfasten the brooch made of lead in the shape of the MacKinnon crest. Reaching up, she unfasted his belt. Carefully, Kandra began unwinding the material from his hips, until it finally slid to the floor at his feet. Her breath hitched when it revealed his hardened manhood.

Cautiously she reached out, touching the tip of him. She traced his hard, silken length. "You are so very hard, like armor, and yet you are so silken." She spoke with wonderment lacing her voice.

Lachlan threw back his head and laughed, "Yer a brazen wench."

Kandra looked up at him eagerly, "Show me." When he merely raised his brows, she gave him a wicked look. "Show me how to pleasure you, as you do me."

He studied her for a long moment, "Give me yer hand, lass." She laid her hand in his larger one. When he brought her hand to him and curled her fingers around his member, she smiled. Slowly, he drew her hand down the length of him then back up and he groaned his pleasure. She caught on quickly and set her own pace. When his eyes drifted closed and his breath hissed between his teeth, she studied him.

Wondering if she could pleasure him with her mouth, much as he did her, she leaned forward, brushing her tongue over the tip of him.

"Kandra," the word came out strangled and hissed.

She stopped and drew back looking up at him as he looked down at her now. "Did I cause you pain?"

"Nay lass, 'tis a feelin' I enjoy much, but 'tis nay an act a lady should perform." He reached down to stroke her cheek tenderly.

Kandra closed her eyes as tears prickled the backs of them, he thought her a true lady. Opening her eyes, she smiled devilishly up at him. "Then you are quite lucky my lord, for I act like no lady, I know."

Before he could reply, she leaned forward taking him into her mouth as her hand began to stroke him once more. His taste was slightly salty and uniquely male. As she suckled him, she swirled her tongue around him, listening for groans of pleasure from him.

Lachlan growled deep in his throat as his head hung back. Reaching out, he quickly removed the braids from her hair and slipped his fingers within her golden tresses, as sheer ecstasy raced through him. The pleasure she wracked through his body was merciless and thorough. Minutes passed as her clever mouth tortured him sweetly. When at last he could take no more, he pulled away from her. "Enough." He growled.

"But I was not through." She whimpered as she frowned up at him.

He watched the candlelight play over her golden hair and features. Her blue eyes held a vast pool of emotions. Reaching out, he caressed her cheek as he whispered in Gaelic to her. "*Tha thu bóidheach.*"

Though she didn't know their meaning, the softly spoken words thrilled her and touched something inside of her that she felt for this man.

Lachlan pulled her to her feet. "If I let ye continue, this would be over far too soon, *gràdh.*"

Kandra stared at him for a long moment then bowed her head.

He placed a finger under her chin, forcing her to look at him. "What 'tis the matter?"

Her blue eyes weary as she confessed, "I do not know what to do from here. I do not know how to love you."

Lachlan took her hand helping her to stand, then raising her hand to his lips. "Undress and I shall teach ye."

"You must think me foolish." She spoke as he moved toward the bed and she began to unlace her stays.

"I think, *Tha thu bòidheach.*" He grinned at her as he sprawled upon the bed, comfortable in his nakedness.

"I do not understand the words you speak." She frowned at him as she removed her dress.

"I told ye, yer beautiful." Lachlan lay there smiling at her.

Kandra blushed at his words. Quickly, she turned from him, bending over to pay attention to unlacing and removing her knee-high boots. Dressed in only her chemise, she offered Lachlan a succulent view of her backside.

When she was finished, she turned to the bed and smiled at him.

Lachlan raised his hand motioning her forward. When she reached the side of the bed, his gaze raked over her.

"Remove yer chemise and come to me." He spoke gruffly as need licked flames of desire higher.

She grasped the hem of her chemise, whipping it over her head. Standing bare before him, she felt vulnerable, yet she trusted this man. Slowly, she climbed upon the bed to kneel at his side.

Reaching over, Lachlan grasped her, pulling her down on top of him. "Kiss me, lass."

Hesitantly, Kandra pressed her lips to his. They were soft and warm. The taste of him filled her. Her kiss grew in strength until she thrust her tongue into his mouth, tasting him. Her fingers found his hair and ran through the silky locks and braids.

Pulling her mouth from his, she looked down into his handsome face. She took in his magnetic green gaze. His eyes were almond shaped with arching black brows and a nose that was fairly large, but perfect for his face. He had a generous mouth with full lips that knew how to make her body sing from their touch. She ran her fingertips over the rough beard of his shadowed cheeks that gave him a dangerous look. Carefully, Kandra memorized every detail of that face, so that on those lonely cold nights when she was alone again, she could recall his face and hope to fade some of the loneliness.

Grasping her waist, Lachlan sat her up to straddle his hips. She could feel his hardened length pressing against her. His fingers traced her breasts then cupped them, feeling their weight. Her head fell back as he rubbed her tight, pebbled nipples.

His fingertips grazed over her flat stomach, circling, teasing. Reaching the golden curls between her spread legs, he brushed a hand over her. Kandra moaned as he parted her tender flesh, sliding his finger into her dampness to find her tiny bud of desire.

There he stroked and coaxed her into a heightened state of desire. As the cord of desire twisted tighter and tighter until she was sure she would shatter, his hand left her long enough to lift her. Before her whimper finished leaving her throat, he had settled her over him. Slowly, he pressed himself into her tight sheath. Her whimper ended in a moan as he began to fill her.

Unable to wait for him to slowly enter her, Kandra sank upon his hardened shaft. A glorious cry left her lips at their joining.

Lachlan grasped her hip to show her the motion. Quickly, Kandra caught the rhythm. She liked the feeling of being in control. Setting her own pace, she rode him until they both reached for the heavens above.

Chapter Twenty

*K*andra lay sprawled across Lachlan's chest. She sighed at the feel of his fingers trailing over her back in lazy circles. Never in her life would she have believed she was truly a desirable woman, but this man who lay beneath her made her feel not only desirable, but beautiful as well.

Her cheek was snuggled against his chest as she listened to the strong steady beat of his heart. How she longed for that heart to belong to her. What would it be like to spend the rest of her life with this man? She was certain they'd make beautiful children together.

Drifting into her thoughts the sound of his voice snapped her back to reality.

"If yer Jonas, was nay yer lover, then who is he?" Lachlan glided his fingers over her shoulder as he enjoyed the feel of her silken skin under his calloused hands.

Folding her hands on his chest, she rested her chin upon them, looking up at him. "He is my brother."

He looked into her eyes incredulously, "I let yer brother go?"

"Yes, you did." She smiled at him. "But you still have me."

"I could have gotten twice the coin for him." He frowned at her.

She stared at him in disbelief for a long silent moment. After everything she had gone through with him and been to him, he could still think a male more valuable than her. Anger surged through her.

Kandra rolled off him to sit on the edge of the bed. She spoke dryly as she stared across the room. "My father would not pay more for either one of us. He does not value one child over the other, male or otherwise."

Lachlan reached out, touching her shoulder and felt her stiffen. "That's nay what..."

"If you are through with me, my lord, I shall seek my own bed." Kandra spoke as she began to rise.

Before she could fully stand, Lachlan snagged her waist, pulling her back on the bed. Quickly, he rolled her under him so that he could look down into her angry face.

Kandra averted her face from his gaze, but she didn't struggle against his grasp.

"That was nay what I meant," he scowled down at her. "I meant, if I had known he was yer brother, he would nay have left here." He waited a moment for her to respond.

"Ye misled me in his identity, *Sasunnach*." He growled accusingly when he was met with only silence.

"I let you believe what you would. You made your own mind up." She glared at him with fire in her eyes. "I never once claimed to be his lover!" She began to struggle, but he easily subdued her.

"I nearly killed that lad because of ye." Lachlan spoke savagely. "The thought of him touchin' ye was near enough to drive me crazy."

At his words, Kandra stopped struggling. She stared up at him in disbelief. "Why?"

Lachlan didn't want to admit his feeling so he skirted them the best he could. "Because I wanted ye."

"You were jealous?" She whispered doubtfully as she searched his face.

For a long moment, he looked down at her. She couldn't fathom someone being jealous when it came to her. Reluctantly, Lachlan spoke, "Aye *Sasunnach*, I was jealous."

She felt the giddy thrill course through her. A soft smile replaced her disbelief. A man, an amazingly handsome man, could be jealous over her. Never had she felt more like a woman than she did in this moment.

"Kiss me," she pleaded with him. She wanted to feel his lips upon hers and she wanted to taste him.

His mouth met hers once again, igniting the flames of their earlier desire. As they mated tongues, they stroked each other into a wild passionate frenzy. Each silently acknowledging something had changed between them.

The rest of the night was spent in desperate lovemaking. The gray light of dawn crept into the room the last time Lachlan turned to her, caressing her.

Sleepily, Kandra looked over at the spot where Lachlan should have been laying. A smile slipped into place as she rolled over onto his side of the bed. Snagging his pillow, she buried her face in it, breathing in his scent. They had been lovers for more than a sennight now, but this was the first night she had spent in his bed all night, since they had first made love.

She enjoyed sharing Lachlan's bed and their lovemaking. Sighing, she looked up at the ceiling, she was sincerely afraid she might be falling in love with Lachlan MacKinnon and *that would be a huge mistake'*, she thought with a frown.

Reluctantly, Kandra began to rise, when a young servant girl bustled in with a tray of food. "The laird sent me with food to break yer fast."

Kandra frowned at the girl as she looked about the room. She didn't want to become gossip for the castle, and this girl would likely run back to the kitchens and prattle to the other women there. With a sigh, Kandra waved the girl toward the table across the room. "Place it upon the table. I will get to it shortly."

"Aye, m'lady. When ye've finished, yer bath shall be brought up." The girl placed the tray upon the table and spoke once more. "The laird is expecting ye in the inner bailey within the hour."

Kandra raised a brow, "Is he?"

"Aye, m'lady," the girl hastened from the room, closing the door behind her.

The food made Kandra's stomach growl. Wrapping the blanket around herself, she made her way to the table and uncovered a bread trencher of porridge that smelled of warm honey, as well as a plate laden with eggs and a rasher of crisp bacon. With it was a mug of warm cider.

Ravenously, she attacked everything before her and drank the entire mug of cider. As she was finishing the last piece of bacon, a tap at the door announced the arrival of her bath.

"Enter," she called out as she wiped her mouth.

The girl was followed by a group of young lads laden with buckets of hot and cold water. A large tub was placed near the hearth. Once the tub was filled and to Kandra's liking, the girl shooed them from the room.

"Would ye, like help with yer bath?" the servant girl laid out soap, a washing cloth and bath sheet for Kandra.

"I can manage on my own," Kandra smiled at the girl who could be no more than three years her junior, placing her at approximately only ten and seven. Kandra herself being a score of years, could not imagine having this girl wait on her. "What is your name?"

"Jinny, m'lady." She performed a quick bob.

"Thank you, Jinny," Kandra smiled at her. "Please tell his lordship, I shall be down directly."

"Aye, m'lady." Jinny left the room quickly.

Kandra immersed herself in the steaming bath. She grabbed the heather scented soap and washed quickly. With that task out of the way, she decided to relax for a few minutes and enjoy the hot water.

When at last she figured, an hour had passed since Jinny had brought her breakfast, she left the cooling tub and dried. Meticulously, she combed out her hair and braided it, letting the braid hang down her back like a golden rope. Dressing in a pair of breeches and a linen shirt, she slipped into her knee-high boots and quickly laced them.

Leaving the laird's chambers, she headed for the bailey. There she found Lachlan waiting patiently for her.

As she walked down the stone steps to where he sat, lounging as he waited, he looked up at her, smiling.

"You summonsed me, my lord." She was extremely disappointed that he was not put out by her tardiness.

"I'd hoped ye would accompany me this morn into the village." He nodded to where Oren was leading her destrier toward them. Following behind them was a lad leading Lachlan's own powerful warhorse.

Kandra strode to meet her horse. She reached out to stroke his nose as he nuzzled her hand. "Hadwin, what a beautiful boy you are. Oh, how I have missed you!"

Lachlan strode behind her. "What is his name?"

"Hadwin, it means good friend in times of war." She let the horse nuzzle her shoulder, looking for treats.

"A wise choice of name," Lachlan stroked the beast's nose. "Though I think it unwise to allow a woman to ride such a powerful beast, but I have seen ye can handle him well enough."

"Thank you, I think." She gave him a frowning look. "If we are to venture out of the castle, then I shall need to retrieve my sword before we leave."

"Ye will have, nay need of it." He gestured to his claymore, strapped to his back. "As you can see I am armed. I can protect us both should the need arise."

Kandra gave him a droll look, "And I suppose I am to sit back, scream and cry whilst you are defending us."

"Nay lass, I expect ye to stay out of the way and keep quiet." He growled surly.

"I will most certainly stay out of the way, because I am not going along with you." She turned on her heels to march away, but he caught her arm, turning her back to face him.

"Do ye nay trust me to protect ye, *Sasunnach*?" He looked into her light blue gaze searchingly. She could see the underlying hurt as well as anger in his green eyes.

Reaching up, she stroked his cheek. "I do trust you, Lachlan, but I am as much a warrior as you are." Her gaze was imploring him to understand what she felt. "Could you leave this castle without your own sword?"

"Nay, I could nay do so." Lachlan shook his dark head as he scowled at the ground between them. He didn't like the idea of her carrying a sword, if they did meet any trouble he knew she wouldn't simply stay out of the way. But then, he himself would feel naked without his own claymore.

"Ye can have yer sword," he gave in with a frustrated sigh. He turned to the lad who had led his horse out of the stables. "Go to the armory and fetch the lady's sword."

"Thank you, Lachlan," she stretched up on her toes to brush a kiss over his lips. It was a huge concession on his part to allow her, her sword, and it didn't go unnoticed by her.

Before she could pull away, he snagged her around the waist. "Promise me ye'll leave the fightin' to me if there is to be any."

She spoke against his lips. "I will not raise my sword unless I feel it is absolutely necessary."

He considered her words for a moment. It was the best he knew he would get from her. "Agreed," he breathed against her lips, then settled his over hers in a searing kiss.

By the time he released her, she was thoroughly breathless. Happily, she watched a few minutes later as the boy brought her sword to her.

"Thank you," she smiled appreciatively at the boy. She quickly fastened the belt around her waist. Taking her sword from its sheath, lovingly, she stroked a hand down the flat of her blade. Carefully, she took a couple of swings to familiarize her with its weight once more.

Lachlan stood back, grinning as she stroked and caressed the sword as a mother would a child. Perhaps he had been right to allow her the sword once more, he thought. The appreciation in her eyes was worth giving into her.

Sheathing her sword, Kandra looked over at Lachlan. "Are you ready, my lord?" She walked over to Hadwin and swung up onto the saddle without waiting for his response.

Lachlan took a sack from one of the kitchen maids and looped the strings over his saddle horn. Lithely he swung up into his own saddle. With a tap of his heels, his destrier Carrick trotted toward the castle gate.

Once out of the castle and in the open countryside, Kandra smiled over at Lachlan. She blew him a kiss then gave Hadwin his head. Like a shot they were off, leaving Lachlan to race after her.

He watched the wind race through her golden hair, making strands of it fly out behind her as the sun filtered through it, causing her to look surreal as she raced across the green countryside. She reminded him of a Fae princess.

Bending low to Hadwin's neck, Kandra glanced over her shoulder. Lachlan was much closer than she wanted him to be. Smiling at him briefly, she turned back to Hadwin and whispered to him.

Lachlan couldn't hear what she said to the horse, but it seemed the beast had understood her and lengthened its strides, for it pulled away from him easily.

Kandra slowed Hadwin once she reached the edge of the village. Coming to a stop, she turned to watch the laird enter the village. A cocky grin spread across her lips.

"You are slow, MacKinnon." She shook her head with a tisk.

"Ye dinna race fair, m'lady." He pulled in rein next to her. Her face was colored with pleasure and excitement. He very much enjoyed seeing this woman happy. The sparkle in her blue eyes caused his heart to turn over. Lachlan knew he couldn't allow himself to have feelings for this *Sasunnach*. She would leave him soon, and he refused to allow her to take his heart with her when she departed.

Hadn't he lost a woman he loved once? Aye, he thought grimly, and it had nearly destroyed him. He wouldn't allow this woman to do the same. He would enjoy her body while she was here, but keep his heart separated.

Kandra stared at the man for a long moment. A sad look passed over his face. Her heart ached for him, she felt the urge to wrap her arms around this brazen man and sooth his hurts.

"What are you thinking, Lachlan?" She titled her head slightly as she watched him. She curbed the temptation to reach out and sooth the line between his brows.

Her words brought him out of his thoughts. "I was thinkin' perhaps we should continue on my rounds and errands before the day wanes on us." He nudged his mounts sides, riding away from her. He had spoken more harshly then he had intended, for that he was remorseful, but he knew he couldn't endear his heart to this woman.

Kandra raised a curious brow as she wondered what could have changed his good humor. Shrugging her shoulders in wonder, she nudged Hadwin to follow him.

She followed behind him as he made his way to a hut at the end of the village. When he dismounted, she reined in and followed suit. Kandra watched as he took a pouch from his horse's saddle and headed for the door. Tethering Hadwin near Lachlan's mount, Kandra watched him.

The door to the cottage swung open, an ancient little woman shuffled out, smiling brightly. "I've been awaitin' ye, laird."

"I've come to see how ye fair, old mother." Lachlan took her gnarled old hand she held out.

"I'm well, laird. 'Tis kind of ye to come." The old woman smiled up at him with real affection. "Ye and yer lass must come in for a spell."

The older woman stepped aside, waving Lachlan through the door. Kandra watched him duck his head to enter the cottage.

"Come with ye now, lass, I've been expectin' ye." The old woman motioned her forward. "Dinna be afraid, girl.

Kandra straightened her shoulders, raised her chin and walked to the house. "I am afraid of nothing." She spoke as she walked past the old woman, entering the cottage. The old woman was nearly half Kandra's size, with her shriveled frame. Her once red hair was now mostly white, but her beautiful blue eyes were crystal clear and took notice of everything.

"Nay of anythin' ye can fight with yer sword, at least." The crone cackled with amusement as she followed Kandra inside.

The cottage was surprisingly airy and fragrant. Kandra looked about at the drying plants hanging from the ceiling. The room was neat as a pin and a pot boiled over the low burning fire. A kettle with warming water hung on another hook.

"Would ye care for a cup of tea, m'lady?" The woman walked over to a shelf, removing cups from it. They were surprisingly beautiful teacups, with tiny roses painted upon them. "Fetch the kettle, lad." The old woman instructed, waving him toward the fire.

Just as Lachlan stood from where he'd been sitting at the table, the kettle began to whistle. Taking a pad from nearby, he removed the hot kettle. He placed it upon the table where the old woman was measuring tea leaves into the tiny teacups.

Kandra watched them work together to fill the teacups. As the tea began to steep, the woman brought out a freshly baked pie that smelled delicious.

"Sit." The old woman motioned Kandra to the table. "Come have some pie."

Kandra sat across the table from Lachlan. She felt his gaze on her, but didn't return it. She was trying to ignore him. Since they had ridden into the village, he had spoken a little over a dozen words to her. She cared not for his cold attitude.

The old woman placed a plate of pie in front of Kandra and Lachlan then settled herself onto her own seat. "It would appear the lad has no intentions of introducing us. I am Maeve." She looked over the younger woman and smiled, she was pretty and a good match for the laird.

"I am Kandra, from Carlisle in Cumbria." Kandra inclined her head regally, "'Tis a pleasure to make your acquaintance, Maeve."

"And ye my fine lady." Maeve smiled broadly, "Ye will do fine." Her eyes held a spark of mischief.

"I will do fine, for what?" Kandra peered at the old woman curiously.

"Ye'll do fine as a wife for this surly, young man." Maeve nodded her head toward Lachlan. "He needs a good wife, he does." She laughed softly, "And ye can keep him on his toes."

"I will be no man's wife, least of all his." Kandra pointed at Lachlan as she addresses Maeve heatedly.

"Aye, good strong bairns ye'll have." Maeve went on as if she had not heard what Kandra said. She turned to the laird, who stared at her wide-eyed. "I could use a bit more firewood, Lachlan."

"What?" He glanced at Kandra then back at Maeve. "What did ye want?"

"Firewood," she shook her head clucking her tongue at him. "Are ye becomin' thick in the head, lad?"

Lachlan stood from the table, "Firewood, aye, I'll be right back." He nearly knocked over his chair in his haste to stand and leave the table and her words behind.

They watched Lachlan stride from the cottage as if the hounds of hell were on his heels. When the door slammed behind him, Maeve threw back her head and cackled. "The boy is scared spit less!" It was good and fitting, she thought.

"I do not find this at all funny." Kandra shook her head, frowning at the woman. "I have no intentions of marrying Lachlan MacKinnon, or anyone else."

"Think what ye will, m'lady. But ye'll give the laird a fine son. I've seen it. Yer heart's already bound to his, nay matter how much ye deny it." Maeve spoke in her no-nonsense tone.

"Are you...are you a witch?" Kandra spoke wearily as she gazed at the old crone. She had heard many strange tales about Scottish witches, a shiver raced down her spine.

"I possess the sight, if that's what yer askin'," Maeve waved away the concerns. "I can nay turn people into toads and such, though the lord and lady ken that most folks deserve nay better." She clucked her tongue.

"But you say you see things?" Kandra inquired with curiosity. She had never met anyone who claimed to have the true gift of sight.

"Aye, visions and such." Maeve held out her hand. "Give me yer hand, lass."

Cautiously, Kandra set her hand into Maeve's. The old woman tisked and tutted, "So verra much sadness in yer young life, yet ye never give up yer hope." A soft smiled played upon her face as her eyes looked around unfocused. "But the love ye have found will make up for yer sadness. Ye'll love little Bryanna

MacKinnon as much as ye'll love the wee bairn yer carryin' now."

Kandra stared at the older woman for a long quiet moment. "I am not carrying a child. It is impossible." She whispered her protest as her mind played over the bed sport she and Lachlan had shared.

"Mark my words, ye are lass. A son 'twill be." Maeve gave her a sad look. "'Twill seem grim for a time, but dinna give up hope. Yer love for him shall be answered."

Before Kandra could say more Lachlan came through the door with his arms loaded with wood. Both women watched him neatly stack the wood near the hearth.

Kandra pulled her hand from Maeve's. She couldn't help but to wonder if the crone was right, her hand drifted to her stomach, touching it lightly. Could she even now be carrying the laird's child? If she was, what could she do? What would become of her child? Her curses had not come yet, but it was not unusual for them to flow late by a week or two, perhaps even more.

"I shall gather the things yer Mam has asked for, if ye'll wait but a moment." Maeve stood from the table and began bustling around the room, gathering herbs.

Within the hour, she was bidding them farewell as they mounted their horses. "Come back to visit soon, the both of ye." She waved them away. "Take care of yer woman, laird."

Each was silent for a long time as they ambled through the village. Kandra took in the homes in disrepair. The fields that lay ready for seeds to be planted. For the first time, she understood why Lachlan needed the money from her ransom. His people had seen hard times and he was desperate for the coin to buy seeds and help his people repair their homes. She couldn't see Lachlan neglecting his people for any other reason.

Lachlan reined in before the blacksmith's. "I've business here. Stay here until I return." He grumbled as he swung off his horse and tied it to a low hanging tree branch.

Kandra didn't agree nor did she disagree, she merely glared down at him from her horse. He was the most annoying man she had ever met.

She watched him stride away to the smithie's shop. Wheeling Hadwin around, she ambled farther through the village. She hadn't made it but just beyond the next cottage when she saw a woman, heavy with child, trying to carry a large basket filled with clothing. Reining in Hadwin, Kandra dismounted and strode toward the woman.

"Would you care for a bit of help?" Kandra looked down at the smaller woman, who was nearly a foot shorter than her.

The young woman stopped and eyed Kandra curiously for a long moment. "Aye, I could nay say I'd mind it."

Kandra dropped Hadwin's reins, "Stay." She told her horse firmly. Turning to the woman, Kandra took the basket from her. The young woman appeared to be near Kandra's own age. Her hair was russet colored and beautiful. Her eyes, a brilliant blue and friendly, shone.

"My thanks m'lady, my back, I fear, will never be the same again after this wee bairn's born." The woman smiled at Kandra. "I'm Maggie."

"I am Kandra." Kandra spoke as she walked alongside the young woman to where a line was strung between two poles.

"'Tis a pleasure to meet ye, m'lady," Maggie held out a hand. "So yer the laird's *Sasunnach*, aye?" She raised a delicate brow.

"I do not belong to anyone. I am a free woman." Kandra growled as she shot Maggie a sharp look. "No man shall ever own me."

Maggie assessed her new friend with a frown. "Yer right, no man should lay claim to a woman, unless she's willin'." Maggie nodded approvingly as she grinned, "But believe me, m'lady, sometimes 'tis a joy to be claimed by a man." She laughed heartily and rubbed her bulging stomach once more.

Kandra looked at the smaller woman for a long moment. A grin slipped out and she couldn't force it back. "Yes, perhaps it is."

Maggie reached into the basket for a garment. Carefully, she hung it over the line. "Can ye, truly use that sword at yer side?"

Kandra set the basket down, handing Maggie another garment, as well as taking one for her to hang, and nodded "Yes, better than a good many men." She shrugged her shoulders, "I suppose we all have our own talents."

"Aye, but some of us have more than others," Maggie gave her a soft smile. She reached over and straightened the garment Kandra had hung.

A soft blush crept over Kandra's face, "I am afraid I am not very good at women's work." She shook her head, "The truth is. I have no clue as to how to be a woman."

Maggie paused a moment in hanging the clothing to turn and look at Kandra, "So stop tryin' so hard, and be who ye are. Let the rest come in time." She smiled, "If he does nay love ye now, give it time and he will."

Kandra reached down for more of the clothing in the basket so that she wouldn't have to look Maggie in the eyes as she spoke. "I do not want him to love me."

"And I'm the bloody Queen of England!" Maggie snorted, taking a garment from Kandra. "Yer besotted with the bloody fool."

Kandra looked at her furiously. Why was everyone so sure of her feelings, when she wasn't? She sighed angrily.

"Dinna look at me thus," Maggie scolded lightly "If ye can nay see it, ye will soon enough." She shook her head, "Lachlan, has a way 'bout him."

"Why does everyone insist that I love him?" Kandra scowled down at her. "I barely like the man!"

Maggie shook her head laughing, "Careful what ye say lass, here comes yer man now, lookin' none too pleased."

Kandra turned to look over her shoulder to where Lachlan strode toward her. A look of disapproval upon his face told her he was not happy that she had disobeyed him. Turning to him, she placed her hands upon her hips and glared right back at him.

"Lachlan MacKinnon," she growled at him, "Take that look off your face, or take me back to the castle right this second."

Lachlan pulled up short at her words. Here she stood, commanding him once more. With his arms crossed over his chest, he glared at her. "Come here, lass."

Kandra mocked his stance all the way down to the arrogant tilt of his head, "No."

With a growl, Lachlan advanced on her, his pride in her grew as she stood there unflinching. He stood toe to toe with her, scowling. "I told ye nay to move."

"You told me to stay here, and I have." She countered.

Lachlan reached out, encircling her throat with his large hand. "Ye ken what I meant."

"I know that you are an overbearing ogre." She spat, glaring back up at him. "If you wish to continue being such unpleasant company, then I shall leave you to it."

She jerked out of his grasp. Bypassing him, she ran to Hadwin, vaulting up into the saddle. Before Lachlan could move, she was galloping out of the village toward the castle.

"I dinna think ye were such a fool, Lachlan MacKinnon." Maggie glared at him then turned, marching back toward her home.

"Damned wench," Lachlan jogged around the building to fetch his own mount.

Chapter
Twenty-One

L achlan raced after her. Spurring his horse on, he was catching up with her.

"Slow down, lass!" He yelled at her as he grew closer.

"No, leave me be!" She called over her shoulder as she looked back at him.

Lachlan's chest seized at the tears shinning in her eyes. "Wait and talk to me, *Sasunnach*."

"I have heard enough from you this day, laird." She spurred Hadwin on. She didn't want to talk to him. She wanted him to go away, for she had done nothing to earn his anger.

Lachlan growled in frustration as she pulled away from him. Swearing in Gaelic, he spurred his destrier to move faster yet. In a burst of speed, he caught up with her.

Before she knew what was happening, Kandra felt herself being plucked off her horse. With a screech, she was plunked down in Lachlan's lap. She turned to hit him, but he captured her wrists in one of his large hands and his reins in the other. "If ye try it, lass, ye'll kill us both."

"You have no right to touch me," she spat as she fought against his hold. Anger surged through her as she battled to free her hands, but it was in vain that she struggled.

"I have every right," he growled in her ear as he slowed his own horse. Reining in, he brought the glossy black destrier to a stop.

Kandra glared up at him. "You are a bastard."

"Bastard I may be, but ye'll listen to what I have to say," he growled down at her.

"I have no interest in what you have to say, MacKinnon." She growled. Kandra looked at his horse, "Sorry old boy."

Before Lachlan could say anything, Kandra kicked the horse, causing him to rear, toppling them both off the back of the horse. Lachlan, who had not expected the fall, released her and tumbled backwards to land on his back.

Kandra pushed herself away from him to tuck and roll as she landed. For a moment, the wind was knocked out of her.

Lachlan landed flat on his back, staring up at the sky with the wind knocked out of him. Anger surged through him. He was going to kill the brazen little wench. He looked up at the sky and imagined his hands around her throat.

Kandra struggled to her feet. Anger burned through her. Without a second thought, she drew her sword, turning to him. "On yer feet, MacKinnon!"

Lachlan scowled over at her as he sat up with a groan. "I swear if ye dinna put that thin' away, I'll give ye the thrashin' of a lifetime, *Sasunnach*."

"Get on your feet and we shall see." She swung her blade with practiced skill. Kandra knew her anger had the best of her, but she didn't care. She'd had enough of this man's commands, rudeness, and his unprovoked anger.

Ambling to his feet, Lachlan glared at her, "Ye swore an oath to me, Kandra. Ye can nay leave until I release ye."

Kandra raised a haughty brow, "I have no intentions of leaving, MacKinnon." She bowed at the waist, "I intend to run you through then I shall return to the castle and await my brother."

Lachlan gave her a long cold look as she stood there, sword at the ready, "Put it down, *Sasunnach*, I have nay intentions to fight ye."

She began slowly circling him, pointing her sword at him. "Well that is a shame, because I have intentions of finishing what we started before."

"I will nay fight ye," Lachlan turned with her as his battle instincts kicked in. "Put down the sword, Kandra lass, I dinna want to hurt ye."

"A shame, because I truly want to hurt you." She came closer. "I give ye one last chance to draw yer sword, MacKinnon."

"Ye will nay kill an unarmed man. Yer English knight's code forbids it." He spoke through clenched teeth.

She watched a muscle in his jaw tick. Kandra laughed bitterly, "Ah, but you forget, I am a mere woman. I do not follow their code, for I am not a knight."

Lachlan watched her anger surge and knew he would have to defend himself, so he drew his claymore. He only prayed he wouldn't hurt her, "Dinna make me do this, sweetin'."

"Too late!" She struck out with her sword. Metal clanged against metal, ringing through the air. Kandra knew he would defend himself if she forced him to. She matched him thrust for thrust, clash for clash, and pare for pare.

Lachlan met her sword to prevent her from taking off his head in one fail swoop. With each thrust and pare that he avoided, he tried to find a way to disarm her without marking her in the least.

"This is foolish, Kandra. What can ye prove?" He spoke as he blocked a blow of her sword.

"That I am equal to you and that you have no right to treat me as you do." She came at him once again. "I have had enough of arrogant men like you."

"I dinna want to hurt ye, lass. Stop this before 'tis too late." Lachlan blocked an angry shot. She was becoming careless as she let her anger unbalance her. He knew he had to wait for the right moment to disarm her.

"Do not...worry...about...uh...me." She hacked at his sword with her own. It annoyed her even more that he fended each of her blows with ease. If she could just draw him into actively participating in the fight, she might get the edge on him with her agility. "You...fight...like...a woman!"

Lachlan couldn't stop the laughter that bubbled out. Kandra narrowed her eyes to angry slits. She met his sword with hard, effort-filled blows. She had lost all control and Lachlan knew this was his moment to disarm her. She was blinded by her own rage. Moving quickly, he twirled his sword around and around hers scrapping metal against metal. Silently, he prayed he would not harm her.

His movement was fast and caught her off guard as he ran his blade around hers in fast circles. Circling lower and lower with each turn, she could only stare. Before she knew it, she lost the grip on her sword. It flew out of her hand and stuck in the ground a few feet away. Her mouth gapped open as she stared at it.

Turning back, she felt the tip of his sword against her chest. Narrowing her eyes, she pressed against it.

"Run me through, throw me in the dungeon, it makes little difference to me." She raised her haughty chin in defiance.

"I've better plans for ye." He grinned wolfishly at her. She was shocked when he threw his sword next to hers.

While she stared in confusion at his discarded sword, he took advantage of the moment. Reaching out, he grabbed her, pulling her up hard against his chest. She gasped as he crushed his mouth over hers.

The kiss was as much searing as it was punishing. She struggled against him as she fought the pull of desire he was creating within her. As he deepened the kiss, she grew placid as her arms slipped up around his neck to thread through his long, silken, black hair. His tongue swept the interior of her mouth as she opened to his probing tongue.

Kandra's fingers bunched in his long, dark hair. Flames of desire licked up her body as she met his hungry kiss and pressed her body to his wantonly. She damned herself for being a fool, but she couldn't deny her lust for this man.

His hands roamed over her body, igniting fires to burn her very soul. She couldn't resist this man even if she tried. Heat coiled in her belly, the familiar throbbing ache he caused in her returned.

"Love me, please Lachlan." She whispered huskily as his mouth tore from hers to taste her jaw and neck. She whimpered as he scraped his teeth along her flesh.

He straightened, looking down into her passion filled blue gaze. "Nay here." Lachlan took her hand and whistled for his horse. The black destrier came trotting to him. Lachlan lifted Kandra, setting her onto the saddle.

She looked down at him, "We cannot ride together."

He looked at her golden hair spread out over her shoulders, where he had let it fall after he had unbraided it to run his fingers through it. She was a warrior Goddess, he thought for a moment. He took the horse's reins, walking over to their swords. Pulling hers from the ground, he held it up. "If ye promise to keep this put away, I shall endeavor to give it back to ye."

"I swear. I have no wish to fight at this moment." She smiled down at him with a sultry look. "Impalement is on my mind, but not with that type of sword."

"Wicked wench," he accused, shaking his head. "I shall have to see if I can tame ye."

"Do your worst, my lord." She turned away from him and scanned the land around them. Looking around, she frowned then she whistled with her fingers in her mouth. The sound was piercing as it went out over the land.

Lachlan swung up behind her. Lifting her bottom, he settled her so that her bottom fit nicely against his loins. Slipping his arms around her, he grasped the reins and set the horse to walking. He held the reins in one hand and had his other hand resting on her stomach.

She felt the tingly butterflies at his touch. As the horse went into a canter, she smiled at the feel of his hand unlacing her breeches. She leaned back into him as his fingers slid inside her breeches to touch just above the curly thatch of hair between her thighs. Reaching up, she wrapped an arm around his neck to play with his long dark hair.

He circled his fingers through the curls that hid her. Slowly, he slid a finger through her woman's curls to find the tiny pearl of her desire. She was already wet for him and he smiled as he pressed a kiss to the side of her neck.

His talented finger stroked and moved with the rhythm of the horse causing the sensations to escalate. Kandra couldn't swallow the moan that escaped her lips. The sound of her cry and feel of her body shuddering against him brought his erection to a painful peek. Her body slid against his, making him hungry and needy for her.

As her body slowed from the pleasure he had brought to her, she stroked her fingers along the nap of his neck. Turning her face up to his, she gave him a soft satisfied smile. Stretching up, she brushed a kiss across his lips.

"Mmm," he sighed as he ran his tongue over the seam of her lips, begging entrance to her. When she opened freely, he delved his tongue deep within the recesses of her mouth. His hand reached up, cupping her breast. Gently, he rolled her erect nipple between his thumb and forefinger.

Kandra pulled her mouth from his. "If you continue to torture me, I will be spent before we can make love." She sighed as his thumb brushed over her erect nipple. Laying a hand to his cheek, she pulled his mouth back down to hers for a kiss.

Lachlan pulled back from this last kiss, inclining his head, "We're almost there."

Turning forward, she saw the woods surrounding the loch ahead of them. Raising a brow, she looked back at him. "We are going in there?"

"Aye, I plan to make love to ye by the loch and eat a long lazy meal." He shrugged then smiled down at her once more, "Perhaps, if we're nay too tired after our meal, we'll make love again."

She smiled up at him with a sultry look, "I cannot wait." Never had she gone on a picnic before and the idea thrilled her.

Lachlan guided his horse through the woods until they reached a clear bank on the side of the loch. Reining in, Lachlan dismounted quickly, walking around to where Kandra sat looking down at him. Reaching up, he lifted her from the horse. She was shocked when he swung her into his arms.

"I am far too heavy for you to carry." She squirmed in his arms, uncomfortable with him holding her like this.

"Quit yer wigglin' 'bout." He scolded good-naturedly. "Yer nay heavy at all." He marched toward his destination and smiled down at her.

Resigned to her fate, Kandra decided to enjoy the feeling as she wrapped her arms around his neck and laid her head upon his shoulder. He walked to the grassy clearing on the bank of the loch, where he knelt and laid her upon the grass.

Leaning over her, he touched his lips to hers, "I'm sorry, but I can nay be patient enough with ye, lass." He stroked his hands over her long lithe body.

Kandra pressed her lips to his firmly, pulling him down with her as she laid back. He let his hands freely roam over her body, unlacing anything in his way. Quickly, he removed her shirt, baring her breasts to him. Tearing his mouth from hers, he bent to lick and suckle her breasts as his fingers worked on removing her boots and breeches.

She worked her hands under his shirt as she raised her hips so that he could remove her breeches. She concentrated on working the shirt to his shoulders, he ripped the shirt over his head, throwing it aside so she could touch him freely and unrestrained. Her hands branded his skin, and her sweet caresses fueled the fire of need burning through him.

Kandra cried out as his mouth left her breast bared to the cool air. Her body hummed as he ran kisses over her stomach then to the inside of her thigh. When he moved between her spread thighs, her body was surging once again with the need for the pleasure only he could give her. Her fingers slid into his glorious black hair as his mouth settled over her intimately. The slide of his tongue and the heat of his mouth made her whimper. Her body arched to press his tongue closer.

Her taste was sweet and he reveled in the passion contained in her cries. Sliding his finger inside her tight sheath, he reveled as she cried out for him. Slowly, he stroked her velvety entrance, taking her higher and higher into the abyss of euphoria.

She came apart in his hands, crying out as waves of pleasure crashed over her. Pulling his mouth from her, he slid up her body as he freed his hardened length. Grasping her hips, he entered her in one powerful thrust. He heard her cry out, but paid no heed as he set a frantic rhythm of thrusts and withdraws.

Kandra felt his animalistic need rear its head as he plundered her and possessed her. She gave herself to him with wild abandon to match his own. The coil of need spiraled high inside her once more. When the coil snapped, she screamed as her orgasm whipped through her whole body. She felt Lachlan stiffen as he strained with his own release.

Lachlan nearly collapsed upon her, but his sated mind thought better of it. He rolled, bringing her to lie stretched over the length of him. Lying there, his breath ragged and labored as his heart pounded, he stroked her long golden hair. Languidly he ran his fingers through it, looking at the way it changed color in the sunlight. With a contented sigh, he looked down at her relaxed face.

Watching the sunlight play upon her face, he felt something inside him shift. She looked like a faery in peaceful slumber. If only he could find it in himself to love her, he wondered for a moment if he would always be as happy as he was right now.

Pushing those thoughts away, he grinned down at her. She would leave him, but he would keep a piece of her even after she was gone. On those long lonely cold winter nights, he would pull these memories out and have her with him again. He felt her begin to stir and stroked her cheek with a fingertip.

Her lashes fluttered up as she woke from her sated rest. She looked up into his soft green gaze and felt her heart clench. The feelings she felt for this brazen Scot was growing day by day. Searching his eyes, she saw something there she had never noticed before. But what was it? Perhaps tenderness and caring? Was it possible for this crude heathen to fall in love with her?

No, she shook herself mentally. He couldn't love her. She wasn't a woman to be a man's wife and mother of his children. She was a warrior with a warrior's cold hardened heart. She sighed, but she would always cherish the memory of this man

Slowly she smiled up at him, "You surprise me, laird."

He raised a brow in question.

"When I thought, I could not feel more, you gave me more." She shook her head laughing. "Do not get yourself a big head, my laird." She saw his prideful smile.

Quickly, he rolled her under him. He looked down at her lying upon the green grass, her golden locks spread out around her. She was beautiful and for the moment, she was his. Leaning down, he brushed a kiss over her already lovely kiss-swollen lips.

"Are ye hungry, lass?" He heard her stomach rumble and laughed. "I've brought us food from the kitchens."

Rolling off her and agilely to his feet, he walked over to where his horse was tethered. He grinned at the sight of Kandra's mount standing near his own horse. Stepping over to Hadwin, Lachlan grasped the reins and tied the horse to the tree.

Taking the sack of food from his destrier's saddle, he walked back to where Kandra sat by the water's edge. Her hair fell around her, shielding much of her body from his gaze. Settling next to her, he removed the contents of the bag and laughed when he heard her moan at the sight of the food.

They feasted upon bread, cheese, slices of salted meat, as well as crisp apples. A skin of wine accompanied the meal. Taking turns, they feed each other bites of bread, meat, and cheese, laughing in general good spirits.

With the apples finished, the wine and the rest of the food consumed, Kandra flopped back on the grass. Lachlan lay next to her on his side so that he could look at her and trace his fingers over her body. He came to a bruise forming on her hip. A frown filled his face as he looked at it.

Looking down to where his hand rested as she spied the bruise. "It is nothing."

"I hurt ye, I should have been gentler with ye." He ran a light finger over the spot. "I always seem to leave marks upon yer bonnie body." He shook his head in self-reproach.

"You did not hurt me." She shook her head. "Think nothing of it." It was trivial that he had given her a bruise, for they had both been eager to make love.

"'Tis wrong to mark a woman in such a way." He continued to frown at the offending mark, unsure why it bothered him so much when she had dismissed it.

"All right, fair is fair," she shoved his shoulder to lay him back. Quickly, she sat up and straddled his hips. Leaning forward, she pressed kisses to his chest. She ran her tongue over his flat male nipple and watched with satisfaction as it hardened. Kissing his neck, his jaw, his mouth, she ran her hands over him, until he was groaning and straining under her.

Settling herself to take him deep within her, she paused and looked down into his handsome face. Slowly, she sank onto him and relished the feeling of him deep inside of her, stretching her, and filling her so completely. Never had she felt so whole then when she was with Lachlan MacKinnon. Gently, she began to move over his silken length. A thrill of power washed over her as she heard him groan in pleasure.

Lachlan's hand cupped her generous breasts then he pulled her forward so that he could take one of her nipples into his warm, wet mouth. He relished the sound of her moan and the way she tightened around his shaft.

Kandra groaned as one of his hands drifted lower across her stomach and his finger slid through her feminine curls. His calloused finger stroked over her sensitive bud and she bit her lip on a moan. He was pushing her until she was teetering on the edge of the abyss of pleasure.

Pulling away from his mouth she sat up and sped the rhythm up, she laughed when he hissed between his teeth, "Yer killin' me, *gràdh*." The tingling sensation she was beginning to get used to when Lachlan truly lost control, slid through her making her pleasure all the greater.

Her passion rocked her as she cried out in release. Lachlan grasped her hips, thrusting deep within her as he found his own release. When at last they were both sated, she lay her head on his chest.

She didn't know the words he whispered in his Gaelic tongue, but somehow, she knew they were good. Collapsing upon him, sated and spent, she sighed as his arms wrapped around her. Pressing her mouth to his chest, the words she felt in her heart were on the tip of her tongue. Carefully, she swallowed them back, afraid to speak them aloud.

Lying there wrapped in each other's embrace they fell into a light satisfied slumber. The warm summer sun shone down upon them, heating them against the cool breeze by the loch. She sighed and felt herself relax as slumber wrapped warmly around her.

With an hour passed, Lachlan stirred, pressing a kiss to her temple to wake Kandra. She muttered, but didn't awaken. Softly, Lachlan began singing to her in Gaelic as he held her.

Slowly, Kandra roused and lay listening to his deep soothing voice. When he finished, she sighed snuggling deeper into him. "What were you singing?"

"A tale about two lovers," he stroked her hair as he told her the story. "They met by the shore of the sea, each were betrothed to another, but they fell desperately in love with each other. Their love was forbidden."

"So, what did they do?" Her blue eyes looked up at him filled with interest. What an odd man her captor is, she thought as she looked into his beautiful Celtic face. He was a gentle warrior. His large hands could cause great harm and yet his fingers were gentle and feather soft when he touched her.

"They ran away together, away where no one 'twould ken them and they could love each other freely." He told her seriously. "They lived happily for a short time, but soon enough the woman's father, as well as the lad's own father, found them."

"What happened to them?" Somehow, she couldn't help but to feel this story was significant to them and their situation.

"The two clans began to feud. The lovers held each other as the fighting surrounded them. They each swore to love one another forever, no matter what happened in the end." He looked to the sky for a long moment. "An arrow was shot from which side 'tis nay ken, but the arrow nay only pierced his heart, but hers as well, for they were standing there, locked in each other's arms. They died together with both families fightin' around them." He spoke as he twisted a lock of her golden hair around his finger.

Lachlan studied that lock of hair intently before he spoke again. "'Tis said that their spirits linger on the shores where they first met and they are together forever." He looked down at her, studying her. His green gaze held a hint of the warmth she felt deep inside of her. "They made a promise to each other, to love each other in life as well as in death." His voice was husky as he spoke.

Kandra sighed at the images he painted for her. She laid her head on his chest, closing her eyes. "Do you believe a love between two people could be that strong?"

He was quiet for a long moment. Kandra raised her head to look up at him with curiosity. Finally, he looked at her and smiled faintly, "Aye, if they truly love each other."

She gave him a wicked smile, "I bet you still believe in fairies, dragons, and magic." She teased lightly.

Lachlan covered his heart with his hand as he gasped at her mockingly. "Aye lass, us Scot's take our Fae, dragons, and magick verra, verra seriously."

Giggling, she shook her head, "You are a little old to believe in magic, are you not?"

He gave her a narrowed eyed look. "Yer tellin' me, ye dinna believe in magick at all?" This lass had much to learn about life.

She shook her head as she sat up to look down to him. "I learned long ago, there is little besides yourself that you can believe in."

"Aye, but there is magick out there," he spoke seriously as he rose to sit facing her. He looked down at his own fingertips and sighed.

"I have never seen real magick. I have seen groups of gypsies perform tricks." She shrugged, "But tell me, Lachlan, where does this magic hide?"

Lachlan raised one knee, resting his forearm upon it. He reached down, plucking a single blade of grass with his free hand. Examining it for a long moment, he frowned, "Have ye never seen a babe take its first breath? Have ye never seen a sunset or sunrise?" He looked at her seriously, "Magick is all around us, *gràdh*. We've only to believe in it."

Kandra turned her head to look across the loch before them. Is love a form of magick, she wanted to ask him, but refrained because she wasn't sure what she truly felt for this man. She knew that the sound of his voice, the touch of his hand, the very sight of him, made her heart gallop. The taste of his lips on hers and the tingle of her skin when he caressed her, made her needy. He made her feel the things other women felt and more. Was that because he was the first man to want her? Or was this immense feeling love?

For a few short moments, she wondered, what did love feel like? How did one tell if they were in love?

Lachlan stroked a hand down her bare leg, "We should be returning to the castle, lass."

She looked back at him. "Yes," she spoke simply as she gained her feet. With little thought, Kandra redressed.

He watched her silent movements and wondered. She had a saddened look about her. Had he done something to hurt her again? Slowly he walked over to stand by her.

Kandra glanced up into his concerned green gaze then went back to lacing and tying her boot. Finishing, she stood to face him, but spoke not a word. She stood there and began to braid her hair carefully.

Raising a hand, he brushed his knuckles across her cheek. "Why are ye sad, lass?" His brows were creased in worry.

Kandra closed her eyes to savor the feel of his caress. She spoke softly as she looked back into his green eyes, "I am not sad, but...confused." She spoke honestly as she finished her braid.

"And what 'tis it that confuses ye?" Lachlan smiled softly as his worry abated a bit.

She looked away from him as she pulled away. "What are we? If I am your whore, then is this how one should act? Should we be picnicking by the loch and such?"

Lachlan listened and watched her rave for a minute. He spoke softly in answer. "What do ye wish us to be?"

She stopped and turned to face him, "I do not know."

"And nor do I, lass." He walked to her, taking her hands in his, "Then we shall take this one day at a time, until we ken what we are, Kandra."

She looked at him solemnly, for a long moment. Slowly she inclined her head, "I would like that."

"We've an accord." His mouth captured hers in a deep searing kiss that left her breathless and her head spinning. "Friends shake hands, lass, lovers kiss." He smiled wickedly down at her.

Kandra looked up into his laughing eyes and shook her head, "If you continue to touch me as you are, Lachlan, we shall not return to the castle before nightfall." She looked behind her to where Lachlan's hands were busy caressing her bottom.

With a laugh, he withdrew his hands from her bottom and caught hold of her hand, entwining it with his. Slowly, he walked her over to her horse. Raising her hand to his lips, he brushed a kiss over her knuckles. Releasing her, he watched as she vaulted into Hadwin's saddle. He untied the reins and handed them to her.

Walking over to his horse, he grasped the reins then gracefully settled himself into the saddle. Turning his mount, he led them out of the woods.

Chapter Twenty-Two

*J*ust outside the edge of the woods, Lachlan reined in with Kandra behind him. Six Scotsmen on horseback stood blocking their path. Looking at the men in front of him, Lachlan couldn't identify even one of them, nor their clan, for they were not wearing their tartans.

"I am the Laird Lachlan MacKinnon of the lowlands and War Chief to the Clan MacKinnon, allow us to pass." Lachlan commanded, looking each Scot in his eye as he spoke regally.

A large redhead with a scruffy beard answered, "Give us the bonnie lass, and we'll let ye be on yer way, laird." He sneered at the end.

Anger surged through Lachlan, "Nay," He growled furiously. "Ye can nay have her, unless ye kill me first."

"Go back into the woods, *Sasunnach*." He spoke to her over his shoulder. "Head for the village as fast as ye can, seek help."

She didn't answer as she turned her mount toward the woods. She wouldn't leave him to fight alone, she only prayed two or three of them would follow her.

To Lachlan's dismay, three broke from the group to follow Kandra. Now, he would have to face three Scotsman of his own as well as worry about her.

Kandra rode for the woods as if the hounds of hell were upon her. She could hear the Scots behind her. Drawing rein, she and Hadwin slid to a stop, causing the Scots to fly past her. Digging her heels into Hadwin's side, she drew her sword, charging on the bandits.

Wheeling their horses, they paused at the sight of her charging upon them. The redheaded leader nudged his horse forward to meet her charge. As they met, Kandra swung her sword, striking his with enough force to unbalance him and knock him from his mount.

If it weren't for the anticipation of the battle singing through her blood, she would have laughed when she saw the look of surprise upon his face as she met him. Kandra let loose of Hadwin's reins, flipping herself to the ground to meet her opponent in combat.

Sword in hand, she approached him as he gained his feet shakily. She blocked the sound of his comrades' laughter. "I will give you but one chance to cry off. For this is lunacy and you shall die!"

The redhead looked at her through narrowed eyes. "Bitch!" He spat as he swiped blood from his mouth. "Ye'll pay dearly for that bit of luck."

"It was not luck, I assure you." She circled him with her sword pointed at his chest. "Beg off, I have no wish to kill you."

The redhead threw back his head and laughed. "Ye, defeat me?" He crowed. "What a prize ye are."

"Then let it begin," she swung her sword neatly around her in swooshing circles, listening to it sing. Extending her sword, she clipped his sword, challenging him.

The Scot took the bait charging her. Kandra dodged him with ease, slicing the back of his leg, dropping him. Before the bandit could react, she turned swinging her sword with all of her might, parting his head from his body. Slowly, she turned to the remaining Scots, giving them a deadly stare, as her enemy's blood dripped from her sword.

The dark-haired man nudge his blond friend, "She killed him! She killed Balfour!"

With a deadly glare in her eyes, she raised her sword, pointing at them. "Do you want to share your companion's fate?"

The two looked at each other then back to her. "We have to kill her, Dorell, she killed Balfour." The dark-haired man nudged his blond partner. Raising their swords, they ran toward her, leaving their horses behind.

Kandra braced for the conflict. As they reached her, swinging their swords at her, she dropped to the ground. Knowing she wouldn't be able to take them on at the same time, she tripped the blond haired one. Regaining her feet, her sword met with the dark-haired scoundrel's sword.

The sound of metal rang out as steel clashed against steel. Kandra matched and pared with her opponent. From the corner of her eye she caught sight of his friend moving in from behind her. As he reached her, she sidestepped the dark-haired man's swing, letting it hit only air. The blond pared at her back, but missed. She turned on him with speed and agility.

As she matched blows and pares from each man as they joined forces to defeat her, she couldn't help but to wonder if she would make it out of this alive?

Within minutes of defending herself against the two, her strength was waning and her breath was labored. It felt like she had been fighting these two large men for hours, they were good and she had already been weary. Soon, she was bleeding from various wounds to her arms, legs, shoulder. However, it was her back that was bleeding profusely. Her head was light and she felt her strength draining, quickly.

With clashing blows, they drove her back, until she tripped over a tree branch behind her. As the two moved in for the kill, Kandra tried to scramble to her feet, but knew she was going to die any moment and she prayed Lachlan had gotten away safely.

From out of thin air came an angry war cry that had the two turning to look right. It gave Kandra the second she needed to regain her feet, but she was wobbly.

She watched as Lachlan charged at the two, his sword raised and a murderous glint in his eyes. Kandra drew the attention of the blond one on the left. With renewed energy, she fought with vigor. Lethally, she drove her enemy back until she was paring and thrusting in lightning like strikes.

Her enemy became furious when she landed a smart blow to his backside. Now, she was just having a bit of sport with him. He grazed her hip, but it barely cut through the material of her jerkin and breeches. Kandra met his sword with vengeance twirling under his sword she faced away from him as she ran him through with her sword through his stomach. She heard him gasp rather than saw it. Pulling her sword from his body she pushed him away from her.

She turned in time to see Lachlan dispatch his opponent. He was larger than life, and she was not sure she would ever want to have him look at her, as he was looking at the man lying upon the ground dying.

Lachlan turned to see her now half-unbound golden hair blowing around her in the breeze. Blood was smeared on her cheek. Her white shirt was ripped where she was cut and bleeding. Her thigh had a gash across it. She stood proudly with her feet braced for fighting and her sword held tight in her fist. The sight of her like this made him die inside. '*She could have been killed! By the Gods she could have died*!' He thought as real fear for the first time in his life threatened to overcome him.

Sheathing his sword, he strode to her. Reaching out, he stroked her cheek. The contact was not enough to satisfy him. Grasping her, he pulled her tight to him, crushing his mouth to hers. His hands roamed her from head to her bottom. He lifted her completely off the ground.

She wrapped her legs around his waist as she dropped her own sword to the ground. Diving into the kiss with pure abandonment, her fingers drove into his long hair and she fingered his braids. When neither could breathe any longer, she pulled her mouth from his and looked down at him.

Lachlan searched her face, "Ye scared ten years off my life, lass." He kissed the corner of her mouth. "Are ye all right, *gràdh*?

"Yes, but if you had not come along when you did, I do not know what I would have done." She rested her forehead against his. "I thank you, Lachlan MacKinnon." She pressed another heartfelt kiss to his mouth. "Thank you." She whispered sincerely.

He held her for a few more minutes just to reassure himself that she was whole and hale. Gently, he set her on her feet. "How bad is the leg and arm?"

"I shall survive those," she told him as she tried to ignore the burning of the wound on her back. "You will have to look at my back for I cannot tell, but I think it is the worst."

Lachlan turned her around, lifting her shirt and jerkin to look. Blood streamed down her back, soaking her breeches. He felt white-hot fury roll through him at the sight of her wound. Removing his shirt and folding it to use as a pad for her wound, he grimaced. He gave a shrilling whistle, calling his mount.

His destrier came bounding toward them, Hadwin from the other direction. Kandra reached out, stroking her mounts muzzle. God, she was so very weary. She looked back at Lachlan who was retrieving her sword from where she had dropped it. Her eyes roamed his bare chest and she felt a very female appreciation at the sight. She smiled at him weakly.

"How bad is it?" She frowned as she surveyed his sullen expression. "It needs stitches does it not?"

"Aye, 'tis nay pretty, lass." Lachlan grasped his mounts reins. Muttering in Gaelic he positioned the horse. Walking over to Kandra, he swept her off her feet.

"What are you doing?" She gasped as she clung to his neck. "I am more than capable of walking," she informed him as he put her upon his horse, "And riding, as well."

"Ye'll ride with me so that I may keep the shirt pressed to yer wound." His tone broke no argument. He didn't want her to ride on her own, not only because of her wound, but because he wanted to hold her close to him. "Dinna argue with me this time, *Sasunnach.*"

She took in his tight-lipped expression and read the concern and she thought, perhaps, fear in his gaze. "I will not die, Lachlan, 'tis a minor wound, barely more than a scratch."

He snorted as he handed her the pad then swung lithely up behind her. Lifting her, he slid into the saddle settling her upon his lap. Raising her shirt, he fit the pad to her back, "Now lean back against me, so as the shirt will stay in place."

Gently, Kandra leaned back against his solid form. Laying her head back against his shoulder, she smiled as she felt his arms wrap around her. Sighing, she let herself enjoy the feeling of being so close to him. As they rode, she felt her weariness growing and her eyes became too heavy to keep open. "I am so cold, Lachlan." She shivered in his arms.

"I ken, *gràdh*." He pressed a kiss to the side of her neck and felt the chill invading her body from blood loss. He held her tighter to him and tried to share his body warmth with her. Holding her so that she was secure in his arms, he set his destrier into a full out run, heading for the castle and the help within its walls.

"I am so very tired," she whispered as her eyes drifted closed, trusting Lachlan to keep her on the horse with him. Her breaths were growing more swallow and it worried him.

"Rest, sweetin'." He brushed his lips against her temple as he whispered to her in Gaelic. To feel her here within the circle of his arms made him know that she was safe. Silently, he swore an oath to the Gods that as long as she was with him, she would never come to harm again.

Kandra slipped into the deep darkness. Slowly, images filled her mind.

'In the lower garden of the MacKinnon castle, she sat upon the white stone bench. A babe swaddled in her arms, Bry was playing with her bow and arrows. Kandra smiled as she looked down upon her tiny babe. A hand upon her shoulder had her looking into the greenest eyes she had ever

known. Lachlan bent, brushing a kiss across her temple. He looked down upon their sleeping son. Gently, he took his son in his arms and smiled.

The sky darkened around them and she felt herself falling. She called out to him and reached for her child, but she couldn't reach him. She stood on a stormy battlefield facing her father seated upon his large white destrier. Her sword was in her hand.

"I have come to take you home," Lord Stafford looked down upon his daughter with anger in his face.

"I do not wish to leave here," she shook her head, "Please father do not make me leave him. I love him so."

"Do you not miss your home and family?" He looked down at her angrily. "Do you not love us any longer?"

"I do father, I love you all, but I love him as well." She tried to explain and make him understand, but it felt hopeless.

"But he does not love you." Her father's voice boomed like thunder. "He is but a heathen Scot!"

"I am sure he loves me and..." she looked down at her stomach as she placed a hand over her child.

"And what?" Her father bellowed, making her cringe. She had always feared displeasing him and she knew this would displease him greatly.

She was silent for a long moment. Finally, reining in her courage, she faced him. "I carry his child."

"You would dishonor me in such a way?" Her father spat the words as his blue eyes blazed with ice cold fire. "You are

no more than a common whore. You are no daughter of mine."

She dropped to her knees, hanging her head, "I am sorry, please forgive me? Please, I beg you, forgive me."

Her father faded away and the darkness of nothingness surrounded her. She was utterly alone, so utterly alone.'

Lachlan reached the castle holding her to him as he galloped through the portcullis. A cry was sent out, Rogan, Ian, Duncan, Aidan, and Ferran were awaiting them. Grim faces met him.

"Och, what happened?" Ian strode forward next to Lachlan's horse, grabbing the reins.

"We were set upon by Scotsmen who wore nay tartans." He held the reins and Kandra as he looked down at his cousin. "Ye must take her carefully, her injury is grave, I fear."

Aidan, Ian, and Duncan reached up for her, taking her from Lachlan's hold. Lachlan slid from his horse, Ferran gasped at the blood smeared across his chest.

"By the Gods Lachlan, how bad are ye hurt?" Ferran paled in terror.

"I've but nicks and bruises, Mam, 'tis Kandra's blood yer seein'." He pushed past his mother to reach Kandra in the arms of Ian. "Give her to me."

"Nay, allow me to carry her." Ian shook his head, "Ye've been through hell, and ye would nay wish her dropped."

"Aye, ye've the right of it, but ye must be careful with her." Lachlan strode after him as Ferran led the way.

When they reached the upper hall, Lachlan stopped them. "I want her taken to my chambers." He turned, striding down the hall until he reached his door. He threw the doors wide, allowing them inside his bedchambers.

Ian strode through the open doors and with the utmost care, he gently placed her upon the bed. He looked down at her pale features and frowned. He would pray for her and for his cousin's heart. If this woman lost her life, Ian was afraid that Lachlan would never get over it.

Silently, Aidan, Duncan, and Ian left the room, closing the chamber doors behind them quietly.

Lachlan stared down at her ghostly pallor and felt his heart stutter in his chest. Carefully, he set on the edge of the bed taking her hand, he stroked her fingers. "You fought bravely lass, but now ye have to fight again. Dinna leave me." He lifted her hand and pressed his lips to it.

Ferran walked over, placing a hand upon her son's shoulder, "We have to get her out of those clothes and have a look at her wounds. Can ye help me, lad?"

"Aye Mam," he looked up at his mother and she could read his heart in his eyes. He cared for this girl very much, if not loved her already.

Lachlan stood. Reaching out to Kandra, he untied her jerkin and linen shirt and began working it to her shoulders. Diligently, they removed her shirt. Lachlan slid her boots and breeches off her. Carefully, he checked the wounds on her arm and leg then rolled her over so that Ferran could examine her back.

The cut was long and slashed from her right shoulder down across her back toward the left hip. Lachlan felt the fury build in him again. If the bastards hadn't been dead already, he would have hunted them down and killed them again.

Ferran brought a washbasin of warm water over to the bed. "Cleanse the wound thoroughly, while I fetch my herbs."

"Aye," he took up the wet rag and began washing the blood from her back and the wound. With the bloodiness of her back, the wound had looked much worse than it did once it was clean. Carefully Lachlan probed the wound.

"I am sorry. I am so sorry." When Kandra cried out, he jerked away.

Gently, he stroked her hair, "Tis all right lass, ye've aught to be sorry for."

"I do not want to go," she whispered to him, "Do not make me, please." Her begging wrenched his heart.

"Ye dinna have to go anywhere, lass." He spoke softly to her. "I will nay let anyone take ye away. I promise ye, Kandra, so long as there's breath in my body, no one will harm ye, ever again."

At his words, she seemed to settle. Lachlan finished cleansing her wounds before his mother came back.

Ferran came into the chamber with a chest of herbs and fresh bandages. "We'll put a poultice upon it and let it draw out any septicemia."

His mother went about stitching the worst of the wound. She made an herbal poultice and bandaged Kandra's back. Lachlan lifted her when necessary to help his mother tend to her wounds.

With the bandages in place and Kandra sound asleep, Lachlan sat in a chair feeling fatigued. He closed his eyes, leaning his head back to rest. His own body ached like the very devil.

When Ferran patted his leg, he looked at her with exhaustion.

"'Tis time I looked at yer wounds, my son." She beckoned him over to a stool near her herbal chest. "Ye've got a few that need at the verra least a good bandage."

Lachlan sighed wearily, "I'm fine Mam, dinna fuss over me."

"Yer woman is safe and sound, 'tis time for ye to have yerself looked at." When he merely shook his head, and waved her away, she struck a defiant pose,

"I will nay take nay for an answer. Lachlan McKinnon, if ye dinna let me look at yer wounds, so help me I shall enlist the help of yer kinsmen."

He looked at her for a long moment, glowering, he knew it was useless to argue with his dear little mother, for she would make good on her promise. Reluctantly, he stood, walked over to the stool and sat without another word.

"Just as I thought, ye've got two that could use a stitch or two." She nodded knowledgeably. Quickly, Ferran sewed and bandaged him up.

She inspected him one last time before she declared him nearly fit. "Now, ye'll take some rest for a while."

"Nay," he shook his dark head, his green eyes defiant. "I shall stay with Kandra through the night."

Ferran shook her head, tisking. "I would nay ask ye to leave her." She cupped her son's cheek and stroked a thumb over it. "Ye care for her a great deal, do ye nay?"

Lachlan closed his eyes and indulged himself in this maternal touch. His mother had always been a large part of his life. His father had died when he and Aidan were still young. She had held the clan together and taught them to be the men they were. Never had he seen her spend a selfish moment upon herself.

He looked back at his mother. He couldn't lie to her. "Aye, verra much, she is a strong, brave woman." He paused and pride filled his eyes, "She took on three armed Scotsmen herself." Anger filled his face, "I should nay have let her out of my sight. If I had been with her, she would nay have gotten hurt."

His mother shook her head, "She ken what she was 'bout. She is a brave warrior, and this will nay be the last time she fights."

Lachlan surged to his feet, "I will nay allow her to fight again!"

"Ye can nay stop her. To cage her would kill her, Lachlan, 'twould break her spirit." Ferran shook her head.

He paced away from his mother, "There must be another way. I will nay allow her to face danger ever again so long as there is a breath in my body."

Ferran shook her head, "So much like yer father, Magnus. Ye can nay make one bow to yer will, Lachlan, nay matter how noble the cause."

He whirled on her, "Make nay mistake, I will find a way." Anger rolled off him in waves.

Ferran walked past him clucking her tongue. She paused at the door, "Then yer a fool." She stood with her back to him and felt his anger, "If she seems in pain give her the drink upon the table, 'twill ease her sufferin'."

With that, she was gone. Lachlan stood looking at the door. His mother was wrong. He would find a way to protect Kandra from herself. So, long as she was with him, he wouldn't allow her a chance to find danger, or it to find her.

Turning, he headed for the bed. Careful not to disturb her, he lay upon the bed. Though he was exhausted, sleep did not find him. Gently, turning to face her, he looked at her golden hair as the fading light of the day streamed through the window. The multicolored golden locks fascinated him. Shades bordering on golden-red, brown, white, and wheat shimmered. His eyes followed the shimmer of her hair down over the sheets. At the ends and throughout there was blood. Hers or her enemies, he wondered?

Reaching out, he stroked her hair, he grimaced when she turned her head and hissed in pain. "Hush lass, 'tis all right. Yer safe."

Her eyes fluttered open, they were glazed from loss of blood and the potion his mother had forced down her throat. She licked her dry lips. "Did you save him?"

Lachlan raised a brow, "Who?"

"The babe?" Her eyes drifted shut, "Did you save our babe?" Her last words were a sigh.

He stared at her for a long moment, "Our bairn?" She mumbled in her sleep. "Aye," he assured her, stroking her head.

Waiting a few moments, he shook her gently, "Kandra. Kandra, are ye carryin' my bairn?"

She looked over at him blurry eyed, "Lachlan?" Reaching out, she winced, but she caressed his cheek.

"Aye lass, 'tis me," he turned his face into her palm, pressing a kiss to it.

"I am so very tired." She sighed as her eyes fluttered shut then reopened.

"Ye lost a bit of blood." He stroked her cheek. "Ye gave me a fright, *gràdh*."

She smiled sleepily, "I am far tougher then I look."

He gave her a smile of his own, "Aye, ye are." He paused a moment then tugged her hair gently. "Ye fought verra bravely."

"High praise coming from you, my lord," She grinned softly then yawned. "Who were they? What did they want?"

"I would say 'twas ye they wanted. And I'm inclined to believe 'twas McNair who sent those bastards." He traced her cheek with his fingertip. "I'm afraid we have nay seen the last of him."

"Then we will defeat him once more should he dare to show his face." She spoke strongly, "We shall defeat him together." A soft smile slid across her face as her eyes closed again.

Lachlan looked at her for a long silent moment as her lashes fluttered sleepily. "He shall be defeated," he spoke at long last.

Her eyelids drooped once more and she yawned. She shifted and hissed at the pain.

"Are ye in much pain, *gràdh*?" He searched her tired face.

"No, I will live." She yawned again. Her sleepy eyes searched his, "Will you stay with me awhile?"

"Aye, as long as ye need me." He leaned forward, brushing a kiss across her mouth, "Sleep now."

"Thank you for saving my life." She closed her eyes and drifted off.

"I'll nay allow anything to hurt ye again, *Sasunnach*." He promised, closing his own eyes. Sleep claimed him quickly as well.

Chapter
Twenty-Three

F or nearly two weeks, Kandra stayed in bed as Lachlan commanded. She didn't lack for entertainment, as there were visitors aplenty. Bry visited for hours on end with stories, books, and women's talk while Kandra brushed and braided her hair. Aidan, with his sweetness, told her stories of his legendary escapades, making her laugh. Ian with his charm, talked politics and other taboo subjects for women. Duncan, with his war stories and their talks of battle strategies, kept her busy. He even brought a chest board, for them to match wits from time to time. She loved them all. Especially Lachlan, with his tenderness and care, he treated her as if she were made of glass.

He refused to make love to her, fearing he would hurt her. His kindness was driving her mad.

With the second week at an end, she knew for certain that Maeve was right. She was carrying

Lachlan's child. After carefully counting the time passed since her last curse was upon her, she knew. She was far too late for it to be anything else.

Now, she had to decide when she would tell Lachlan. She didn't know how she would tell him and feared what he would say. Would he cast her out? Would he demand she gave him the child once it was born and keep it from her? Would he care at all for her and their babe, or turn his back on them both?

Doubts and worries plagued her mind. Shoving those thoughts and worries from her mind, she decided it was time she left her sickbed. Throwing back the covers, she swung her feet over the edge of the mattress. The cool stone floor greeted her feet. She wiggled her toes and smiled.

Pushing off the bed, she walked around the room once. The sunlight shinning, through the window drew her to it. The Scottish fields were covered with wild heather in the late summer sun were beautiful. She closed her eyes, letting the warmth from the sun sink into her.

The door creaked open and Lachlan entered. He looked at the empty bed then around the room. Kandra stood bathed in a golden ray, making her look ethereal. His breath seized at the sight of her, she was so glorious to look at. He locked the door behind him so that he could have a few moments alone with her.

His knees felt weak as he strode across the room to stand behind her. Gently, he wrapped his arms around her waist, pulling her back against him. As he nuzzled her neck, she tilted her head to give him better access.

She gave a shudder and sighed at the feel of his body surrounding hers. She had missed him and the feelings only he could give to her. "I have missed you."

"I have been right here, *gràdh*." He continued to nuzzle her neck. "I have gone nay where."

"You have not loved me in two weeks. I have missed you." She reached down between them to stroke the bulge in the front of his kilt. His groan made her smile. She slipped around in his hold to face him. "I want you to make love to me."

He frowned down at her, "Nay, I would hurt ye if we tried."

She took his face in her hands, "I am nearly healed. Even your mother says so." She stretched up to brush a kiss over his reluctant lips. "If you do not make love to me, Lachlan MacKinnon, I will be forced to take advantage of you."

Lachlan couldn't stop the smile that her words caused. He threw back his head and let out a roaring laugh. When his laughter died, he looked back down at her, raising a brow, "Yer a mighty brave, bonnie, lass."

"Do you doubt me, laird?" She began pushing him backwards. "I have felled mightier men then you."

"Aye, but ye've got nay sword." He smiled as she continued to move him backwards.

She reached down stroking his groin, smiling wickedly, "That's quite all right. I intend to borrow yours."

Lachlan groaned as her hand found its way under his kilt to stroke him. Her other hand began tugging his shirt from his waist. "Ye dinna play fair, *Sasunnach*."

"No, I play to win." She began working his shirt up.

"We can nay do this." He spoke in a strained voice as he grasped her wrist. "If ye keep that up lass, there'll be nay turning back."

"I do not wish to stop now." She pressed him onto the bed when his knees hit it. With a hand to his chest, she pressed him back. She straddled his hips. "I intend, my lord, to have my wicked way with you."

Smiling, he grasped her hips. Who was he to argue with a temptress? Lifting her, he impaled her on his rigid throbbing staff.

When she cried out, he froze. "Did I hurt ye, *gràdh*."

She leaned down, brushing a kiss across his lips, "No, you have given me only pleasure." She stroked his cheek with a finger then brushed his lips once more. Sliding her hands down his chest, she sat up, taking him fully inside her.

She began slowly riding him and as her desire and need to reach ecstasy coiled tighter, she rode him harder and faster. She shattered and quaked around him, her inner muscles squeezing his long hard shaft.

Lachlan grasped her hips, thrusting himself into her harder and faster until he found his own release. As the world broke apart around him, he cried her name.

Kandra fell upon his chest in a boneless, numb heap. She sighed as his fingers gently circled the lower half of her back, but avoided her wound. Snuggling into him, she smiled as springy hair on his chest tickled her cheek.

Sedately, she smiled, "Can we stay like this forever?"

Looking at her, Lachlan's hand stilled on her back as he spoke. "Aye, if ye wish it, *gràdh*." Then he began tracing her scar on her side.

"It is impossible," she smiled up at him, "you would tire of me before long."

He looked gravely down at her, "I dinna think that could ever happen."

Her smile faded, "Lachlan, there is something I must..."

The knocking upon the door interrupted her. "Kandra, are ye in there?" The knocking continued, "Why is the door locked?" Bryanna's voice called through the wood.

Lachlan sighed, "If we're quiet do ye think she'll go away?"

Kandra smacked his chest as she called to the little girl on the other side of the door, "Give me a moment Bry, and I shall unlock the door." She scrambled off Lachlan and hissed, "Get dressed, she cannot find us like this."

Grudgingly, he left the bed and straightened his clothing. Once they were decent, Kandra opened the door.

A frowning Bry walk in, "Why did ye lock the door?"

Lachlan answered the question, "I was checkin' Kandra's wound."

Bry gasped in appalled shock, "'Tis nay right, Gram will skin ye if she finds out."

He pinched the bridge of his nose as he regained his composure. Kandra jumped to the rescue, "Bry darling, your father saved my life when we were attacked. He helped your Gram tend my wounds."

The little girl nodded as if this all made sense. She smiled up at her father, "Since Kandra is out of bed now, can she come see how well I shoot my bow?"

"I dinna..."

"Please, please, please Da." Bry clasped her tiny hands and begged him. Then she turned to Kandra herself, "Ye feel well enough, aye?"

Kandra turned her blue eyes on Lachlan, "I do feel quite well, and as we know exercise is good for me." She smiled up at him and held her laughter back.

Lachlan gave her a hard glare. With a pair of green eyes and a pair of blue eyes giving him a begging look, grudgingly, he gave in. "All right, but ye'll nay walk all that way, and we must have a comfortable chair ready for ye to sit upon."

Kandra rolled her eyes and Bry followed suit. Lachlan was far too protective.

Later that day, Kandra sat in the courtyard like a queen, in a chair padded with cushions and a quilt over her legs. She felt like an invalid. As Bry took aim for the fourth time and missed, Kandra sighed, "Lachlan, I cannot take this anymore."

She threw aside the blanket and stood. Ignoring his protests, she walked over to Bryanna. "I will show you a better way."

Bryanna beamed up at her, "Will ye teach me to hit the target?"

"Yes, and more." Kandra took an arrow and the bow from the girl. Though the bow was little, she aimed the arrow and pulled back. When the arrow hit the target dead center, Bry cheered loudly.

Kandra knelt and took the child in her arms, "Now, watch carefully." She demonstrated the movements. "You may not hit it your first time, but each time you practice you will get better and better, until you can hit it every time."

Bry notched the arrow, aimed for the target and pulled back.

"Now, imagine it going into the center." Kandra whispered from behind the little girl. "See it in your mind."

Letting go of the arrow, it flew through the air and hit just short of the target. Bry frowned and looked up at Kandra. "I seen it goin' in, but I still missed."

Kandra squatted down to be at Bry's level. "A very wise man once told me that nothing ever happens overnight. And if you want it, you must work very hard for it, so practice, practice, practice, Sweetheart." Kandra tucked a stray wisp of black hair behind Bry's ear. "Before you know it, you will hit the middle every time." She brushed a kiss over Bry's forehead.

Bry thought on her words for a minute then smiled. "One day, I'll be as good a warrior as ye."

"No, you shall be even better." Kandra pulled the child into a hug, smiling. She only wished she would be around to see the day this small girl became a warrior.

Lachlan came over, smiling brightly at his daughter, "Good shot dumplin', perhaps soon ye'll be replacing one of my archers."

"I'm goin' to practice verra, verra hard, Da, and become a warrior, like Kandra." She smiled at him proudly.

His heart sank. He didn't want his daughter to become a warrior, for he could lose her just as he had come so close to losing Kandra. His smile was stiff as he replied, "Aye, ye just might."

Kandra raised a questioning brow, but kept silent. The look of horror on his face worried her. Was he afraid of what would become of his daughter? Was he afraid Bry would be looked at as unusual and strange? Did he look at her in the same light?

She pushed these thoughts aside. "It is time for me to return to my bed. I am afraid I am not as strong as I had thought. I bid you both a good evening."

She turned to go, but Lachlan's hand on her arm stopped her. "Wait and I shall see ye up to the solar."

"That is not necessary, my lord." She shook her head, but her voice was weak.

"I'll see ye to bed, dinna argue with me, *gràdh*." He growled softly. She was a stubborn woman, but he did not suffer fools. For her to walk all that way alone was foolish. The deep shadows under her eyes told him she was fatigued. He should never have allowed her out here in the first place.

"As you wish, laird." She inclined her head regally. To argue in front of Bryanna would be no use.

"When ye have finished yer practice, take care of yer things, Bryanna." He smiled at her. "I'll see Kandra to bed and stay with her a bit, then we'll take a ride."

Bry clapped her hands, "On yer horse, Da?"

"Aye."

"I'll be ready." She beamed. It was rare for her father to allow her to ride with him upon his giant warhorse, and she treasured the times. One day she vowed to have a warhorse of her own.

"I'll have yer uncles sent to oversee yer practice." Lachlan turned back to Kandra, "Come my lady, 'tis time ye were tucked back in yer bed." Before she could protest, he swept her off her feet and carried her into the keep.

Over the next few days, Lachlan treated Kandra as if she were as fragile as spun glass. Kandra let herself enjoy some of his fussing, but she made a stand at him carrying her everywhere.

"I am not an invalid, Lachlan. I can walk." She stood with her arms crossed as she glared at him from across the room. "If you make one move to carry me, I swear I shall box your ears."

Lachlan frowned at her, "I dinna want ye strainin' yerself, *gràdh*." She was a vexing woman and the shadows under her eyes had not lessened. The sight of those shadows worried him.

"I will not over tax myself walking to the morning meal." She admonished, shaking her head woefully.

Lachlan stood with his hands upon his hips, facing her, "We could have our meal brought up to us." He tried to compromise with hope that she would relax and those dark smudges would disappear.

She crossed her arms over her chest and gave him a look that was sheer determination. "No, we shall walk down to break our fast together with the rest of the castle."

Lachlan knew when he was defeated. Holding up his hands, he approached her. "All right lass, ye win. But if ye start to feelin' weary, ye'll tell me, will ye nay?"

Kandra tipped her face up to his, "Lachlan, I appreciate what you have done for me, but I can take care of myself." She reached up, caressing his cheek. She still hadn't found a way or a time to tell him about the baby.

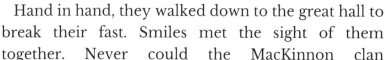

Hand in hand, they walked down to the great hall to break their fast. Smiles met the sight of them together. Never could the MacKinnon clan remember seeing their laird looking quite so happy.

By midafternoon, Kandra had convinced Lachlan that sitting in the garden with the fresh air would do her good. Though she tried to persuade him to go about his duties, he refused and accompanied her and Bry to play.

Bryanna chased after her kitten through the garden paths as Kandra and Lachlan lay in a patch of shaded grass. Lachlan rolled onto his side looking at Kandra. Gently, he stroked his fingertips from the side of her breast to her hip.

She opened her eyes and looked over at him, "If you continue in such a fashion, my dear laird, I shall have to take retributive action."

Lachlan's green eyes laughed, "Are ye threatenin' me, *gràdh*?"

Kandra rolled over and pushed him onto his back. She hovered over him. "No, I am simply making a promise." She nipped his bottom lip.

Lachlan rolled her onto her back very gently so that he was above her now. He read the passion in her blue gaze. His thumb grazed her cheek as his mouth descended to taste hers. His lips brushed over hers in a sweet loving kiss.

At the sound of the warning alarm being called out, Lachlan snapped his head up, concern filling his eyes.

Kandra looked around then turned her gaze to Lachlan in question. She bit her lower lip, worried that it was her father and the whole of the English army.

"'Tis time for ye and Bry to return to the keep." He spoke quietly, but gave her a serious look as he caressed her cheek, "Take her to our chamber and keep her there." He didn't tell her about the cold dread filling him.

"What is wrong?" She could see his anxiousness. She watched him rise nimbly to his feet. He held out a hand, but she ignored it as she gained her own feet. "Tell me what is amiss, Lachlan."

"'Tis aught to worry over right now, lass." He shook his dark head then took her hand. Bringing it to his lips, he pressed a kiss to the inside of her palm. "I want ye to take Bry inside and keep her with ye in our chambers until I fetch ye. Swear it to me, lass, ye'll keep her there, safe with ye."

Kandra searched his green gaze. She knew, no matter how much she begged and pleaded he would tell her nothing until he was ready. Inclining her head, she gave him a stern look. "I will promise you that, but I expect you to tell me what is happening as soon as you return to the keep."

"I will tell ye, what I think ye need to ken, *Sasunnach*." Lachlan smiled down at her, cupping her cheek, he brushed his thumb over her lips. "Dinna worry lass, 'tis most likely aught."

She pressed a kiss to his thumb. Kandra couldn't stop the feeling of dread that their time together was nearly over. "Be safe." She whispered before she pulled away from him.

He watched her gather Bry and head indoors with his daughter and her kitten in tow, then he turned to make his way to the battlements and see what was afoot.

Chapter
Twenty-Four

*L*achlan reached the battlements to find Ian, Aidan, Duncan, and Rogan already there. He scanned the hills and saw the men dotting it. Horsemen, as well as foot soldiers, stood waiting.

"Can ye tell who 'tis?" Lachlan squinted into the sun. Dread filled him at a single thought, "The English Lord come to claim Kandra?" He spat the words.

All four men heard the note of panic as well as heat in his voice, but chose to ignore it.

"We can nay tell from this distance, laird, but we have scouts out already." Rogan spoke from his post at the wall.

"Are the villagers in danger?" Aidan looked over at the village to their left. "Should we move them within the walls?"

Lachlan looked at the hostile group on the hill. "Aye, but we must do so quickly."

"I shall send riders out to warn them." Rogan turned and strode away, shouting orders as he went.

"I fear this is only the beginnin' of somethin' verra, verra bad." Lachlan spoke ominously as he looked from the men outside his castle to his brother and cousins. Fear of losing Kandra curled in his belly, making him want to run and hide her where her English father would never find her.

It was not long before riders left the ranks on the hill. Well before they reached the castle, their MacNair and MacDonald plaids were seen. Four men came within shouting distance of the wall.

"Lachlan MacKinnon, laird of this keep and War Chieftain of the Clan MacKinnon," Angus MacNair shouted.

Lachlan walked to the edge of the wall. "Why are ye trespassin' upon my lands, McNair? Yer nay welcome here."

"I want the English woman." Angus called back. "If ye dinna hand her over, we shall lay siege to yer castle and take her by force."

"Yer a bigger fool than I had thought, Angus. And ye shall fall with him, MacDonald." Lachlan shook his head, "She's mine, Angus, ye can nay have her."

"Then yer fate 'tis sealed." Angus shook his fist angrily at Lachlan. He wheeled his horse around and charged back to his waiting men. The MacDonald laird followed behind him.

Lachlan shook his head. "We must hurry in getting our people inside the castle walls. I fear MacNair and MacDonald shall take it out upon them."

"Aye, laird, we'll have the clan behind the walls soon." Rogan frowned in concentration.

"Check the battlements, armory, and stores. From the look of things, we may be well out numbered." Lachlan looked at his cousins and his brother. "I will need every available sword." He paused and frowned, "Send rides out to our allies for aid."

"Aye," the four men said in unison.

"Start yer inspections and I shall join ye shortly. I've to speak with Kandra." He turned and hurried toward the keep.

He stormed through the keep, shouting orders for the castle to make ready to house the villagers. Up to the solar, he strode. Reaching his chambers, he threw open the door.

Kandra and Bryanna sat upon the bed reading and when he stormed in, they merely looked up at him. What a picture they made, he thought for a long moment. The lass with her golden locks and his dark-haired daughter sitting together. It was a sight that spoke to his heart.

Kandra closed the book. "We shall continue this later, darling." She pressed a kiss to the top of Bryanna's dark head.

"Bry, go find yer Gram and ask her to seek out Rogan and help prepare for the villagers to arrive." He watched Bry scoot off the bed and run for the door. When it closed, Kandra stood from the bed and pulled her sword from under the pillow next to her. After sheathing her sword, she faced him expectantly.

She looked into his green gaze and tilted her head, "What is it?"

"MacNair is here and he's brought the MacDonald clan with him." Lachlan reached out, pulling her into his arms.

"They are here for me, are they not?" She looked up into his eyes for the truth. "What are you not telling me?"

He avoided her gaze. "Yer right, they're here for ye," he looked back into her eyes as he spoke, "But I will nay let them near ye, I swear this to ye, as long as there is breath still left in my body, *gràdh*, I will protect ye."

His words made her melt. No man had ever treated her so wonderfully, or treasured her so very much. She caught his face in her hands, "Tell me the rest, I have a right to know."

Silence spread between them as he debated the issue. She was right, she may as well know. "'Twould appear we're out numbered as well, but we will ken more tonight when our scouts return."

"How bad do you think it is?" She frowned in concern as she released his face. She could offer the help of her men, as well as herself. It would be a minor boon, but she feared it wouldn't help nearly enough.

He sighed in frustration, "We'll need every sword we can lay our hands on, but I still dinna like the look of things."

"You have the service of my men and myself." She offered without hesitation. If she asked it, her men would fight side by side with these Scotsmen.

"I thank ye, lass, we could use yer men." He frowned, "'Twill nay make a large difference I fear, but every man helps."

"You have my sword as well." She stepped away from him as he glared down at her.

"I will nay allow ye to fight." He growled resoundingly. "Ye could be captured or killed. I will nay allow it."

"Then you are a fool to turn my sword away." She strode away from him to the open window. "Perhaps it would be wiser to send me out now and save the bloodshed."

Lachlan roared with fury. "I will nay allow MacNair to have ye." He strode over to her, grasping her shoulder, spinning her around to face him. "Yer mine, and only mine! Nay other man will ever have ye!"

She jerked from his grasp. "I am your wench, your whore, but I do not belong to you, Lachlan MacKinnon. I belong to no man."

"In that, yer wrong, lass," he ran an assessing eye over her. "Ye will nay belong to any other man, save me." He turned away angrily, stomping toward the door.

"Lachlan wait," she called out to him. He turned to look at her silently. "I want to fight by your side."

"Nay lass. Even if I have to chain ye and lock ye away, ye'll nay fight." With that, he turned and walked out the door.

Kandra had never been so angry with him. He was a fool to throw away a good sword arm for pride's sake. With a determined step, Kandra left their chambers to seek out her men.

In the storeroom, where her men were being held, the men sat huddled and speaking in hushed tones. When Kandra entered, they fell to silence. Raff stepped forward to greet her.

"It is about time you came for us girl." He hugged her to him. "We're brimming with questions."

"I have to make a request of all of you." She looked around the group. "The castle is under siege and the MacKinnon's are sorely out numbered." She paused as she looked from man to man. "I ask you to pledge yourselves to battle for the MacKinnon laird."

"Why should we, he is our captor?" A voice came from the rear of the men.

"Yes, that he is, but these men outside the gates wish to do me harm. They want to kidnap me and use me." She spoke, then shivered at the thought. "I will fight with you, side by side."

"No girl, you will not." Raff spoke gruffly, "If these men want you, it would be foolhardy for you to leave the castle walls."

"Perhaps you are right, Raff." She bowed her head. Though she knew she wouldn't sit idly by while these men fought for her, if there was any way to fight beside her men and Lachlan, she would find it. She would be in the fray of things when the time came.

"I wish you to pledge yourselves to his lordship for the coming battle." She didn't see one man who wouldn't carry arms to defend her and honor her request.

In turn, each one dropped to his knee saying, "Yes, m'lady."

"Bless all of you, please follow me and I shall take you to the MacKinnon laird." She turned from the room, letting her men follow in her wake. As they crossed the courtyard, many of the MacKinnons working to prepare for battle stopped to stare at the English Knights following their lady.

Lachlan stood at the armory with Ian. He turned when Ian tapped him on the shoulder. Kandra led her men to him, kneeling with them, in front of the laird.

"We are here to pledge our English swords to your cause, Lachlan MacKinnon." She looked up at him and grasped the hand he offered.

"I accept and appreciate yer help. 'Twill nay be an easy battle." He shook his head, "We are sorely outnumbered."

One young soldier stepped forward. "We are willing to lay down our lives for our Lady."

Lachlan lifted her hand to his lips, "Ye inspire loyalty, lass."

"Because my men know that I would willingly lay down my life for them as well." She looked defiantly into his green gaze.

"We've been through this, *Sasunnach*, I will nay allow ye to fight." Lachlan growled down at her, "I forbid ye to fight."

"Could I not at least man a bow on the wall?" She glared at him.

"Nay. No." the voices of Raff and Lachlan came at the same time.

"We've been through this, *gràdh*," Lachlan shook his head in frustration.

"As have we, girl." Raff glared at her.

Kandra once again bowed her head demurely. "I would think you would appreciate another person skilled in battle." With that said, she turned and stormed off, muttering under her breath.

Raff watched her walk away and shook his head. "She gave in far too easily, watch her laird, or you shall find her on the battlefield beside us." He gave Lachlan a hard stare. "Do not give into her, no matter how hard she tries to fight you. If she goes upon that field, I fear we are fighting a losing battle."

"Aye, I agree with ye." Lachlan shook his head, "Is she always so stubborn?"

"I am afraid she was born that way." Raff laughed, "And she gets worse with age."

"Tell us where you wish us to help, my lord." Raff gestured to his men.

Lachlan directed them to where he had need of them most. Each man was given back a sword and his armor. He sighed in relief when he sensed no animosity between his people and the Englishmen.

The rest of the day and that night were quiet. Lachlan had men stationed throughout the castle along the walls, watching for trouble. After the evening repast, he escorted Kandra to his chambers.

He was weary, but he was filled with lust for his woman as well.

She walked in ahead of him, her back stiff and straight, her shoulders back and her demeanor hostile, but silent. Walking over to the chest of drawers, where her hairbrush laid, she began unpinning her hair in angry movements with her back to Lachlan.

He watched her angry movements and frowned. As her hair tumbled over her shoulders, he moved forward. She picked up her hairbrush and began the vigorous strokes. Taking the brush from her hand made she gasp in surprise. He placed a staying hand upon her shoulder, not allowing her to turn around. "I'll brush it for ye, *gràdh.*"

She scowled at the tapestry covered wall with her arms crossed. "Should you not be out fighting a war, my lord?"

Lachlan ignored the sarcasm that dripped from her voice. "I do believe I have one on my hands already."

She pulled away from him. Turning, she faced him with open fury. "It is unfair of you all. How many times, must I prove myself to you, before you will acknowledge me as a warrior?" She railed at him as anger and hurt spilled over into her voice.

He stepped toward her, but she skirted him, "I ken what a fine warrior ye are. But I can nay let ye go out there." He stalked after her, "Yer still hurt, what if yer wound reopens?"

She slipped away from him knowing that if his arms made it around her, her argument would be lost. "What if you are killed? It is war Lachlan, anything can happen."

As she went to move around him, he reached out snagging her waist. Though she protested, she didn't put up much of a fight. "Aye, right ye are. I could die on the morrow."

"Let go of me." She struggled slightly, but without much sincerity.

Ignoring her protests, he swept her into his arms and placed her upon the bed. His large body covered hers. Looking down at her, he trapped her hands on either side of her head. "I dinna want ye out there for selfish reasons, *gràdh*." Lachlan was silent for a long moment as he memorized her beautiful face. Grudgingly, he admitted his fear, "I can nay let ye fight. For my heart 'twould die if somethin' happened to ye, *Sasunnach*. If ye were out there I would nay be able to concentrate for worryin' about ye."

Kandra let her lashes drift shut as she took in his words. A single tear escaped her eyes and ran down her cheek. When she finally looked back up at him, her eyes shimmered with unshed tears. "I do not want to think of you dying either, Lachlan. I care for you far too much." She swallowed audibly, "But I do not think I can sit here in this castle awaiting the end of this battle and for you to come back to me. I need to be with you out there, for I am as much a warrior as you."

He thought for a long moment then leaned forward to brush his lips over hers. "I care for ye as well, *gràdh*." His look turned thoughtful, "I want ye to consider this as well, ye may be carrying my bairn in yer belly. If ye fight ye would risk more than yerself."

Kandra stared at him in shock. She licked her dry lips. "Lachlan, I ..." She just couldn't say it. Kandra couldn't tell him what she knew. She was uncertain as to how he would react.

He could read the uncertainty in her eyes. If she knew she was carrying his child, she would tell him, wouldn't she? "What *gràdh*? Tell me."

"I...I..." She just couldn't take the chance. This man cared for her, but didn't love her. "Make love to me, please, Lachlan."

He looked at her for a long moment. Deep in his heart, he had wished she would tell him she was with child. He would have wasted no time getting her to a priest and making her his forever. To hell with the coin and even her father.

Lachlan made slow love to her, memorizing every curve, every hollow and plain of her body. His fingers touched, and stroked her. She arched and cried out when he brought her to pleasure over and over again.

Kandra touched him everywhere, kissing, caressing, and stroking him into a wild frenzy. In the back of her mind, she feared this would be one of the last nights she would spend in this man's arms. Tears coursed down her cheeks as he made such sweet, aching love to her.

When at last they were sated, she curled into him. Desperately, she clung to him. "Do not leave me." She whispered into the darkness around them.

Lachlan curled his body around hers as he stroked her hair and kissed her soundly, "Nay before I have to, *gràdh*."

Kandra peered up at him and smiled softly, "What does that word mean?"

"*Gràdh?*" He raised his brow in question. When she nodded, he smiled, "'tis an endearment, such as darlin' or love" he spoke softly then brushed a soft kiss over her lips. This sparked another round of tender passionate lovemaking.

They dozed for a short time. When they woke once more, they made hard desperate love that left them panting and weak.

Again, they slept and again, twice more, they made slow tender love. Lachlan lay awake for a long time after their last round of lovemaking and thought of how he would keep Kandra from fighting on the morrow. He couldn't let her leave the castle. With firm determination, he made his plan. She would be angry and hurt, but later, he prayed that perhaps, she would understand his decision. He feared she would not understand and he would lose her forever, but at least she would be safe, he reasoned.

Looking down at her face in the glow of the candlelight, he brushed his thumb over her lower lip. "*Mo ghaol ort.*" He leaned forward and whispered his words of love against her lips. Lachlan finally gave into his heart and allowed it to love again. He loved this woman with his entire heart and soul, but he couldn't tell her.

Chapter
Twenty-Five

*T*hough they tried to hold back the dawn, it came against Kandra's wishes. She looked at the gray morning and frowned. She looked at the man who lay next to her. His long, black hair was spread out over the pillow. His face was relaxed and boyish as he slept. Lips parted in slumber, his breathing even, she wanted to reach out and touch his bristly cheek.

Kandra leaned over him, memorizing his face. She would betray his trust this day, she would defy him and she would fight. And worst of all, she would lose him.

"I love you, Lachlan McKinnon." She whispered, then bent, brushing a kiss to his lips. He came awake under her lips. His mouth met with hers. She stroked his cheek and tried to hold back the tears she felt pricking at the back of her eyes.

She would be damned if Angus MacNair would kill the man she loved. She'd kill Angus with her own blade. Lachlan would have her at his back whether he wanted her there or not.

Lachlan rolled her over to cover her body with his own. He stroked her cheeks, her hair and tasted her lips. "Yer enough to make a man want to stay abed all day," he nipped her bottom lip.

"Is that an offer, laird?" She spoke with a sultry look.

"Perhaps after I have driven the MacNairs and MacDonalds from my lands, we'll stay abed for a day." He brushed another kiss over her lips. "For now, I must join my men."

'So, must I', she thought to herself. "Let me help you dress, Lachlan." She pushed off the bed and began the task of gathering his shirt and boots.

Walking to where he stood, after his morning absolutions, she helped him to dress. Walking back to his chest, she pulled his MacKinnon tartan from it. She held it to her face breathing in his scent. Pressing a kiss to it, she handed it to him.

With great care and pride, Lachlan laid out his plaid and began folding the complicated pleats in the material, and quickly donned the garment in the traditional Scottish fashion. Sadness filled her, unshed tears shimmered in her eyes. "Come *gràdh*." He held out his hand to her when he was finished. When she took it, he sat upon the bed, pulling her onto his lap.

"I will nay fall this day." He used his fingers under her chin to make her look at him, "I shall come back to ye." He kissed her soundly.

Slipping off his lap, she stood proudly before him, "Allow me to fight beside you." She was every inch the warrior he had come to know and respect. But she was still the woman he loved and he was afraid to lose her.

"Nay lass, ye will nay fight." Lachlan shook his dark head, crossing his arms over his massive chest. "We're outnumbered nigh on two to one, even with yer men fightin' beside us."

"And one man can turn the tide in our favor. Allow me to fight beside you." She stepped toe to toe with him, looking him straight in the eyes. "Please, Lachlan?"

Lachlan reached out, grasping her arms as he shook her slightly, "Yer a woman, nay a man, and I will nay risk yer life!"

Kandra tried to pull away from him, but she couldn't break his grip. "I am a warrior."

"Nay lass, yer a woman and ye will nay be in this battle." He frowned down at her as he loosened his grip. He couldn't risk her life. Damn it, he thought, he wouldn't risk it. If he lost her as he had Kerra, he didn't know how he would go on living. "I forbid ye to bear arms this day."

"Then you are a fool, fighting for nothing!" She spat at him. She wouldn't be sitting docilely by while he was off fighting for her. She needed no one to fight for her. She could fight for herself. Raising her chin haughtily, she glared at him, "I do not need you to protect me, I can take care of myself."

"Yer a stubborn wench!" He glowered at her. "Understand me, Kandra, ye will nay leave this castle, or heaven save ye from me."

She blanched slightly at his menacing words and his threatening tone, "You do not scare me, MacKinnon." She crossed her arms over her chest as she spoke haughtily.

Lachlan grabbed her and pulled her to him and up on her tiptoes so that they were nose to nose as he spoke. "I dinna care what yer a'scared of, but if I see yer bothersome hide upon that battlefield, I shall run ye through myself."

Kandra jerked out of his hold. "You are such a stubborn fool!" She paced away from him. "I could be helpful with my sword or my bow, but you refuse because of your stupid pride."

"Promise me, Kandra, ye'll stay within the castle walls." He spoke softly as he watched her pace.

She stood mutely before him, crossing her arms over her chest stubbornly. She would not make him a promise she couldn't keep.

"Fine lass, be stubborn, but heed me, ye will nay fight this day." Lachlan reached out, grasping her. Before she could so much as utter a sound, he pulled her to him. His mouth crushed over hers in a consuming kiss that left her breathless and shaken.

Releasing her, he grabbed his sword sheathing it as he went, he reached the door and looked back at her flushed face, "*Mo ghaol ort.*" He whispered. Opening the door, he walked through it without a backwards glance. Closing it behind him, he locked it firmly. She would rail at him later, but she would be alive, he assured himself.

Kandra heard the door lock and ran to it. Pounding on it, she called to him, "Do not do this, Lachlan, please?"

Her unshed tears trickled down her face as she beat upon the door, "I cannot bear the thought of you out there with me locked in here." She waited for a response then, she hit the door, with her fist, one last time. "Damn you, Lachlan MacKinnon, damn you!" She rested her forehead against the cool wooden door.

Lachlan strode away, "I am already damned, my love." He whispered to himself.

As he reached the great hall, he strode to his mother. "I have locked Kandra in my chamber. She is to remain there until this is over, or unless ye must use the passageway for escape.

Ferran looked up into his pain filled eyes, "I shall only allow her out if needs be."

He inclined his head regally. "I shall join my kinsmen to break my fast, then we shall deal with the bastards at our door." He turned and joined the ranks of his men at their tables, ignoring the high table, for today Lachlan was just another warrior.

Ferran went to the kitchen to fetch a tray for Kandra. She hurried up the stairs to the solar. She swung open the door to find Kandra braiding her hair.

"Look lively lass, break yer fast to give ye strength." Ferran smiled at her. "I'll be back with yer things soon enough. But ye will nay go off to battle if ye dinna eat somethin'." She admonished the younger woman.

Kandra stared at Ferran in disbelief. "You are going to help me get out of here?"

"Aye, but ye can nay go without yer armor, or yer sword." Ferran turned back to the door. "Eat while I fetch yer things."

Kandra walked over and sat at the table. She ate no more than a few bites, as she had no stomach for more than that. Ferran appeared, towing her armor and sword, Kandra stared at her in disbelief.

"Come with ye now, lass, times a wastin'. We must prepare ye for battle." Ferran waved her forward.

Kandra stood before the smaller woman, who helped her don her armor. "Will Lachlan not be angry with you?"

"Ye worry about fightin' those MacNairs and MacDonalds. I'll worry about my son's wrath." She smiled as she fastened Kandra's breastplate. "Now we must disguise ye so that Lachlan and the others dinna ken 'tis ye."

Ferran pulled a cloak from Lachlan's chest, she tutted and frowned. Rummaging through, she pulled a MacKinnon tartan from the depths of the chest. "Aye, these shall do nicely."

She fastened the tartan over Kandra's armor then secured the cloak in place with a broach of Lachlan's. Looking up at the younger woman, Ferran smiled softly. "Oren will meet ye with yer mount. He'll tell ye where to go from there. Ye dinna want to be discovered by Lachlan and the other men."

Kandra impulsively hugged Ferran to her, "Thank you Ferran, for all you have done for me."

"Ye make sure to guard my sons' backs. I want all of my boy's back safely." She shook her head, "Dinna reveal yerself, 'til the battle has started. Then kill Angus MacNair, the men will pay ye little enough heed being a woman."

Kandra bowed to Ferran's wisdom, "I shall do everything within my power to keep them safe." She turned for the door, but Ferran's voice stopped her.

"Be safe, daughter of my heart." Ferran shooed Kandra out the door. "Go with the Gods, my brave warrior daughter." Tears shined in the older woman's eyes.

Kandra flashed Ferran a smile then fled down the hall, her long dark cloak billowing out behind her as she ran. Reaching the bottom of the stairs, she pulled the cloak farther over her face, shielding it from people as she passed. Racing through the courtyard, she slipped into the stables, where Hadwin stood saddled already. Oren came over to her.

"M'lady, yer to blend into the ranks of our men. With yer tartan shown it will make it all the more, easy. Dinna let Lachlan, or any of the others, get a look at ye. 'Twill be hell to pay if the laird should catch sight of ye." Oren held Hadwin while she swung up into the saddle. "One more thing." He handed her a bow and quiver of arrows. "I've heard yer quite handy with these."

"I am," she smiled down at him. "Thank you, Oren, for all of your help." She took the hand that he offered her and shook it.

"Come back to us safely, lass." Oren inclined his head to her.

"I shall, I promise." She squeezed his hand slightly. She liked Oren and his kind ways. Kandra wished she could repay Ferran and Oren for their kindness. Perhaps she could, she thought for a moment and smiled slightly.

"Let the Gods watch over ye, lass." He released her hand and waved her off, "The ranks are beginnin' to form. Join in the fourth row back from the laird. 'Twill keep ye close enough to watch over his stubborn hide."

Kandra turned her mount and walked him out of the stables. Making sure her hood was well drawn on this chilly Scottish morning, leaving her face well hidden. She settled Hadwin in the middle of the fourth row back from Lachlan. Looking around her, she noticed she wasn't the only one wearing a cloak and that made her sigh in relief. For a moment, she wondered if this could be Ferran's doing. Kandra smiled to herself, she dealt well with the Lady Ferran, as they were much alike.

Silently, she said a prayer to protect her men, herself, and the MacKinnon's alike. As they rode out of the castle, she felt the calm of battle readiness wash over her. Her palm itched to draw her sword and lay waste to the MacNair and the MacDonald bastards.

The MacNairs and the MacDonalds were ready for them as they rode into battle. Kandra took up her bow and arrows as she sped through the ranks. Within moments, she found herself in the front of the line. Using her knees, she guided Hadwin, as her hands fired arrow after arrow taking down MacNairs as well as MacDonalds.

As they drew in upon their enemy, she replaced her bow over her shoulders and pulled her sword. The clash of men and steal was fierce. Men cried out, horses screamed, but Kandra concentrated on killing as many of the enemy as she could get to with her sword.

Losing her grip on Hadwin, who reared, she fell to the ground. Rolling, she quickly rose to her feet. Her sword swinging as she engaged in battle. The cloak was a nuance. She ripped it from her throat, throwing it to the ground. Her opponent hesitated and she dispatched him quickly with a slice across his midsection.

She spied Lachlan engaged with a MacDonald, not far from her. Kandra gasped as she saw another MacDonald coming up behind Lachlan's back. She was still too far away to do anything with her sword. Sheathing her sword, she removed her bow from her shoulder and an arrow from her quiver. She shot and watched the arrow pierce the man's neck. He screamed and she drew her sword, just as a MacNair swung his sword at her.

Kandra worked her way toward Lachlan, slashing, fighting, and killing. When she spotted Duncan, she smiled when he saluted her. Ian gave her a wink, but there was no sign of Aidan and that worried her.

She turned back to where Lachlan was fighting and watched, in albeit horror, as Angus MacNair came up behind Lachlan to deliver a killing blow. She was only a few feet from Lachlan, but it felt like miles.

Grasping her sword tight, she ducked, swinging swords and blocked blows to meet Angus MacNair. Just as his sword swung down to kill Lachlan, she met his sword, staggering under his strength. She smiled viciously up at him.

A ringing blow near his head had Lachlan looking over his shoulder. He froze when he saw Kandra blocking the fatal blow Angus would have delivered. With no option, he turned back to his own fight as two men were trying to make short work of him. He would deal with her damnable hide later, he thought angrily.

Angus looked at her in shock. "What are ye doin' here, lass?"

Kandra pushed his sword away easily, "Saving Lachlan's life." She swung her sword at Angus.

"I dinna want to fight ye, lass." He blocked her advances.

"Then runaway and take your men with you." She spoke as she struck her blade against his, driving him back.

"I can nay do that, lass, I've come for ye. I want ye to be my wife. I am in love with ye." He huffed as he blocked her blows once more.

"Well I am not in love with you!" She moved her blade swiftly to his throat. "I love Lachlan." Kandra told him as she pressed the tip of her sword in his neck.

Though she had Angus subdued, the MacKinnons were severely out numbered. All around her, men were falling. They had little hope of winning.

"Ye can try to kill me lass, but it will nay save the MacKinnons. They will die here today." Angus spat angrily. "Yer Lachlan, he will be cut to ribbons and lay dying in a river of his own blood."

Kandra looked over her shoulder to where Lachlan was fighting, two on one. "No," she whispered in despair.

It was the opportunity Angus was waiting for. He moved her blade and swung with his. Kandra turned back, meeting him, but he drove her to her knees with the force of the blow. She rolled out from under his sword and met him from the side.

"I will kill you!" She spoke between clenched teeth. "If we die on this field today at least I shall have the honor of killing you first."

Though he was stronger, she was quicker and fleeter of foot than he was. She dodged his blade. Kandra pared and thrust with her own sword, until he was running around in circles. When she saw, him falter, she took the killing shot. Her blade slid into his stomach, running him through.

As Angus fell at her feet, she heard the familiar sound of trumpeters. Turning, she saw a regiment of horses pouring over the hill, carrying the Stafford banners bearing a golden Falcon on a black background. Her heart thumped in her chest.

Was it Jonas, or was it her father? Kandra let out a cry and ran for the horses. Placing her fingers between her lips she gave a shrill whistle. Hadwin came running to her. She grasped his saddle and pulled herself up at a run. Taking the reins, she rode, hell bent for leather toward the approaching soldiers.

A grin split her face as she looked upon her brother and father leading the way. She reined in, turning Hadwin so that she could ride with them as they met.

She prodded Hadwin once they we closer. She rode easily with her father and brother. "We have to help the MacKinnons, Father."

Lord Stafford raised a brow at her, but said not a word. She spoke quickly. "They are fighting for me, father. Raff and the rest are in there somewhere." She explained shortly with a worried expression upon her face.

With more than two hundred men pouring over the hill, the MacDonalds, and the MacNairs, decided to turn tail and run. The MacKinnons didn't give chase as they rallied around their laird, ready for a new battle with the English.

Raff strode forward to meet Lord Stafford. "Greetings, my lord."

Lord Stafford reined in, in front of Raff. "What has happened here, Raff?"

"Those cowards wished to relieve Lord MacKinnon of your daughter, but the MacKinnons fought for her." Raff explained with a grin.

"Where is the man who dares hold my daughter for ransom?" Lord Stafford bellowed.

Lachlan pushed his way through the crowd to face the English lord. "I am Lachlan MacKinnon, laird of this land and War Chieftain of the Clan MacKinnon."

Lord Stafford took in the man before him, he was battle weary, blood dripped from his claymore, and he was cut in numerous places. "You dare to hold my daughter for ransom? Do you wish for war, Lord MacKinnon?"

"Nay sir, yer daughter attacked me and my men in haste and unprovoked." Lachlan looked over at Kandra. His eyes scanned her for signs of injury. He wanted to take her in his arms, to thrash her, then to kiss her senseless. She had disobeyed him and he was determined to seek his retribution, but at the same time, he was dying just to hold her and assure himself she was safe. "I felt it would teach her a lesson, but I will admit, my lord, I thought her a lad, until she removed her helm."

Lord Stafford had not missed the assessing gaze this Scotsman gave his daughter. He saw the anxious look upon his daughter's face as well. Something was going on here that he was not yet privy to, but in time, he would find out. "And still, you presume to take her prisoner?" Edward boomed.

Lachlan shook his head then looked back at the Englishman, "Lord Stafford, if ye wish to battle, we may, but if nay then I've wounded to see to." He gave Kandra a hard look, "We shall discuss yer wayward daughter later."

She was surprised when Lachlan turned his back on her father and began issuing orders for the wounded and the dead to be taken care of. Kandra nudged her mount forward, but her father put out a hand.

"Where do you think, you are going?" He growled at her.

"These people laid down their lives to save me, I will go help with the wounded, and stay with them until this is settled." Kandra gave him a hard look.

Lord Stafford inclined his head, "You are an honorable woman, your mother would have been proud of you."

Kandra smiled softly, "Thank you father." Nudging Hadwin, she galloped after Lachlan.

Lord Stafford watched his daughter ride away, then turned to his son. "What do you know about this?" He waved after his daughter.

Jonas frowned, "All that I know father is that the heathen bastard took us captive and kept us separated." Jonas glared at MacKinnon, "I fear he has ruined her. Before I left, she told me he had not harmed her, but treated her as a woman instead of a warrior."

"Ah," Lord Stafford turned his horse, "We shall make camp here. Inform the ranks." He grunted, "I think we may be here for a while."

Chapter
Twenty-Six

*K*andra headed for the castle far behind Lachlan. Meeting Oren at the stables, she handed over Hadwin to him. She hurried into the great hall that had been turned into an infirmary to help with the wounded.

Kneeling over a young MacKinnon man, she brushed back a lock of dark hair, "Thank you," she whispered after she had finished bandaging his leg.

From patient to patient, she worked on minor wounds. She stood, rubbing her aching back after more than three hours of bending over wounded men.

Hands on her back had her gasping, she turned to see Lachlan standing behind her. When he pulled her to him and reached around her with his large hands on her back, she groaned at the immense pleasure of his touch.

After a few minutes, he stopped massaging her back. Before she could utter a word, Lachlan swept her off her feet. Heading for the solar, he climbed the stairs. He strode down the hall toward his chambers with true purpose. Walking through the open door, he kicked it shut behind them. Arriving at the bed, he dumped her unceremoniously upon it.

Hands braced on his hips, he scowled down at her, "What the bloody hell were ye doin' out there? Did I nay forbid ye to fight, and yet ye did so anyhow, *Sasunnach*?" He growled down at her.

Kandra came up on her knees to meet his anger, "I saved your life." She choked on the lump of emotion in her throat, "You promised me you would come back to me, but you would not have without me." Tears coursed down her face and she seemed unaware. "He was going to kill you, but I stopped him. I stopped him. I could not let him harm you."

The sight of her kneeling on his bed with tears streaming down her cheeks, and the hurt written upon her face, broke his heart. "Dinna cry, *Sasunnach*. Shh, *gràdh*." He sat upon the bed and gathered her into his arms as he rained kisses over her tear streaked face. His words in Gaelic she couldn't understand, but she wrapped her arms around him just to hold him and know he was safe. "*Tha gaol agam ort.*" He whispered over and over as he pressed kisses to the top of her head, her face, then her cheeks.

As her tears subsided, he lifted her to stand on the floor. Slowly, he removed her clothing, checking her for wounds as he went. He breathed a sigh of relief when she appeared unharmed.

Taking her hand in his, he led her to the washstand. Wetting a cloth, he cleansed her whole body. By the time, he was through, her entire body was humming with need for him.

Giving as good as she got, Kandra took the cloth and set it aside as she began undressing Lachlan little by little, running her hands over his wounded skin. She found only nicks and scraps, all of which had already stopped bleeding. Taking a new cloth, she began bathing him slowly, gently, and enticingly.

Lachlan could take no more of her sweet torture. His body was hard, aching with need to be inside of his woman. Pulling the cloth from her hand, he threw it aside. He swept her into his arms.

As he strode to the bed, she pressed kisses to the hollow of his throat. Nibbling and nuzzling, she tasted the saltiness of him. She squeezed her eyes shut as she tried to memorize the taste of him.

He gently laid her upon the bed. Standing over her, he looked down upon her glorious body. Slowly, his eyes roamed over her, taking in every detail of her from her golden hair spread across the coverlet down over her flat stomach to the slightly darker golden curls at the apex of her thighs. His hungry gaze devoured her long, sensuous legs. He imprinted a picture of her in his mind. Forever would he see her, gloriously naked, upon his bed, with passion filling her seductive blue eyes. He would see her playing with Bry, or laughing in the garden. An image of her dancing in the great hall, smiling radiantly, would haunt him.

Neither spoke the words, but each knew this would be the last time they would be together. As Lachlan joined her on the bed, she clung to him, running her fingers through his long, thick hair, fingering his braids. His lips roamed her face and he tasted her tears.

His large hand cupped her cheek, his thumb caressing it and wiping those tears away. He didn't want her to be sad. "Dinna cry, *gràdh*. I want to see a smile in yer beautiful eyes as I love ye." He kissed away her tears.

"Love me, Lachlan." She whispered as she met his mouth in a soft kiss that turned urgent. She wanted him more than she had ever wanted anything in this world. She poured every ounce of her love for him into this one kiss.

Lachlan pressed her down into the bedding as he devoured her. His hands stroked her, causing her to sigh into his mouth. The taste of her was driving him mad with need.

The desperation she felt was building. She had no clue how she would walk away from this man when the time came. If only he loved her, she would stay. She would give him her heart. But, he didn't love her.

Lachlan could feel the urgency in her kisses, in her hands running over his hardened, muscled body. He rolled her on top of him, letting her sprawl above him.

Kandra took advantage of the situation, kissing his broad chest, swiping her tongue across his flat male nipple. His groan made her feel powerful. Her mouth trailed farther down his body until she reached his hard, throbbing erection. Flicking the tip of her tongue over his throbbing crown, she heard him hiss and she laughed. Tasting him only made her want him more. When she took him into her mouth, his fingers slid into her hair as he encouraged her.

Lachlan thought he would die from the pleasure she assailed him with. The feel of her mouth upon him was driving him mad with desire. He tried to tug her away when he teetered on the edge of ecstasy. When she wouldn't relent, he held on like a drowning man and let her send him spiraling into the abyss of pleasure. Her name was a horse cry upon his lips.

When at last she pulled away, she smiled a satisfied, slightly smug, smile. She leaned down pressing a kiss to his hard, muscled thigh. Lovingly, she ran her hands up his body until she lay next to him with her head upon his broad shoulder.

As he made to speak, she placed a finger over his lips, "Please, no words. Not now, just hold me, love me."

He kissed her finger then rolled her beneath him so that he could look into the depths of her beautiful blue eyes. "Aye," was the only word he spoke to her. He began the slow pleasurable torture upon her body with his hands and nimble fingers. He stroked and teased while his mouth traced a path of fire that fanned the flames of her desire to scorching heights. She was sure if he didn't give her some release from the need coiling within her, she would burst into an inferno of desire.

Tugging at his hair in an attempt to make him finally give her some release by loving her, he merely laughed and caught hold of her wrists, holding them to her sides, as he made his way to the golden, fleeced vee between her thighs. His mouth nuzzled and brushed the curls, causing her to sob his name. With his tongue, he parted her heated, slick folds. Finding the tiny bud of her desire, he swirled his tongue around it. Kandra moved against him, seeking the release only he could give her. His tongue licked and laved, turning her frantic. As she neared her release, he let lose her hands, grasping her hips, pressing his mouth tight to her as he drove his tongue inside of her with quick thrusting motions.

Threading her fingers into his hair, she pulled him closer as she crashed over the edge into the paradise only he could create for her. Wave after wave of climax washed over her, as Lachlan's skilled tongue laved her.

When his mouth left her, she cried out once more, but as he rose over her, she opened eagerly for him. Grasping her hips in his hands, he lifted her, thrusting into her with one smooth motion. Her cry of pleasure was music to his ears.

They danced to a rhythm as old as time itself, a rhythm only they could hear. Each one met the other and drove the pleasure higher. When they reached the heavens that only love could bring, they cried out together, falling as they clung to each other.

Both were panting and coated in sweat, but sated. Carefully, Lachlan rolled off her, pulling her with him to sprawl over him. He was reluctant to lose the contact he had with her. He didn't want to open his arms for fear she would leave him all the sooner.

Kandra sighed, closing her eyes as the painful love she felt for him washed over her. Shifting, she slid to his side, laying her head upon his shoulder. Sated from their lovemaking, she let sleep claim her.

Weary from the battle and sated from what they had shared, Lachlan fell into a heavy sleep. His dreams revolved around the woman in his arms.

The new day had arrived and shadows had grown long by the time Kandra's eyes fluttered open. She looked up at Lachlan's sleeping face. Peaceful and blissful, she thought with a sigh. Swallowing back her tears, she knew their time had run out. It was time to leave. With great care and gentle movements so as not to disturb him, Kandra rose from the bed.

Dressing, she tried not to look at the bed. She glanced around the room for something left that needed her attention. Kandra knew she was only putting off the inevitable. She slowly walked to the door, but his voice drew her up short.

"Stay," Lachlan's rough voice spoke the one word from behind her as he lay on the bed.

"I cannot." She didn't turn around to look at him, bowing her head. It killed her to say that.

"I could make ye." He rose from the bed, padding over to stand behind her. He yearned to bend her to his will, to keep her no matter what.

"You would not." She closed her eyes, feeling the tear slip down her cheek. Try as she might, Kandra couldn't stop that one tear, but she refused to cry any more than that.

"Stay with me." He growled from behind her. "Stay because ye want to." Damn it he wanted her, wanted her more than anyone, or anything.

She was silent for a long moment, "Do not take the coin my father offers." It was impossible and she knew it, but if only he said he loved her, loved her so much he couldn't live without her, she would stay.

He bit out an oath in Gaelic, causing her to flinch. "Ye ken I can nay do that, *Sasunnach*." His responsibility was to his people, damn his needs and damn his desires, he had to uphold his duty to his clan.

She pulled the door open, "Farewell, Lachlan. I shall never forget you." She meant every word she spoke, she loved him with all of her heart.

He grasped her arm, spinning her into him. His arms pinned her to him as he claimed her mouth for a long desperate kiss. When she pulled from him with a sob, she was shaking.

She wanted to stay, to give him her heart, but she couldn't take the risk of not being loved by him. Shaking so badly she didn't think her legs would hold her much longer, Kandra pressed a hand to her lips and fled through the open door.

Her heart splintered in her chest as she moved through the door. She could have sworn that her heart broke so loudly the entire castle could have heard it. For as she walked away from him, her heart shattered painfully inside of her, leaving a void she knew she would never fill again. Kandra ran down the hall with tears streaking down her face. Passing

Aidan, she spoke not a word, but bowed her head to keep him from seeing her silent tears.

Bursting from the keep, she raced to the stables. Hastily, she grabbed Hadwin, not caring that he had no saddle or bridle. She rode from the castle with only one intent, getting away from the pain. Hitting the open field between the castle and her father's encampment, Kandra felt the pain rip through her at the loss of the man she loved. She knew in that moment that she had already given Lachlan MacKinnon her heart totally and completely for all times.

Her tears blinded her as she rode into the camp. Jonas ran to her, catching her as she flew from the horse into his arms. Wrapping his arms around her, he allowed her to weep on his shoulder. Quickly, he ushered her into his tent, where she was afforded a bit of privacy.

She made him swear to secrecy before she would tell him a word of what had caused her tears. When she had his oath, she told him everything, down to the child she was carrying.

His anger boiled as he paced the tent, hurling insults upon Lachlan's head, "I shall kill MacKinnon for dishonoring you." He growled with the end of her tale.

She stood, shaking, "No, please, Jonas. Promise me you will do nothing." He gave her a silent heated look. He was furious and wanted to extract his pound of flesh to defend her honor. "Promise me, Jonas. I love him, and I love you. Do nothing and say nothing, I beg of you."

Kandra dropped to her knees imploringly. It broke his heart to see his once proud sister upon her knees. He knelt before her. "I promise not to act upon this, but what will you tell father?"

"I do not know." Kandra looked at him searchingly. "But I cannot remain at home for long. When I start to noticeably increase, I shall have to have a plan to leave."

He took her hands, "Then we shall plan together. I shall not allow you to leave alone."

She fell into his arms, "You are my best friend, Jonas, and I love you, but I cannot allow you to sacrifice your life for me."

"It is no sacrifice. We have always stood together." Jonas gave her a smile as he pecked a kiss upon her cheek. "Cheer up, love, we will get through this together."

She smiled warmly at him, but said nothing. Kandra wouldn't allow him to sacrifice himself for her and her child. No, when the time came, she would leave him behind.

"You look peaked," he studied her face. "Take my pallet and rest." He rose to his feet, taking his sister with him. Pulling her by the hand, he led her to the pile of furs in the corner of the tent. "I shall wake you for the evening meal."

Kandra watched him turn to leave, "Thank you, Jonas." Kandra spoke sincerely to him as her eyes conveyed her gratitude.

"Thank me not, Kandra, for I am your brother, 'tis my place to look out for you." He nodded then left her to sleep.

Wearily, she removed her boots and crawled onto the pile of furs. Hot tears coursed down her cheeks. She cried herself to sleep then slept like the dead.

When Jonas came to wake her for the evening meal, she was peacefully asleep. He had not the heart to wake her, but brought her food in case she woke later in the night.

⊢─────────

The next morning, Kandra woke early. She smiled at the food Jonas had left her. He was far to kind to her. With a weary sigh, she sat up and put her boots back on. Running her fingers through her golden locks, she quickly braided it and found a piece of leather to tie it with.

The sun was barely peeking through the morning mist as she walked around the camp. She left the perimeter and walked toward the loch. For a long time, she stared at the water, remembering the day she and Lachlan had spent making love by its side. A soft, sad smile touched her lips as she wrapped her arms around her waist.

"It is a sight, is it not?" He father's voice startled her out of her revere.

"Yes, a beautiful sight." She hugged herself, trying to keep from looking at him. The last thing she wanted was for her father to look in her eyes and see her pain.

"Tell me what bothers you, daughter?" He spoke quietly. Edward grasped her chin, turning her to face him. "I see the sadness in your eyes. They do not sparkle anymore."

"I am fine." Though she tried not to let it, her voice wavered. Tears and heartache shone in her eyes. Without a word, she walked into her father's arms. He held her, rocking her as he stroked her fair hair.

He spoke nonsense words to her, soothingly. When, at last, she pulled away to look at him, she shook her head. "I do not wish to talk about it right now."

"My darling girl, you have to face it sometime." He stroked her cheek with a finger. Edward could remember the moment she was born, a tiny, pink, squalling bundle, kicking at her swaddling. Now here she stood before him all grown up. "My how you have become a beautiful woman." He paused, fingering her golden braid. "So much like your mother. She would have been so very proud of you, as I am."

"When you lose someone, you love, it can eat at your soul, or you can go on loving them, but living." He smiled at her. "Love is a complicated game, much like chess, but if you give up then you lose forever."

She stretched up to place a kiss upon his cheek, "A wise man taught me that sometimes in battle it is better to retreat and fight another day then to lose all together."

"You learned your lessons well." He smiled brightly at her. "A true warrior you have become."

"Thank you, Father." She hugged him tightly. She pulled from his embrace, feeling better than she had, "I love you."

As the camp broke, a soldier who had taken the ransom to Lachlan and retrieved her belongs returned, but he wasn't alone. Lachlan, Aidan, Ian, Duncan and Ferran accompanied him. Lachlan dismounted, walking to Lord Stafford.

"My lord," Lachlan inclined his head. "I wish a word with yer daughter 'afore ye depart."

"I am afraid she has already left." Lord Stafford shook his head. Looking at the woman on horseback, he reached into his cloak's pocket and pulled out some rolled parchment. "She has asked me to give you this, Lady MacKinnon." He walked over, handing it to her.

Ferran smiled tearfully, taking the scrolls, "Yer daughter 'tis truly a remarkable woman, my lord."

"Aye," the agreement came from the three men still on horseback. "She will be missed." Aidan frowned at his brother's back.

"She is a remarkable warrior," Duncan smiled proudly, though he would miss her greatly.

Ferran held out a bundle to him, "Would ye see that she's given these?"

Jonas came over to where they stood. The anger on his face was obvious. His stance was belligerent as he scowled at Lachlan.

Lord Stafford ignored his son's behavior. If what he thought had happened, then Jonas had every right to be angry with this Scotsman. He, himself, was none too thrilled with the man for breaking his baby girl's heart. "I believe all is in order, it is time we head home."

He held out his hand to the laird, "I want you to know, MacKinnon, that not every story has to have an unhappy ending." Edward paused as he looked into Lachlan's eyes then he spoke, "My daughter cares a great deal for you."

Lachlan looked at the Englishman with raised brows. "I'm afraid I can nay turn back time. What 'tis done, 'tis done."

Stafford nodded as he climbed onto his mount. "You value a prize more if you fight for it,

MacKinnon, and there is no greater treasure than love." He inclined his head to the group and wheeled away. He hoped the laird would realize before long what a treasure his daughter was.

Jonas stepped toe to toe with Lachlan. "I swear to you MacKinnon, one day you shall answer for what you have done to my sister."

"That day 'tis nay today, unless ye wish to draw yer sword, English." Lachlan glared down at Jonas, challenging him.

"That day 'tis not today, only because I made a vow to my sister, but one day I shall hunt you down like the dog that you are." Jonas turned on his heels and swung onto his horse. Taking up the reins, he wheeled his mount and shot off to catch up with his sister and make certain she was all right.

Back in the MacKinnon castle, Lachlan held out his hand to his mother, "I want to read that letter."

She shook her head, "'Tis written for me, nay ye." With that, she turned and walked away angrily.

Lachlan watched her retreating back, but had not the will to fight with her over it. He knew she was angry with him for not fighting to keep Kandra, but he had done what was right for his clan. They needed the coin, or by next year they would be desperate if he didn't take it.

He looked around his castle and it felt empty to him. Aimlessly, he walked through the great hall then out to the gardens where he swore he could almost see Kandra stretched out beneath one of the trees.

That night he tossed and turned in his bed as the scent of Kandra pervaded his dreams. Reaching over, he grabbed the coverlet she had slept upon and held it to his nose, Gods how he missed the troublesome lass.

Climbing from his bed, he paced his chambers, telling himself he had to get her out of his mind. But all the while he wondered how he would get her out of his heart.

Chapter
Twenty-Seven

*F*or two and a half months Kandra had been home and she still missed Lachlan as much as she had the day she left. Her heart ached with love for him. Day in and day out, she dreamt of returning to his castle and loving him.

The leaves were turning toward autumn and bright colors graced the forests, but she felt no enthusiasm for the coming winter. Her heart was truly broken.

Sitting in the cool autumn of the garden, she pulled Lachlan's tartan more firmly around her to block the chill. Ferran had sent her the three gowns she had made as well as one of Lachlan's own tartans. The note inside had told her of how much she would be missed and how much the MacKinnons loved her. All of Lachlan's family loved her except the one person who mattered most of all, Lachlan.

Kandra placed a hand over her stomach that was ever increasing. The small mound was visible and she smiled as she thought of their child tucked safely inside of her womb. She wanted this child, for it would fulfill a part of her dreams, the dreams to have a husband and children of her own. She would love this child with all her heart and she would tell everyone, including her child, that the baby's father had died in battle.

The mound where her child rested was ever increasing and noticeable. Even the breeches she was wearing were barely laced, because she was increasing so rapidly. She knew she would have to leave the castle before long, her plans were laid and ready.

As usual, her thoughts slipped to Lachlan, she couldn't help but to wonder what he was doing? Did he miss her? And little Bry, Kandra's heart pained her with missing the girl. She wondered if Bry had hit the target yet. A smile crossed her lips at the thought of the child.

A fine sheen of tears filled her eyes as she thought of the MacKinnon clan. She missed all of them, but especially their laird. Her heart ached with missing him. Why couldn't he have loved her? Why couldn't they have found a way? By God, she was dead inside without him. A small moan escaped her lips as she wiped at the tears that had slipped down her cheeks.

A sound behind her startled her out of her thoughts. She wiped her tears away and forced a smile for the woman who had become her stepmother. "How are you fairing, Rowena?"

"I could ask the same of yourself?" She raised a brow then glanced at Kandra's stomach pointedly. "Is all well with both of you?"

Kandra paled as she searched the woman's face. "You know? How?"

"I can see it in you and your clothes and in the glow, you give off when you are not so saddened." Rowena laid a reassuring hand on her stepdaughter's arm, "Do not fear, your father appears to have no idea, and I will not be the one to tell him." She sighed, "But perhaps you should."

Kandra shook her head, "I cannot. He would disown me."

"Then tell me what will you do?" She raised a brow, "Will you return to the father?"

Kandra frowned, "No, he does not love me." She gave a bitter laugh, "I was foolish enough to lose my heart to him, but I will not risk losing my child to him."

"So, he does not know of his child?" Rowena was stunned and concerned.

Kandra laughed, "If I had told him, he would have insisted that I stay with him until the child was born. Then what? Cast me out without my child? No, I would not take that chance."

"Are you sure he does not love you?" Rowena spoke softly as she looked out over the garden.

"No, I am sure. If he did would he not have come for me?" Kandra felt the familiar hurt and anger at Lachlan. Yet she ached to be with him once more.

"Do not be too sure of yourself, there is still time for him to come to his senses and to come for you." Rowena smiled softly at her.

Kandra shook her head, "I fear time has run out. If you can see my increasing, it will not be long before everyone else can and I shall not dishonor my father in such a way." Tears filled her eyes once more. The idea of leaving and living on her own saddened her.

"I beg you, Kandra, give it just a wee bit more time.

Rowena grasped the younger woman's hands as she pleaded.

Kandra searched her face, "What would be the use?" she frowned.

"Perhaps your man is just lost." Rowena smiled lightly then hugged Kandra softly. "Promise me you shall not leave now. Give it one more month. If he does not come for you, I shall give you all the money I have to care for your child."

Kandra sighed as she considered what Rowena had said. "All right, but promise you will not speak a word of this to my father."

"I swear it." Rowena promised solemnly then hugged her again. She would have to work quickly if she were to help resolve things between Kandra and her man.

Lachlan had been miserable since the day Kandra left. Sleep eluded him and he ached to hold her. His grumpiness was causing his people to be weary of him. His chest ached with the loss of her and the need to retrieve her.

All his dreams revolved around his *sasunnach*, and their time together. His body ached for her. His arms felt empty. To make matters worse, there was nowhere in the castle he could go and not be reminded of her. For neigh on three whole, long, pitiful months he had stormed around the castle looking for a peaceful place, and had yet to find one. Even his daughter reminded him of what he had lost.

Lachlan sat in his study staring at the fire burning in the hearth. His mind remembering the times he had spent with his beautiful golden haired, *sasunnach*. He groaned as he wondered if she had found herself another man already. Was there some man betrothed to her, touching her, kissing her? Was she sleeping in his bed? Lachlan's temper snapped as fury built inside of him.

Ferran marched through the castle, she was sincerely sick of Lachlan's growling and muttering. Poor Bry missed Kandra wholeheartedly and did nothing but mope. Nothing seemed to truly cheer the child up. Like her father, Bry was in love with the golden haired, *sasunnach*. Kandra had brightened all of their lives.

With that thought, Ferran held the rolled parchment in her hand as she entered Lachlan's private study unannounced. When he merely glared up at her, she stood with hands to her hips. "I've had enough of yer moping and Bryanna's tears. Here." She thrust the parchment at him.

He looked at the scrolls as if it were going to bite him. "Take it and read it, perhaps it will help that thick head of yer's to open up."

Reluctantly, he took it. Once it was in his hand, Ferran marched from the room, slamming the door behind her. He set the scroll down and stared at it. She had left him, he had asked her to stay, but she had chosen to leave. There was no way a piece of paper was going to make him see differently. She hadn't wanted to stay with him. She hadn't loved him as he had loved her.

He sat for half an hour debating about reading the letter. Finally, he couldn't fight the urge any longer. This letter was a link to her.

Lachlan quickly unrolled the scroll and out dropped another rolled parchment that was sealed with wax.

He stared at it for a long moment, reading his name written upon it. He looked back to the letter in his hand and read.

Dear Ferran,

I leave all of you with a heavy heart. I have no choice but to leave. For my staying with you will only make it harder when the day came that I was no longer welcomed among all of you. In the short time that I have lived with you, I have grown to love you all. Please explain to Bryanna for me that I have no choice, but to leave. I love her so very much and will miss her dearly for all the rest of my days. Please tell her, I am sorry I had to leave her. I will pray every day that she grows into the warrior she dreams of.

Please give these messages to the following: Ian, I will miss your sense of humor and your wonderful heart. Duncan, no one can fight with quite your style, blade to blade, my brother in arms. Aidan, your kind words and concern helped my heart. I will pray you find a woman one day who will appreciate you fully. I will miss all of you, my friends.

Ferran, you have become the mother of my heart. Thank you, for all you have done for me. I will always treasure you and your kindness.

Lastly, my dear friend, I ask that you hold the letter I have enclosed for Lachlan for one year. Please give it to him so that he may understand why I had to leave all of you.

Forever all of you will be in my heart.
Kandra

Lachlan stared at the letter for a long moment. Turning his attention to his letter, he reached for it with shaky hands. He broke the seal, took a breath and began to read.

Lachlan, my love,

My heart broke as I walked out that door and left you behind. God only knows how much I wanted to stay with you, to be with you forever, but I could not. I needed so very much to know how you felt about me. Was I your prisoner, leman, or the woman you loved? And now I know that you could never love me the way I love you.

I have come to realize how important the coin was to you and your people. I do not blame you for taking it. If I were you, I would have done the same.

I hope by the time you read this, you will have found someone you can truly love, and that happiness has blessed you. Know, that I will always love you, Lachlan MacKinnon, and your daughter Bryanna, with all of my heart. You gave me a wonderful gift that I shall cherish for the rest of my life.

Forever my love,
Kandra

He closed his eyes and set down the letter. Good God, he hadn't known that she loved him. If he had known, he would never have let her leave him. His heart beat an uneven tattoo, as sorrow washed over him. Gods, he loved that woman, but it was too late. What was done was done, he couldn't change what had happened between them.

Lachlan frowned down at the letter, shaking his head. There was no way to get her back. His people needed the coin from the ransom to help them through the winter and to rebuild. She was lost to him, for he couldn't go after her.

With a heavy heart, he left his study to attend the noon meal. Walking into the great hall, he stopped short. It looked as if his entire clan was present. He looked about the room at the solemn faces before him, and raised a questioning brow.

Ferran stepped forward, "What are ye goin' to do 'bout her?"

Lachlan glared at his mother, "Aught, for I can nay do a thing 'bout her."

Ian, stepped forward, "Ye have to Lachlan, she loves ye, ye thick headed fool."

"There is aught to be done," he growled at the group. "I have taken the coin and we needed it." Lachlan looked around the room at the somber faces. "'Tis over, get on with the meal. I've nay more patients for it." He turned to walk away, but a voice stopped him.

Maggie stepped forward, "laird," she took his hand, she carefully set a gold coin in his palm. "'Tis nay much, but if 'twill help ye to get her back 'tis more than worth it. We'll make do." Her solemn eyes pled with him. "Love is far more important."

Lachlan frowned down at the coin, "It would buy much needed seeds and repair homes with leaky roofs."

Ferran walked forward, she closed his fist around the coin. "It would bring a greater gift, Lachlan, it would bring love." She looked up into his brilliant green eyes and saw just how much his sacrifice was costing him. "We all want ye to have this, and we'll make do."

Aidan walked over and clapped him on the back. "So, when do we leave for England, big brother?" Aidan smiled at Lachlan and the smile was returned.

Chapter Twenty-Eight

*K*andra had waited three and a half more weeks and she could wait no longer. Rowena would have to face that she was wrong. Lachlan wasn't coming for her and the thought once again caused Kandra's heart to ache. She sank down onto the edge of her bed and sighed. She shouldn't have listened to Rowena and gotten her hopes up in the first place. Kandra knew love was not meant for her. No man could ever love her. She looked down at her stomach and smiled as she ran a loving hand over her babe. This child would love her, she thought as she stood up and began to hum a soft tune.

She had just about finished packing her satchel when she heard the first faint sounds of music. Turning, she stared at the window, she frowned and thought, it couldn't be. Rushing to the window, she threw it open.

The beautiful strands of a familiar Scottish melody filled the air from what sounded like bagpipes. Faintly, she could see the group heading toward the castle. A whole group of them riding over the hill, there had to be fifty men at least. Four men broke off and rode toward the castle gates and a thrill went through her at the sight of their plaids.

Rowena burst into the room, smiling broadly. "I told you he'd come." She looked at the bag of clothing and frowned. "You will wait, will you not?"

"Yes, but do not get your hopes up." Kandra turned from the window and frowned, "How do I look?"

Rowena frowned, "I do not think he will notice."

"I pray not," Kandra frowned, shaking her head. "I have increased considerably in the last few weeks."

"Put on yer cloak, for 'tis chilly out this day." Rowena instructed, and helped Kandra into her heavy black cloak. "Perfect." She announced as the cloak hid her stepdaughter's pregnancy.

Kandra stood on the stairs of the keep as Lachlan, Ian, Duncan, and Aidan rode into the inner bailey. Dismounting, the group moved up the stairs as stable boys took the reins of their horses. They walked up the stairs of the keep and greeted her father cordially, but the whole time Kandra was aware of Lachlan's gaze, though she would not return it.

"My lord," Lachlan greeted her father. "I have come to speak with ye." He greeted Rowena and exclaimed over her beauty. Not a word was exchanged between him and Jonas, who stood there glaring at the laird.

When at last Lachlan reached Kandra he studied her, she was radiant. She nearly shone with beauty. He looked her over from head to toe. She was different, almost glowing, though she wouldn't quite meet his gaze. The heavy cloak around her shoulders made him frown, it was not cold enough for such a heavy garment. He took her hand and brought it to his lips placing a kiss to her palm. "*Gràdh*, I have missed ye."

Her gaze shot to his at the endearment. Then she looked at her father, he didn't appear to have heard it, or he was just ignoring it as he spoke quietly with Ian.

Though, one look at Jonas showed he had heard the words Lachlan had spoken to her and was not happy at all. Jonas looked as if he would like to kill Lachlan with his bare hands.

She finally looked back at Lachlan and raised a brow, "What, pray tell, brings you to our home?"

"Urgent business to be discussed with yer father, *gràdh*." He told her with a cocky grin.

"Stop calling me that." She hissed at him and he only smiled at her. It aggravated her that he could be so happy, when she had been so miserable. She held back her tears, this was all the proof she needed Lachlan had never and would never love her as she loved him.

He turned his attention back to her father, overlooking Jonas' belligerent glare. "Lord Stafford, I seek a private word with ye if ye would grant me the time."

"Of course, MacKinnon, follow me." He turned to his wife, "Would ye show these men into the hall and have them served with refreshments and something to eat if they wish it."

Rowena inclined her red head. "My lords, this way if you will." She waved them into the great hall.

Edward beckoned Lachlan through the doors and into the castle keep. They walked through the great hall, then down a corridor to a large wooden door. Lord Stafford ushered him into his study. The room held a large fireplace and a polished oak desk, as well as two chairs that faced the hearth. A chessboard set between those two chairs. The room's walls were covered with weapons, some of which were like nothing Lachlan had ever seen.

Lachlan noted that Jonas took up residence at the hearth and stood there glaring at him. "My lord, I ask for a private word."

"I will not allow you to be alone with my father." Jonas growled, "After what you have done to my sister, I owe you a death sentence."

"That is enough, Jonas," Edward gave his son a stern look. "Let the laird be." He turned to Lachlan, "I will not ask my son to leave, as he and his sister are very close. I assume this has to do with my daughter."

"If that is yer wish," Lachlan inclined his head. "And aye, has everything to do with her."

Edward walked over to the decanter sitting upon a table, "Would you care for a glass of whiskey, laird?"

"My thanks." Lachlan inclined his head as he began to pace the room. When he was handed his drink, he downed it in one swallow.

"Am I to assume you are here to ask for my daughter's hand in marriage?" Edward settled into the chair behind his desk to assess the man prowling the room before him.

"Aye, I wish to marry her, with yer permission of course, my lord." Lachlan stopped his pacing to look at Lord Stafford. He waited a long moment and held his breath.

"It is about time. You have certainly waited long enough, MacKinnon. I thought perhaps you were too cowardly to own up to ruining my daughter and leaving her in such a state." Edward shook his head. "Before I give my blessing though, allow me to ask you something."

He released his pent-up breath. "Aye?" Lachlan raised a brow at Kandra's father.

"Do you love my daughter, MacKinnon?" Edward watched the man carefully.

Lachlan was quiet for a moment then smiled. "My lord, I love her so much it nigh on kills me. She has become my life, my whole world." He paused then gave Edward a serious look. "I have come to realize what a gift she is, my lord. When we marry, I shall treasure her always."

Lord Stafford was silent for a long while. Finally, he sighed, "You may call me, Edward." He held out his hand to Lachlan, "I give you my blessing, but I warn you, Lachlan, you must get her to agree as well, or there will be no marriage."

"Edward, by fair or by foul, she shall say aye, because I dinna intend to return to Scotland without her." He gave him a serious look. "Now about the coin..."

"You will not marry my sister!" Jonas growled and pushed away from the hearth. "I shall kill you before I allow you anywhere near Kandra ever again!"

Lachlan turned to meet Kandra's brother, "Ye've nay say in this, English." He snarled at the younger man.

"I have every say," Jonas growled menacingly. "You kidnapped her, used her, broke her heart then threw her away like kitchen scraps, you blackguard." He stepped up to Lachlan. "You should be horse whipped for the way you have hurt her."

The fight went out of Lachlan and he closed his eyes and pinched the bridge of his nose, "Aye, ye've the right of it, English." He sighed, "I was a bloody bastard for hurtin' yer sister." Lachlan looked back at Jonas and smiled, "But I'm nay a daft bastard, she loves me and I love her more than life itself. So, English, if ye wish to extract yer pound of flesh, be my guest." Lachlan held out his arms, but wasn't quite ready when Jonas hit him in the jaw. He landed on his ass on the floor. "Och English." He rubbed at his jaw, "Ye pack a mighty wicked punch."

Jonas stepped forward and held out his hand. When he pulled Lachlan up to stand, he pressed a dagger to his neck. "I shall kill you if you ever endeavor to hurt my sister again."

"I dinna intend too." Lachlan clapped Jonas on the back. "I intend to spend the rest of my days making her happy."

"This does not mean you and I are finished, laird." Jonas growled, "But she loves you, so I have no choice, but to accept you."

Lachlan smiled at Jonas, "She does love me, and I love her verra much." He shook his dark hair back behind him, "I can nay think of a woman better suited to be my wife and mother to my children."

Jonas gave a hearty laugh, "Glad I am to hear you say as much." He shook his head, but remained silent on the reasoning. Let the laird figure it out for himself.

Lachlan turned to Edward. "I've most of the coin..."

Edward held up at hand, stopping Lachlan in mid-sentence. "Consider the coin I gave you, part of a wedding present."

"Thank ye." He inclined his head. Lachlan gave his soon to be father-in-law and brother-in-law a cocksure smile. "Now if ye'd excuse me, I've someone to find."

"She's gone to her room. It is the third door on the right." Jonas grinned at Lachlan. "Good luck ol' boy, you're going to need it."

"I thank ye." Lachlan saluted Jonas then turned on his heel and marched away from them, a man on a mission.

Kandra was in her room, finishing packing her satchel. She couldn't stay here, even if Lachlan had come to confess his undying love. When he found out she was carrying his child and hadn't told him, he would be angry and scorn her. She couldn't face his hatred.

Throwing clothing in her bag haphazardly, she let out a startled cry when her door suddenly opened. Her eyes looked into brilliant green depths. She froze, her heart pounding, her breath stilled.

Lachlan raised a brow, "Goin' somewhere, *gràdh*?"

"I...I...Yes I am." She reined in her courage, raised her chin, and continued packing. Walking over to her vanity, she removed her silver backed hair brush and hand held mirror that had been her mother's.

Lachlan reached her in three steps. "And just where would ye be goin'?"

"That is not any of your concern." She stepped away from him and moved back to the satchel, and placed her brush and mirror inside it.

He looked at her for a full minute, "I want ye to marry me, Kandra."

She froze and gasped, "You cannot be serious."

"I am *gràdh*, I want ye to become my wife." He stepped over to her and she shied back. "What's wrong, love?"

"N...N...Nothing." She stumbled as she tried to find a way to get away from him. To hide her stomach, she held a shirt in front of it. "Lachlan, you do not want to marry me."

"I do."

"No, you do not!"

"Damn it Kandra, I love ye!" He growled at her. What the hell was wrong with the bloody woman? Lachlan wondered as he scowled at her.

She dropped the shirt, going pale. "Do not say such a thing." Feeling light headed, she touched her fingers to her lips and blinked back the tears that threatened to spill over.

"Why? Ye love me." He informed her confidently. "Admit it, *Sasunnach*."

"You are completely mad." She replied instead of denying it or answering him. God help her, he was absolutely right and it was killing her.

"Aye, for ye, *gràdh.*" He reached out, pulling her to him.

"No, do not touch me, Lachlan." She fought, pushing him away. Panic surged through her. If he pulled her close, then he would feel the baby.

"I read yer letter, lass." He sighed, "I was a fool nay to tell ye how I felt about ye. I love ye."

Tears swam in her eyes, "Please do not tell me that now, Lachlan, or I will not be able to live the rest of my life without you." A sob broke from her as tears rained down her cheeks. How could she live with those words haunting her?

As Lachlan reached out and pulled her to him, she lowered her head to his chest. Gently, he swept her up in his arms and laid her upon the bed. He lay next to her and pressed kisses to her face. "Hush *gràdh,* ye dinna have to live without me. We shall be together always. *Tha gaol agam ort*, I love ye."

She sniffed, "You do not understand..."

Kandra broke off as he pulled her to him and he froze. His hand slid down between them to caress the small mound in her stomach. Brows furrowed, he looked at her. "How long have ye ken, lass?" He prayed she would say after she had left him.

"Before the battle with the MacNairs." She spoke softly, not looking at him.

"Why?" He searched her eyes as he raised her chin making her look at him.

"Because I was afraid. I did not know how you felt, and I did not know what you would have done." She raged at him. Quickly, she rolled away from him, covering her babe with her arms crossed over it. "I did not want to lose my babe."

He was silent for what seemed an eternity and it frightened her more than any battle she had ever fought. "You gave me this wonderful gift, Lachlan. I will always treasure this babe." She whispered the last softly.

"Do ye truly love me, lass?" He asked of her.

She was quiet for a long moment, then sighed, knowing she could not lie to him. "Yes, more than almost anything in this world."

When his arms came around her, she flinched. His face nuzzled her neck and one hand slipped around her to cradle their child. "*Grádh*, ye have given me the greatest of gifts."

He laid her back down so that he could look down at her. Gently, he brushed a kiss over her lips. "I love ye, Kandra." He brushed another kiss across her lips.

"Let me take ye home as my wife and mother to my children."

She looked at him. For a long moment, she looked into his brilliant green gaze and saw the love she needed shining there. Joy filled her, "I will not be a perfect wife and I tend to argue and disobey." She flashed him a sultry smile. "I refuse to bow down to your tyranny, laird. And I will use my sword when I see fit, because I am a warrior." She brushed her lips across his, "And I will always love you, Lachlan MacKinnon."

"And I will always love ye, my temperamental, disobedient, stubborn, warrior wife." He whispered against her lips then deepened the kiss until it became searing and they were both breathless.

Epilogue

The wedding was beautiful. Lachlan, Kandra and Bryanna stood before the MacKinnon priest and exchanged vows. Kandra wore a light blue dress trimmed in gold and Bryanna wore a matching one, the only difference was that the bride was wrapped in a MacKinnon tartan. Lachlan was honored to see his woman wearing the MacKinnon plaid proudly.

Ferran and Rowena cried together and hugged as Lachlan kissed Kandra. Edward, Jonas, Ian, Duncan and Aidan all cheered loudly and whistled. The rest of the MacKinnon clan congratulated Lachlan and Kandra exuberantly.

Kandra looked down at Bryanna as she tugged upon her gown. "Yes sweetheart?" Kandra ran a hand over Bry's dark little head.

"Does this make ye my Mam now?" Bry asked Kandra seriously.

Kandra leaned down to look her in the eyes, "I guess this does," she pulled Bry to her and hugged her, "But you do not have to call me, Mam, if you do not want to. But you will always be my daughter, because I love you, Bry."

"Can I call ye Mam if I want to?" She looked up imploringly at Kandra.

"I would love for you to call me Mam, if you want to." Kandra grew misty eyed and pressed a kiss to the top of her daughter's head.

Bryanna threw her arms around Kandra's neck, "I want to be just like ye when I grow up, Mam." She pressed a kiss to Kandra's cheek, *"Mo ghaol ort."*

"And I love you, Bryanna MacKinnon." Kandra hugged her new daughter to her.

Lachlan picked up Bryanna as the hug finished. He wrapped an arm around Kandra, pulling her to him. "And I love ye both." He pressed a kiss to his daughter's cheek then turned and pressed a kiss to Kandra's lips. "Ye've given me back my greatest wish, lass."

Kandra looked up at him and frowned, "What is that?"

"To have a family and a woman I love." Lachlan set down Bryanna, as her Grandmother Rowena called her over. Rowena was sure to spoil her some more, he thought with a smile. Rowena had taken a special liking to Bryanna and spoiled the girl mercilessly.

Gathering Kandra into his arms, he brushed a kiss over her lips and whispered words of love to her as the wedding feast went on around them unobserved.

Duncan MacKinnon stood across the room and watched his cousin and his new wife. How he himself wished for what Lachlan had found. He begrudged his cousin nothing, but he wished for a wife and bairns of his own. He watched the way Kandra glowed with her pregnancy and smiled, at least the lass was happy.

Ian walked over and clapped Duncan on the shoulder. "They look good together."

"Aye, they do."

"What's with that look?" Ian raised a brow in question.

Duncan looked at his brother seriously. "I envy him, for his family." He sighed, "I want a family of my own."

Ian clapped his brother on the shoulder, "'Tis what we all desire. But it takes findin' the right lady."

Rowena turned to Duncan and touched his arm. "Your woman awaits you, Duncan. She must be freed from her captor." She turned to Ian and smiled. "You will find her, but not where you expect." With that said, she wandered off to talk with Kandra.

Ian looked at his brother and frowned. "Do you think she could be right?"

"I've nay clue," Duncan shrugged, but something inside of him was thrilled by her prediction. Though it sounded like a stretch of imagination, he hoped to find his woman soon and he couldn't wait.

Three months later

*T*he door burst open and Bryanna raced in the room to see her new baby brother. She scrambled up on the bed at Kandra's side. "Can I see him, Mam?"

The single word Mam from Bry's little lips made Kandra's heart soar. She held the babe down for his sister's inspection.

Bry wrinkled her nose in disdain. "He's too little and wrinkly." She shook her head, "How can we teach him to be a warrior like us?" She looked inquisitively at Kandra.

"He's too little now, but he'll grow soon enough." Lachlan spoke as he strode across the room to the bed where his family was. He sat upon the bed and held out his hands for his son. "Braydon MacKinnon will be a mighty warrior, as well as laird someday."

Lachlan held his son and smiled at his daughter. One day soon Bryanna MacKinnon would make a fine warrior in her own right. Especially with help from her mother, one of the fiercest warrior's he knew.

"Give him back to me, so that I can feed him." Kandra held out her hands for the babe as he started to fuss.

Lachlan handed the bairn back to her then pressed a kiss to her mouth. "Thank ye, my love, for the most wonderful son a man could ask for." He cupped her cheek, "I love ye, Kandra MacKinnon."

"And I love you." She pressed a kiss to his lips once more. Kandra was happier than she had ever thought to be possible. Never had she believed she would have a daughter she adored, a baby so perfect, and a man who loved her just exactly as she was, and she knew in her heart that he would love her forever.

Keep reading for a Preview Of
The MacKinnon's
Raven!
Coming August 2017

Prologue

The highland mist surrounded them, as Ian MacKinnon and his brother Duncan, separated to surround the MacLeod men who lay sleeping in their beds on MacKinnon land. Ian had received word of the attack planned against his clan. As Chieftain of his people, he would see to their safety and welfare, driving the enemy from MacKinnon lands.

With a smile, Duncan MacKinnon took twenty men with him to the right. Ian's younger cousin Aidan MacKinnon, from the Border Lands, broke off to the left, and let Ian take the center position to thwart the MacLeods.

On the edge of the MacLeod's encampment, Ian asked the Gods to protect his men, then gave the signal for the men to enter the camp of their sleeping enemy.

Duncan felt the hum of battle singing through his veins as he made his way through the sleeping MacLeods. Taking his dagger from between his teeth, he slit the first man's throat. He made it through four MacLeod men, before the alarm was raised. The MacKinnon men shouted their battle cry, *"Cumnich Bas Alpin*!"* 'Remember the death of Alpin!' raced through their minds.

Claymore in hand, Duncan sliced his way into the middle of the fray. The clash of metal was all around him. Cries of rage and death filled the air. His skills with a blade were excellent. He was after all, a highland warrior from the top of his war braids, to the depths of his soul. Duncan wore the MacKinnon tartan with pride.

He dispatched one MacLeod only to turn and engage another. This one was well skilled with a blade, he thought. Duncan relished the fight and countered the moves of his opponent. As the man swung his claymore toward Duncan's head, he blocked with his own sword, then thrust his dagger into the man's stomach. Bringing his own claymore around, Duncan ran the man through.

Pulling his sword from the man's gullet, he turned to engage yet another MacLeod meeting him in a bloody clash of swords. This one was young, no more than a score of years. He was barely a man and probably was not yet married or had bairns of his own. There was no doubt that this was one of his first battles, and sadly, he would most likely not live to see the rise of the sun.

At more than a score and ten years Duncan had lived a full happy life. It wasn't until this last year that he had even thought of finding a woman and making her his, or considered the possibility of wee bairns of his own. Duncan was a warrior with a warrior's heart and a love for battle. However, since he had returned from the border lands and the home of his cousin Lachlan MacKinnon's, his mind had turned to settling down with a woman of his own.

Duncan pared and thrust with the lad hoping to wound the boy, and put him out of the battle, and not kill him. he watched patiently for an opening. From the corner of his eye, he saw his older brother Ian, in the middle of battle with the MacLeod chieftain. From behind Ian, came another enemy with claymore in hand, Ian was too involved with the fight at hand, to have seen the other man. Duncan took his dagger from its sheath in his boot and threw it, hitting the dirty bastard in the neck.

At the sound of the cry behind him, Ian noticed the man for the first time and looked to where his brother was. With a small salute, Ian thanked his brother, then stood horrified as he watched the young man his brother was fighting stab Duncan with his own dagger in the chest. In slow motion Duncan looked down at his chest then his deep blue eyes met his brother's similar gaze. He dropped to his knees as his claymore slipped from his fingers.

As Ian watched his brother fall in battle, anger erupted in him. In that moment, Ian lost all thought and fought like a Viking berserker, bringing down the MacLeod chieftain in one mighty blow. With blood dripping from his sword, Ian went after the lad that had killed his brother. There would be no mercy for the lad now. His life would not be spared...

Look for the next epic installment in the
Immortal MacKinnons Saga,
'The MacKinnon's Raven'
Coming in August 2017.
Go to www.treasakloth.com for sneak peaks and
subscribe for updates on new releases and amazing
giveaways!

About the Author

Treasa Klöth is a contemporary writer with a flair for writing engaging adventures, in a wide variety of romantic genres. She enjoys the great outdoors, camping with her family, getting up with the sunrise to do photography, and appreciating nature. She has a menagerie of animals ranging from bossy cats, demanding dogs and a grumpy bunny.

She is a believer in true love, as she eventually married her high school sweetheart, and they have spent a good portion of their lives raising four children of their own and many of other children. All while living in her small home town outside of Kalamazoo, Michigan.

Treasa has worked for a newspaper, as a reporter, and columnist, and has completed her B.A. in History and Communication.

If you enjoyed this adventure, please visit her website at **www.treasakloth.com** and check out the coming additions to the Immortal MacKinnon Saga, and revisit with Lachlan and Kandra in future adventures. If you get a chance leave a comment or two about your thoughts on the novel, on her site or on amazon, as Treasa enjoys hearing from readers and getting to know them. Also subscribe to her site, to get the latest information on the next installment of the Immortal MacKinnons, Raven along with exclusive giveaways!

94726998R00276

Made in the USA
Columbia, SC
01 May 2018